The White Chief
A Legend Of Northern Mexico

By

Captain Mayne Reid

The White Chief
A Legend Of Northern Mexico
by Captain Mayne Reid

ISBN: 978-93-61154-59-1

Published by

DOUBLE 9 BOOKS

2/13-B, Ansari Road
Daryaganj, New Delhi – 110002
info@double9books.com
www.double9books.com
Tel. 011-40042856

ABOUT THE AUTHOR

Thomas Mayne Reid, an Irish-American novelist, participated in the Mexican–American War. His numerous books on American life discuss colonial policy in the American colonies, the horrors of slave labor, and the lifestyles of American Indians. "Captain" Reid created adventure stories similar to those of Frederick Marryat and Robert Louis Stevenson. They were primarily situated in the American West, Mexico, South Africa, the Himalayas, and Jamaica. He admired Lord Byron. Dion Boucicault turned his anti-slavery novel Quadroon (1856) into a drama called The Octoroon (1859), which was staged in New York. Reid was born in Ballyroney, a hamlet near Katesbridge in County Down, Northern Ireland, as the son of Rev. Thomas Mayne Reid Sr., a senior clerk of the General Assembly of the Presbyterian Church in Ireland, and his wife. Reid's father intended him to become a Presbyterian pastor, so he enrolled at the Royal Belfast Academical Institution in September 1834. He stayed for four years, but lacked the ambition to finish his studies and graduate. He returned to Ballyroney to teach at a school.

CONTENTS

Chapter One

Deep in the interior of the American Continent—more than a thousand miles from the shores of any sea—lies our scene.

Climb with me yonder mountain, and let us look from its summit of snow.

We have reached its highest ridge. What do we behold?

On the north a chaos of mountains, that continues on through thirty parallels to the shores of the Arctic Sea! On the south, the same mountains,—here running in separate sierras, and there knotting with each other. On the west, mountains again, profiled along the sky, and alternating with broad tables that stretch between their bases.

Now turn we around, and look eastward. Not a mountain to be seen! Far as the eye can reach, and a thousand miles farther, not a mountain. Yonder dark line rising above the plain is but the rocky brow of another plain—a *steppe* of higher elevation.

Where are we? On what summit are we standing? On the Sierra Blanca, known to the hunter as the "Spanish Peaks." We are upon the western rim of the *Grand Prairie*.

Looking eastward, the eye discovers no signs of civilisation. There *are* none within a month's journeying. North and south,—mountains, mountains.

Westward, it is different. Through the telescope we can see cultivated fields afar off,—a mere strip along the banks of a shining river. Those are the settlements of Nuevo Mexico, an oasis irrigated by the Rio del Norte. The scene of our story lies not there.

Face once more to the eastward, and you have it before you. The mountain upon which we stand has its base upon a level plain that expands far to the east. There are no foot-hills. The plain and the mountain touch, and at a single step you pass from the naked turf of the one to the rocky and pine-clad declivities of the other.

The aspect of the plain is varied. In some places it is green, where the gramma-grass has formed a sward; but in most parts it is sterile as the Sahara. Here it appears brown, where the sun-parched earth is bare; there it is of a sandy, yellowish hue; and yonder the salt effervescence renders it as white as the snow upon which we stand.

The scant vegetation clothes it not in a livery of verdure. The leaves of the agave are mottled with scarlet, and the dull green of the cactus is still further obscured by its thickly-set spines. The blades of the yuccas are dimmed by dust, and resemble clusters of half-rusty bayonets; and the low scrubby copses of acacia scarce offer a shade to the dusky *agama* and the ground rattlesnake. Here and there a solitary palmetto, with branchless stem and tufted crown, gives an African aspect to the scene. The eye soon tires of a landscape where every object appears angular and thorny; and upon this plain, not only are the trees of that character, but the plants,— even the *very* grass carries its thorns!

With what sensations of pleasure we turn to gaze into a lovely valley, trending eastward from the base of the mountain! What a contrast to the arid plain! Its surface is covered with a carpet of bright green, enamelled by flowers that gleam like many-coloured gems; while the cotton-wood, the wild-china-tree, the live-oak, and the willow, mingle their foliage in soft shady groves that seem to invite us. Let us descend!

We have reached the plain, yet the valley is still far beneath us—a thousand feet at the least—but, from a promontory of the bluff projecting over it, we command a view of its entire surface to the distance of many miles. It is a level like the plain above; and gazing down upon it, one might fancy it a portion of the latter that had sunk into the earth's crust, so as to come within the influence of a fertilising power denied to the higher region.

On both sides of it, far as the eye can reach, run the bordering cliffs, stepping from one level to the other, by a thousand feet sheer, and only passable at certain points. There is a width of ten miles from cliff to cliff; and these, of equal height, seem the counterparts of each other. Their grim savage fronts, overhanging the soft bright landscape of the valley, suggest the idea of a beautiful picture framed in rough oak-work.

A stream, like a silver serpent, bisects the valley—not running in a straight course, but in luxuriant windings, as though it loved to tarry in the midst of that bright scene. Its frequent curves and gentle current show that it passes over a surface almost plane. Its banks are timbered, but not continuously. Here the timber forms a wide belt, there only a fringe scarce shadowing the stream, and yonder the grassy turf can be distinguished running in to the very water's edge.

Copse-like groves are scattered over the ground. These are of varied forms; some perfectly circular, others oblong or oval, and others curving like the cornucopias of our gardens. Detached trees meet the eye, whose full round tops show that Nature has had her will in their development. The whole scene suggests the idea of some noble park, planted by design, with just timber enough to adorn the picture without concealing its beauties.

Is there no palace, no lordly mansion, to correspond? No. Nor palace nor cottage sends up its smoke. No human form appears within this wild paradise. Herds of deer roam over its surface, the stately elk reposes within the shade of its leafy groves, but no human being is there. Perhaps the foot of man never—

Stay! there is one by our side who tells a different tale. Hear him.

"That is the valley of San Ildefonso." Wild though it appears, it was once the abode of civilised man. Near its centre you may note some irregular masses scattered over the ground. But for the trees and rank weeds that cover them, you might there behold the ruins of a city.

"Yes! on that spot once stood a town, large and prosperous. There was a *Presidio* with the flag of Spain flying from its battlements; there was a grand Mission-house of the Jesuit padrés; and dwellings of rich miners and 'hacendados' studded the valley far above and below. A busy populace moved upon the scene; and all the passions of love and hate, ambition, avarice, and revenge, have had existence there. The hearts stirred by them are long since cold, and the actions to which they gave birth are not chronicled by human pen. They live only in legends that sound more like romance than real history.

"And yet these legends are less than a century old! One century ago, from the summit of yonder mountain could have been seen, not only the settlement of San Ildefonso, but a score of others—cities, and towns, and villages—where to-day the eye cannot trace a vestige of civilisation. Even the names of these cities are forgotten, and their histories buried among their ruins!

"The Indian has wreaked his revenge upon the murderers of Moctezuma! Had the Saxon permitted him to continue his war of retaliation, in one century more—nay, in half that time—the descendants of Cortez and his conquerors would have disappeared from the land of Anahuac!

"Listen to the 'Legend of San Ildefonso'!"

Chapter Two

Perhaps in no country has religion so many devoted days as in Mexico. The "fiestas" are supposed to have a good effect in Christianising the natives, and the saints' calendar has been considerably enlarged in that pseudo-holy land. Nearly every week supplies a festival, with all its mummery of banners, and processions, and priests dressed as if for the altar-scene in "Pizarro," and squibs, and fireworks, and silly citizens kneeling in the dust, and hats off all round. Very much like a London Guy-Fawkes procession is the whole affair, and of about like influence upon the morals of the community.

Of course the *padrés* do not get up these ceremonial exhibitions for mere amusement—not they. There are various little "blessings," and "indultos," and sprinklings of sacred water, to be distributed on these occasions—not *gratuitously*—and the wretched believer is preciously "plucked" while he is in the penitent mood—at the same time he is promised a short and easy route to heaven.

As to any solemnity in the character of the ceremonials, there is nothing of the sort. They are in reality days of amusement; and it is not uncommon to see the kneeling devotee struggling to keep down the cackle of his fighting-cock, which, full-galved, he carries under the folds of his *serapé*! All this under the roof of the sacred temple of God!

On days of fiesta, the church genuflexions are soon over; and then the gambling-booth, the race-course, bull-baiting, the cock-pit, and various minor amusements, come into full operation. In all these you may meet the robed priest of the morning, and stake your dollar or doubloon against his, if you feel so inclined.

"San Juan" is one of the *"fiestas principales"*—one of the most noted of Mexican ceremonials. On this day—particularly in a *New* Mexican village—the houses are completely deserted. All people turn out, and proceed to some well-known locality, usually a neighbouring plain, to witness the sports—which consist of horse-racing, "tailing the bull," "running the cock," and the like. The intervals are filled up by gambling, smoking, and flirtation.

There is much of republican equality exhibited on these occasions. Rich and poor, high and low, mingle in the throng, and take part in the amusements of the day.

It is the day of San Juan. A broad grassy plain lies just outside the town of San Ildefonso, and upon this the citizens are assembled. It is the scene of the festival, and the sports will soon begin. Before they do, let us stroll through the crowd, and note its component parts. All classes of the community—in fact, all the community—appear to be present. There go the two stout *padrés* of the mission, bustling about in their long gowns of coarse serge, with bead-string and crucifix dangling to their knees, and scalp-lock close shaven. The Apache will find no trophy on their crowns.

There is the *cura* of the town church, conspicuous in his long black cloak, shovel hat, black silk stockings, pumps, and buckles. Now smiling benignly upon the crowd, now darting quick Jesuitical glance from his dark ill-meaning eyes, and now playing off his white jewelled fingers, as he assists some newly-arrived "señora" to climb to her seat. Great "ladies' men" are these same black-gowned bachelor-churchmen of Mexico.

We have arrived in front of several rows of seats raised above one another. Let us observe who occupy them. At a glance it is apparent they are in possession of the "*familias principales*," the aristocracy of the settlement. Yes—there is the rich "*comerciante*," Don José Rincon, his fat wife, and four fat sleepy-looking daughters. There, too, is the wife and family of the "Alcalde," and this magistrate himself with tasselled official staff; and the Echevarrias—pretty creatures that they think themselves—under care of their brother, the beau, who has discarded the national costume for the *mode de Paris!* There is the rich "*hacendado*," Señor Gomez del Monte, the owner of countless flocks and broad acres in the valley; and there are others of his class with their señoras and señoritas. And there, too, observed of all, is the lovely Catalina de Cruces, the daughter of Don Ambrosio, the wealthy miner. He will be a lucky fellow who wins the smiles of Catalina, or rather perhaps the good graces of her father—for Don Ambrosio will have much to say in the matter of her marriage. Indeed, it is rumoured that that matter is already arranged; and that Captain Roblado, second in command at the Presidio, is the successful suitor. There stands he, in full moustache, covered with gold-lace, back and front, and frowning fiercely on every one who dares to rest eye for a moment upon the fair Catalina. With all his gold-lace and gallant strut, Catalina displays no great taste in her choice;—but is he her choice? Maybe not—maybe he is the choice of Don Ambrosio; who, himself of plebeian origin, is ambitious that his blood should be mingled with that of the military hidalgo. The soldier has no money—beyond his pay; and that is mortgaged for months in advance; but he is a true *Gachupino*, of "blue blood," a genuine "hijo de algo." Not a singular ambition of the old miser, nor uncommon among parvenus.

Vizcarra, the Comandante, is on the ground—a tall colonel of forty—laced and plumed like a peacock. A lively bachelor is he; and while chatting with padré, cura, or alcalde, his eye wanders to the faces of the pretty *poblanas* that are passing the spot. These regard his splendid uniform with astonishment, which he, fancying himself "Don Juan Tenorio," mistakes for admiration, and repays with a bland smile.

There, too, is the third officer—there are but the three—the *teniente*, Garcia by name. He is better looking, and consequently more of a favourite with both poblanas and rich señoritas, than either of his superiors. I wonder the fair Catalina does not give her preference to him. Who can tell that she does not? A Mexican dame does not carry her soul upon her sleeve, nor upon her tongue neither.

It would be a task to tell of whom Catalina is thinking just now. It is not likely at her age—she is twenty—that her heart is still her own; but whose? Roblado's? I would wager, no. Garcia's? That would be a fairer bet. After all, there are many others—young "hacendados," employés of the mines, and a few merchant dandies of the town. Her choice may be some one of these. *Quien sabe?*

Let us on through the crowd!

We see the soldiers of the garrison, with tinkling spurs and long trailing sabres, mingling fraternally with the serapé-clad tradesmen, the *gambucinos*, and *rancheros* of the valley. They imitate their officers in strut and swagger—the very character of which enables one to tell that the military power is here in the ascendant. They are all dragoons—infantry would not avail against an Indian enemy—and they fancy that the loud clinking of their spurs, and the rattle of their steel scabbards, add greatly to their importance. They have their eyes after the poblanas, and the sweethearts of the poblanas keep their eyes after them in a constant vigil of jealousy.

The "poblanas" are the pretty girls of the place; but, pretty or plain, all the girls are out to-day in their best and gayest apparel. Some wear *enaguas* of blue—others of scarlet—others of purple; and many of them tastefully flounced at the bottoms with a trimming of narrow lace. They wear the embroidered chemisette, with its snow-white frills, and the blueish *reboso*, gracefully arranged, so as to conceal neck, bosom, arms, and, in some cases of coquetry, even the face! Ere night this jealous garment will have lost half its prudery. Already the prettier faces peep forth; and you may see, from the softness of the complexion, that they have been just washed free of the "allegria" that for the last two weeks has rendered them hideous.

The "rancheros" are in their full and beautiful costume—velveteen trousers, wide at the bottoms and open up the sides; *botas* of unstained leather; jackets of tanned sheepskin; or velveteen richly embroidered; fancy-worked shirts underneath; and scarfs of rich red silk around the waist. Over all the broad-brimmed *sombrero*, of black glaze, with silver or gold band, and tags of the same, screwed into the crown. Some have no jacket, but the serapé, hanging negligently from their shoulders, serves in place of one. All of these men have horses with them; and on their feet may be seen spurs full five pounds in weight, with rowels three, four, and even five inches in diameter!

The "gambucinos," and young men of the town, the smaller tradespeople, are very similarly attired; but those of higher class—the officials and "comerciantes"—are clad in broad-cloth jackets and pantaloons, not exactly of European cut, but approaching it—a sort of compromise between Paris fashions and the native costume of the country.

Another costume may be noticed, worn by many of the crowd. This is the dress of the native "Pueblos", or *Indios mansos*—the poor labourers of the mines, and the neophytes of the mission. It is a simple dress, and consists of an upper garment, the *tilma*, a sort of coat without sleeves. A coffee-sack with a hole ripped in the bottom for the head to pass through, and a slit cut in each side for the arms, would make the "tilma." It has no waist, and hangs nearly to the hips without other fastening than the support at the shoulders. The tilma is usually a piece of coarse rug—a cheap woollen cloth of the country, called "gerga," of a whitish colour, with a few dyed threads to give the semblance of a pattern. This with a pair of dressed sheepskin breeches and rude sandals—*guaraches*—constitutes the wear of most of the "Indios mansos" of Mexico. The head is bare; and the legs, from the knee to the ankle, shine forth in all their copper-coloured nakedness.

Of these dark aborigines—the "peons" of the mission and the mines—there are hundreds stalking about, while their wives and daughters sit squatted upon the ground in rear of their *petatés*; upon which are piled the fruits of the soil—the *tuñas*, *petahayas*, plums, apricots, grapes, *sandias*, and other species of melons, with roasted nuts of the piñon-tree, the produce of the neighbouring mountains. Others keep stands of *dulces* and *agua-miel* or *limonada*; while others sell small loaves—*piloncilios*—of corn-stalk sugar, or baked roots of the agave. Some squat before fires, and prepare *tortillas* and *chilé Colorado*; or melt the sugared chocolate cake in their urn-like earthen *ollas*. From these humble "hucksters," a hot peppery stew, a dish of *atole*, or a bowl of *piñole*, is to be had for a few *clacos*. There are other stands where you can buy cigarillos of *punche*, or a drink of the fiery *aguardiente* from

Taos or El Paso; and these stands are favourite resorts of the thirsty miners and soldiers. There are no "booths," but most of the hucksters protect themselves from the sun by a huge screen of palmetto mat (*petaté*) placed umbrella-like over their heads.

There is one class of persons yet to be spoken of—an important class at the festival of San Juan—they who are to be competitors in the sports—the real wrestlers in the games.

These are young men of all grades in society, and all of them mounted—of course, each in the best way he can. There they go, prancing over the ground, causing their gaily caparisoned steeds to caper and curvet, especially in front of the tiers of seated señoritas. There are miners among them, and young *hacendados*, and *rancheros*, and *vaqueros*, and *ciboleros*, and young merchants who ride well. Every one rides well in Mexico—even the dwellers in cities are good horsemen.

Nearly a hundred are there of these youths who intend to take part in the various trials of skill in equitation.

Let the sports begin!

Chapter Three

The first exhibition on the programme was to be the *coleo de toros*, which may be rendered in English as "tailing the bull." It is only in the very large cities of Mexico where a regular *plaza de toros*, or arena for the bull-fight, is to be found; but in every tillage, however insignificant, the spoil of bull-tailing may be witnessed, as this only requires an open plain, and as wild a bull as can be procured. The sport is not quite so exciting as the bull-fight, as it is less perilous to those engaged in it. Not unfrequently, however, a gored horse or a mutilated rider is produced by the "coleo;" and fatal accidents have occurred at times. The horses, too, sometimes stumble, and both horse and rider are trampled by the others crowding from behind, so that in the pellmell drive awkward accidents are anything but uncommon. The coleo is, therefore, a game of strength, courage, and skill; and to excel in it is an object of high ambition among the youth of a New Mexican settlement.

The arrangements having been completed, it was announced by a herald that the coleo was about to begin. These arrangements were simple enough, and consisted in collecting the crowd to one side, so that the bull, when let loose, would have a clear track before him in the direction of the open country. Should he not be allowed this favour he might head *towards* the crowd,—a thing to be apprehended. In fear of this, most of the women were to be seen mounting into the rude *carretas*, scores of which were upon the ground, having carried their owners to the spectacle. Of course the señoras and señoritas on the raised benches felt secure.

The competitors were now drawn up in a line. There were a dozen detailed for this first race,—young men of all classes, who were, or fancied themselves, "crack" riders. There were rancheros in their picturesque attire, smart arrieros, miners from the hills, townsmen, hacendados of the valley, vaqueros from the grazing-farms, and ciboleros, whose home is for the most part on the wide prairies. Several dragoons, too, were arrayed with the rest, eager to prove their superiority in the *manège* of the horse.

At a given signal the bull was brought forth from a neighbouring *corral*. He was not led by men afoot,—that would have been a dangerous undertaking. His conductors were well-mounted vaqueros, who, with their lazoes around his horns, were ready, in case of his showing symptoms of mutiny, to fling him to the earth by a jerk.

A vicious-looking brute he appeared, with shaggy frontlet and scowling lurid eye. It was *plain* that it only needed a little goading to make him a still more terrible object; for he already swept his tail angrily against his flanks, tossed his long straight horns in the air, snorted sharply, and beat the turf at intervals with his hoofs. He was evidently one of the fiercest of a fierce race—the race of Spanish bulls.

Every eye was fixed upon him with interest, and the spectators freely commented upon his qualities. Some thought him too fat, others alleged he was just in the condition to make a good run—as, in the coleo, speed, not courage, is the desirable quality. This difference of opinions led to the laying of numerous wagers on the result,—that is, the time that should elapse from the start until the bull should be "tailed" and "thrown." The throwing of the bull, of course ends the chase.

When it is considered that the brute selected is one of the strongest, swiftest, and fiercest of his kind, and that no weapon—not even the lazo—is allowed, it will be admitted this is a matter of no easy accomplishment. The animal goes at full run, almost as fast as the horse can gallop; and to bring him to the ground under these circumstances requires the performance of a feat, and one that demands skill, strength, and the best of horsemanship. That feat is to seize the bull by the tail, and jerk the animal off his legs!

The bull was led out some two hundred yards beyond the line of horsemen, where he was halted, with his head turned to the open plain. The lazoes, that held him by a leash-knot, were then cautiously slipped, two or three fire-squibs, pointed and barbed, were shot into his hips, and away he went amidst the yells of the spectators!

Next moment the riders spurred after, each shouting in his own fashion.

Soon the line was broken, and a confused spread of horsemen, like a "field" of fox-hunters, was seen scouring over the plain. Each moment the troop became elongated, until what had started in line was now strung out in double and single file to a length of several hundred yards. Still on they went, whipping, and spurring, and urging their steeds to the utmost.

The bull, maddened by the arrowy squibs, and terrified by their hissing, ran at the top of his speed in a nearly direct line. The start he had been allowed was not so easily taken up, even by fast riders, and he had got a full mile or more before any one neared him. Then a dragoon, mounted on a large bay horse, was seen pressing him closely, and at length laying hold of the tail. He was observed to give it a jerk or two, as though endeavouring to fling the brute by sheer strength. It was a failure, however; for the next moment the bull shot out in a side direction, and left his pursuer behind.

A young hacendado, splendidly horsed, was next upon his flanks; but each time he reached forth to grasp the tail it was whisked beyond his reach. He succeeded at length in seizing it; but the bull, making a sudden lurch, whipped his tail from the rider's hands, and left him also in the rear.

One condition of the "coleo" was, that each competitor, after having once failed, should retire from the ground; so that the hacendado and the dragoon were now actually *hors de chasse*.

These were seen riding back, though not directly in front of the spectators. They preferred making a roundabout thing of it, so that their fallen faces might not be too closely scanned on their return.

On went the bull, and after him the eager and excited horsemen. Another dragoon soon tried his "pluck," and also failed; and then a vaquero, and another horseman, and another, with like success—each failure being hailed by a groan from the crowd. There were several tumbles, too, at which the spectators laughed heartily; and one horse was badly gored, having headed the bull and got entangled upon his horns.

In less than ten minutes eleven out of the twelve competitors were seen returning from the chase.

Only one now remained to make his trial. The bull had proved a splendid fellow, and was already in high favour, and loudly applauded by the spectators.

"*Bravo, toro! bravissimo!*" was heard on all sides. All eyes were now turned upon the enraged animal, and his one remaining pursuer. Both were still near enough to be well observed, for the chase had led hitherto, not in one line, but in different directions over the plain; so that the bull was actually no farther from the crowd than when first overtaken by the dragoon. He was at this moment running in a cross course, so that every movement of both pursuer and pursued could be well observed from the stand.

At the first glance it was plain that the bull had now behind him the handsomest horse and horseman upon the field—would they prove the best? That was to be tried.

The horse was a large coal-black *mustang*, with a long full tail, pointed at the tip, and carried like the brush of a running fox. Even while in gallop, his neck slightly curved, and his proud figure, displayed against the smooth sward, called forth expressions of admiration.

The rider was a young man of twenty or over; and his light curling hair and white-red complexion distinguished him from all his competitors—

who were, without exception, dark-skinned men. He was dressed in full ranchero costume, with its rich broidery and trappings; and instead of the usual "serapé," he wore a purple *manga*—a more graceful, as well as costlier garment. The long skirts of this he had flung behind him, in order to have his arms free; and its folds, opening to the breeze, added to the gracefulness of his carriage in the saddle.

The sudden appearance of this splendid horseman—for, hanging in the rear with folded manga, he seemed not to have been noticed before,—caused unusual attention, and many were heard inquiring his name.

"*Carlos the cibolero!*" cried a voice, loud enough to satisfy all at once.

Some evidently knew who "Carlos the cibolero" was, though by far the greater number on the ground did not. Of the former, one was heard inquiring—

"Why hasn't he come up before?—He could have done so if he had wished."

"*Carrambo!* yes," added another. "He might have done so. He only hung back to give the others a trial. He knew none of them could throw *that* bull. *Mira!*"

The speaker's conjecture was, no doubt, correct.

It was plain, at first sight, that this rider could easily overtake the bull. His horse was still in a gentle gallop, and, though his ears were set and his red nostrils staring open, it was only through the excitement of the chase, and chafing at being hitherto checked. The bridle-rein was, in fact, still tightly drawn.

As the speaker uttered the cautionary phrase "*Mira!*" a change was suddenly observed in the manner of the horseman. He was about twenty paces from the chase and directly in the rear. All at once his horse sprang forward at double his former speed, and in a few stretches laid himself alongside the bull. The rider was observed to grasp the long outstretched tail, and then lean forward and downward. The next moment he raised himself with a sudden jerk, and the huge horned creature turned sprawling upon his back. The whole thing seemed to cost him no more effort than if the bull had been a tom-cat. Loud "*vivas!*" broke from the spectators, and the victorious horseman rode back in front of the stand, modestly bowed his thanks, and then retired into the depth of the crowd.

There were not wanting those who fancied that in bowing the eyes of the cibolero were directed on the fair Catalina de Cruces; and some went so far as to assert that she smiled and looked content; but that could not be. The heiress of the rich Don Ambrosio smile to a compliment from a cibolero!

There was one, however, who *did* smile. That was a fair-haired, fair-skinned girl, who stood upon one of the carretas, by the side of which the victor had placed himself. Side by side those two faces seemed one. They were of one blood,—one colour,—one race: were they not brother and sister? Yes,—the fair girl was the sister of the cibolero. She was smiling from happiness at the thought of her brother's triumph.

A strange-looking woman was seated in the bottom of the carreta—an old woman, with long flowing hair, white as flax. She was silent, but her sharp eyes were bent upon the cibolero with a triumphant expression. Some regarded her with curiosity, but most with fear, akin to awe. These knew something of her, and whispered strange tales to one another.

"*Esta una bruxa!—una hechicera!*" (She is a witch! a charmer!) said they.

This they muttered in low tones lest they might be heard by Carlos or the girl. *She was their mother!*

Chapter Four

The sports continue. The bull thrown by the cibolero, now cowed, walks moodily across the plain. He would not serve for a second run, so he is lazoed and led off,—to be delivered to the victor as his prize.

A second is brought forth and started, with a fresh dozen of horsemen at his heels.

These seem to be better matched, or rather the bull has not run off so well, as all overtake him at once, riding past him in their headlong speed. Most unexpectedly the animal turns in his tracks, and runs back, heading directly for the stand!

Loud screams are heard from the poblanas in the carretas—from the señoras and señoritas. No wonder. In ten seconds the enraged brute will be in their midst!

The pursuing horsemen are still far behind him. The sudden turning in their headlong race threw them out of distance. Even the foremost of them cannot come up in time.

The other horsemen are all dismounted. No man on foot will dare to check the onward rush of a goaded bull!

Confusion and loud shouting among the men, terror and screaming among the women, are the characteristics of the scene. Lives will be lost—perhaps many. None know but that they themselves may be the victims!

The strings of carretas filled with their terrified occupants flank the stand on each side; but, running farther out into the plain, form with it a sort of semicircle. The bull enters this semicircle, and guided by the carretas rushes down, heading directly for the benches, as though determined to break through in that direction. The ladies have risen to their feet, and, half-frantic, seem as though they would leap down upon the very horns of the monster they dread! It is a fearful crisis for them.

Just at this moment a man is seen advancing, lazo in hand, in front of the carretas. He is afoot. As soon as he has detached himself from the crowd, he spins the lazo round his head, and the noose shooting out is seen to settle over the horns of the bull.

Without losing a moment the man runs to a small tree that stands near the centre of the semicircle, and hastily coils the other end of the lazo around its trunk. Another moment, and he would have been too late.

The knot is scarcely tied, when a heavy pluck announces that the bull has reached the end of his rope, and the foiled brute is now seen thrown back upon his hips, with the *lazo* tightly noosed over his horns. He has fallen at the very feet of the spectators!

"*Bravo! viva!*" cried a hundred voices, as soon as their owners had sufficiently recovered from their terror to call out.

"*Viva. Viva!* Carlos the cibolero!"

It was he who had performed this second feat of skill and daring.

The bull was not yet conquered, however. He was only confined within a certain range—the circle of the lazo—and, rising to his feet, with a furious roar he rushed forward at the crowd. Fortunately the lazo was not long enough to enable him to reach the spectators on either side; and again he tumbled back upon his haunches. There was a scattering on all sides, as it was feared he might still slip the noose; but the horsemen had now come up. Fresh lazoes were wound about his neck, others tripped up his legs, and he was at length flung violently upon the ground and his quarters well stretched.

He was now completely conquered, and would run no more; and as but two bulls had been provided for the occasion, the "coleo de toros" was for that day at an end.

Several lesser feats of horsemanship were next exhibited, while preparations were being made for another of the grand games of the day. Those were by way of interlude, and were of various kinds. One was throwing the lazo upon the foot of a person running at full speed, noosing him around the ankle, and of course tripping him up. This was done by men both mounted and afoot; and so many accomplished it, that it could hardly be deemed a "feat:" nor was it regarded as such among the more skilful, who disdained to take part in it.

Picking up the hat was next exhibited. This consisted in the rider throwing his hat upon the ground, and then recovering it from the saddle, while his horse swept past at full gallop. Nearly every rider on the spot was equal to this feat, and only the younger ones looked upon it as a proof of skill. Of these some twenty could now be seen wheeling about at a gallop and ducking down for their sombreros, which they had previously dropped.

But it is not so easy to pick up smaller objects, and a piece of coin lying flat upon the ground tries the skill of the best "cavallero."

The Comandante Vizcarra now stepped forth and commanded silence. Placing a Spanish dollar upon the smooth turf, he called out—

"This to the man who can take it up at the first trial. Five gold onzas that Sergeant Gomez will perform the feat!"

There was silence for a while. Five gold "onzas" (doubloons) was a large sum of money. Only a "rico" could afford to lose such a sum.

After a pause, however, there came a reply. A young ranchero stepped forth:—

"Colonel Vizcarra," said he, "I will not bet that Sergeant Gomez cannot perform the feat; but I'll wager there's another on the ground can do it as well as he. Double the amount if you please."

"Name your man!" said Vizcarra.

"Carlos the cibolero."

"Enough—I accept your wager. Any one else may have their trial," continued Vizcarra, addressing the crowd. "I shall replace the dollar whenever it is taken up—only one attempt, remember!"

Several made the attempt and failed. Some touched the coin, and even drew it from its position, but no one succeeded in lifting it.

At length a dragoon mounted on a large bay appeared in the list, who was recognised as the Sergeant Gomez. He was the same that had first come up with the bull, but failed to fling him; and no doubt that failure dwelling still in his thoughts added to the natural gloom of his very sallow face. He was a man of large size, unquestionably a good rider, but he lacked that symmetrical shape that gives promise of sinewy activity.

The feat required little preparation. The sergeant looked to his saddle-girths, disencumbered himself of his sabre and belts, and then set his steed in motion.

In a few minutes he directed his horse so as to shave past the shining coin, and then, bending down, he tried to seize it. He succeeded in lifting it up from the ground; but, owing to the slight hold he had taken, it dropped from his fingers before he had got it to the height of the stirrup.

A shout, half of applause and half of disapprobation, came from the crowd. Most were disposed to favour him on Vizcarra's account. Not that they loved Colonel Vizcarra, but they *feared* him, and that made them loyal.

The cibolero now rode forth upon his shining black. All eyes were turned upon him. His handsome face would have won admiration, but for its very *fairness*. Therein lay a secret prejudice. They knew *he was not of their race*!

Woman's heart has no prejudice, however; and along that line of dark-eyed "doncellas" more than one pair of eyes were sparkling with admiration for the blond "Americano," for of such race was Carlos the cibolero.

Other eyes than woman's looked favourably on the cibolero, and other lips murmured applause. Among the half-brutalised Tagnos, with bent limbs and downcast look, there were men who dreamt of days gone by; who knew that their fathers were once free; who in their secret assemblies in mountain cave, or in the deep darkness of the "estufa," still burned the "sacred fire" of the god Quetzalcoatl—still talked of Moctezuma and Freedom.

These, though darker than all others, had no prejudice against the fair skin of Carlos. Even over their benighted minds the future had cast some rays of its light. A sort of mysterious presentiment, apparently instinctive, existed among them, that their deliverers from the yoke of Spanish tyranny would yet come from the East—from beyond the great plains!

The cibolero scarce deigned to make any preparation. He did not even divest himself of his manga, but only threw it carelessly back, and left its long skirt trailing over the hips of his horse.

Obedient to the voice of his rider, the animal sprang into a gallop; and then, guided by the touch of the knees, he commenced circling round the plain, increasing his speed as he went.

Having gained a wide reach, the rider directed his horse towards the glittering coin. When nearly over it he bent down from the saddle, caught the piece in his fingers, flung it up into the air, and then, suddenly checking his horse underneath, permitted it to drop into his outstretched palm!

All this was done with the ease and liability of a Hindoo juggler. Even the prejudiced could not restrain their applause; and loud *vivas* for "Carlos the cibolero" again pealed upon the air.

The sergeant was humiliated. He had for a long time been victor in these sports—for Carlos had not been present until this day, or had never before taken part in them. Vizcarra was little better pleased. His favourite humbled—himself the loser of ten golden onzas—no small sum, even to the Comandante of a frontier Presidio. Moreover, to be jibed by the fair señoritas for losing a wager he had himself challenged, and which, no doubt, he felt certain of winning. From that moment Vizcarra liked not "Carlos the cibolero."

The next exhibition consisted in riding at full gallop to the edge of a deep "zequia" which passed near the spot. The object of this was to show the courage and activity of the rider as well as the high training of the steed.

The zequia—a canal used for irrigation—was of such width that a horse could not well leap over it, and deep enough to render it no very pleasant matter for a horseman to get into. It therefore required both skill and daring to accomplish the feat. The animal was to arrive upon the bank of the canal in full run, and to be drawn up suddenly, so that his four feet should rest upon the ground inside a certain line. This line was marked at less than two lengths of himself from the edge of the drain. Of course the bank was quite firm, else the accomplishment of such a feat would have been impossible.

Many succeeded in doing it to perfection; and an admirable piece of horsemanship it was. The horse, suddenly checked in his impetuous gallop, upon the very brink of the zequia, and drawn back on his haunches, with head erect, starting eyeballs, and open smoking nostrils, formed a noble picture to look upon. Several, however, by way of contrast, gave the crowd a ludicrous picture to laugh at. These were either faint-hearted riders, who stopped short before arriving near the bank, or bold but unskilful ones, who overshot the mark, and went plunge into the deep muddy water. Either class of failure was hailed by groans and laughter, which the appearance of the half-drowned and dripping cavaliers, as they weltered out on the bank, rendered almost continuous. On the other hand, a well-executed manoeuvre elicited *vivas* of applause.

No wonder that, under such a system of training and emulation, these people are the finest riders in the world, and such they certainly are.

It was observed that Carlos the cibolero took no part in this game. What could be the reason? His friends alleged that he looked upon it as unworthy of him. He had already exhibited a skill in horsemanship of a superior kind, and to take part in this would be seeking a superfluous triumph. Such was in fact the feeling of Carlos.

But the chagrined Comandante had other views. Captain Roblado as well—for the latter had seen, or fancied he had seen, a strange expression in the eyes of Catalina at each fresh triumph of the cibolero. The two "militarios" had designs of their own. Base ones they were, and intended for the humiliation of Carlos. Approaching him, they inquired why he had not attempted the last feat.

"I did not think it worth while," answered the cibolero, in a modest tone.

"Ho!" cried Roblado, tauntingly; "my good fellow. You must have other reasons than that. It is not so contemptible a feat to rein up on the edge of that 'zanca.' You fear a ducking, I fancy?"

This was uttered in a tone of banter, loud enough for all to hear; and Captain Roblado wound up his speech with a jeering laugh.

Now, it was just this ducking that the militarios wished to see. They had conceived hopes, that, if Carlos attempted the feat, some accident, such as the slipping or stumbling of his horse, might lead to that result; which to them would have been as grateful as it would have been mortifying to the cibolero. A man floundering out of a muddy ditch, and drenched to the skin, however daring the attempt that led to it, would cut but a sorry figure in the eyes of a holiday crowd; and in such a situation did they wish to see Carlos placed.

Whether the cibolero suspected their object did not appear. His reply does not show. When it was heard, the "zequia" and its muddy water were at once forgotten. A feat of greater interest occupied the attention of the spectators.

Chapter Five

Carlos, seated in his saddle, was silent for a while. He seemed puzzled for a reply. The manner of the two officers, as well as Roblado's speech, stung him. To have proceeded to the performance of this very common feat after all others had given over, merely on the banter of Roblado and the Comandante, would have been vexatious enough; and yet to refuse it would lay him open to jeers and insinuations; and, perhaps, this was their design.

He had reason to suspect some sinister motive. He knew something of both the men—of their public character—he could not otherwise, as they were lords paramount of the place. But of their private character, too, he had some knowledge, and that was far from being to their credit. With regard to Roblado, the cibolero had particular reasons for disliking *him*—very particular reasons; and but that the former was still ignorant of a certain fact, he had quite as good a reason for reciprocating the dislike. Up to this moment Roblado knew nothing of the cibolero, who for the most part of his time was absent from the valley. Perhaps the officer had never encountered him before, or at all events had never changed words with him. Carlos knew *him* better; and long ere this encounter, for reasons already hinted at, had regarded him with dislike.

This feeling was not lessened by the conduct of the officer on the present occasion. On the contrary, the haughty jeering tones fell bitterly upon the ear of the cibolero. He replied, at length, "Captain Roblado, I have said it is not worth my while to perform what a *muchachito* of ten years old would hardly deem a feat. I would not wrench my horse's mouth for such a pitiful exhibition as running him up on the edge of that harmless gutter; but if—"

"Well, if what?" eagerly inquired Roblado, taking advantage of the pause, and half suspecting Carlos' design.

"If *you* feel disposed to risk a doubloon—I am but a poor hunter, and cannot place more—I shall attempt what a muchachito of ten years *would* consider a feat perhaps."

"And what may that be, Señor Cibolero?" asked the officer, sneeringly.

"I will check my horse at full gallop *on the brow of yonder cliff!*"

"Within two lengths from the brow?"

"Within two lengths—less—the same distance that is traced here on the banks of the zequia!"

The surprise created by this announcement held the bystanders for some moments in silence. It was a proposal of such wild and reckless daring that it was difficult to believe that the maker of it was in earnest. Even the two officers were for a moment staggered by it, and inclined to fancy the cibolero was not serious but mocking them.

The cliff to which Carlos had pointed was part of the bluff that hemmed in the valley. It was a sort of promontory, however, that jutted out from the general line, so as to be a conspicuous object from the plain below. Its brow was of equal height with the rest of the precipice, of which it was a part—a sort of buttress—and the grassy turf that appeared along its edge was but the continuation of the upper plateau. Its front to the valley was vertical, without terrace or ledge, although horizontal seams traversing its face showed a stratification of lime and sandstone alternating with each other. From the sward upon the valley to the brow above the height was one thousand feet sheer. To gaze up to it was a trial to delicate nerves—to look down put the stoutest to the proof.

Such was the cliff upon whose edge the cibolero proposed to rein up his steed. No wonder the proposal was received with a surprise that caused a momentary silence in the crowd. When that passed, voices were heard exclaiming,—"Impossible!"

"He is mad!"

"Pah! he's joking!"

"*Esta burlando los militarios!*" (He's mocking the military gents); and such-like expressions.

Carlos sat playing with his bridle-rein, and waiting for a reply.

He had not long to wait. Vizcarra and Roblado muttered some hasty words between themselves; and then, with an eagerness of manner, Roblado cried out—

"I accept the wager!"

"And I another onza!" added the Comandante.

"Señores," said Carlos, with an air of apparent regret, "I am sorry I cannot take both. This doubloon is all I have in the world; and it's not likely I could borrow another just now."

As he said this Carlos regarded the crowd with a smile, but many of these were in no humour for smiling. They were really awed by the terrible fate which they believed awaited the reckless cibolero. A voice, however, answered him:—

"Twenty onzas, Carlos, for any other purpose. But I cannot encourage this mad project."

It was the young ranchero, his former backer, who spoke.

"Thank you, Don Juan," replied the cibolero. "I know you would lend them. Thank you all the same. Do not fear! I'll win the onza. Ha! ha! ha! I haven't been twenty years in the saddle to be bantered by a *Gachupino*."

"Sir!" thundered Vizcarra and Roblado in a breath, at the same time grasping the hilts of their swords, and frowning in a fierce threatening manner.

"Oh! gentlemen, don't be offended," said Carlos, half sneeringly. "It only slipped from my tongue. I meant no insult, I assure you."

"Then keep your tongue behind your teeth, my good fellow," threatened Vizcarra. "Another slip of the kind may cost you a fall."

"Thank you, Señor Comandante," replied Carlos, still laughing. "Perhaps I'll take your advice."

The only rejoinder uttered by the Comandante was a fierce "Carrajo!" which Carlos did not notice; for at this moment his sister, having heard of his intention, sprang down from the carreta and came running forward, evidently in great distress.

"Oh, brother Carlos!" she cried, reaching out her arms, and grasping him by the knees, "Is it true? Surely it is not true?"

"What, *hermanita*?" (little sister), he asked with a smile.

"That you—"

She could utter no more, but turned her eyes, and pointed to the cliff.

"Certainly, Rosita, and why not? For shame, girl! Don't be alarmed—there's nought to fear, I assure you—I've done the like before."

"Dear, dear Carlos, I know you are a brave horseman—none braver—but oh! think of the danger—*Dios de mi alma*! think of—"

"Pshaw, sister! don't shame me before the people—come to mother!—hear what she will say. I warrant she won't regard it." And, so saying, the cibolero rode up to the carreta, followed by his sister.

Poor Rosita! Eyes gleamed upon you at that moment that saw you for the first time—eyes in whose dark orbs lay an expression that boded you no good. Your fair form, the angelic beauty of your face—perhaps your very grief—awakened interest in a heart whose love never meant else than ruin to its object. It was the heart of Colonel Vizcarra.

"*Mira*! Roblado!" muttered he to his subordinate and fellow-villain. "See yonder! *Santisima Virgen*! Saint Guadalupe! Look, man! Venus, as I'm a Christian and a soldier! In the name of all the saints, what sky has she fallen from?"

"For *Dios*! I never saw her before," replied the captain; "she must be the sister of this fellow: yes—hear them! they address each other as brother and sister! She *is* pretty!"

"*Ay de mi*!" sighed the Comandante. "What a godsend! I was growing dull—very dull of this monotonous frontier life. With this new excitement, perhaps, I may kill another month. Will she last me that long, think you?"

"Scarcely—if she come and go as easily as the rest. What! already tired of Inez?"

"Poh! poh! loved me too much; and that I can't bear. I would rather too little if anything."

"Perhaps this blonde may please you better in that respect. But, see! they are off!"

As Roblado spoke, Carlos and his sister had moved forward to the carreta which held their aged mother, and were soon in conversation with her.

The Comandante and his captain, as well as a large number of the spectators, followed, and crowded around to listen.

"She wants to persuade me against it, mother," Carlos was heard to say. He had already communicated his design. "Without *your* consent, I will not. But hear me, dear mother; I have half pledged myself, and I wish to make good my pledge. It is a *point of honour*, mother."

The last phrase was spoken loudly and emphatically in the ear of the old woman, who appeared to be a little deaf.

"Who wants to dissuade you?" she asked, raising her head, and glancing upon the circle of faces. "Who?"

"Rosita, mother."

"Let Rosita to her loom, and weave rebosos—that's what she's fit for. You, my son, can do great things—deeds, ay, deeds; else have you not in your veins the blood of your father. *He* did deeds—*he*—ha! ha! ha!"

The strange laugh caused the spectators to start, accompanied, as it was, with the wild look of her who uttered it.

"Go!" cried she, tossing back her long flax-coloured locks, and waving her arms in the air—"go, Carlos the cibolero, and show the tawny cowards—slaves that they are—what a free American can do. To the cliff! to the cliff!"

As she uttered the awful command, she sank back into the carreta, and relapsed into her former silence.

Carlos interrogated her no further. The expressions she had let slip had rendered him somewhat eager to close the conversation; for he noticed that they were not lost on several of the bystanders. The officers, as well as the priests and alcalde, exchanged significant glances while she was uttering them.

Placing his sister once more in the carreta, and giving her a parting embrace, Carlos leaped to the back of his steed, and rode forth upon the plain. When at some distance he reined in, and bent his eyes for a moment upon the tiers of benches where sat the señoras and señoritas of the town. A commotion could be observed among them. They had heard of the intended feat, and many would have dissuaded the cibolero from the perilous attempt.

There was one whose heart was full to bursting—full as that of Carlos' own sister; and yet she dared not show it to those around. She was constrained to sit in silent agony, and suffer.

Carlos knew this. He drew a white handkerchief from his bosom, and waved it in the air, as though bidding some one an adieu. Whether he was answered could not be told; but the next moment he wheeled his horse, and galloped off towards the cliffs.

There were conjectures among the señoras and señoritas, among the poblanas too, as to who was the recipient of that parting salute. Many guesses were made, many names mentioned, and scandal ran the rounds. One only of all knew in her heart for whom the compliment was meant—in her heart overflowing with love and fear.

Chapter Six

All who had horses followed the cibolero, who now directed himself towards a path that led from the valley to the table above. This path wound up the cliffs by zigzag turnings, and was the only one by which the upper plain could be reached at that point. A corresponding road traversed the opposite bluff, so that the valley might be here crossed; and this was the only practicable crossing for several miles up and down.

Though but a thousand feet separated the valley and table-land, the path leading from one to the other was nearly a mile in length; and as it was several miles from the scene of the festival to the bottom of the cliff, only those accompanied Carlos who were mounted, with a few others determined to witness every manoeuvre of this fearful attempt. Of course, the officers were of the party who went up. The rest of the people remained in the valley, but moved forward in the direction of the cliffs, so that they would be able to observe the more interesting and thrilling part of the spectacle.

For more than an hour those on the plain were kept waiting; but they did not allow the time to pass unimproved. A *monte* table had been spread out over which both gold and silver changed hands rapidly, the two padrés of the mission being among the highest bettors; and the señoras, among themselves, had a quiet little game of their favourite *chuza*. A "main" between a pair of sturdy chanticleers, one belonging to the alcalde and the other to the *cura* (!), furnished the interlude for another half-hour. In this contest the representative of the Church was triumphant. His grey cock ("pardo") killed the alcalde's red one at a single blow, by striking one of his long steel galves through the latter's head. This was regarded as a very interesting and pleasant spectacle by all on the ground—ladies included, and alcalde excepted.

By the time the cock-fight was finished, the attention of the crowd became directed to the movements of the party who had gone up to the upper plain. These were now seen along the edge of the cliff, and by their manoeuvres it was evident they were engaged in arranging the preliminaries of the perilous adventure. Let us join them.

The cibolero, on gaining the ground, pointed out the spot where he had proposed to execute his daring design. From the plain above the cliffs were not visible, and even the great abyss of the valley itself could not be seen a hundred paces back from the edge of the bluff. There was no escarpment or slope of any kind. The turf ran in to the very edge of the precipice, and on the same level with the rest of the plain. It was smooth and firm—covered with a short sward of *gramma* grass. There was neither break nor pebble to endanger the hoof. No accident could arise from that cause.

The spot chosen, as already stated, was a sort of buttress-like promontory that stood out from the line of bluffs. This formation was more conspicuous from below. Viewing it from above, it resembled a tongue-like continuation of the plain.

Carlos first rode out to its extremity, and carefully examined the turf. It was just of the proper firmness to preclude the possibility of a horse's hoof either sliding or sinking into it. He was accompanied by Vizcarra, Roblado, and others. Many approached the spot, but kept at a safe distance from the edge of the horrid steep. Though denizens of this land of grand geological features, there were many present who dreaded to stand upon the brow of that fearful ledge and look below.

The cibolero sat upon his horse, on its very edge, as calm as if he had been on the banks of the zequia, and directed the marking of the line. His horse showed no symptoms of nervousness. It was evident he was well-trained to such situations. Now and then he stretched out his neck, gazed down into the valley, and, recognising some of his kind below, uttered a shrill neigh. Carlos purposely kept him on the cliff, in order to accustom him to it before making the terrible trial.

The line was soon traced, less than two lengths of the horse from the last grass on the turf. Vizcarra and Roblado would have insisted upon short measure; but their proposal to curtail it was received with murmurs of disapprobation and mutterings of "Shame!"

What did these men want? Though not evident to the crowd, they certainly desired the death of the cibolero. Both had their reasons. Both hated the man. The cause or causes of their hatred were of late growth,—with Roblado still later than his Comandante. He had observed something within the hour that had rendered him furious. He had observed the waving of that white kerchief; and as he stood by the stand he had seen to whom the "adios" was addressed. It had filled him with astonishment and indignation; and his language to Carlos had assumed a bullying and brutal tone.

Horrible as such a supposition may seem, both he and Vizcarra would have rejoiced to see the cibolero tumble over the bluff. Horrible indeed it seems; but such were the men, and the place, and the times, that there is nothing improbable in it. On the contrary, cases of equal barbarity—wishes and *acts* still more inhuman—are by no means rare under the skies of "Nuevo Mexico."

The young ranchero, who had accompanied the party to the upper plain, insisted upon fair play. Though but a ranchero, he was classed among the "ricos," and, being a fellow of spirit, urged Carlos' rights, even in the face of the moustached and scowling militarios.

"Here, Carlos!" cried he, while the arrangements were progressing; "I see you are bent on this madness; and since I cannot turn you from it, I shall not embarrass you. But you sha'n't risk yourself for such a trifle. My purse! bet what sum you will."

As he said this, he held out a purse to the cibolero, which, from its bulk, evidently contained a large, amount.

Carlos regarded the purse for a moment without making answer. He was evidently gratified by the noble offer. His countenance showed that he was deeply touched by the kindness of the youth. "No," said he, at length; "no, Don Juan. I thank you with all my heart, but I cannot take your purse— one onza, nothing more. I should like to stake one against the Comandante."

"As many as you please," urged the ranchero.

"Thank you, Don Juan! only one—that with my own will be two.— Two onzas!—that, in faith, is the largest bet I have ever made. *Vaya*! a poor cibolero staking a double onza!"

"Well, then," replied Don Juan, "if you don't, I shall. Colonel Vizcarra!" said he aloud, addressing himself to the Comandante, "I suppose you would like to win back your wager. Carlos will now take your bet for the onza, and I challenge you to place ten."

"Agreed!" said the Comandante, stiffly.

"Dare you double it?" inquired the ranchero.

"Dare I, sir?" echoed the Colonel, indignant at being thus challenged in the presence of the spectators. "Quadruple it, if you wish, sir."

"Quadruple then!" retorted the other. "Forty onzas that Carlos performs the feat!"

"Enough! deposit your stakes!"

The golden coins were counted out, and held by one of the bystanders, and judges were appointed.

The arrangements having been completed, the spectators drew back upon the plain, and left the cibolero in full possession of the promontory — alone with his horse.

Chapter Seven

All stood watching him with interested eyes. Every movement was noted.

He first alighted from the saddle, stripped off his manga, had it carried back and placed out of the way. He next looked to his spurs, to see that the straps were properly buckled. After this he re-tied his sash, and placed the sombrero firmly on his head. He buttoned his velveteen calzoneros down nearly to his ankles, so that their leathern bottoms might not flap open and discommode him. His hunting-knife along with his "whip" were sent back to the charge of Don Juan.

His attention was next turned to his horse, that stood all this while curving his neck proudly as though he divined that he was to be called upon for some signal service. The bridle was first scrutinised. The great bit—a Mameluke—was carefully examined, lest there might be some flaw or crack in the steel. The head-strap was buckled to its proper tightness, and then the reins were minutely scanned. These were of the hair of wild horses' tails closely and neatly plaited. Leather might snap, there was no fear of breaking such cords as these.

The saddle now had its turn. Passing from side to side, Carlos tried both stirrup-leathers, and examined the great wooden blocks which formed the stirrups. The girth was the last as well as most important object of his solicitude. He loosed the buckles on both sides, and then tightened them, using his knees to effect his purpose. When drawn to his liking, the tip of the finger could not have been passed under the strong leathern band.

No wonder he observed all this caution. The snapping of a strap, or the slipping of a buckle, might have hurled him into eternity.

Having satisfied himself that all was right, he gathered up the reins, and leaped lightly into the saddle.

He first directed his horse at a walk along the cliff, and within a few feet of its edge. This was to strengthen the nerves both of himself and the animal. Presently the walk became a trot, and then a gentle canter. Even this was an exhibition fearful to behold. To those regarding it from below it was a beautiful but terrible spectacle.

After a while he headed back towards the plain, and then stretching into a fair gallop—the gait in which he intended to approach the cliff—he suddenly reined up again, so as to throw his horse nearly on his flanks. Again he resumed the same gallop and again reined up; and this manoeuvre he repeated at least a dozen times, now with his horse's head turned towards the cliffs, and now in the direction of the plain. Of course this gallop was far from being the full speed of the animal. That was not bargained for. To draw a horse up at race-course speed within two lengths of himself would be an utter impossibility, even by sacrificing the life of the animal. A shot passing through his heart would not check a racer in so short a space. A fair gallop was all that could be expected under the circumstances, and the judges expressed themselves satisfied with that which was exhibited before them. Carlos had put the question.

At length he was seen to turn his horse towards the cliff, and take his firmest seat in the saddle. The determined glance of his eyes showed that the moment had come for the final trial.

A slight touch of the spur set the noble brute in motion, and in another second he was in full gallop, and heading directly for the cliff!

The gaze of all was fixed with intense earnestness upon that reckless horseman. Every heart heaved with emotion; and, beyond their quick breathing, not an utterance escaped from the spectators. The only sounds heard were the hoof-strokes of the horse as they rang back from the hard turf of the plain.

The suspense was of short duration. Twenty strides brought horse and horseman close to the verge, within half-a-dozen lengths. The rein still hung loose—Carlos dared not tighten it—a touch he knew would bring his horse to a halt, and that before he had crossed the line would only be a failure.

Another leap,—another,—yet another! Ho! he is inside—Great God! He will be over!

Such exclamations rose from the spectators as they saw the horseman cross the line, still in a gallop; out the next moment a loud cheer broke from both crowds, and the "vivas" of those in the valley were answered by similar shouts from those who witnessed the feat from above.

Just as the horse appeared about to spring over the horrid brink, the reins were observed suddenly to tighten, the fore-hoofs became fixed and spread, and the hips of the noble animal rested upon the plain. He was poised at scarce three feet distance from the edge of the cliff! While in this attitude the horseman raised his right hand, lifted his sombrero, and after waving it round returned it to his head!

A splendid picture from below. The dark forms of both horse and rider were perceived as they drew up on the cliff, and the imposing and graceful attitude was fully developed against the blue background of the sky. The arms, the limbs, the oval outlines of the steed, even the very trappings, could be seen distinctly; and for the short period in which they were poised and motionless, the spectator might have fancied an equestrian statue of bronze, its pedestal the pinnacle of the cliff!

This period was but of a moment's duration, but, during its continuance, the loud "vivas" pealed upon the air. Those looking from below saw the horseman suddenly wheel, and disappear beyond the brow-line of the bluff.

The daring feat was ended and over; and hearts, but a moment ago throbbing wildly within tender bosoms, now returned to their soft and regular beating.

Chapter Eight

When the cibolero returned to the plain, he was received with a fresh burst of vivas, and kerchiefs were waved to greet him. One only caught his eye,—but that was enough. He saw not the rest, nor cared to see them. That little perfumed piece of cambric, with its lace border, was to him an ensign of hope—a banner that would have beckoned him on to achieve deeds of still higher daring. He saw it held aloft by a small jewelled hand, and waved in triumph for *him*. He was happy.

He passed the stand, rode up to the carreta, and, dismounting, kissed his mother and sister. He was followed by Don Juan, his backer;—and there were those who noticed that the eyes of the blonde were not always upon her brother: there was another on the ground who shared their kind glances, and that other was the young ranchero. No one, not even the dullest, could fail to notice that these kind glances were more than repaid. It was an affair of mutual and understood love, beyond a doubt.

Though Don Juan was a rich young farmer, and by courtesy a "Don," yet in rank he was but a degree above the cibolero—the degree which wealth confers. He was not one of the high aristocracy of the place,—about that he cared little; but he had the character of being a brave, spirited young fellow; and in time, if he desired it, might mingle with the "sangre azul." It was not likely he ever should—at least through the influence of marriage. Any one who was witness to the ardent glances exchanged between his eyes and those of the cibolero's sister, would prophesy with ease that Don Juan was not going to marry among the aristocracy.

It was a happy little group around the carreta, and there was feasting, too,—dulces, and orgeat, and wine from El Taso of the best vintage. Don Juan was not afraid to spend money, and he had no reason on that occasion, with fifty onzas of clear gain in his pocket—a fact that by no means sat easily on the mind of the Comandante.

The latter was observed, with a clouded countenance, strolling around, occasionally approaching the carreta, and glancing somewhat rudely towards the group. His glances were, in fact, directed on Rosita, and the consciousness of his almost despotic power rendered him careless of concealing his designs. His admiration was expressed in such a manner that many could perceive it. The poor girl's eyes fell timidly when they encountered his, and Don Juan, having noticed it, was not without feelings of anger as well as uneasiness. He knew the character of the Comandante, as well as the dangerous power with which he was armed. O Liberty! what a glorious thing art thou! How many hopes are blighted, how many loves crossed, and hearts crushed, in a land where thou art not! where the myrmidons of tyranny have power to thwart the purpose of a life, or arrest the natural flow of its affections!

Several games were yet carried on upon the plain, but they were without general interest. The splendid feat of the cibolero had eclipsed all lesser exhibitions for the time; besides, a number of the head men were out of humour. Vizcarra was sad, and Roblado savage—jealous of Catalina. The alcalde and his assistant were in a vexed state, as both had bet heavy sums on the red cock. Both the padrés had lost at *monté,* and they were no longer in a Christian spirit. The cura alone was in good spirits, and ready to back the "pardo" for another main.

The concluding game was at length heralded. It was to be the "*Correr el gallo*" (running the cock). As this is rather an exciting sport, the "*monté*" tables and other minor amusements were once more put aside; and all prepared to watch "el gallo."

"Running the cock" is a New Mexican game in all its characteristics. It is easily described. Thus: A cock is suspended by the limbs to a horizontal branch, at just such a height that a mounted man may lay hold of his head and neck hanging downward. The bird is fastened in such a manner that a smart pluck will detach him from the tree; while, to render this the more difficult, both head and neck are well covered with soap. The horseman must be in full gallop while passing under the branch; and he who succeeds in plucking down the cock is pursued by all the others, who endeavour to rob him of the prize. He has a fixed point to run round, and his goal is the tree from which he started. Sometimes he is over, taken before reaching this, the cock snatched from him,—or, as not infrequently happens, torn to pieces in the contest. Should he succeed in getting back—still retaining the bird entire—he is then declared victor. The scene ends by his laying his prize at the feet of his mistress; and she—usually some pretty poblana—appears that same evening at the fandango with the feathered trophy under her arm—thus signifying her appreciation of the compliment paid her, as well as giving to the *fandangueros* ocular proof of the fact that some skilful horseman is her admirer. It is a cruel sport, for it must be remembered that the poor cock who undergoes all this plucking and mangling is a *living bird*! It is doubtful whether a thought of the *cruelty* ever entered the mind of a New Mexican. If so, it must have been a New Mexican *woman*; for the humanity of these is in an inverse ratio to that of their lords. For the women it may be urged that the sport is a custom of the country; and what country is without its cruel sports? Is it rational or consistent to weep over the sufferings of Chanticleer, while we ride gaily upon the heels of poor broken Reynard?

There are two modes of the "Correr el gallo." The first has been described. The second only differs from it in the fact that the cock, instead of being tied to a tree, is buried up to his shoulders in the earth. The horsemen, as before, pass in routine—each bending from his saddle, and striving to pluck the bird out of the ground. For the rest the conditions are the same as before.

The first cock was hung to a branch; and the competitors having taken their places in a line, the game commenced.

Several made the attempt, and actually seized the bird's head, but the soap foiled them.

The dragoon sergeant was once more a competitor; but whether his colonel made any further bet upon him is not known. The Comandante had gambled enough for that day; and but for a little peculation which he enjoyed upon the mining "derechos," and other little customs dues, he would have felt his losses still more severely. Out of the derechos, however, he knew he could square himself at the expense of the vice-regal government.

The sergeant, who, as already stated, had the advantage of a tall figure and a tall horse, was able to get a full grasp at the neck of the bird; and being already provided, as was afterwards ascertained, with a fistful of sand, he took the prize with him, and galloped off.

But there were swifter horses than his on the ground; and before he could double the turning-post he was overtaken by an active vaquero, and lost a wing of his bird. Another wing was plucked from him by a second pursuer; and he returned to the tree with nothing but a fragment left! Of course he received neither *vivas* nor cheers.

Carlos the cibolero took no part in this contest. He knew that he had won glory enough for that day—that he had made both friends and enemies, and he did not desire to swell the list of either. Some of the bystanders, however, began to banter him, wishing, no doubt, to see him again exhibit his fine horsemanship. He withstood this for some time, until two more cocks were plucked from the tree—the vaquero already alluded to carrying one of them clear, and laying it at the feet of his smiling sweetheart.

A new thought seemed now to have entered the mind of Carlos, and he was seen riding into the lists, evidently about to take part in the next race.

"It will be some time before I can be present at another fiesta," remarked he to Don Juan. "Day after to-morrow I start for the plains. So I'll take all the sport I can out of this one."

An innovation was now introduced in the game. The bird was buried in the ground; and its long neck and sharp-pointed bill showed that it was no cock, but a snow-white "gruya," one of the beautiful species of herons common in these regions. Its fine tapering neck was not soiled with soap, but left in its natural state. In this case the chances of failure lay in the fact that, loosely buried as it was, the gruya would not allow its head to be approached by a hand, but jerked it from side to side, thus rendering it no easy matter to get hold of it.

The signal being given, away went the string of horsemen! Carlos was among the last, but on coming up he saw the white bending neck still there. His hand was too quick for the bird, and the next moment it was dragged from the yielding sand, and flapping its snowy wings over the withers of his horse.

It required not only speed on the part of Carlos, but great adroitness, to pass the crowd of horsemen, who now rushed from all points to intercept him. Here he dashed forward—there reined up—anon wheeled round a rider, and passed behind him; and, after a dozen such manoeuvres, the black horse was seen shooting off towards the turning-post alone. This passed, he galloped back to the goal, and holding up his prize, unstained and intact, received the applause of the spectators.

There was a good deal of guessing and wondering as to who would be the recipient of the trophy. Some girl of his own rank, conjectured the crowd; some poblana or ranchero's daughter. The cibolero did not seem in haste to gratify their curiosity; but, after a few minutes, he astonished them all, by flinging the gruya into the air, and suffering it to fly off. The bird rose majestically upward, and then, drawing in its long neck, was seen winging its way toward the lower end of the valley.

It was observed that before parting with the bird Carlos had plucked from its shoulders the long gossamer-like feathers that distinguish the heron species. These he was tying into a plume.

Having accomplished this, he put spurs to his horse, and, galloping up to the front of the stand, he bent gracefully forward, and deposited the trophy at the feet of *Catalina de Cruces*!

A murmur of surprise ran through the crowd, and sharp censure followed fast. What! a cibolero,—a poor devil, of whom nothing was known, aspire to the smiles of a rico's daughter? It was not a compliment. It was an insult! Presumption intolerable!

And these critiques were not confined to the señoras and señoritas. The poblanas and rancheros were as bitter as they. These felt themselves slighted—passed by—regularly jilted—by one of their own class. Catalina de Cruces, indeed!

Catalina—her situation was pleasant, yet painful—painful, because embarrassing. She smiled, then blushed, uttered a soft *"Gracias, cavallero!"* yet hesitated a moment whether to take up the trophy. A scowling father had started to his feet on one side, on the other a scowling lover. The last was Roblado.

"Insolent!" cried he, seizing the plume, and flinging it to the earth; "insolent!"

Carlos bent down from his saddle, once more laid hold of the plume, and stuck it under the gold band of his hat. Then, turning a defiant glance upon the officer, he said, "Don't lose your temper, Captain Roblado. A jealous lover makes but an indifferent husband." And transferring his look to Catalina, he added with a smile, and in a changed tone, "Gracias, señorita!"

As he said this he doffed his sombrero, and, waving it gracefully, turned his horse and rode off.

Roblado half drew his sword, and his loud "Carrajo!" along with the muttered imprecations of Don Ambrosio, reached the ears of the cibolero. But the captain was far from brave, with all his swagger; and seeing the long *machete* of the horseman strapped over his hips, he vented his spite in threats only, and suffered Carlos to depart.

The incident had created no small excitement, and a good deal of angry feeling. The cibolero had roused the indignation of the aristocracy, and the jealousy and envy of the democracy; so that, after all his brilliant performances, he was likely to leave the field anything but a favourite. The wild words of his strange old mother had been widely reported, and national hatred was aroused, so that his skill called forth envy instead of admiration. An angel indeed, should he have been to have won friendship there—he an Americano—a "heretico"—for in this far corner of the earth fanaticism was as fierce as in the Seven-hilled City itself during the gloomiest days of the Inquisition!

Mayhap it was as well for Carlos that the sports were now ended, and the fiesta about to close.

In a few minutes the company began to move off. The mules, oxen, and asses, were yoked to the carretas — the rancheros and rancheras climbed inside the deep boxes; and then, what with the cracking of quirts, the shouts of drivers, and the hideous screaming of the ungreased axles, a concert of sounds arose that would have astonished any human being, except a born native of the soil.

In half-an-hour the ground was clear, and the lean coyote might be seen skulking over the spot in search of a morsel for his hungry maw.

Chapter Nine

Though the field-sports were over, the fiesta of San Juan was not yet ended. There were still many sights to be seen before the crowd scattered to their homes. There was to be another turn at the church—another sale of "indultos," beads, and relics,—another sprinkling of sacred water, in order that the coffers of the padrés might be replenished toward a fresh bout at the *monté* table. Then there was an evening procession of the Saint of the day (John), whose image, set upon a platform, was carried about the town, until the five or six fellows who bore the load were seen to perspire freely under its weight.

The Saint himself was a curiosity. A large wax and plaster doll, dressed in faded silk that had once been yellow, and stuck all over with feathers and tinsel. A Catholic image Indianised, for the Mexican divinities were as much Indian as Roman. He appeared bored of the business, as, the joinings between head and neck having partially given way, the former drooped over and nodded to the crowd as the image was moved along. This nodding, however, which would have been laughed at as supremely ridiculous in any other than a priest-ridden country, was here regarded in a different light. The padrés did not fail to put their interpretation upon it, pointing it out to their devout followers as a mark of condescension on the part of the Saint, who, in thus bowing to the crowd, was expressing his approbation of their proceedings. It was, in fact, a regular miracle. So alleged both padrés and cura, and who was there to contradict them? It would have been a dangerous matter to have said nay. In San Ildefonso no man dared to disbelieve the word of the Church. The miracle worked well. The religious enthusiasm boiled up; and when Saint John was returned to his niche, and the little "cofre" placed in front of him, many a "peseta," "real," and "cuartillo," were dropped in, which would otherwise have been deposited that night in the *monté* bank. Nodding Saints and "winking Madonnas" are by no means a novel contrivance of the Holy Church. The padrés of its Mexican branch have had their wonderful saints too; and even in the almost *terra ignota* of New Mexico can be found a few of them that have performed as *smart* miracles as any recorded in the whole jugglery of the race.

A pyrotechnic display followed—and no mean exhibition of the sort neither—for in this "art" the New Mexicans are adepts. A fondness for "fireworks" is a singular but sure characteristic of a declining nation. Give me the statistics of pyrotechnic powder burnt by a people, and I shall tell you the standard measure of their souls and bodies. If the figure be a maximum, then the physical and moral measure will be the minimum, for the ratio is inverse.

I stood in the Place de Concorde, and saw a whole nation—its rich and its poor—gazing on one of these pitiful spectacles, got up for the purpose of duping them into contentment. It was the price paid them for parting with their liberty, as a child parts with a valuable gem for a few sugar-plums. They were gazing with a delight that seemed enthusiasm! I looked upon scrubby, stunted forms, a foot shorter than were their ancestors. I looked upon eyes that gleamed with demoralised thought.

These were the representatives of a once great people, and who still deem themselves the first of mankind. I felt sure that this was an illusion. The pyro-spectacle and its reception convinced me that I saw before me a people who had passed the culminating point of their greatness, and were now gliding rapidly down the declining slope that leads to annihilation and nothingness.

After the fireworks came the "fandango." There we meet the same faces, without much alteration in the costumes. The señoras and señoritas alone have doffed their morning dresses, and here and there a pretty poblana has changed her coarse woollen "nagua" for a gay flounced muslin.

The ball was held in the large saloon of the "Casa de Cabildo," which occupied one side of the "Plaza." On this festival day there was no exclusiveness. In the frontier towns of Mexico not much at any time, for, notwithstanding the distinctions of class, and the domineering tyranny of the government authorities, in matters of mere amusement there is a sort of democratic equality, a mingling of high and low, that in other countries is rare. English, and even American travellers, have observed this with astonishment.

All were admitted to the "Salon de baile" who chose to pay for it; and alongside the rico in fine broad-cloth you might see the ranchero in his leathern jacket and velveteen calzoneros; while the daughter of the rich comerciante danced in the same set with the "aldeana," whose time was taken up in kneading tortillas or weaving rebosos!

The Comandante with Roblado and the lieutenant figured at the fandango in full uniform. The alcalde was there with his gold-headed cane and tassel; the *cura* in his shovel hat; the padrés in their swinging robes; and all the "familias principales" of the place.

There was the rich comerciante, Don José Rincon, with his fat wife and four fat sleepy-looking daughters—there, too, the wife and family of the alcalde—there the Echevarrias, with their brother the "beau" in full Paris costume, with dress coat and crush hat—the only one to be seen in the saloon. There, too, the rich hacendado, Señor Gomez del Monté, with his lean wife and several rather lean daughters—differing in that respect from the hundreds of kine that roam over the pastures of his "ganada." And there, too, observed of all, was the lovely Catalina de Graces, the daughter of the wealthy miner Don Ambrosio, who himself is by her side, keeping a watchful eye upon her.

Besides these grand people there were employés of the mines of less note, clerks of the comerciantes, young farmers of the valley, gambucinos, vaqueros, ciboleros, and even "*leperos*" of the town, shrouded in their cheap serapés. A motley throng was the fandango.

The music consisted of a bandolon, a harp, and fiddle, and the dances were the waltz, the *bolero*, and the *coona*. It is but just to say that finer dancing could not have been witnessed in the saloons of Paris. Even the peon, in his leathern spencer and calzoneros, moved as gracefully as a professor of the art; and the poblanas, in their short skirts and gay coloured slippers, swept over the floor like so many coryphées of the ballet.

Roblado, as usual, was pressing his attentions on Catalina, and danced almost every set with her; but her eye wandered from his gold epaulettes and seemed to search the room for some other object. She was evidently indifferent to the remarks of her partner, and tired of his company.

Vizcarra's eyes were also in search of some one that did not appear to be present, for the Comandante strolled to and fro, peering into every group and corner with a dissatisfied look.

If it was the fair blonde he was looking for, he would be unsuccessful. She was not there. Rosita and her mother had returned home after the exhibition of the fireworks. Their house was far down the valley, and they had gone to it, accompanied by Carlos and the young ranchero. These, however, had returned to be present at the fandango. It was late before they made their appearance, the road having detained them. This was why the eye of Catalina wandered. Unlike Vizcarra, however, she was not to meet with disappointment.

While the dance was going on two young men entered the saloon, and soon mingled with the company. One of them was the young ranchero, the other was Carlos. The latter might easily have been distinguished by the heron-plume that waved over his black sombrero.

The eye of Catalina was no longer restless. It was now directed upon an object, though its glances were not fixed, but quick and stolen—stolen, because of the observation of an angry father and a jealous lover.

Carlos assumed indifference, though his heart was burning. What would he not have given to have danced with her? But he knew the situation too well. He knew that the offer of such a thing would lead to a scene. He dared not propose it.

At times he fancied that she had ceased to regard him—that she even listened with interest to Roblado—to the beau Echevarria—to others. This was but Catalina's fine acting. It was meant for other eyes than those of Carlos, but he knew not that, and became piqued.

He grew restless, and danced. He chose for his partner a very pretty "aldeana," Inez Gonzales by name, who was delighted to dance with him. Catalina saw this, and became jealous in turn.

This play continued for a length of time, but Carlos at length grew tired of his partner, and sat down upon the *banqueta* alone. His eyes followed the movements of Catalina. He saw that hers were bent upon him with glances of love,—love that had been avowed in words,—yes, had already been plighted upon oath. Why should they suspect each other?

The confidence of both hearts was restored; and now the excitement of the dance, and the less zealous guardianship of Don Ambrosio, half drunk with wine, gave confidence to their eyes, and they gazed more boldly and frequently at one another.

The ring of dancers whirling round the room passed close to where Carlos sat. It was a waltz. Catalina was waltzing with the beau Echevarria. At each circle her face was towards Carlos, and then their eyes met. In these transient but oft-recurring glances the eyes of a Spanish maid will speak volumes, and Carlos was reading in those of Catalina a pleasant tale. As she came round the room for the third time, he noticed something held between her fingers, which rested over the shoulder of her partner. It was a sprig with leaves of a dark greenish hue. When passing close to him, the sprig, dexterously detached, fell upon his knees, while he could just bear, uttered in a soft whisper, the word—"*Tuya!*"

Carlos caught the sprig, which was a branch of "tuya," or cedar. He well understood its significance; and after pressing it to his lips, he passed it through the button-hole of his embroidered "jaqueta." As Catalina came round again, the glances exchanged between them were those of mutual and confiding love.

The night wore on—Don Ambrosio at length became sleepy, and carried off his daughter, escorted by Roblado.

Soon after most of the ricos and fashionables left the saloon, but some tireless votaries of Terpsichore still lingered until the rosy Aurora peeped through the "rejas" of the Casa de Cabildo.

Chapter Ten

The "Llano Estacado," or "Staked Plain" of the hunters, is one of the most singular formations of the Great American Prairie. It is a table-land, or "steppe," rising above the regions around it to a height of nearly one thousand feet, and of an oblong or leg-of-mutton form, trending from north to south.

It is four hundred miles in length, and at its widest part between two and three hundred. Its superficial area is about equal to the island of Ireland. Its surface aspect differs considerably from the rest of prairie-land, nor is it of uniform appearance in every part. Its northern division consists of an arid steppe, sometimes treeless, for an extent of fifty miles, and sometimes having a stunted covering of mezquite (*acacia*), of which there are two distinct species. This steppe is in several places rent by chasms a thousand feet in depth, and walled in on both sides by rugged impassable precipices. Vast masses of shapeless rocks lie along the beds of these great clefts, and pools of water appear at long intervals, while stunted cedars grow among the rocks, or cling from the seams of the cliffs.

Such chasms, called "cañons," can only be crossed, or even entered, at certain points; and these passes are frequently a score of miles distant from each other.

On the upper plain the surface is often a dead level for a hundred miles, and as firm as a macadamised road. There are spots covered with a turf of grass of the varieties known as gramma, buffalo, and mezquite; and sometimes the traveller encounters a region where shallow ponds of different sizes stud the plain—a few being permanent, and surrounded by sedge. Most of these ponds are more or less brackish, some sulphurous, and others perfectly salt. After heavy rains such aqueous deposits are more numerous, and their waters sweeter; but rain seems to fall by accident over this desolate region, and after long spells of drought the greater number of these ponds disappear altogether.

Towards the southern end of the Llano Estacado the surface exhibits a very singular phenomenon—a belt of sand-hills, nearly twenty miles in breadth and full fifty in length, stretching north and south upon the plain. These hills are of pure white sand, thrown up in ridges, and sometimes in cones, to the height of a hundred feet, and without tree, bush, or shrub, to break their soft outlines, or the uniformity of their colour. But the greatest anomaly of this geological puzzle is, that water-ponds are found in their very midst—even among their highest ridges—and this water not occasional, as from rains, but lying in "lagunas," with reeds, rushes, and *nymphae* growing in them, to attest that the water is permanent! The very last place where water might be expected to make a lodgment.

Such formations of drift-sand are common upon the shores of the Mexican Gulf, as well as on European coasts, and there their existence is easily explained; but here, in the very heart of a continent, it cannot be regarded as less than a singular phenomenon.

This sand-belt is passable at one or two points, but horses sink to the knees at every step, and but for the water it would be a perilous experiment to cross it.

Where is the Llano Estacado? Unroll your map of North America. You will perceive a large river called the Canadian rising in the Rocky Mountains, and running, first southerly, and then east, until it becomes part of the Arkansas. As this river bends eastwardly, it brushes the northern end of the Llano Estacado, whose bluffs sometimes approach close to its banks, and at other times are seen far off, resembling a range of mountains—for which they have been frequently mistaken by travellers.

The boundary of the west side of the "Staked Plain" is more definite. Near the head-waters of the Canadian another large river has its source. This the Pecos. Its course, you will observe, is nearly south, but your map is not correct, as for several hundred miles the Pecos runs within a few degrees of east. It afterwards takes a southerly direction, before it reaches its embouchure in the Rio Grande. Now the Pecos washes the whole western base of the Llano Estacado; and it is this very plain, elevated as it is, that turns the Pecos into its southerly course, instead of leaving it to flow eastward, like all the other prairie-streams that head in the Rocky Mountains.

The eastern boundary of the Llano Estacado is not so definitely marked, but a line of some three hundred miles from the Pecos, and cutting the head-waters of the Wichita, the Louisiana Bed, the Brazos, and Colorado, will give some idea of its outline. These rivers, and their numerous tributaries, all head in the eastern "ceja" (brow) of the Staked Plain, which is cut and channelled by their streams into tracts of the most rugged and fantastic forms.

At the south the Llano Estacado tapers to a point, declining into the mezquite plains and valleys of numerous small streams that debouch into the Lower Rio Grande.

This singular tract is without one fixed dweller; even the Indian never makes abode upon it beyond the few hours necessary to rest from his journey, and there are parts where he—inured as he is to hunger and thirst—dare not venture to cross it. So perilous is the "Jornada," or crossing of the Llano Estacado, that throughout all its length of four hundred miles there are only two places where travellers can effect it in safety! The danger springs from the want of water, for there are spots of grass in abundance; but even on the well-known routes there are, at certain seasons, stretches of sixty and eighty miles where not a drop of water is to be procured!

In earlier times one of these routes was known as the "Spanish Trail," from Santa Fé to San Antonio de Bexar, of Texas; and lest travellers should lose their way, several points were marked with "palos," or stakes. Hence the name it has received.

The Llano Estacado is now rarely travelled, except by the ciboleros, or Mexican buffalo-hunters, and "Comancheros," or Indian traders. Parties of these cross it from the settlements of New Mexico, for the purpose of hunting the buffalo, and trafficking with the Indian tribes that roam over the plains to the east. Neither the hunt nor the traffic is of any great importance, but it satisfies a singular race of men, whom chance or inclination has led to the adopting it as a means of subsistence.

These men are to the Mexican frontier pretty much what the hunter and backwoodsman are upon the borders of the Anglo-American settlements. They are, however, in many respects different from the latter—in arms and equipments, modes of hunting, and otherwise. The outfit of a cibolero, who is usually also a *coureur de bois*, is very simple. For hunting, he is mounted on a tolerable—sometimes a fine—horse and armed with a bow and arrows, a hunting-knife, and a long lance. Of fire-arms he knows and cares nothing—though there are exceptional cases. A lazo is an important part of his equipment. For trading, his stock of goods is very limited—often not costing him twenty dollars! A few bags of coarse bread (an article of food which the prairie Indians are fond of), a sack of "piñole," some baubles for Indian ornament, some coarse serapés, and pieces of high-coloured woollen stuffs, woven at home: these constitute his "invoice." Hardware goods he does not furnish to any great extent. These stand him too high in his own market, as they reach it only after long carriage and scandalous imposts. Fire-arms he has nothing to do with: such prairie Indians as use these are furnished from the eastern side; but many Spanish pieces—fusils and escopettes—have got into the hands of the Comanches through their forays upon the Mexican towns of the south.

In return for his outlay and perilous journey, the cibolero carries back dried buffalo-flesh and hides—some the produce of his own hunting, some procured by barter from the Indians.

Horses, mules, and asses, are also articles of exchange. Of these the prairie Indians possess vast herds—some individuals owning hundreds; and most of them with Mexican brands! In other words, they have been stolen from the towns of the *Lower* Rio Grande, to be sold to the towns of the *Upper* Rio Grande, and the trade is deemed perfectly legitimate,—at least, there is no help for it as the case stands.

The cibolero goes forth on the plains with a rare escort. Sometimes a large number of these men, taking their wives and families with them, travel together just like a tribe of wild Indians. Generally, however, one or two leaders, with their servants and equipage, form the expedition. They experience less molestation from the savages than ordinary travellers. The Comanches and other tribes know their object, and rather encourage them to come amongst them. Notwithstanding, they are often cheated and ill-used by these double-faced dealers. Their mode of transport is the pack-mule, and the "carreta" drawn by mules or oxen. The carreta is of itself a picture of primitive locomotion. A pair of block-wheels, cut out of a cotton-wood tree, are joined by a stout wooden axle. The wheels usually approach nearer to the oval, or square, than the circular form. A long tongue leads out from the axle-tree, and upon top of this a square, deep, box-like body is placed. To this two or more pairs of oxen are attached in the most simple manner—by lashing a cross-piece of wood to their horns which has already been made fast to the tongue. The animals have neither yoke nor harness, and the forward push of the head is the motive power by which the carreta is propelled. Once in motion, the noise of the wooden axle is such as to defy description. The cries of a whole family, with children of all sizes, in bitter agony, can alone represent the concert of terrible sounds; and we must go to South Mexico to find its horrid equal in a troop of howling monkeys.

Chapter Eleven

About a week after the fiesta of Saint John, a small party of ciboleros was seen crossing the Pecos, at the ford of the "Bosque Redondo." The party was only five in number, and consisted of a white man, a half-blood, and three pure-bred Indians, having with them a small *atajo* of pack-mules, and three ox-team carretas. The crouching trot of the Indians, as well as their tilma dresses and sandalled feet, showed that they were "Indios mansos." They were, in fact, the hired *peons* of Carlos the cibolero—the white man, and chief of the party.

The half-blood—Antonio by name—was "arriero" of the mule-train, while the three Indians drove the ox-teams, guiding them across the ford with their long goads. Carlos himself was mounted upon his fine black horse, and, muffled in a strong serapé, rode in front to pilot the way. His beautiful manga had been left behind, partly to save it from the rough wear of such an expedition, and also that it might not excite the cupidity of the prairie Indians, who, for such a brilliant mantle as it was, would not hesitate to take his scalp. Besides the manga, the embroidered jacket, the scarlet scarf, and velveteen calzoneros, had all been put off, and others of a coarser kind were now worn in their place.

This was an important expedition for Carlos. He carried with him the largest freight he had ever taken upon the prairies. Besides the three carretas with four oxen each, the atajo consisted of five pack-mules, all loaded with merchandise—the carretas with bread, piñole, Spanish beans, Chilé peppers; and the packs were made up of serapé blankets, coarse woollen cloth, and a few showy trinkets, as also some Spanish knives, with their pointed triangular blades. It was his bold luck on the day of the fiesta that had enabled him to provide such a stock. In addition to his own original onza and the two he had won, the young ranchero, Don Juan, had insisted upon his accepting the loan of five others towards an outfit for this expedition.

The little troop, having safely forded the Pecos, headed towards the "ceja" of the Llano Estacado, that was not far distant from the crossing of Bosque Redondo. A sloping ravine brought them to the top of the "mesa," where a firm level road lay before them—a smooth plain without break or bush to guide them on their course.

But the cibolero needed no guide. No man knew the Staked Plain better than he; and, setting his horse's head in a direction a little south of east, the train moved on. He was striking for one of the head branches of the Red River of Louisiana, where he had heard that for several seasons past the buffalo had appeared in great numbers. It was a new route for him—as most of his former expeditions had been made to the upper forks of the Texan rivers Brazos had Colorado. But the plains around these rivers were at this time in undisputed possession of the powerful tribe of Comanches, and their allies, the Kiawas, Lipans, and Tonkewas. Hence, these Indians, uninterrupted in their pursuit of the buffalo, had rendered the latter wild and difficult of approach, and had also thinned their numbers. On the waters of the Red River the case was different. This was hostile ground. The Wacoes, Panés, Osages, and bands from the Cherokee, Kickapoo, and other nations to the east, occasionally hunted there, and sanguinary conflicts occurred among them; so that one party or another often lost their season's hunt by the necessity of keeping out of each other's range; and the game was thus left undisturbed. It is a well-known fact that in a neutral or "hostile ground" the buffalo, as well as other game, are found in greatest abundance, and are there more easily approached than elsewhere.

With a knowledge of these facts, Carlos the cibolero had determined to risk an expedition to the Red River, whose head-waters have their source in the eastern "ceja" of the Llano Estacado, and *not* in the Rocky Mountains as laid down upon maps.

Carlos was well armed for hunting the buffalo—so was the half-blood Antonio—and two of the three peons were also experienced hunters. Their arms consisted of the bow and lance, both weapons being preferable to fire-arms for buffalo-hunting. In one of the carretas, however, might be seen a weapon of another kind—a long brown American rifle. This Carlos kept for other and higher game, and he well knew how to use it. But how came such a weapon into the hands of a Mexican cibolero? Remember Carlos was not of Mexican origin. The weapon was a family relic. It had been his father's.

We shall not follow Carlos and his "caravan" through all the details of their weary "journeyings" across the desert plain. At one place they made a "Jornada" of seventy miles without water. But the experienced Carlos knew how to accomplish this without the loss of a single animal.

He travelled thus. Having given his cattle as much as they would drink at the last watering-place, he started in the afternoon, and travelled until near daybreak. Then a halt of two hours was made, so that the animals should graze while the dew was still on the grass. Another long march followed, continuing until noon, then a rest of three or four hours brought the cool evening, when a fresh spell of marching brought the "Jornada" to its end, far on in the following night. Such is the mode of travelling still practised on the desert steppes of Chihuahua, Sonora, and North Mexico.

After several days' travelling the cibolero and his party descended from the high "mesa," and, passing down its eastern slope, arrived on a tributary of the Red River. Here the scenery assumed a new aspect—the aspect of the "rolling" prairie. Gentle declivities, with soft rounded tops declining into smooth verdant vales, along which meandered streams of clear and sparkling water. Here and there along the banks stood groves of trees, such as the evergreen live-oak, the beautiful "pecan" with its oblong edible nuts, the "overcup" with its odd-looking acorns, the hackberry with its nettle-shaped leaves and sweet fruits, and the silvery cotton-wood. Along the swells could be seen large trees standing apart, and at almost equal distances, as though planted for an orchard. Their full leafy tops gave them a fine appearance, and their light pinnate leaves, with the long brown legumes hanging from their branches, told they were the famous "mezquite" trees—the American acacia. The red mulberry could be seen in the creek bottoms, and here and there the beautiful wild-china-tree with its pretty lilac flowers. The whole surface both of hill and valley was clad in a rich mantle of short *buffalo* grass, which gave it the aspect of a meadow lately mown, and springing into fresh verdure. It was a lovely landscape, and no wonder the wild bulls of the prairies chose it for their favourite range.

The cibolero had not travelled far through this favoured region until he came upon the buffalo sign—"roads", "wallows", and "bois de vache;" and next morning he found himself in the midst of vast herds, roaming about like tame cattle, and browsing at their leisure. So little shy were they, they scarce deigned to make off at his approach!

Of course he had reached the end of his journey. This was his great stock-farm. These were his own cattle—as much his as any one else's; and he had nothing more to do but set to killing and curing.

As to his trade with the Indians, that would take place whenever he should chance to fall in with a party—which he would be certain to do in the course of the season.

Like all men of the prairie, rude trappers as well as Indians, Carlos had an eye for the picturesque, and therefore chose a beautiful spot for his camp. It was a grassy bottom, through which ran a clear "arroyo" of sweet water, shaded by pecan, mulberry, and wild-china-trees, and under the shadow of a mulberry grove his carretas were halted and his tent was pitched.

Chapter Twelve

Carlos had commenced his hunt, and was making rapid progress. In the first two days he had slaughtered no less than twenty buffaloes, and had them all carried to camp. He and Antonio followed the buffalo and shot them down, while two of the peons skinned the animals, cut up the meat, and packed it to camp. There, under the hands of the third, it underwent the further process of being "jerked," that is, cut into thin slices and dried in the sun.

The hunt promised to be profitable. Carlos would no doubt obtain as much "tasajo" as he could carry home, besides a large supply of hides, both of which found ready sale in the towns of New Mexico.

On the third day, however, the hunters noticed a change in the behaviour of the buffalo. They had suddenly grown wild and wary. Now and then vast gangs passed them, running at full speed, as if terrified and pursued! It was not Carlos and his companion that had so frighted them. What then had set them a-running?

Carlos conjectured that some Indian tribe was in the neighbourhood engaged in hunting them.

His conjecture proved correct. On ascending a ridge which gave him a view of a beautiful valley beyond, his eye rested upon an Indian encampment.

It consisted of about fifty lodges, standing like tents along the edge of the valley, and fronting towards the stream. They were of a conical form, constructed of a framework of poles set in a circle, drawn together at their tops, and then covered with skins of the buffalo.

"Waco lodges!" said the cibolero, the moment his practised eye fell upon them.

"Master," inquired Antonio, "how do you tell that?" Antonio's experience fell far short of that of his master, who from childhood had spent his life on the prairies.

"How!" replied Carlos, "by the lodges themselves."

"I should have taken it for a Comanche camp," said the half-blood. "I have seen just such lodges among the 'Buffalo-eaters.'"

"An estampeda!" said the cibolero, in a husky voice; "my poor mules—all gone—*every* one of them! A curse upon Indian duplicity!"

Carlos had not the slightest doubt but that the marauders were the Wacoes—the very same from whom he had purchased the mules. He knew that such an occurrence was by no means rare—that oftentimes the traders are robbed in this way; and not unusual is it for them to purchase a second time the very animals thus carried off, and from the same Indians who have stolen them!

"A curse upon Indian duplicity!" he repeated with indignant emphasis. "No wonder they were so free and generous in their barter! It was but a plot on the part of the cowardly thieves to take from me my whole cargo, without daring to do so openly. *Carajo!* I am lost!"

This last phrase was uttered in a tone that partook equally of anger and grief.

The cibolero was certainly placed in an unpleasant situation. All his hopes—lately running so high—were crushed in a single moment. His whole property taken from him—the object of his enterprise lost—his long, perilous, and painful journeyings made for nothing. He should return empty-handed, poorer than when he set out—for his own five pack-mules were gone among the rest. The oxen, and his faithful steed, tied to the carretas, alone remained. These would scarce serve to carry provision for himself and party on their journey home; no cargo—not a bale of hides—not a "bulta" of meat more than would be required for their own food!

These reflections all passed through the mind of the cibolero in the space of a few moments, as he stood gazing in the direction in which the marauders had gone. He made no attempt to follow—that would have been worse than useless. On his splendid horse he might have overtaken them—only to die on the points of their lances!

"A curse upon Indian duplicity!" he once more repeated; and then, rising to his feet, walked back to the corral, and gave orders for the oxen to be drawn close up and firmly fastened to the carretas. Another surprise might be attempted by some lingering party of the savages; and, as it would be unsafe to go to sleep, the cibolero and his four companions remained awake and on the alert for the remainder of the night.

Chapter Fourteen

That was a *noche triste* to Carlos—a night of painful reflections. Bereft of his property—in the midst of hostile Indians, who might change their minds, return, and massacre him and his party—many hundred miles from home, or from any settlement of whites—a wide desert to be traversed—the further discouragement that there was no object for his going home, now that he was stripped of all his trading-stock—perhaps to be laughed at on his return—no prospect of satisfaction or indemnity, for he well knew that his government would send out no expedition to revenge so humble an individual as he was—he knew, in fact, that no expedition of Spanish soldiery could penetrate to the place, even if they had the will; but to fancy Vizcarra and Roblado sending one on his account! No, no; there was no hope of his obtaining satisfaction. He was cruelly robbed, and he knew that he must endure it; but what a blighted prospect was before him!

As soon as day broke he would go to the Waco camp—he would boldly upbraid them for their treachery. But what purpose would that serve? Besides, would he find them still there? No; most likely they were moving off to some other part at the time they had planned the robbery!

Several times during the night a wild idea occurred to him. If he could not have indemnity he might obtain revenge. The Wacoes were not without enemies. Several bordering tribes were at war with them; and Carlos knew they had a powerful foe in the Panés.

"My fortune is bitter," thought Carlos; "but revenge is sweet! What if I seek the Pané,—tell him my intention,—offer him my lance, my bow, and my true rifle? I have never met the Pané. I know him not; but I am no weak hand, and now that I have a cause for vengeance he will not despise my aid. My men will follow me—I know they will—anywhere; and, tame 'Tagnos' though they be, they can fight when roused to revenge. I shall seek the Pané!"

The last thought was uttered half aloud, and with emphasis that spoke determination. The cibolero was a man of quick resolves, and this resolve he had actually come to. It is not to be wondered at, His indignation at being treated in such a cruel and cowardly manner—the poor prospect before him on returning to the settlement—his natural desire to punish those who had placed him in such a predicament—as well as some hope which he still entertained of recovering at least a part of his lost property,—all influenced him to this resolve. He had determined upon it, and was just on the point of communicating his determination to his companions, when he was interrupted by the half-blood Antonio.

"Master," said the latter, who appeared to have been for some time busied with his own thoughts, "did you notice nothing strange?"

"When, Antonio?"

"During the estampeda."

"What was there strange?"

"Why, there appeared to be a good number, full half, of the rascals afoot."

"True; I observed that."

"Now, master, I have seen a *cavallada* stampeded by the Comanches more than once—they were always mounted."

"What signifies that? These are Wacoes, not Comanches."

"True, master; but I have heard that the Wacoes, like the Comanches, are true Horse-Indians, and never go afoot on any business."

"That is indeed so," replied the cibolero in a reflective mood. "Something strange, I confess."

"But, master," continued the half-blood, "did you notice nothing else strange during the stampede?"

"No," answered Carlos; "I was so annoyed—so put out by the loss—I scarce noticed anything. What else, Antonio?"

"Why, in the midst of these yellings, did you not hear a shrill whoop now and then—a *whistle*?"

"Ha! did you hear that?"

"More than once—distinctly."

"Where were my ears?" asked the cibolero of himself. "You are sure, Antonio?"

"Quite sure, master."

Carlos remained for a moment silent, evidently engaged in busy reflection. After a pause, he broke out in a half-soliloquy:—

"It may have been—it must have been—by Heavens! it must—"

"What, master?"

"The Pané whistle!"

"Just what I was thinking, master. The Comanches never whoop so—the Kiawa never. I have not heard that the Wacoes give such a signal. Why not Pané? Besides, their being afoot—that's like Pané!"

A sudden revulsion had taken place in the mind of the cibolero. There was every probability that Antonio's conjecture was correct. The "whistle" is a peculiar signal of the Pané tribes. Moreover, the fact of so many of the marauders being on foot—that was another peculiarity. Carlos knew that among the Southern Indians such a tactic is never resorted to. The Panés are *Horse*-Indians too, but on their marauding expeditions to the South they often go afoot, trusting to return mounted—which they almost invariably do.

"After all," thought Carlos, "I have been wronging the Wacoes—the robbers are Panés!"

But now a new suspicion entered his mind. It was still the Wacoes that had done it. They had adopted the Pané whistle to deceive him! A party of them might easily be afoot—it was not such a distance to their camp,—besides, after the estampeda they had gone in that very direction!

No doubt, should he go there on the morrow, they would tell him that Panés were in the neighbourhood, that it was they who had stolen his mules—the mules of course he would not see, as these would be safely concealed among the hills.

"No, Antonio," he said, after making these reflections, "our enemies are the Wacoes themselves."

"Master," replied Antonio, "I hope not."

"I hope not, too, camarado. I had taken a fancy to our friends of but yesterday: I should be sorry to find them our foes—but I fear it is even so."

With all, Carlos was not confident; and now that he reflected, another circumstance came to his mind in favour of the Wacoes. His companions had also noted it.

That circumstance was the running of the buffaloes observed during the past few days. The gangs had passed from the north, going southward; and their excited manner was almost a proof that they were pressed by a party of hunters. The Wacoes were all this time hunting to the south of the cibolero's camp! This would seem to indicate that some other Indians were upon the north. What more likely than a band of Panés?

Again Carlos reproached himself for his too hasty suspicions of his new friends. His mind was filled with doubts. Perhaps these would be resolved by the light of the morning.

As soon as day should arrive, he had resolved to go to the Waco camp, and satisfy himself, or at all events openly make his inquiries.

The first streaks of daylight were just falling upon the prairie, when the quick keen eye of the half-blood, ranging the ground in every direction, was arrested by the appearance of something odd upon the grass. It lay near the spot where the *mulada* had been picketed. It was a darkish object in a recumbent position. Was it bushes or gorse? No. It could not be that. Its outlines were different. It was more like some animal lying down—perhaps a large wolf? It was near the place where they had fancied that they saw something in the darkness, and at which Carlos had fired.

Antonio, on first perceiving the object, called his master's attention to it, and both now gazed over the box of the carreta, scanning it as well as the grey light would permit them.

As this became brighter, the object was seen more distinctly, while at each moment the curiosity of the ciboleros increased. They would have long since gone out to examine it more closely; but they were not yet free from apprehensions of a second attack from the Indians; and they prudently remained within the corral.

At length, however, they could forego an examination no longer. They had formed their suspicion of what the object was; and Carlos and Antonio climbed over the carretas, and proceeded towards it.

On arriving at the spot they were not so much surprised—for they had partially anticipated such a thing—at finding the body of a dead Indian. It was lying flat upon the grass, face downwards; and, on closer examination, a wound, from which much blood had run, was perceived in the side. There was the mark of a rifle bullet—Carlos had not fired in vain! They bent down, and turned over the body to examine it. The savage was in full war-costume—that is, naked to the waist, and painted over the breast and face so as to render him as frightful as possible: but what struck the ciboleros as most significant was the *costume of his head*! This was close shaven over the temples and behind the ears. A patch upon the top was clipped short, but in the centre of the crown one long lock of hair remained uncut, and this lock was intermingled with plumes, and plaited so as to hang, queue-like, down the back. The naked temples were stained with vermilion, and the cheeks and bosom daubed in a similar manner. These brilliant spots contrasted with the colourless and deathly hue of the skin, and, with the blanched lips and glazed eyeballs, gave to the corpse a hideous appearance.

Carlos, after gazing upon it for some moments, turned to his companion with a look of intelligence; and, pointing to the shaved head, and then to the moccasins upon the Indian's feet, in a tone that expressed the satisfaction he felt at the discovery, pronounced the word,—"Pané!"

Chapter Fifteen

The dead Indian was a Pané beyond doubt. The tonsure of his hair, the cut of his moccasins, his war-paint, enabled Carlos to tell this.

The cibolero was glad that he was a Pané. He had several reasons for being so. First, it gratified him to know that his Waco friends were still true; secondly, that he had punished one of the robbers; and, lastly, the knowledge that they were Panés gave him some hope that he might yet recover, *by the help of the Wacoes,* some of the stolen mules.

This was not improbable. As already stated, the Wacoes and Panés were sworn foes; and as soon as the former should hear that the latter were in the neighbourhood, Carlos felt sure they would go in pursuit of them. He would share in this pursuit with his little band, and, in the event of the Panés being defeated, might get back his *mulada.*

His first impulse, therefore, was, to gallop to the Waco camp—apprise them of the fact that the Pané was on the war-trail, and then join them in search of the latter.

Just then both he and Antonio remembered that the Panés had themselves gone in the direction of the Waco camp! It was not two miles distant—they could hardly fail to find it, even in the night. What if they had taken the Wacoes by surprise, and had already made their attack!

It was quite probable—more than probable. The time and the hour were just in keeping. The estampeda had occurred before midnight. No doubt they were then on their way to the Waco village. They would just be in time to make their attack, at the usual hour for such forays, between midnight and morning.

Carlos feared he might be too late to give warning. His Waco friends may have already perished! Whether or no, he determined to proceed at once to their encampment.

Leaving Antonio and the peons with directions to guard and defend his own camp to the last, he rode off, armed both with rifle and bow. It was yet but grey day, but he knew the trail leading to the Waco village, and followed it without difficulty. He rode with caution, scanning the timber copses before approaching them; and running his eye along the crests of the ridges as he advanced.

This caution was not unnecessary. The Panés could not be far off—they might still be in ambush between him and the Waco camp, or halted among the hills.

The cibolero had but little fear of meeting one or two of them. He rode a horse in which he had full confidence; and he knew that no Pané could overtake him; but he might be surrounded by numbers, and intercepted before he could reach the Waco lodges. That was the reason why he advanced with so much caution.

His ears were set to listen attentively. Every sound was noted and weighed—the "gobble" of the wild turkey from the branches of the oak; the drumming of the ruffed grouse on some dry knoll; the whistling of the fallow-deer; or the tiny bark of the prairie marmot. All these were well-known sounds; and as each was uttered, the cibolero stopped and listened attentively. Under other circumstances he would not have heeded them, but he knew that these sounds could be imitated, and his ear was bent to detect any counterfeit. He could distinguish the Pané trail of the previous night. A strong band there must have been, by the numerous tracks on the grass. At the crossing of a stream Carlos could detect the prints of moccasins in the sand. There were still some of the party afoot then, though, no doubt, the stolen *mulada* had mounted a good many.

Carlos rode on with more caution than ever. He was half-way to the Waco village, and still the Pané trail led in that direction. Surely these could not have passed without finding it? Such skilled warriors as the Panés would not. They would see the trail of the Wacoes leading to the cibolero's own camp—they would soon discover the lodges—perhaps they had already made their attack—perhaps—

The reflections of the cibolero were suddenly interrupted; distant sounds fell upon his ear—shouts and cries of fearful import—with that continued murmur that results from the mingling of many voices in loud and confused clamour. Now and then was heard a whoop, or a cheer, or a shrill whistle, rising above the ordinary noises, and carrying far over the plain its tones of triumph or revenge.

Carlos knew the import of those shouts and cries—they were the sounds of battle!—of terrible and deadly strife!

They came from behind the hill—the cibolero was just climbing it.

He spurred his horse, and, galloping forward to its crest, looked down into the valley. The conflict was raging before him!

He had a full view of the dreadful scene. Six hundred dusky horsemen were riding about on the plain; some dashing at each other with couched lances—some twanging their bows from a distance; and others close together in the hand-to-hand combat of the deadly tomahawk! Some were charging in groups with their long spears—some wheeling into flight, and others, dismounted, were battling on foot! Some took shelter among the timber islands, and sprang out again as they saw an opportunity of sending an arrow, or lancing a foeman in the back; and so the red contest continued.

Not a shot was heard—neither bugle nor drum sent forth their inspiring notes—no cannon rolled its thunder—no rocket blazed—no smoke spread its sulphury cloud upon the air; but without these sights and sounds there was no fear of mistaking that contest for a mimic game—a tournament of the prairies. The wild war-whoop, and the wilder whistle—the earnest onslaught—the fierce charging cheer—the cries of triumph and vengeance—the neighing steeds without riders—here and there the prostrate savage, with skinless scalp, glaring red in the sun—the spears and hatchets crimsoned with blood,—all were evidence of real and deadly strife, and Carlos did not doubt for a moment the character of the scene. Before him was an Indian fight—Waco and Pané engaged in the earnest struggle of life and death!

All this he comprehended at a glance, and, after regarding the fight for a moment, he could distinguish the warriors of both tribes from one another. The Panés, in full war-costume, were easily recognised by their tufted scalp-locks; while the Wacoes, who had, no doubt, been taken by surprise, were many of them in hunting-shirts and leggings. Some, however, were nearly as naked as their adversaries; but easily distinguished from them by their full flowing hair.

The first impulse of the cibolero was to gallop forward and mingle in the fight,—of course, taking side with the Wacoes. The sound of the conflict roused his blood, and the sight of the robbers who had so lately ruined him rendered him eager for revenge. Many of them were mounted upon the very mules they had taken from him, and Carlos was determined to have some of them back again.

He was about to put spurs to his horse, and dash forward, when a sudden change seemed to occur in the conflict that decided him to remain where he was. The Panés were giving way!

Many of them were seen wheeling out of the plain, and taking to flight.

As Carlos looked down the hill, he saw three of the Pané warriors in full run, making up to the spot where he stood. Most of the band were still fighting, or had fled in a different direction; but these, cut off from the rest, came directly up the hill at a gallop.

The cibolero had drawn his horse under the cover of some trees, and was not perceived by them until they were close to the spot.

At this moment the war-cry of the Wacoes was heard directly in their rear, and Carlos saw that two mounted warriors of that tribe were in pursuit. The fugitives looked back, and, seeing only two adversarios after them, once more wheeled round and gave fight.

At their first charge one of the pursuers was killed, and the other—whom Carlos now recognised as the Waco chief—was left alone against three assailants.

The whip-like crack of the cibolero's rifle sounded on the air, and one of the Panés dropped out of his saddle. The other two, ignorant of whence the shot had come, continued their onset on the Waco chief, who, dashing close up, split the skull of one of there with his tomahawk. His horse, however, bore him rapidly past, and before he could wheel round, the remaining Pané—an active warrior—rushed after and thrust his long spear into the back of the chief. Its head passed clear through his body, completely impaling him; and with a death-whoop, the noble Indian fell from his horse to the ground.

But his enemy fell at the same time. The arrow of the cibolero was too late to save, though not to avenge, the Waco's fall. It pierced the Pané just at the moment the latter had made his thrust, and he fell to the ground simultaneously with his victim, still clutching the handle of the spear!

A fearful group lay dead upon the sward; but Carlos did not stay to contemplate it. The fight still raged in another part of the field, and, putting spurs to his horse he galloped off to take part in it.

But the Panés had now lost many of their best warriors, and a general panic had seized upon them, ending in their full flight. Carlos followed along with the victorious pursuers, now and then using his rifle upon the fleeing robbers. But fearing that a stray party of them might attack his own little camp he turned from the line of pursuit, and galloped in that direction. On arriving, he found Antonio and the peons fortified within their corral, and all safe. Stray Indians had passed them, but all apparently too much frightened to have any desire for an attack upon the little party.

As soon as the cibolero had ascertained these facts, he turned his horse and rode back toward the scene of the late conflict.

Chapter Sixteen

As Carlos approached the spot where the chief had been slain he heard the death-wail chanted by a chorus of voices.

On getting still nearer, he perceived a ring of warriors dismounted and standing around a corpse. It was that of the fallen chief. Others, fresh from the pursuit, were gathering to the place; each taking up the melancholy dirge as he drew nigh.

The cibolero alighted, and walked forward to the ring. Some regarded him with looks of surprise, while others, who knew he had aided them in the fight, stepped up and grasped him by the hand. One old warrior taking Carlos' arm in his, led him forward to the ring, and silently pointed to the now ghastly features, as though he was imparting to the cibolero the news that their chief was dead!

Neither he nor any of the warriors knew what part Carlos had borne in the affair. No one, now alive, had been witness to the conflict in which the chief had fallen. Around the spot were high copses that hid it from the rest of the field, and, at the time this conflict occurred, the fight was raging in a different direction. The warrior, therefore, thought he was imparting to Carlos a piece of news, and the latter remained silent.

But there was a *mystery* among the braves, and Carlos saw this by their manner. Five Indians lay dead upon the ground *unscalped*! That was the mystery. They were the three Panés, and the chief with the other Waco. They could not have slain each other, and all have fallen on the spot. That was not probable. The Waco and one of the Panés lay apart. The other three were close together, just as they had fallen, the chief impaled by the Pané spear, while his slayer lay behind him still grasping the weapon! The red tomahawk was clutched firmly in the hands of the chief, and the cleft skull of the second Pané showed where it had last fallen.

So far the Indians translated the tableau, but the mystery lay not there. Who had slain the slayer of their chief? That was the puzzle. Some one must have survived this deadly strife, where five warriors had died together!

If a Pané, surely he would not have gone off without that great trophy which would have rendered him famous for life,—the scalp of the Waco chief? If a Waco, where and who was he?

These questions passed from lip to lip. No one was found to answer them, but there were yet some warriors to return from the pursuit, and the inquiry was suspended, while the death-song was again chanted over the fallen chief.

At length all the braves had arrived on the spot, and stood in a circle around the body. One of the warriors stepped forward to the midst, and by a signal intimated that he wished to be heard. A breathless silence followed, and the warrior began:—

"Wacoes! our hearts are sad when they should otherwise rejoice. In the midst of victory a great calamity has fallen upon us. We have lost our father,—our brother! Our great chief—he whom we all loved—has fallen. Alas! In the very hour of triumph, when his strong right hand had hewn down his enemy on the field—in that moment has he fallen!

"The hearts of his warriors are sad, the hearts of his people will long be sad!

"Wacoes! our chief has not fallen unrevenged. His slayer lies at his feet pierced with the deadly dart, and weltering in his blood. Who of you hath done this?"

Here the speaker paused for a moment as if waiting for a reply. None was given.

"Wacoes!" he continued, "our beloved chief has fallen, and our hearts are sad. But it glads them to know that his death has been avenged. There lies his slayer, still wearing his hated scalp. What brave warrior claims the trophy? Let him stop forth and take it!"

Here there was another pause, but neither voice nor movement answered the challenge.

The cibolero was silent with the rest. He did not comprehend what was said, as the speech was in the Waco tongue, and he understood it not. He guessed that it related to the fallen chief and his enemies, but its exact purport was unknown to him.

"Brothers!" again resumed the orator, "brave men are modest and silent about their deeds. None but a brave warrior could have done this. We know that a brave warrior will avow it. Let him fear not to speak. The Wacoes will be grateful to the warrior who has avenged the death of their beloved chief."

Still the silence was unbroken, except by the voice of the orator.

"Brother warriors!" he continued, raising his voice and speaking in an earnest tone, "I have said that the Wacoes will be grateful for this deed. I have a proposal to make. Hear me!"

All signified assent by gestures.

"It is our custom," continued the speaker, "to elect our chief from the braves of our tribe. I propose that we elect him *now* and *here*—here! on the red field where his predecessor has fallen. *I propose for our chief the warrior who has done this deed!*" And the orator pointed to the fallen Pané.

"*My* voice for the brave who has avenged our chief!" cried one.

"And mine!" shouted another.

"And mine! and mine! and mine!" exclaimed all the warriors.

"Then solemnly be it proclaimed," said the orator, "that he to whom belongs this trophy," he pointed to the scalp of the Pané, "shall be chief of the Waco nation!"

"Solemnly we avow it!" cried all the warriors in the ring, each placing his hand over his heart as he spoke.

"Enough!" said the orator. "Who is chief of the Waco warriors? Let him declare himself on the spot!"

A dead silence ensued. Every eye was busy scanning the faces around the circle, every heart was beating to hail their new chief.

Carlos, unconscious of the honour that was in store for him, was standing a little to one side, observing the movements of his dusky companions with interest. He had not the slightest idea of the question that had been put. Some one near him, however, who spoke Spanish, explained to him the subject of the inquiry, and he was about to make a modest avowal, when one of the braves in the circle exclaimed—

"Why be in doubt longer? If modesty ties the tongue of the warrior, let his weapon speak. Behold! his arrow still pierces the body of our foe. Perhaps it will declare its owner,—it is a marked one!"

"True!" ejaculated the orator. "Let us question the arrow!"

And, stepping forward, he drew the shaft from the body of the Pané, and held it aloft.

The moment the eyes of the warriors fell upon its barbed head, an exclamation of astonishment passed from their lips. The head was of *iron*! No Waco ever used such a weapon as that!

All eyes were instantly turned on Carlos the cibolero, with looks of inquiry and admiration. All felt that it must be from his bow had sped that deadly shaft; and they were the more convinced of this because some who had noticed the third Pané pierced with a rifle bullet, had just declared the fact to the crowd.

Yes, it must be so. The pale-face was the avenger of their chief!

Chapter Seventeen

Carlos, who by this time had become aware of the nature of their inquiries, now stepped forward, and, in modest phrase, detailed through the interpreter how the chief had fallen, and what part he himself had borne in the conflict.

A loud murmur of applause broke from the circle of warriors, and the more excited of the young men rushed forward and grasped the cibolero's hand, uttering as they did so expressions of gratitude. Most of the warriors already knew that to him they were indebted for their safety. It was the report of his rifle, fired in the night, that had put them on their guard, and prevented the Panés from surprising their encampment, else the day's history might have been *very* different. In fact, the Panés, through this very signal having been heard, had been themselves surprised, and that was the true secret of their disaster and sanguinary retreat.

When, in addition to this service, it was seen how the cibolero had fought on their side, killing several of their foes, the hearts of the Wacoes were filled with gratitude; but now that it became known that the pale-faced warrior was the avenger of their beloved chief, their gratitude swelled into enthusiasm, and for some minutes their loud expressions of it alone could be heard.

When the excitement had to some extent subsided, the warrior who seemed to be recognised as the orator of the tribe, and who was regarded with great deference, again stood forth to speak. This time his speech was directed to Carlos alone.

"White warrior!" he said. "I have spoken with the braves of our nation. They all feel that they owe you deep gratitude, which words cannot repay. The purport of our recent deliberations has been explained to you. Upon this ground we vowed that the avenger of him who lies cold should be our future chief. We thought not at the time that that brave warrior was our white brother. But now we know; and should we for that be false to our vow—to our promised word? No!—not even in thought; and here, with equal solemnity, we again repeat that oath."

"We repeat it!" echoed around the ring of warriors, while each with solemnity of manner placed his hand over his heart.

"White warrior!" continued the speaker, "our promise remains sacred. The honour we offer you is the greatest that we can bestow. It has never been borne but by a *true* warrior of the Waco tribe, for no impotent descendant of even a favourite chief has ever ruled over the braves of our nation. We do not fear to offer this honour to you. We would rejoice if you would accept it. Stranger! we will be proud of a *white* chief when that chief is a warrior such as you! We know you better than you think. We have heard of you from our allies the Comanche—we have heard of *Carlos the Cibolero!*

"We know you are a great warrior; and we know, too, that in your own country, among your own people, you are nothing. Excuse our freedom, but speak we not the truth? We despise your people, who are only tyrants and slaves. All these things have our Comanche brothers told us, and much more of *you*. We know who you are, then; we knew you when you came amongst us, and were glad to see you. We traded with you as a friend.

"We now hail you as a brother, and thus say,—If you have no ties that bind you to your ungrateful nation, we can offer you one that will not be ungrateful. Live with us,—be our chief!"

As the speaker ended, his last words were borne like an echo from lip to lip until they had gone round the full circle of warriors, and then a breathless silence ensued.

Carlos was so taken by surprise that for some moments he was unable to make reply, he was not alone surprised by the singular proposal thus singularly made to him; but the knowledge which the speaker betrayed of his circumstances quite astonished him. True, he had traded much among the Comanches, and was on friendly terms with that tribe, some of whom, in times of peace, even visited the settlement of San Ildefonso; but it seemed odd that these savages should have noticed the fact—for fact it was—that the cibolero was somewhat of an outcast among his own people. Just then he had no time to reflect upon the singularity of the circumstances, as the warriors waited his reply.

He scarcely knew what reply to make. Hopeless outcast that he was, for a moment the proposal seemed worthy of acceptance. At home he was little better than a slave; here he would be ruler, the lord elect of all.

The Wacoes, though savages by name, were warriors, were men of hearts, human and humane. He had proofs of it before him. His mother and sister would share his destiny; but Catalina,—ha! that one thought resolved him; he reflected no further.

"Generous warriors!" he replied; "I feel from the bottom of my heart a full sense of the honour you have offered to confer upon me. I wish that by words I could prove how much I thank you, but I cannot. My words, therefore, shall be few and frank. It is true that in my own land I am not honoured,—I am one of the poorest of its people; but there is *a tie* that binds me to it—*a tie of the heart* that calls upon me to return. Wacoes, I have spoken!"

"Enough!" said the orator; "enough, brave stranger: it is not for us to inquire into the motives that guide your acts. If not our chief, you will remain our friend. We have yet a way—a poor one—left us to show our gratitude: you have suffered from our enemies; you have lost your property, but that has been recovered, and shall be yours again. Further we entreat you to remain with us for some days, and partake of our rude hospitality. *You* will stay with us?"

The invitation was promptly echoed by all, and as promptly accepted.

About a week after this time an atajo of pack-mules—nearly fifty in number—loaded with buffalo-hides and tasajo, was seen struggling up the eastern ceja of the Llano Estacado, and heading in a north-westerly direction over that desert plain. The arriero, mounted upon the *mulera*, was a half-blood Indian. Three carretas, drawn by oxen and driven by dusky peons, followed the mule-train, making noise enough to frighten even the coyotes that behind skulked through the coverts of mezquite. A dashing horseman mounted upon a fine black steed rode in advance, who, ever and anon turning in his saddle, looked back with a satisfied glance upon the fine atajo. That horseman was *Carlos*.

The Wacoes had not forgotten to be generous. That train of mules and those heavy packs were the gift of the tribe to the avenger of their chief. But that was not all. In the breast-pocket of the cibolero's jacket was a "bolsa," filled with rare stuff, also a present from the Wacoes, who promised some day that their guest should have more of the same. What did that bolsa contain? coin? money? jewels? No. It contained only dust; but that dust was yellow and glittering. It was *gold*!

Chapter Eighteen

On the second day after the fiesta there was a small dining party at the Presidio. Merely a few bachelor friends of the Comandante—the *beaux esprits* of the place—including the fashionable Echevarria. The cura was among the number, and also the mission padrés, both of whom enjoyed the convivialities of the table equal to any "friar of orders grey."

The company had gone through the numerous courses of a Mexican meal—the "pucheros," "guisados," and endless mixtures of "chilé,"—and the dinner was at that stage when the cloth has been carried off, and the wine flows freely, "Canario" and "Xeres," "Pedro do Ximenes," "Madeira," and "Bordeos," in bottles of different shapes, stood upon the table; and for those who liked a stronger beverage there was a flask of golden "Catalan," with another of Maraschino. A well-stored cellar was that of the Comandante. In addition to his being military governor, he was, as already hinted, collector of the *derechos de consume*, or custom-house dues. Hence he was the recipient of many a little present, as now and then a basket of champagne or a dozen of Bordeaux.

His company had got fairly into the wine. The cura had thrown aside his sanctity and become *human* like the rest; the padrés had forgotten their sackcloth and bead-roll, and the senior of them, Padré Joaquin, entertained the table with spicy adventures which had occurred to him *before* he became a monk. Echevarria related anecdotes of Paris, with many adventures he had encountered among the grisettes.

The Spanish officers being the hosts were, of course, least talkative, though the Comandante—vain as any young sub who wore his epaulettes for the first time—could not refrain from alluding occasionally to his terrible list of *bonnes fortunes* among the fair Sevillanas. He had long been stationed at the city of oranges, and "la gracia Andalusiana" was ever his theme of admiration.

Roblado believed in the belles of the Havannah, and descanted upon the plump, material beauty which is characteristic of the Quadroons; while the lieutenant expressed his *penchant* for the small-footed *Guadalaxareñas*—not of old Spain, but of the rich Mexican province Guadalaxara. *He* had been quartered there.

So ran the talk—rough and ribald—upon that delicate theme—woman. The presence of the trio of churchmen was no restraint. On the contrary, both padrés and cura boasted of their *liaisons* with as much bawd and brass as the others, for padrés and cura were both as depraved as any of their dining companions. Any little reserve either might have shown upon ordinary occasions had disappeared after a few cups of wine; and none of them feared the company, which, on its part, stood as little in awe of them. The affectation of sanctity and self-denial was meant only for the simple poblanos and the simpler peons of the settlement. At the dinner-table it was occasionally assumed by one or the other, but only by way of joke,—to give point and piquancy to the relation of some adventure. In the midst of the conversation, which had grown somewhat general and confused, a name was pronounced which produced a momentary silence. That name was "Carlos the cibolero."

At the mention of this name several countenances changed expression. Roblado was seen to frown; on Vizcarra's face were portrayed mixed emotions; and both padrés and cura seemed to know the name unfavourably.

It was the beau Echevarria who had mentioned it.

"'Pon the honour of a cavallero! the most impudent thing I ever witnessed in all my life, even in republican Paris! A fellow,—a demned trader in hides and tasajo—in short, a butcher of demned buffaloes to aspire—*Parbleu!*"

Echevarria, though talking Spanish, always swore in French. It was more polite.

"Most insolent—intolerable!" cried several voices.

"I don't think the lady seemed over angry withal," remarked a blunt young fellow, who sat near the lower end of the table.

A chorus of voices expressed dissent from this opinion. Roblado's was the loudest.

"Don Ramon Diaz," said he, addressing himself to the young fellow, "you certainly could not have observed very carefully on that occasion. I who was beside the lady know that she was filled with disgust—" (this was a lie, and Roblado knew it), "and her father—"

"Oh, her *father*, yes!" cried Don Ramon, laughing. "Any one could see that *he* was angry—that was natural enough. Ha! ha!"

"But who is the fellow?" inquired one.

"A splendid rider," replied Don Ramon. "The Comandante will admit that." And the free speaker looked at Vizcarra with a smile of intelligence. The latter frowned at the observation.

"You lost a good sum, did you not?" inquired the cura of Vizcarra.

"Not to him," replied the Comandante, "but to that vulgar fellow who seems his friend. The worst of it is, when one bets with these low people there is no chance of getting a *revanche* at some other time. One cannot meet them in the ordinary way."

"But who is the fellow?" again inquired one.

"Who? Why, a cibolero—that's all."

"True, but is there nothing about his history? He's a *gilero*, and that is odd for a native! Is he a Criollo? He might be a Biscayan."

"Neither one nor the other. 'Tis said he's an Americano."

"Americano!"

"Not exactly that—his father was; but the padré here can tell all about him."

The priest thus appealed to entertained the company with some facts in the history of the cibolero. His father had been an Americano, as it was supposed—some stray personage who had mysteriously found his way to the valley and settled in it long ago. Such instances were rare in the settlements of New Mexico; but what was rarer still, in this case the "Americano" was accompanied by an "Americana"—the mother of Carlos—and the same old woman who attracted so much attention on the day of San Juan. All the efforts of the padrés to christianise either one or the other had been in vain. The old trapper—for such he was—died as he had lived—a blaspheming "heretico;" and there was a general belief in the settlement that his widow held converse with the devil. All this was a scandal to the Church, and the padrés would long since have expelled the güero family, but that, for some reason or other, they were protected by the old Comandante—Vizcarra's predecessor—who had restrained the zealous priests in their good intention.

"But, caballeros!" said the padré, glancing towards Vizcarra, "such heretics are dangerous citizens. In them lie the seeds of revolution and social disturbance; and when this güero is at home, he is seen only in the company of those we cannot watch too closely: he has been seen with some of the suspected Tagnos, several of whom are in his service."

"Ha! with them, indeed!" exclaimed several. "A dangerous fellow!—he should be looked after."

The sister of the cibolero now became the subject of conversation; and as remarks were made more or less complimentary to her beauty, the expression upon the face of Vizcarra kept constantly changing. That villain was more interested in the conversation than his guests were aware, and he had already formed his plans. Already his agents were out on the accomplishment of his atrocious designs.

The transition from the cibolero's sister to the other belles of the place, and to the subject of woman in general, was natural; and the company were soon engaged in their original conversation, which, under the influence of additional wine, grew more "racy" than ever.

The scene ended by several of the party becoming "boracho;" and the night being now far advanced, the guests took their leave, some of them requiring to be conducted to their homes. A soldier apiece accompanied the cura and padrés, all three of whom were as "drunk as lords;" and it was no new thing for them.

Chapter Nineteen

The Comandante, with his friend Roblado, alone remained in the room, and continued the conversation with a fresh glass and cigar.

"And you really think, Roblado, that the fellow had encouragement. I think so too, else he would never have dared to act as he did."

"I am quite sure of it now. That he saw her last night, and alone, I am certain. As I approached the house I saw a man standing before the reja, and leaning against the bars, as if conversing with some one inside. Some friend of Don Ambrosio, thought I.

"As I drew nearer, the man, who was muffled in a manga, walked off and leaped upon a horse. Judge my surprise on recognising in the horse the black stallion that was yesterday ridden by the cibolero!

"When I entered the house and made inquiries as to who were at home, the servants informed me that master was at the *mineria*, and that the Señorita had retired, and could see no one that night!

"By Heaven! I was in such a passion, I hardly knew what I said at the moment. The thing's scarce credible; but, that this low fellow is on secret terms with her, is as sure as I am a soldier."

"It does seem incredible. What do you mean to do, Roblado?"

"Oh! I'm safe enough about her. She shall be better watched for the future. I've had a hint given to Don Ambrosio. You know my secret well enough, colonel. Her *mine is my loadstone*; but it is a cursed queer thing to have for one's rival such a fellow as this! Ha! ha! ha!"

Roblado's laugh was faint and unreal. "Do you know," continued he, striking on a new idea, "the padré don't like the güero family. That's evident from the hints he let drop to-night. We may get this fellow out of the way without much scandal, if the Church will only interfere. The padrés can expel him at once from the settlement if they can only satisfy themselves that he is a 'heretico.' Is it not so?"

"It is," coldly replied Vizcarra, sipping his wine; "but to expel *him*, my dear Roblado, *some one else* might be also driven off. The rose would be plucked along with the thorn. You understand?"

"Perfectly."

"That, then, of course, I don't wish—at least not for the present. After some time we may be satisfied to part with rose, thorn, bush, roots, and all. Ha! ha! ha!"

"By the way, colonel," asked the captain, "have you made any progress yet?—have *you* been to the house?"

"No, my dear fellow; I have not had time. It's some distance, remember. Besides, I intend to defer my visit until this fellow is out of the way. It will be more convenient to carry on my courtship in his absence."

"Out of the way! what do you mean?"

"That the cibolero will shortly start for the Plains—to be gone, perhaps, for several months, cutting up buffalo-beef, tricking the Indians, and such-like employments."

"Ho! that's not so bad."

"So you see, querido camarado, there's no need for violence in the matter. Have patience—time enough for everything. Before my bold buffalo-hunter gets back, both our little affairs will be settled, I trust. You shall be the owner of rich mines, and I—"

A slight knock at the door, and the voice of Sergeant Gomez was heard, asking to see the Comandante.

"Come in, sergeant!" shouted the colonel. The brutal-looking trooper walked into the room, and, from his appearance, it was plain he had just dismounted from a ride.

"Well, sergeant?" said Vizcarra, as the man drew near; "speak out! Captain Roblado may know what you have to say."

"The party, colonel, lives in the very last house down the valley,—full ten miles from here. There are but the three, mother, sister, and brother—the same you saw at the fiesta. There are three or four Tagno servants, who help the man in his business. He owns a few mules, oxen, and carts, that's all. These he makes use of in his expeditions, upon one of which he is about to start in three or four days at the furthest. It is to be a long one, I heard, as he is to take a new route over the Llano Estacado."

"Over the Llano Estacado?"

"Such, I was told, was his intention."

"Anything else to say, sergeant?"

"Nothing, colonel, except that the girl has a sweetheart—the same young fellow who bet so heavily against you at the fiesta."

"The devil!" exclaimed Vizcarra, while a deep shadow crossed his forehead.

"He, indeed! I suspected that. Where does he live?"

"Not far above them, colonel. He is the owner of a rancho, and is reputed rich—that is for a ranchero."

"Help yourself to a glass of Catalan, sergeant."

The trooper stretched out his hand, laid hold of a bottle, and, having filled one of the glasses, bowed respectfully to the officers, and drank off the brandy at a draught. Seeing that he was not wanted further, he touched his shako and withdrew.

"So, camarado, you see it is right enough, so far as you are concerned."

"And for you also!" replied Roblado.

"Not exactly."

"Why not?"

"I don't like the story of this sweetheart—this ranchero. The fellow possesses money—a spirit, too, that may be troublesome. He's not the man one would be called upon to fight—at least not one in my position; but *he* is one of these people—what the cibolero is not—and has their sympathies with him. It would be a very different thing to get involved with him in an affair. Bah! what need I care? I never yet failed. Good night, camarado!"

"*Buenos noches!*" replied Roblado; and both, rising simultaneously from the table, retired to their respective sleeping-rooms.

Chapter Twenty

The "ranchos" and "haciendas" of the valley extended nearly ten miles along the stream below San Ildefonso. Near the town they were studded more thickly; but, as you descended the stream, fewer were met with, and those of a poorer class. The fear of the "Indios bravos" prevented those who were well off from building their establishments at any great distance from the Presidio. Poverty, however, induced others to risk themselves nearer the frontier; and, as for several years the settlement had not been disturbed, a number of small farmers and graziers had established themselves as far as eight or ten miles distance below the town.

Half-a-mile beyond all these stood an isolated dwelling—the last to be seen in going down the valley. It seemed beyond the pale of protection—so far as the garrison was concerned—for no patrol ever extended its rounds to so distant a point. Its owner evidently trusted to fate, or to the clemency of the Apaches—the Indians who usually troubled the settlement,—for the house in question was in no other way fortified against them. Perhaps its obscure and retired situation contributed to its security.

It stood somewhat off the road, not near the stream, but back under the shadow of the bluff; in fact, almost built against the cliff.

It was but a poor rancho, like all the others in the valley, and, indeed, throughout most parts of Mexico, built of large blocks of mud, squared in a mould and sun-dried. Many of the better class of such buildings showed white fronts, because near at hand gypsum was to be had for the digging. Some of greater pretension had windows that looked as though they were glazed. So they were, but not with glass. The shining plates that resembled it were but *laminae* of the aforesaid gypsum, which is used for that purpose in several districts of New Mexico.

The rancho in question was ornamented neither with wash nor windows. It stood under the cliff, its brown mud walls scarce contrasting with the colour of the rock; and, instead of windows, a pair of dark holes, with a few wooden bars across them, gave light to the interior.

This light, however, was only a supplement to that which entered by the door, habitually kept open.

The front of the house was hardly visible from the valley road. A traveller would never have noticed it, and even the keen eye of an Indian might have failed to discover it. The singular fence that surrounded it hid it from view,—singular to the eye of one unaccustomed to the vegetation of this far land, it was a fence of columnar cacti. The plants that formed it were regular fluted columns, six inches thick and from six to ten feet high. They stood side by side like pickets in a stockade, so close together that the eye could scarce see through the interstices, still further closed by the thick beard of thorns. Near their tops in the season these vegetable columns became loaded with beautiful wax-like flowers, which disappeared only to give way to bright and luscious fruits. It was only after passing through the opening in this fence that the little rancho could be seen; and although its walls were rude, the sweet little flower-garden that bloomed within the enclosure told that the hand of care was not absent.

Beyond the cactus-fence, and built against the cliff, was another enclosure—a mere wall of *adobe* of no great height. This was a "corral" where cattle were kept, and at one corner was a sort of shed or stable of small dimensions. Sometimes half-a-dozen mules and double the number of oxen might be seen in that corral, and in the stable as fine a horse as ever carried saddle. Both were empty now, for the animals that usually occupied them were out. Horse, mules, and oxen, as well as their owner, were far away upon the prairies.

Their owner was Carlos the cibolero. Such was the home of the buffalo-hunter, the home of his aged mother and fair sister. Such had been their home since Carlos was a child.

And yet they were not of the people of the valley nor the town. Neither race—Spanish nor Indian—claimed them. They differed from both as widely as either did from the other. It was true what the padré had said. True that they were Americans; that their father and mother had settled in the valley a long time ago; that no one knew whence they had come, except that they had crossed the great plains from the eastward; that they were *hereticos*, and that the padrés could never succeed in bringing them into the fold of the Church; that these would have expelled, or otherwise punished them, but for the interference of the military Comandante; and furthermore, that both were always regarded by the common people of the settlement with a feeling of superstitious dread. Latterly this feeling, concentrated on the mother of Carlos, had taken a new shape, and they looked upon her as a *hechicera*—a witch—and crossed themselves devoutly whenever she met them. This was not often, for it was rare that she made her appearance among the inhabitants of the valley. Her presence at the fiesta of San Juan was the act of Carlos, who had been desirous of giving a day's amusement to the mother and sister he so much loved.

Their American origin had much to do with the isolation in which they live. Since a period long preceding that time, bitter jealousy existed between the Spano-Mexican and Anglo-American races. This feeling had been planted by national animosity, and nursed and fomented by priestcraft. Events that have since taken place had already cast their shadows over the Mexican frontier; and Florida and Louisiana were regarded as but steps in the ladder of American aggrandisement; but the understanding of these matters was of course confined to the more intelligent; but all were imbued with the bad passions of international hate.

The family of the cibolero suffered under the common prejudice, and on that account lived almost wholly apart from the inhabitants of the valley. What intercourse they had was mostly with the native Indian population— the poor Tagnos, who felt but little of this anti-American feeling.

If we enter the rancho of Carlos we shall see the fair-haired Rosita seated upon a *petaté*, and engaged in weaving rebosos. The piece of mechanism which serves her for a loom consists of only a few pieces of wood rudely carved. So simple is it that it is hardly just to call it a machine. Yet those long bluish threads stretched in parallel lines, and vibrating to the touch of her nimble fingers, will soon be woven into a beautiful scarf to cover the head of some coquettish poblana of the town. None in the valley can produce such rebosos as the cibolero's sister. So much as he can beat all the youth in feats of horsemanship, so much does she excel in the useful art which is her source of subsistence.

There are but two rooms in the rancho, and that is one more than will be found in most of its fellows. But the delicate sentiment still exists in the Saxon mind. The family of the cibolero are not yet Indianised.

The kitchen is the larger apartment and the more cheerful, because lighted by the open door. In it you will see a small "brazero," or altar-like fireplace—half-a-dozen earthen "ollas," shaped like urns—some gourd-shell cups and bowls—a tortilla-stone, with its short legs and inclined surface— some *petatés* to sit upon—some buffalo-robes for a similar purpose—a bag of maize—some bunches of dried herbs, and strings of red and green chilé— but no pictures of saints; and perhaps it is the only house in the whole valley where your eye will *not* be gratified by a sight of these. Truly the family of the cibolero are "hereticos."

Not last you will see an old woman seated near the fire, and smoking *punche* in a pipe! A strange old woman is she, and strange no doubt her history but that is revealed to no one. Her sharp, lank features; her blanched, yet still luxuriant hair; the wild gleam of her eyes; all render her appearance singular. Others than the ignorant could not fail to fancy her a being different from the common order. No wonder, then, that these regard her as "una hechicera!"

Chapter Twenty One

Rosita knelt upon the floor, passing her little hand-shuttle through the cotton-woof. Now she sang—and sweetly she sang—some merry air of the American backwoods that had been taught her by her mother; anon some romantic lay of Old Spain—the "Troubadour," perhaps—a fine piece of music, that gives such happy expression to the modern song "Love not." This "Troubadour" was a favourite with Rosita; and when she took up her bandolon, and accompanied herself with its guitar-like notes, the listener would be delighted.

She was now singing to beguile the hours and lighten her task; and although not accompanied by any music, her silvery voice sounded sweet and clear.

The mother had laid aside her pipe of *punche*, and was busy as Rosita herself. She spun the threads with which the rebosos were woven. If the loom was a simple piece of mechanism, much more so was the spinning-machine—the "huso," or "malacate"—which was nothing more or less than the "whirligig spindle." Yet with this primitive apparatus did the old dame draw out and twist as smooth a thread as ever issued from the "jenny."

"Poor dear Carlos! One, two, three, four, five, six—six notches I have made—he is just in his sixth day. By this time he will be over the Llano, mother. I hope he will have good luck, and get well treated of the Indians."

"Never fear, niña—my brave boy has his father's rifle, and knows how to use it—well he does. Never fear for Carlos!"

"But then, mother, he goes in a new direction! What if he fall in with a hostile tribe?"

"Never fear, niña! Worse enemies than Indians has Carlos—worse enemies nearer home—cowardly slaves! they hate us—both *Gachupinos* and *Criollos* hate us—Spanish dogs! they hate our Saxon blood!"

"Oh, mother, say not so! They are not *all* our enemies. We have some friends."

Rosita was thinking of Don Juan.

"Few—few—and far between! What care I while my brave son is there? He is friend enough for us. Soft heart—brave heart—strong arm—who like my Carlos? And the boy loves his old mother—his strange old mother, as these *pelados* think her. He still loves his old mother. Ha! ha! ha! What, then, cares she for friends? Ha! ha! ha!"

Her speech ended in a laugh of triumph, showing how much she exulted in the possession of such a son.

"O my! what a *carga*, mother! He never had such a carga before! I wonder where Carlos got all the money?"

Rosita did not know exactly where; but she had some fond suspicions as to who had stood her brother's friend.

"*Ay de mi!*" she continued; "he will be very rich if he gets a good market for all those fine things—he will bring back troops of mules. How I shall long for his return! One—two—three—six—yes, there are but six notches in the wood. Oh! I wish it were full along both edges—I do!"

Rosita's eyes, us she said this, were bent upon a thin piece of cedar-wood that hung against the wall, and upon which six little notches were observable. That was her clock and calendar, which was to receive a fresh mark each day until the cibolero's return—thus keeping her informed of the exact time that had elapsed since his departure.

After gazing at the cedar-wood for a minute or two, and trying to make the six notches count seven, she gave it up, and went on with her weaving.

The old woman, laying down her spindle, raised the lid of an earthen "olla" that stood over a little fire upon the brazero. From the pot proceeded a savoury steam; for it contained a stew of *tasajo* cut into small pieces, and highly seasoned with *cebollas* (Spanish onions) and *chilé Colorado* (red capsicum).

"Niña, the *guisado* is cooked," said she, after lifting a portion of the stew on a wooden spoon, and examining it; "let us to dinner!"

"Very well, mother," replied Rosita, rising from her loom; "I shall make the tortillas at once."

Tortillas are only eaten warm—that is, are fit only for eating when warm—or fresh from the "*comal.*" They are, therefore, to be baked immediately before the meal commences, or during its continuance.

Rosita set the olla on one side, and placed the comal over the coals. Another olla, which contained maize—already boiled soft—was brought forward, and placed beside the "metate," or tortilla-stone; and then, by the help of an oblong roller—also of stone—a portion of the boiled maize was soon reduced to snow-white paste. The metate and roller were now laid aside, and the pretty, rose-coloured fingers of Rosita were thrust into the paste. The proper quantity for a "tortilla" was taken up, first formed into a round ball, and then clapped out between the palms until it was only a wafer's thickness. Nothing remained but to fling it on the hot surface of the comal, let it lie but for an instant, then turn it, and in a moment more it was ready for eating.

These operations, which required no ordinary adroitness, were performed by Rosita with a skill that showed she was a practised "tortillera."

When a sufficient number were piled upon the plate, Rosita desisted from her labour, and her mother having already "dished" the guisado, both commenced their repast, eating without knife, fork, or spoon. The tortillas, being still warm, and therefore capable of being twisted into any form, served as a substitute for all these contrivances of civilisation, which in a Mexican rancho are considered superfluous things.

Their simple meal was hardly over when a very unusual sound fell upon their ears.

"Ho! what's that?" cried Rosita, starting to her feet, and listening.

The sound a second time came pealing through the open door and windows.

"I declare it's a bugle!" said the girl. "There must be soldiers."

She ran first to the door, and then up to the cactus-fence. She peered through the interstices of the green columns.

Sure enough there were soldiers. A troop of lancers was marching by twos down the valley, and not far off. Their glittering armour, and the pennons of their lances, gave them a gay and attractive appearance. As Rosita's eyes fell upon them, they were wheeling into line, halting, as they finished the movement, with their front to the rancho, and not a hundred paces from the fence. The house was evidently the object of their coming to a halt.

What could soldiers want there? This was Rosita's first reflection. A troop often passed up and down the valley, but never came near the rancho, which, as already stated, was far from the main road. What business could the soldiers be upon, to lead them out of their usual track?

Rosita asked herself these questions; then ran into the house and asked her mother. Neither could answer them; and the girl turned to the fence, and again looked through.

As she did so she saw one of the soldiers—from his finer dress evidently an officer—separate from the rest, and come galloping towards the house. In a few moments he drew near, and, reining his horse close up to the fence, looked over the tops of the cactus-plants.

Rosita could just see his plumed hat, and below it his face, but she knew the face at once. It was that of the officer who on the day of San Juan had ogled her so rudely. She knew he was the Comandante Vizcarra.

Chapter Twenty Two

The officer, from his position, had a full view of the girl as she stood in the little enclosure of flowers. She had retreated to the door, and would have gone inside, but she turned to call off Cibolo, a large wolf-dog, who was barking fiercely, and threatening the new-comer.

The dog, obedient to her voice, ran back into the house growling, but by no means satisfied. He evidently wanted to try his teeth on the shanks of the stranger's horse.

"Thank you, fair Señorita," said the officer. "It is very kind of you to protect me from that fierce brute. I would he were the only clangour I had to fear in this house."

"What have you to fear, Señor?" inquired Rosita, with some surprise.

"*Your eyes*, sweet girl: more dangerous than the sharp teeth of your dog,—they have already wounded me."

"Cavallero," replied Rosita, blushing and averting her face, "you have not come here to jest with a poor girl. May I inquire what is your business?"

"Business I have none, lovely Rosita, but to see *you*,—nay, do not leave me!—I *have* business—that is, I am thirsty, and halted for a drink: you will not refuse me a cup of water, fair Señorita?"

These last phrases, broken and hastily delivered, were meant to restrain the girl from cutting short the interview, which she was about to do by entering the house. Vizcarra was not thirsty, neither did he wish for water; but the laws of hospitality would compel the girl to bring it, and the act might further his purposes.

She, without replying to his complimentary harangue, stepped into the house, and presently returned with a gourd-shell filled with water. Carrying it to the gate-like opening of the fences, she presented it to him, and stood waiting for the vessel.

Vizcarra, to make his request look natural, forced down several gulps of the fluid, and then, throwing away the rest, held out the gourd. The girl stretched forth her hand to receive it, but he still held it fast, gazing intently and rudely upon her.

"Lovely señorita," he said, "may I not kiss that pretty hand that has been so kind to me?"

"Sir! please return me the cup."

"Nay, not till I have paid for my drink. You will accept this?"

He dropped a gold onza into the gourd.

"No, Señor, I cannot accept payment for what is only an act of duty. I shall not take your gold," she added, firmly.

"Lovely Rosita! you have already taken my heart, why not this?"

"I do not understand you, Señor; please put back your money, and let me have the cup."

"I shall not deliver it up, unless you take it with its contents."

"Then you must keep it, Señor," replied she, turning away. "I must to my work."

"Nay, further, Señorita!" cried Vizcarra; "I have another favour to ask,—a light for my cigar? Here, take the cup! See! the coin is no longer in it! You will pardon me for having offered it?"

Vizcarra saw that she was offended, and by this apology endeavoured to appease her.

She received the gourd-shell from his hands, and then went back to the house to bring him the light he had asked for.

Presently she reappeared with some red coals upon a small "brazero."

On reaching the gate she was surprised to see that the officer had dismounted, and was fastening his horse to a stake.

As she offered him the brazero, he remarked, "I am wearied with my ride; may I beg, Señorita, you will allow me a few minutes' shelter from the hot sun?"

Though annoyed at this request, the girl could only reply in the affirmative; and the next moment, with clattering spur and clanking sabre, the Comandante walked into the rancho.

Rosita followed him in without a word, and without a word he was received by her mother, who, seated in the corner, took no notice of his entrance, not even by looking up at him. The dog made a circuit around him, growling angrily, but his young mistress chided him off; and the brute once more couched himself upon a petaté, and lay with eyes gleaming fiercely at the intruder.

Once in the house, Vizcarra did not feel easy. He saw he was not welcome. Not a word of welcome had been uttered by Rosita, and not a sign of it offered either by the old woman or the dog. The contrary symptoms were unmistakeable, and the grand officer felt he was an intruder.

But Vizcarra was not accustomed to care much for the feelings of people like these. He paid but little regard to their likes or dislikes, especially where these interfered with his pleasures; and, after lighting his cigar, he sat down on a "banqueta," with as much nonchalance as if he were in his own quarters. He smoked some time without breaking silence.

Meanwhile Rosita had drawn out her loom, and, kneeling down in front of it, went on with her work as if no stranger were present.

"Oh, indeed!" exclaimed the officer, feigning interest in the process, "how very ingenious! I have often wished to see this! a reboso it is? Upon my *word*! and that is how they are woven? Can you finish one in a day, Señorita?"

"*Si, Señor,*" was the curt reply.

"And this thread, it is cotton; is it not?"

"Si, Señor."

"It is very prettily arranged indeed. Did you place it so yourself?"

"Si, Señor."

"Really it requires skill! I should like much to learn how the threads are passed."

And as he said this he left his seat upon the banqueta, and, approaching the loom, knelt down beside it.

"Indeed, very singular and ingenious. Ah, now, do you think, pretty Rosita, you could teach me?"

The old woman, who was seated with her eyes bent upon the ground, started at hearing the stranger pronounce her daughter's name, and glanced around at him.

"I am really serious," continued he; "do you think you could teach me this useful art?"

"No, Señor!" was the laconic reply.

"Oh! surely I am not so stupid! I think I could learn it—it seems only to hold this thing so,"—here he bent forward, and placed his hand upon the shuttle, so as to touch the fingers of the girl,—"and then put it between the threads in this manner; is it not—?"

At this moment, as if carried away by his wild passions, he seemed to forget himself; and, turning his eyes upon the blushing girl, he continued in an under tone, "Sweetest Rosita! I love you,—one kiss, fairest,—one kiss!" and before she could escape from his arms, which had already encircled her, he had imprinted a kiss upon her lips!

A scream escaped from the girl, but another, louder and wilder, answered it from the corner. The old woman sprang up from her crouching position, and running across the floor launched herself like a tigress upon the officer! Her long bony fingers flew out, and in an instant were clutching his throat!

"Off! beldame! off!" cried he, struggling to escape: "off I say; or my sword shall cut short your wretched life, off!—off!—I say!"

Still the old woman clutched and screamed, tearing wildly at his throat, his epaulettes, or whatever she could lay hold of.

But sharper than her nails were the teeth of the great wolf-dog that sprang almost simultaneously from his lair, and, seizing the soldier by the limbs, caused him to bellow out at the top of his voice—

"Without there! Sergeant Gomez! Ho! treason! to the rescue! to the rescue!"

"Ay! dog of a Gachupino!" screamed the old woman,—"dog of Spanish blood! you may call your cowardly myrmidons! Oh! that my brave son were here, or my husband alive! If they were, you would not carry a drop of your villain blood beyond the threshold you have insulted!—Go!—go to your poblanas—your *margaritas*! Go—begone!"

"Hell and furies! This dog—take him off! Ho, there! Gomez! your pistols. Here! send a bullet through him! Haste! haste!"

And battling with his sabre, the valiant Comandante at length effected a retreat to his horse.

He was already well torn about the legs, but, covered by the sergeant, he succeeded in getting into the saddle.

The latter fired off both his pistols at the dog, but the bullets did not take effect; and the animal, perceiving that his enemies outnumbered him, turned and ran back into the house.

The dog was now silent, but the Comandante, as he sat in his saddle, heard a derisive laugh within the rancho. In the clear soft tones of that jeering laughter he distinguished the voice of the beautiful güera!

Chagrined beyond measure, he would have besieged the rancho with his troop, and insisted on killing the dog, had he not feared that the cause of his ungraceful retreat might become known to his followers. That would be a mortification he did not desire to experience.

He returned, therefore, to the troop, gave the word to march, and the cavalcade moved off, taking the backward road to the town.

After riding at the head of his men for a short while, Vizcarra—whose heart was filled with anger and mortification—gave some orders to the sergeant, and then rode off in advance, and in full gallop.

The sight of a horseman in blue manga, passing in the direction of the rancho—and whom he recognised as the young ranchero, Don Juan—did not do much towards soothing his angry spirit. He neither halted nor spoke, but, casting on the latter a malignant glance, kept on.

He did not slacken his pace until he drew bridle in the saguan of the Presidio.

His panting horse had to pay for the bitter reflections that tortured the soul of his master.

Chapter Twenty Three

The first thing which Rosita did, after the noise without had ceased, was to glide forth and peep through the cactus-fence. She had heard the bugle again, and she wished to be sure that the intruders were gone.

To her joy, she beheld the troop some distance off, defiling up the valley.

She ran back into the house and communicated the intelligence to her mother, who had again seated herself, and was quietly smoking her pipe of *punche*.

"Dastardly ruffians!" exclaimed the latter. "I knew they would be gone. Even an old woman and a dog are enough. Oh, that my brave Carlos had been here! He would have taught that proud Gachupino we were not so helpless! Ha! that would Carlos!"

"Do not think of it any more, dear mother; I don't think they will return. You have frightened them away,—you and our brave Cibolo. How well he behaved! But I must see," she added, hastily casting her eyes round the room; "he may be hurt. Cibolo! Cibolo! here, good fellow! Come, I've got something for you. Ho, brave dog!"

At the call of her well-known voice the dog came forth from his hiding-place, and bounded up, wagging his tail, and glancing kindly in her face.

The girl stooped down, and, passing her hands through his shaggy coat, examined every part of his body and limbs, in fear all the while of meeting with the red stain of a bullet. Fortunately the sergeant's aim had not been true. Neither wound nor scratch had Cibolo received; and as he sprang around his young mistress, he appeared in perfect health and spirits.

A splendid animal he was,—one of those magnificent sheep-dogs of New Mexico, who, though half-wolf themselves, will successfully defend a flock of sheep from the attack of wolves, or even of the more savage bear. The finest sheep-dogs in the world are they, and one of the finest of his race was Cibolo.

His mistress, having ascertained that he was uninjured, stepped upon the banqueta, and reached up towards a singular-looking object that hung over a peg in the wall. The object bore some resemblance to a string of ill-formed sausages. But it was not that, though it was something quite as good for Cibolo, who, by his sparkling eyes and short pleased whimpers, showed that he knew what it was. Yes, Cibolo had not to be initiated into the mysteries of a string of tasajo. Dried buffalo-meat was an old and tried favourite; and the moment it reached his jaws, which it did immediately after, he gave proof of this by the earnest manner in which he set to work upon it.

The pretty Rosita, still a little apprehensive, once more peeped through the cactus-fence to assure herself that no one was near.

But this time some one *was* near, and the sight did not cause her any fear,—quite the contrary. The approach of a young man in a blue manga, mounted upon a richly-caparisoned horse, had a contrary effect altogether, and Rosita's little heart now beat with confidence.

This young horseman was Don Juan the ranchero. He rode straight up to the opening, and seeing the güera cried out in a frank friendly voice, "*Buenos dias, Rosita!*"

The reply was as frank and friendly—a simple return of the salutation—

"*Buenos dias, Don Juan!*"

"How is the Señora your mother to-day?"

"*Muchas gracias*, Don Juan! as usual she is. Ha! ha! ha! ha! ha! ha!"

"*Hola!*" exclaimed Don Juan. "What are you laughing at, Rosita?"

"Ha! ha! ha! Saw you nothing of the fine soldiers?"

"True, I did. I met the troop as I came down, going up the valley in a gallop, and the Comandante riding far ahead, as if the Apaches were after him. In truth, I thought they had met the Indios bravos—for I know that to be their usual style of riding after an interview with these gentry."

"Ha! ha! ha!" still laughed the little blonde, "but did you notice nothing odd about the officer?"

"I think I did. He looked as though he had ridden through the chapparal; but I had scarce a glance at him, he passed so quickly. He gave *me* one that was anything but friendly. No doubt he remembers the loss of his gold onzas at San Juan. Ha! ha! But, dear Rosita, what may you be laughing at? Have the soldiers been here? Anything happened?"

Rosita now gave an account of the Comandante's visit; how he had called to light his cigar and get a drink of water; how he had entered the house and been attacked by Cibolo, which caused the precipitate retreat to his horse, and his hasty departure from the place. She was silent, however, about the most important particulars. She said nothing of the insulting speeches which Vizcarra had made—nothing of the kiss. She feared the effect of such a communication on Don Juan. She knew her lover was of a hot rash disposition. He would not hear these things quietly; he would involve himself in some trouble on her account; and these considerations prompted her to conceal the cause that had led to the "scene." She, therefore, disclosed only the more ludicrous effects, at which she laughed heartily.

Don Juan, even knowing only so much, was inclined to regard the affair more seriously. A visit from Vizcarra—a drink of water—light his cigar—enter the rancho—all very strange circumstances, but not at all laughable, thought Don Juan. And then to be attacked and torn by the dog—to be driven from the house in such a humiliating manner—in presence of his own troop, too!—Vizcarra—the vainglorious Vizcarra—the great militario of the place—the hero of a hundred Indian battles that never were fought—he to be conquered by a cur! Seriously, thought Don Juan, it was not an affair to laugh at. Vizcarra would have revenge, or try hard to obtain it.

The young ranchero had other unpleasant thoughts in connexion with this affair. What could have brought the Comandante to the rancho? How had he found out that interesting abode,—that spot, sequestered as it was, that seemed to him (Don Juan) to be the centre of the world? Who had directed him that way? What brought the troop out of the main road, their usual route of march?

These were questions which Don Juan put to himself. To have asked them of Rosita would have been to disclose the existence of a feeling he would rather keep concealed—jealousy.

And jealous he was at the moment. The drink, she had served him of course,—the cigar, she had lit it for him—perhaps invited him in! Even now she appeared in the highest spirits, and not at all angry at the visit that had been paid her!

Don Juan's reflections had suddenly grown bitter, and he did not join in the laugh which his sweetheart was indulging in.

When after a short while she invited him in, his feelings took a turn, and he became himself again. He dismounted from his horse, and followed Rosita through the garden into the house.

The girl sat down by the loom and continued her work, while the young ranchero was allowed to kneel upon the petaté beside her, and converse at will. There was no objection to his occasionally assisting her to straighten out the woof or untwist a fouled thread; and, on these occasions, their fingers frequently met, and seemed to remain longer in contact than was necessary for the unravelling of the knot.

But no one noticed all this. Rosita's mother was indulging in a siesta; and Cibolo, if he saw anything amiss, said nothing about it to any one, but wagged his tail, and looked good-humouredly at Don Juan, as if he entirely approved of the latter's conduct.

Chapter Twenty Four

When Vizcarra reached his sumptuous quarters, the first thing he did was to call for wine. It was brought, and he drank freely and with fierce determination.

He thought by that to drown his chagrin; and for a while he succeeded.

There is relief in wine, but it is only temporary: you may make jealousy drunk and oblivious, but you cannot keep it so. It will be sober as soon—ay, sooner than yourself. Not all the wine that was ever pressed from grapes can drown it into a complete oblivion.

Vizcarra's heart was filled by various passions. There was love—that is, such love as a libertine feels; jealousy; anger at the coarse handling he had experienced; wounded self-love, for with his gold-lace and fine plumes he believed himself a conqueror at first sight; and upon the top of all, bitter disappointment.

This last was the greater that he did not see how his suit could be renewed. To attempt a similar visit would lead to similar chagrin,—perhaps worse.

It was plain the girl did not care for him, with all his fine feathers and exalted position. He saw that she was very different from the others with whom he had had dealings—different from the dark-eyed doncellas of the valley, most of whom, if not all, would have taken his onza without a word or a blush!

It was plain to him he could go no more to the rancho. Where, then, was he to meet her—to see her? He had ascertained that she seldom came to the town—never to the amusements, except when her brother was at home. How and where, then, was he to see her? His was a hopeless case—no opportunity of mending his first *faux pas*—none, any more than if the object of his pursuit was shut up in the cloisters of a nunnery! Hopeless, indeed! Thus ran his reflections.

Though uttering this phrase, he had no belief in its reality. He had no intention of ending the affair so easily. He—the lady-killer, Vizcarra—to fail in the conquest of a poor ranchera! He had never failed, and would not now. His vanity alone would have urged him farther in the affair; but he had a sufficient incentive to his strong passion, — for strong it had now grown. The opposition it had met — the very difficulty of the situation — only stimulated him to greater energy and earnestness.

Besides, jealousy was there, and that was another spur to his excited pride.

He was jealous of Don Juan. He had noticed the latter on the day of the fiesta. He had observed him in the company of the cibolero and his sister. He saw them talking, drinking, feasting together. He was jealous *then*; but that was light, for then he still anticipated his own easy and early triumph. That was quiet to the feeling that tortured him now — now that *he had failed* — now that he had seen in the very hour of his humiliation that same rival on his road to the rancho — welcome, no doubt — to be told of all that had happened — to join her in jeering laughter at his expense — to — Furies! the thought was intolerable.

For all that the Comandante had no idea of relinquishing his design. There were still means — foul, if not fair — if he could only think of them. He wanted some head cooler than his own. Where was Roblado?

"Sergeant! tell Captain Roblado I wish to speak with him."

Captain Roblado was just the man to assist him in any scheme of the sort. They were equally villains as regarded women; but Vizcarra's *métier* was of a lighter sort — more of the genteel-comedy kind. His forte lay in the seductive process. He made love *à la Don Giovanni*, and carried hearts in what he deemed a legitimate manner; whereas Roblado resorted to any means that would lead most directly to the object — force, if necessary and safe. Of the two Roblado was the coarser villain.

As the Comandante had failed in his way, he was determined to make trial of any other his captain might suggest; and since the latter knew all the "love stratagems," both of civilised and savage life, he was just the man to suggest something.

It chanced that at this time Roblado wanted counsel himself upon a somewhat similar subject. He had proposed for Catalina, and Don Ambrosio had consented; but, to the surprise of all, the Señorita had rebelled! She did not say she would *not* accept Captain Roblado. That would have been too much of a defiance, and might have led to a summary interference of paternal authority. But she had appealed to Don Ambrosio for time—she was not ready to be married! Roblado could not think of time—he was too eager to be rich; but Don Ambrosio had listened to his daughter's appeal, and there lay the cause of the captain's trouble.

Perhaps the Comandante's influence with Don Ambrosio might be the means of overruling this decision and hastening the wished-for nuptials. Roblado was therefore but too eager to lay his superior under an obligation.

Roblado having arrived, the Comandante explained his case, detailing every circumstance that had happened.

"My dear colonel, you did not go properly to work. I am astonished at that, considering your skill and experience. You dropped like an eagle upon a dovecot, frightening the birds into their inaccessible holes. You should not have gone to the rancho at all."

"And how was I to see her?"

"In your own quarters; or elsewhere, as you might have arranged it."

"Impossible!—she would never have consented to come."

"Not by your sending for her direct; I know that."

"And how, then?"

"Ha! ha! ha!" laughed Roblado; "are you so innocent as never to have heard of such a thing as an 'alcahuete'?"

"Oh! true—but by my faith I never found use for one."

"No!—you in your fine style have deemed that a superfluity; but you might find use for one now. A very advantageous character that, I assure you—saves much time and trouble—diminishes the chances of failure too. It's not too late. I advise you to try one. If that fails, you have still another string to your bow."

We shall not follow the conversation of these ruffians further. Enough to say that it led into details of their atrocious plans, which, for more than an hour, they sat concocting over their wine, until the whole scheme was set forth and placed in readiness to be carried out.

It *was* carried out, in fine, but led to a different ending from what either anticipated. The "lady" who acted as "alcahuete" soon placed herself *en rapport* with Rosita; but her success was more equivocal than that of

Vizcarra himself; in fact, I should rather say unequivocal, for there was no ambiguity about it.

As soon as her designs were made known to Rosita, the latter communicated them to her mother; and the scratches which the Comandante had received were nothing to those which had fallen to the lot of his proxy. The "alcahuete" had, in fact, to beg for her life before she was allowed to escape from the terrible Cibolo.

She would have sought legal revenge, but that the nature of her business made it wiser for her to pocket the indignities, and remain silent.

Chapter Twenty Five

"Now, Roblado," asked the Comandante, "what is the other string to my bow?"

"Can't you guess, my dear colonel?"

"Not exactly," replied Vizcarra, though he well knew that he could. It was not long since the other string had been before his mind. He had even thought of it upon the day of his first defeat, and while his anger was hot and revengeful. And since then, too—often, often. His question was quite superfluous, for he well knew Roblado's answer would be "force."

It *was* "force." That was the very word. "How?"

"Take a few of your people, go by night, and carry her off. What can be more simple? It would have been the proper way at first, with such a prude as she! Don't fear the result. It's not so terrible to them. I've known it tried before. Long ere the cibolero can return, she'll be perfectly reconciled, I warrant you."

"And if not?"

"If not, what have you to fear?"

"The talk, Roblado—the talk."

"Bah! my dear colonel, you are timid in the matter. You have mismanaged it so far, but that's no reason you should not use tact for the future. It can be done by night. You have chambers here where no one is allowed to enter— some *without windows*, if you need them. Who's to be the wiser? Pick your men—those you can trust. You don't require a whole troop, and half-a-dozen onzas will tie as many tongues. It's as easy as stealing a shirt. It is only stealing a chemisette. Ha! ha! ha!" and the ruffian laughed at his coarse simile and coarser joke, in which laugh he was joined by the Comandante.

The latter still hesitated to adopt this extreme measure. Not from any fineness of feeling. Though scarce so rough a villain as his companion, it was not delicacy of sentiment that restrained him now. He had been accustomed all his life to regard with heartless indifference the feelings of those he had wronged; and it was not out of any consideration for the future happiness or misery of the girl that he hesitated now. No, his motive was of a far different character. Roblado said true when he accused him of being timid. He was. It was sheer cowardice that stayed him.

Not that he feared any bodily punishment would ever reach him for the act. He was too powerful, and the relatives of his intended victim too weak, to give him any apprehensions on that score. With a little policy he could administer death,—death to the most innocent of the people,—and give it a show of justice. Nothing was more easy than to cause suspicion of treason, incarcerate, and slay—and particularly at that time, when both Pueblo revolt and Creole revolution threatened the Spanish rule in America.

What Vizcarra feared was "talk." Such an open rape could not well be kept secret for long. It would leak out, and once out it was too piquant a piece of scandal not to have broad fame: all the town would soon enjoy it. But there was a still more unpleasant probability. It might travel beyond the confines of the settlement, perhaps to high quarters, even to the Vice-regal ear! There find we the secret of the Comandante's fears.

Not indeed that the Vice-regal court at the time was a model of morality. It would have been lenient enough to any act of despotism or debauchery done in a quiet way; but such an open act of rapine as that contemplated, on the score of policy, could hardly be overlooked. In truth, Vizcarra's prudence had reason. He could not believe that it would be possible to keep the thing a secret. Some of the rascals employed might in the end prove traitors. True, they would be his own soldiers, and he might punish them for it at his will, but what satisfaction would that give him? It would be locking the stable after the steed had been stolen!

Even without their playing him false, how could he hope to keep the affair concealed? First, there was an angry brother. True, he was out of the way; but there was a jealous lover on the ground, and the brother would return in time. The very act of the rape would point to him, Vizcarra. His visit, the attempt of the "alcahuete," and the carrying off of the girl, would all be pieced together, and put down to his credit; and the brother—such a one—and such a lover too—would not be silent with their suspicious. He might take measures to get rid of both, but these measures must needs be violent and dangerous.

Thus reasoned Vizcarra with himself, and thus he argued with Roblado. Not that he wished the latter to dissuade him—for the end he desired with all his heart—but in order that by their united wisdom some safer means of reaching it might be devised.

And a safer plan *was* devised. Roblado, deeper in head, as well as bolder in heart, conceived it. Bringing his glass to the table with a sudden stroke, he exclaimed—

"*Vamos*, Vizcarra! By the Virgin, I have it!"

"*Bueno — bravo!*"

"You may enjoy your sweetheart within twenty four hours, if you wish, and the sharpest scandalmonger in the settlement will be foiled; at least, you will have nothing to fear. What a devil of a lucky thought! — the very thing itself, amigo!"

"Don't keep me in suspense, camarado! your plan! your plan!"

"Stop till I've had a gulp of wine. The very thought of such a glorious trick makes me thirsty."

"Drink then, drink!" cried Vizcarra, filling out the wine, with a look of pleasant anticipation.

Roblado emptied the goblet at a draught, and then, leaning nearer to the Comandante, he detailed what he had conceived in a low and confidential tone. It seemed to satisfy his listener, who, when the other had finished, uttered the word "Bravo!" and sprang to his feet like one who had received some joyful news. He walked back and forth for some minutes in an excited manner, and then, bursting into a loud laugh, he cried out, "*Carrambo*, comrade! you *are* a tactician! The great Conde himself would not have shown such strategy. *Santisima Virgen!* it is the very master-stroke of design; and I promise you, camarado, it shall have speedy execution."

"Why delay? Why not set about it at once?"

"True, — at once let us prepare for this *pleasant masquerade!*"

Chapter Twenty Six

Circumstances were arising that would be likely to interrupt the Comandante and his captain in the execution of their design. At least so it might have been supposed. In less than twenty-four hours after the conversation described, a rumour of Indian incursions was carried to the town, and spread through every house in the valley. The rumour said that a band of "Indios bravos," —whether Apache, Yuta, or Comanche, was not stated,—had made their appearance near the settlement, in full *war-paint and costume*!

This of course denoted hostile intentions, and an attack might be expected in some part of the settlement. The first rumour was followed by one still more substantial,—that the Indians had attacked some shepherds in the upper plain, not far from the town itself. The shepherds had escaped, but their dogs had been killed, and a large number of sheep driven off to the mountain fastnesses of the marauders!

This time the report was more definite. The Indians were Yutas, and belonged to a band of that tribe that had been hunting to the east of the Pecos, and who had no doubt resolved upon this plundering expedition before returning to their *home*, near the heads of the Del Norte. The shepherds had seen them distinctly, and knew the *Yuta paint*.

That the Indians were Yutas was probable enough. The same tribe had lately made a foray upon the settlements in the fine valley of Taos. They had heard of the prosperous condition of San Ildefonso, and hence their hostile visit. Besides, both Apaches and Comanches were *en paz* with the settlement, and had for some years confined themselves to ravaging the provinces of Coahuila and Chihuahua. No provocation had been given to these tribes to recommence hostilities, nor had they given any signs of such an intention.

Upon the night of the same day in which the sheep were carried off, a more important robbery was committed. That took place in the settlement itself. A large number of cattle were driven off from a grazing-farm near the lower end of the valley. The Indians had been seen in the act, but the frightened vaqueros were but too glad to escape, and shut themselves up in the buildings of the farm.

No murders had as yet been committed, but that was because no resistance had been made to the spoliations. Nor had any houses been yet attacked. Perhaps the Indians were only a small band; but there was no knowing how soon their numbers might be increased, and greater outrages attempted.

The people of the valley, as well as those in the town, were now in a state of excitement. Consternation prevailed everywhere. Those who lived in the scattered ranchos forsook their homes during the night, and betook themselves to the town and the larger haciendas for shelter. These last were shut up as soon as darkness approached, and regular sentries posted upon their azoteas, who kept watch until morning. The terror of the inhabitants was great,—the greater because for a long period they had lived on good terms with the Indios bravos, and a visit from them was novel as unexpected.

No wonder that they were alarmed. They had cause for it. They well knew that in these hostile incursions the savage enemy acts with the utmost barbarity,—murdering the men, and sparing only the younger women, whom they carry off to a cruel captivity. They well knew this, for at that very date there were thousands of their countrywomen in the hands of the wild Indians, lost to their families and friends for ever! No wonder that there was fear and trembling.

The Comandante seemed particularly on the alert. At the head of his troops he scoured the neighbouring plains, and made incursions towards the spurs of the mountains. At night his patrols were in constant motion up and down the valley. The people were admonished to keep within their houses, and barricade their doors in case of attack. All admired the zeal and activity of their military protectors.

The Comandante won golden opinions daily. This was the first real opportunity he had had of showing them his "pluck," for there had been no alarm of Indians since he arrived. In the time of his predecessor several had taken place, and on these occasions it was remembered that the troops, instead of going abroad to search for the "barbaros," shut themselves up in the garrison till the latter were gone clear out of the valley, after having carried off all the cattle they could collect! What a contrast in the new Comandante! What a brave officer was Colonel Vizcarra!

This excitement continued for several days. As yet no murders had been committed, nor any women, carried off; and as the Indians had only appeared in the night, the probability was that they were in but small force,—some weak band of robbers. Had it been otherwise, they would have long since boldly shown themselves by daylight, and carried on their depredations on a much larger scale.

During all this time the mother and sister of the cibolero lived in their lone rancho without any protection, and were, perhaps, less in dread of the Indians than any other family in the whole valley. This was to be attributed to several causes. First, their training, which had taught them to make light of dangers that terrified their less courageous neighbours. Secondly, their poor hut was not likely to tempt the cupidity of Indian robbers, whose design was evidently plunder. There were too many well-stocked ranchos a little farther up the valley. The Indians would not be likely to molest them.

But there was still a better reason for this feeling, of confidence on their part, and that was somewhat of a family secret. Carlos, having traded with all the neighbouring tribes, was known to the Indians, and was on terms of friendship with nearly every one of their chiefs. One cause of this friendship was, that Carlos was known to them as an *American*. Such was their feeling in regard to Americans that, at this time, and for a long period after, both the trappers and traders of that nation could pass through the whole Apache and Comanche range in the smallest parties without molestation, while large caravans of Mexicans would be attacked and robbed! It was only long after that these tribes assumed a fierce hostility against the Saxon whites; and this was brought about by several acts of barbarism committed by parties of the whites themselves.

In his dealings with the Indios bravos, then, the cibolero had not forgotten his little rancho at home; and he had always counselled his mother and sister not to fear the Indians in his absence, assuring them that these would not molest them.

The only tribe with which Carlos was not on friendly terms was the Jicarilla, a small and miserable band that lived among the mountains north-east of Santa Fé. They were a branch of the Apaches, but lived apart, and had little in common with the great freebooters of the south—the *Mezcaleros* and *Wolf-eaters*.

For these reasons, then, the little Rosita and her mother, though not entirely without apprehension, were yet less frightened by the current rumours of the time than their neighbours.

Every now and then Don Juan rode over to the rancho, and advised them to come and stay at his house—a large strong building well defended by himself and his numerous peons. But the mother of Rosita only laughed at the fears of Don Juan; and Rosita herself, from motives of delicacy, of course refused to accede to his proposal.

It was the third night from the time the Indians had been first heard of. The mother and daughter had laid aside their spindle and loom, and were about to retire to their primitive couches on the earthen floor, when Cibolo was seen to spring from his petaté, and rush towards the door, growling fiercely.

His growl increased to a bark—so earnest, that it was evident some one was outside. The door was shut and barred; but the old woman, without even inquiring who was there, pulled out the bar, and opened the door.

She had scarcely shown herself when the wild whoop of Indians rang in her ears, and a blow from a heavy club prostrated her upon the threshold. Spite the terrible onset of the dog, several savages, in all the horrid glare of paint and feathers, rushed into the house yelling fearfully, and brandishing their weapons; and in less than five minutes' time, the young girl, screaming with terror, was borne in their arms to the outside of the rancho, and there tied upon the back of a mule.

The few articles which the Indians deemed of any value were carried away with them; and the savages, after setting fire to the rancho, made off in haste.

Rosita saw the blaze of the rancho as she sat tied upon the mule. She had seen her mother stretched upon the door-step, and was in fact dragged over her apparently lifeless form; and the roof was now in flames!

"My poor mother!" she muttered in her agony; "O God! O God! what will become of my poor mother?"

Almost simultaneously with this attack, or a little after it, the Indians appeared before the house of the ranchero, Don Juan; but, after yelling around it and firing several arrows over the azotea and against the door, they retired.

Don Juan was apprehensive for his friends at the rancho. As soon as the Indians had gone away from about his own premises, he stole out; and, trusting to the darkness, made his way in that direction.

He had not gone far before the blaze of the building came under his eyes, causing the blood to rush cold through his veins.

He did not stop. He was afoot, but he was armed, and he dashed madly forward, resolved to defend Rosita, or die!

In a few minutes he stood before the door of the rancho; and there, to his horror, lay the still senseless form of the mother, her wild and ghastly features illuminated by the blaze from the roof. The fire had not yet reached her, though in a few moments more she would have been buried in the flames!

Don Juan drew her forth into the garden, and then rushed frantically around calling on Rosita.

But there was no reply. The crackling blaze—the sighing of the night wind—the hooting of the cliff owl, and the howling of the *coyote*, alone answered his anxious calls.

After remaining until all hope had vanished, he turned towards the prostrate body, and knelt down to examine it. To his surprise there was still life, and, after her lips had been touched with water, the old woman showed symptoms of recovery. She had only been stunned by the heavy blow.

Don Juan at length lifted her in his arms, and taking the well-known path returned with his burden, and with a heavy heart, to his own house.

Next morning the news of the affair was carried through all the settlement, adding to the terror of the inhabitants. The Comandante with a large troop galloped conspicuously through the town; and after much loud talk and empty demonstrations, went off on the trail which the Indians were supposed to have taken.

Long before night the troopers returned with their usual report, "*los barbaros no pudimos alcanzar.*" (We could not overtake the savages.)

They said that they had followed the trail to the Pecos, where the Indians had crossed, and that the savages had continued on towards the Llano Estacado.

This piece of news gave some relief, for it was conjectured, if the marauders had gone in that direction, their plundering would end. They had probably proceeded to join the rest of their tribe, known to be somewhere in that quarter.

Chapter Twenty Seven

Vizcarra and his gay lancers passed up the valley, on their return from the pursuit at an early hour of the evening.

Scarcely had a short hour elapsed when another cavalcade, dusty and wayworn, was seen moving along the same road, and heading towards the settlements. It could hardly be termed a cavalcade, as it consisted of an atajo of pack-mules, with some carretas drawn by oxen. One man only was on horseback, who, by his dress and manner, could be recognised as the owner of the atajo.

Despite the fatigue of a long march, despite the coating of dust which covered both horse and rider, it was not difficult to tell who the horseman was. Carlos the cibolero!

Thus far had he reached on his homeward way. Another stretch of five miles along the dusty road, and it would halt before the door of his humble rancho. Another hour, and his aged mother, his fond sister, would fling themselves into his arms, and receive his affectionate embrace!

What a surprise it would be! They would not be expecting him for weeks—long weeks.

And what a surprise he had for them in another way! His wonderful luck! The superb mulada and cargo,—quite a little fortune indeed! Rosita should have a new dress,—not a coarse woollen nagua, but one of silk, real foreign silk, and a manta, and the prettiest pair of satin slippers—she should wear fine stockings on future fiesta days—she should be worthy of his friend Don Juan. His old mother, too—she should drink tea, coffee, or chocolate, which she preferred—no more *atole* for her!

The rancho was rude and old—it should come down, and another and better one go up in its place—no—it would serve as a stable for the horse, and the new rancho should be built beside it. In fact, the sale of his mulada would enable him to buy a good strip of land, and stock it well too.

What was to hinder him to turn ranchero, and farm or graze on his own account? It would be far more respectable, and would give him a higher standing in the settlement. Nothing to hinder him. He would do so; but first one more journey to the plains—one more visit to his Waco friends, who had promised him—Ha! it was this very promise that was the keystone of all his hopes.

The silk dress for Rosita, the luxuries for his old mother, the new house, the farm, were all pleasant dreams to Carlos; but he indulged a dream of a still pleasanter nature—a dream that eclipsed them all; and his hopes of its realisation lay in that one more visit to the country of the Wacoes.

Carlos believed that his poverty alone was the barrier that separated him from Catalina. He knew that her father was not, properly speaking, one of the "rico" class. True, he was a rico now: but only a few years ago he had been a poor "gambucino"—poor as Carlos himself. In fact, they had once been nearer neighbours; and in his earlier days Don Ambrosio had esteemed the boy Carlos fit company for the little Catalina.

What objection, then, could he have to the cibolero—provided the latter could match him in fortune? "Certainly none," thought Carlos. "If I can prove to him that I, too, am a 'rico,' he will consent to my marrying Catalina. And why not? The blood in my veins—so says my mother—is as good as that of any hidalgo. And, if the Wacoes have told me the truth, one more journey and Carlos the cibolero will be able to shew as much gold as Don Ambrosio the miner!"

These thoughts had been running in his mind throughout the whole of his homeward journey. Every day—every hour—did he build his aery castles; every hour did he buy the silk dress for Rosita—the tea, coffee, and chocolate for his mother; every hour did he erect the new rancho, buy the farm, show a fortune in gold-dust, and demand Catalina from her father! *Châteaux en Espagne!*

Now that he was close to his home, these pleasant visions grew brighter and seemed nearer; and the countenance of the cibolero was radiant with joy. What a fearful change was soon to pass over it!

Several times he thought of spurring on in advance, the sooner to enjoy the luxury of his mother's and sister's welcome; and then he changed his mind again.

"No," muttered he to himself; "I will stay by the atajo. I will better enjoy the triumph. We shall all march up in line, and halt in front of the rancho. They will think I have some stranger with me, to whom belong the mules! When I announce them as my own they will fancy that I have turned Indian, and made a *raid* on the southern provinces, with my stout retainers. Ha! ha! ha!" And Carlos laughed at the conceit.

"Poor little Rosy!" he continued; "she *shall* marry Don Juan this time! I won't withhold my consent any longer? It would be better, too. He's a bold fellow, and can protect her while I'm off on the plains again: though one more journey, and I have done with the plains. One more journey, and I shall change my title from Carlos the cibolero to Señor Don Carlos R—, Ha! ha! ha!"

Again he laughed at the prospect of becoming a "rico," and being addressed as "Don Carlos."

"Very odd," thought he, "I don't meet anyone. I don't see a soul upon the road up or down. Yet it's not late—the sun's above the bluff still. Where can the people be? And yet the road's covered thick with fresh horse-tracks! Ha! the troops have been here! they have just passed up! But that's no reason why the people are not abroad; and I don't see even a straggler! Now I could have believed there was an alarm of Indians had I not seen these tracks; but I know very well that, were the Apaches on their war-trail, my Comandante and his Whiskerandos would never have ventured so far from the Presidio—that I know.

"Well, there's something extraordinary! I can't make it out. Perhaps they're all up to the town at some fiesta. Anton, my boy, you know all the feast-days! Is this one?"

"No, master."

"And where are all the folks?"

"Can't guess, master! Strange we don't see some!"

"So I was thinking. You don't suppose there have been wild Indians in the neighbourhood?"

"No, master—*mira*! They're the tracks of the 'lanzeros'—only an hour ago. No Indians where they are!"

As Antonio said this, both his accent and look had an expression which guided his master to the true meaning of his words, which might otherwise have been ambiguous. He did not mean that the fact of the lancers having been on the ground would prevent the Indians from occupying it, but exactly the reverse. It was, not "lancers no Indians," but "Indians no lancers," that Antonio meant.

Carlos understood him; and, as this had been his own interpretation of the tracks, he burst out into a fit of laughter.

Still no travellers appeared, and Carlos did not like it. As yet he had not thought of any misfortune to those he loved; but the unpeopled road had an air of loneliness about it, and did not seem to welcome him.

As he passed on a feeling of sadness came stealing over him, which after it had fairly taken possession he could not get rid of.

He had not yet passed a settlement. There were none before reaching his own rancho, which, as already stated, was the lowest in the valley. Still the inhabitants fed their flocks far below that; and it was usual, at such an hour, to see them driving their cattle home. He neither saw cattle nor vaqueros.

The meadows on both sides, where cattle used to graze, were empty! What could it mean?

As he noticed these things an indefinite sense of uneasiness and alarm began to creep over him; and this feeling increased until he had arrived at the turning which led to his own rancho.

At length he headed around the forking angle of the road; and having passed the little coppices of evergreen oaks, came within sight of the house. With a mechanical jerk he drew his horse upon his haunches, and sat in the saddle with open jaw and eyes glaring and protruded.

The rancho he could not see—for the covering interposal columns of the cacti—but through the openings along their tops a black line was visible that had an unnatural look, and a strange film of smoke hung over the azotea!

"God of heaven! what can it mean?" cried he, with a choking voice; but, without waiting to answer himself, he lanced the flanks of his horse till the animal shot off like an arrow.

The intervening ground was passed; and, flinging himself from the saddle, the cibolero rushed through the cactus-fence.

The atajo soon after came up. Antonio hurried through: and there, inside the hot, smoke-blackened walls, half-seated, half-lying on the banqueta, was his master, his head hanging forward upon his breast, and both hands nervously twisted in the long curls of his hair.

Antonio's foot-fall caused him to look up—only for a moment.

"O God! My mother—my sister!" And, as he repeated the words, his head once more fell forward, while his broad breast rose and fell in convulsed heaving. It was an hour of mortal agony; for some secret instinct had revealed to him the terrible truth.

Chapter Twenty Eight

For some minutes Carlos remained stupefied with the shock, and made no effort to rouse himself.

A friendly hand laid upon his shoulder caused him to look up; Don Juan the ranchero was bending over him.

Don Juan's face wore a look as wretched as his own. It gave him no hope; and it was almost mechanically the words escaped his lips—

"My mother? my sister?"

"Your mother is at my house," replied Don Juan.

"And Rosita?"

Don Juan made no reply—the tears were rolling down his cheeks.

"Come, man!" said Carlos, seeing the other in as much need of consolation as himself; "out with it—let me know the worst! Is she dead?"

"No,—no,—no!—I hope not *dead*!"

"Carried off?"

"Alas, yes!"

"By whom?"

"The Indians."

"You are sure by *Indians*?"

As Carlos asked this question, a look of strange meaning glanced from his eyes.

"Quite sure—I saw them myself—your mother?"

"My mother! What of her?"

"She is safe. She met the savages in the doorway, was knocked senseless by a blow, and saw no more."

"But Rosita?"

"No one saw her; but certainly she was taken away by the Indians."

"You are sure they were *Indians*, Don Juan?"

"Sure of it. They attacked my house almost at the same time. They had previously driven off my cattle, and for that, one of my people was on the look-out. He saw them approach; and, before they got near, we were shut up and ready to defend ourselves. Finding this, they soon went off. Fearing for your people, I stole out as soon as they were gone, and came here. When I arrived the roof was blazing, and your mother lying senseless in the doorway. Rosita was gone! *Madre de Dios*! she was gone!"

And the young ranchero wept afresh.

"Don Juan!" said Carlos, in a firm voice; "you have been a friend—a brother—to me and mine. I know you suffer as much as I do. Let there be no tears! See! mine are dried up! I weep no more—perhaps sleep not—till Rosita is rescued or revenged. Let us to business, then! Tell me all that is known about these Indians—and quick, Don Juan! I have a keen appetite for your news!"

The ranchero detailed the various rumours that had been afloat for the three or four days preceding—as well as the actual occurrences,—how the Indians had been first seen upon the upper plain; their encounter with the shepherds and the driving off of the sheep; their appearance in the valley, and their raid upon his own cattle—for it was his *ganaderia* that had suffered—and then the after circumstances already known to Carlos.

He also informed the latter of the activity shown by the troops; how they had followed that morning upon the trail of the robbers; how he had desired to accompany them with some of his people; and how the request was refused by the Comandante.

"Refused?" exclaimed Carlos, interrogatively.

"Yes," replied Don Juan; "he said we would only hinder the troops! I fancy his motive was his chagrin with me. He does not like me ever since the fiesta."

"Well! what then?"

"The troops returned but an hour ago. They report that they followed the trail as far as the Pecos, where it crossed, striking direct for the Llano Estacado; and, as the Indians had evidently gone off to the great plains, it would have been useless to attempt pursuing them farther. So they alleged.

"The people," continued Don Juan, "will be only too glad that the savages have gone away, and will trouble themselves no farther about it. I have been trying to get up a party to follow them, but not one would venture. Hopeless as it was, I intended a pursuit with my own people; but, thank God! *you* have come!"

"Ay, pray God it may not be too late to follow their trail. But no; only last night at midnight, you say? There's been neither rain nor high wind—it will be fresh as dew; and if ever hound—Ha! where's Cibolo?"

"At my house, the dog is. He was lost, this morning; we thought he had been killed or carried off; but at midday my people found him by the rancho here, covered with mud, and bleeding where he had received the prick of a spear. We think the Indians must have taken him along, and that he escaped from them on the road."

"It is strange enough—Oh! my poor Rosita!—poor lost sister!—where art thou at this moment?—where?—where?—Shall I ever see you again?—My God! my God!"

And Carlos once more sunk back into his attitude of despair.

Then suddenly springing to his feet, with clenched fist and flashing eyes, he cried out—

"Wide though the prairie plains, and faint the trail of these dastardly robbers, yet keen is the *eye* of Carlos the cibolero! I shall find thee yet—I shall find thee, though it cost me the search of a life. Fear not, Rosita! fear not, sweet sister! I come to your rescue! If thou art wronged, woe, woe, to the tribe that has done it!" Then turning to Don Juan, he continued,—"The night is on—we can do nothing to-night. Don Juan!—friend, brother!—bring me to her—to my mother."

There is a wild poetry in the language of grief, and there was poetry in the words of the cibolero; but these bursts of poetic utterance were brief, and he again returned to the serious reality of his situation. Every circumstance that could aid him in his purposed pursuit was considered and arranged in a sober and practical manner. His arms and accoutrements, his horse, all were cared for, so as to be ready by the earliest hour of light. His servants, and those of Don Juan, were to accompany him, and for these horses were also prepared.

Pack-mules, too, with provisions and other necessaries for a long journey—for Carlos had no intention of returning without the accomplishment of his sworn purpose—rescue or revenge. His was no pursuit to be baffled by slight obstacles. He was not going to bring back the report "*no los pudimos alcanzar*" He was resolved to trail the robbers to the farthest point of the prairies—to follow them to their fastens, wherever that might be.

Don Juan was with him heart and soul, for the ranchero's interest in the result was equal to his own—his agony was the same.

Their peons numbered a score—trusty Tagnos all, who loved their masters, and who, if not warriors by trade, were made so by sympathy and zeal.

Should they overtake the robbers in time, there would be no fear of the result. From all circumstances known, the latter formed but a weak band. Had this not been the case, they would never have left the valley with so trifling a booty. Could they be overtaken before joining their tribe, all might yet be well. They would be compelled to give up both their plunder and their captive, and, perhaps, pay dearly for the distress they had occasioned. Time, therefore, was a most important consideration, and the pursuers had resolved to take the trail with the earliest light of the morning.

Carlos slept not—and Don Juan only in short and feverish intervals. Both sat up in their dresses,—Carlos by the bedside of his mother, who, still suffering from the effects of the blow, appeared to rave in her sleep.

The cibolero sat silent, and in deep thought. He was busied with plans and conjectures—conjectures as to what tribe of Indians the marauders could belong to. Apaches or Comanches they were not. He had met parties of both on his return. They treated him in a friendly manner, and they said nothing of hostilities against the people of San Ildefonso. Besides, no bands of these would have been in such small force as the late robbers evidently were. Carlos wished it had been they. He knew that in such a case, when it was known that the captive was *his* sister, she would be restored to him. But no; they had nothing to do with it. Who then?—the Yutas? Such was the belief among the people of the valley, as he had been told by Don Juan. If so, there was still a hope—Carlos had traded with a branch of this powerful and warlike tribe. He was also on friendly terms with some of its chiefs, though these were now at war with the more northern settlements.

But the Jicarillas still returned to his mind. These were Indians of a cowardly, brutal disposition, and his mortal foes. They would have scalped him on sight. If his sister was *their* captive, her lot was hard indeed; and the very thought of such a fate caused the cibolero to start up with a shudder, and clench his hands in a convulsive effort of passion.

It was near morning. The peons were astir and armed. The horses and mules were saddled in the patio, and Don Juan had announced that all were ready. Carlos stood by the bedside of his mother to take leave. She beckoned him near. She was still weak, for blood had flown freely from her, and her voice was low and feeble.

"My son," said she, as Carlos bent over her, "know you what Indians you are going to pursue?"

"No, mother," replied Carlos, "but I fear they are our enemies the Jicarillas."

"Have the Jicarillas *beards on their faces and jewels on their fingers*?"

"No mother; why do you ask such a question?—you know they have no beards! My poor mother!" added he, turning to Don Juan; "this terrible stroke has taken her senses!"

"Follow the trail, then!" she continued, without noticing the last remark uttered by Carlos in a whisper; "follow the trail—perhaps it will guide thee to—" and she whispered the rest into his ear.

"What, mother?" said he, starting, as if at some strange information. "Dost thou think so?"

"I have some suspicion—only *suspicion*—but follow the trail—it will guide thee—follow it, and be satisfied!"

"Do not doubt me, mother; I shall be satisfied of *that*."

"One promise before you go. Be not rash—be prudent."

"Fear not, mother! I will."

"If it be so—"

"If it be so, mother, you'll soon see me back. God bless you!—My blood's on fire—I cannot stay!—God bless you, mother!—Farewell!"

Next minute the train of mounted men, with Don Juan and Carlos at its head, passed out of the great gate, and took the road that led out from the valley.

Chapter Twenty Nine

It was not yet daybreak when the party left the house, but they had not started too early. Carlos knew that they could follow the road so far as the lancers had gone, in the darkness; and it would be light enough by the time they had got to the point where these had turned back.

Five miles below the house of Don Juan the road forked—one, leading southward, was that by which Carlos had returned the evening before; the other, or left fork, led nearly in a direct line towards the Pecos, where there was a ford. The left fork had been that taken by the troopers, as their horse-tracks showed.

It was now day. They could have followed the trail at a gallop, as it was a much-travelled and well-known path. But the eye of the cibolero was not bent upon this plain trail, but upon the ground on each side of it, and this double scrutiny caused him to ride more slowly.

On both sides were cattle-tracks. These were, no doubt, made by the cattle stolen from Don Juan—in all numbering about fifty. The cibolero said they must have passed over the ground two days before. That would correspond with the time when they had been taken.

The trackers soon passed the limits of the valley, and entered the plain through which runs the Pecos. They were about approaching that stream in a direct line, and were still two miles from its banks, when the dog Cibolo, who had been trotting in advance of the party, suddenly turned to the left, and ran on in that direction. The keen eye of Carlos detected a new trail upon which the dog was running, and which parted from the track of the troopers. It ran in a direction due north.

What appeared singular both to Carlos and Don Juan was the fact of Cibolo having taken this new route, as it was not marked by a road or path of any kind, but merely by the footprints of some animals that had lately passed over it!

Had Cibolo gone that way before?

Carlos dismounted to examine the tracks.

"Four horses and one mule!" he said, speaking to Don Juan. "Two of the horses shod on the fore feet only; the other two, with the mule, barefoot. All of them mounted—the mule led—perhaps with a pack."

"*No!*" he added, after a little further examination, "it's not a pack-mule!"

It scarce cost the cibolero five minutes to arrive at these conclusions. How he did so was a mystery to most of his companions,—perhaps to all, except the half-blood, Antonio. And yet he was right in every particular.

He continued to scrutinise the new trail for some moments longer.

"The time corresponds," said he, still addressing Don Juan. "They passed yesterday morning before the dew was dry. You are sure it was not midnight when they left your house?"

"Quite sure," replied the ranchero. "It was still only midnight when I returned with your mother from the rancho. I am quite sure of that."

"One more question, Don Juan: How many Indians, think you, were in the party that made their appearance at your house—few or many?"

"Not many I think. Two or three only could be heard yelling at once; but the trees prevented us from seeing them. I fancy, from their traces left, that the band was a very small one. It might be the same that burned the rancho. They could have arrived at my house afterwards. There was time enough."

"I have reason to believe they *were* the same," said Carlos, still bending over the hoof-prints, "and *this may be their trail.*"

"Think you so?" inquired Don Juan.

"I do.—See—there! Is this not strange?"

The speaker pointed to the dog, who, meanwhile, had returned to the spot, and stood whimpering, and showing an evident desire to proceed by the trace newly discovered!

"Very strange," replied Don Juan. "He must have travelled it before!"

"Perhaps so," said Carlos. "But it will not spoil by an hour's keeping. Let us first see where these valiant troopers have been to. I want to know that before I leave this main path. Let us on, and briskly!"

All spurred their animals into a gentle gallop, the cibolero leading as before. As before, also, his eyes swept the ground on both sides in search of any trail that might diverge from that on which they travelled.

Now and then cross paths appeared, but these were old. No horses had passed recently upon them, and he did not slacken his pace to examine them.

After a twenty minutes' gallop the party halted upon the bank of the Pecos, at the ford. It was plain that the troopers had also halted there, and turned back without crossing! But cattle had crossed two days before—so said the cibolero—and mounted drivers. The tracks of both were visible in the mud. Carlos rode through the shallow water to examine the other side. At a glance he saw that no troops had crossed, but some forty or fifty head of cattle.

After a long and careful examination, not only of the muddy bank, but of the plain above, he beckoned to Don Juan and the rest to ford the stream and join him.

When Don Juan came up, the cibolero said to him, in a tone full of intelligence—

"*Amigo*! you stand a fair chance to recover your cattle."

"Why do you think so?"

"Because their drivers, four in number, have been near this spot not much over twenty-four hours ago. The animals, therefore, cannot be far off."

"But how know you this?"

"Oh, that is plain enough," coolly responded the cibolero. "The men who drove your beasts were mounted on the same horses that made yonder trail." The speaker indicated the trail which he had halted to examine, and continued,—"Very probably we'll find the herd among the spurs of the ceja yonder."

As Carlos said this, he pointed to a number of ragged ridges that from the brow of the Llano Estacado jutted out into the plain. They appeared to be at the distance of some ten miles from the crossing.

"Shall we push on there?" asked Don Juan.

The cibolero did not give an immediate answer. He had evidently not decided yet, and was debating in his own mind what course to pursue.

"Yes," he replied, at length, in a solemn and deliberate voice. "It is better to be sure. With all my terrible suspicions, I may be wrong. *She* may be wrong. *The two trails may yet come together.*"

The latter part of this was spoken in soliloquy, and, though it reached the ears of Don Juan, he did not comprehend its meaning. He was about to ask his companion for an explanation, when the latter, suddenly collecting his energies, struck the spurs into his horse, and, calling to them to follow, galloped off upon the cattle-track.

After a run of ten miles, which was made in less than an hour, the party entered a large ravine or point of the plain that protruded, like a deep bay, into the mountain-like side of the high steppe. As they entered this, a singular spectacle came under their eyes. The ravine, near its bottom, was covered with zopilotes, or black vultures. Hundreds of them were perched upon the rocks, or wheeling overhead in the air; and hundreds of others hopped about upon the plain, flapping their broad wings as if in full enjoyment. The coyote, the larger wolf, and the grizzly bear, were seen moving over the ground, or quarrelling with each other, though they need not have quarrelled—the repast was plenteous for all. Between forty and fifty carcases were strewed over the ground, which Don Juan and his vaqueros as they drew near recognised as the carcases of his own cattle.

"I told you so, Don Juan," said Carlos, in a voice now husky with emotion; "but I did not expect this. What a deep-laid plan! They might have strayed back! and that—oh! horrible villain! My mother was right—*it is he! it is he!*"

"Who, Carlos! What mean you?" inquired Don Juan, wondering at these strange and incongruous phrases.

"Ask me not now, Don Juan! Presently I shall tell you all—presently, but not now; my brain's too hot—my heart is burning: presently—presently. The mystery is past—I know all—I had suspicion from the first—I saw him at the fiesta—I saw his bad ruffian gaze bent upon her. Oh, despot! I'll tear your heart out! Come, Don Juan!—Antonio—comrades!—After me on the trail! It's easily followed. *I know where it will lead*—well I know.—On!"

And driving the spur into the flanks of his horse, the cibolero galloped off in the direction of the crossing.

The wondering troop—Don Juan among the rest—set their animals in motion, and galloped after.

There was no halt made at the ford. Carlos dashed his horse through the water, and the rest imitated his example. There was no halt either on arriving at the trace that led northward. The dog scampered along it, yelping at intervals; and the troop kept close after his heels.

They had not followed it quite a mile when it suddenly turned at right angles, and *took the direction of the town*!

Don Juan and the rest expressed surprise, but there was nothing in all this to surprise the cibolero. *He* was expecting that. The expression on his face was not that of astonishment. It was far different—far more terrible to behold!

His eyes were sunk in their sockets and gleaming with a lurid light, as if fire was burning within them. His teeth were firmly set—his lips white and tightly drawn, as if he was meditating, or had already made, some desperate resolve. He scarce looked at the tracks, he needed their guidance no longer. *He knew there he was going*!

The trail crossed a muddy arroyo. The dog sweltered through, and the red clay adhered to his shaggy coat. It corresponded with that with which he had been already besmeared!

Don Juan noticed the circumstance, and pointed it out.

"He has been here before!" said he.

"I know it," replied Carlos; "I know it all—all. There is no mystery now. Patience, amigo! You shall know all, but now let me *think*. I have no time for aught else."

The trail still led in the direction of the town. It did not re-enter the valley, but passed over a sloping country to the upper plain, and then ran nearly parallel with the bluffs.

"Master!" said Antonio, riding up by the side of Carlos, "these are not the tracks of Indian horses, unless they have stolen them. Two of them are *troop* horses. I know the *berradura* well. They are *officers' horses*, too—I can tell that from the shoeing."

The cibolero showed no signs of being astonished by this information, nor made he reply. He seemed engrossed with his thoughts.

Antonio, thinking he had not been heard or understood, repeated what he had said.

"Good Antonio!" said the cibolero, turning his eyes on his follower, "do you think me blind or stupid?"

This was not said angrily. Antonio understood its meaning, and fell back among his companions.

On moved the trackers—now at a gallop, now more slowly, for their animals were by this time somewhat jaded. On they moved, still keeping the trail, and still heading straight for the town!

At length they reached a point where a road from the upper plain led by a zigzag path to the valley below. It was the same by which Carlos had ascended to perform his great feat on the day of the fiesta. At the top of the descent Carlos ordered the party to halt, and with Don Juan rode forward to the edge of the projecting cliff—at the very spot where he had exhibited his skill—the cliff of *Niña Perdida*.

Both drew up when near the edge. They commanded a full view of the valley and the town.

"Do you see that building?" inquired the cibolero, pointing to the detached pile which lay between them and the town.

"The Presidio?"

"The Presidio."

"Yes—what of it?"

"*She is there!*"

Chapter Thirty

At that moment upon the *azotea* a man was pacing to and fro. He was not a sentinel, though at opposite angles of the building two of these could be seen who carried carbines—their heads and shoulders just appearing above the crenated top of the battlement towers.

The man *en promenade* was an officer, and the part of the azotea *upon* which he moved was the roof of the officers' quarter, separated from the rest by a wall of equal height with the parapet. It was, moreover, a sacred precinct—not to be disturbed by the tread of common troopers on ordinary occasions. It was the "quarterdeck" of the Presidio.

The officer was in full dress, though not on any duty; but a single glance at the style and cut of his uniform would convince any one that he was a "dandy soldier," and loved to appear at all times in fine feathers. The gold-lace and bright-coloured broad-cloth seemed to affect him as his rich plumage does the peacock. Every now and again he paused in his promenade, glanced down at his lacquered boots, examined the tournure of his limbs, or feasted his eyes upon the jewels that studded his delicate white fingers.

He was no beauty withal nor hero either; but that did not prevent him from indulging in the fancy that he was both—a combination of Mars and Apollo.

He was a colonel in the Spanish army, however, and Comandante of the Presidio—for the promenader in question was Vizcarra himself.

Though satisfied with his own appearance, he was evidently not satisfied about something else. There was a cloud upon his features that not even the contemplation of the lacquered boots or lily-white hands could banish. Some disagreeable thought was pressing upon his mind, causing him at intervals to make fitful starts, and look nervously around him.

"Bah! 'twas but a dream!" he muttered to himself. "Why should I think of it? 'twas only a dream!"

His eyes were bent downward as he gave expression to these abrupt phrases, and as he raised them again chance guided his look in the direction of "La Niña Perdida." No, it was not chance, for La Niña had figured in his dream, and his eyes were but following his thoughts.

The moment they rested on the cliff he started back as if some terrible spectre were before him, and mechanically caught hold of the parapet. His cheeks suddenly blanched, his jaws fell, and his chest heaved, in hurried and convulsive breathing!

What can cause these symptoms of strong emotion? Is it the sight of yonder horseman standing upon the very pinnacle of the bluff, and outlined against the pale sky? What is there in such an appearance to terrify the Comandante—for terrified he is? Hear him!

"My God! my God!—it is *he*! The form of his horse—of himself—just as he appeared—it is he! I fear to look at him! I cannot—"

And the officer averted his face for a moment, covering it with his hands.

It was but a moment, and again he looked upwards. Not curiosity, but the fascination of fear, caused him to look again. The horseman had disappeared. Neither horse nor man—no object of any sort—broke the line of the bluffs!

"Surely I have been dreaming again?" muttered the still trembling caitiff. "Surely I have? There was no one there, least of all—. How could he? He is hundreds of miles off! It was an illusion! Ha! ha! ha! What the devil is the matter with my senses, I wonder? That horrid dream of last night has bewitched them! *Carrambo!* I'll think no more of it?"

As he said this he resumed his pace more briskly, believing that that might rid him of his unpleasant reflections. At every turn, however, his eyes again sought the bluff, and swept along its edge with a glance that betokened fear. But they saw no more of the spectre horseman, and their owner began to feel at ease again.

A footstep was heard upon the stone steps of the "escalera." Some one was ascending to the roof.

The next moment the head and shoulders of a man were visible; and Captain Roblado stepped out upon the azotea.

The "buenos dias" that passed between him and Vizcarra showed that it was their first meeting for that day. In fact, neither had been long up; for the hour was not yet too late for fashionable sleepers. Roblado had just breakfasted, and come out on the azotea to enjoy his Havannah.

"Ha! ha! ha!" laughed he, as he lighted the cigar, "what a droll masquerade it has been! 'Pon my soul! I can scarce get the paint off; and my voice, after such yelling, won't recover for a week! Ha! ha! Never was maiden wooed and won in such a romantic, roundabout way. Shepherds attacked—sheep driven off and scattered to the winds—cattle carried away and killed in regular *battue*—old woman knocked over, and rancho given to the flames—besides three days of marching and countermarching, travestying Indian, and whooping till one is hoarse; and all this trouble for a poor *paisana*—daughter of a reputed witch! Ha! ha! ha! It would read like a chapter in some Eastern romance—Aladdin, for instance—only that the maiden was not rescued by some process of magic or knight-errantry. Ha! ha ha!"

This speech of Roblado will disclose what is, perhaps, guessed at already—that the late incursion of "los barbaros" was neither more nor less than an affair got up by Vizcarra and himself to cover the abduction of the cibolero's sister. The Indians who had harried the sheep and cattle—who had attacked the hacienda of Don Juan—who had fired the rancho and carried off Rosita—were Colonel Vizcarra, his officer Captain Roblado, his sergeant Gomez, and a soldier named José—another minion of his confidence and will.

There were but the four, as that number was deemed sufficient for the accomplishment of the atrocious deed; and rumour, backed by fear, gave them the strength of four hundred. Besides, the fewer in the secret the better. This was the prudence or cunning of Roblado.

Most cunningly, too, had they taken their measures. The game, from beginning to end, was played with design and execution worthy of a better cause. The shepherds were first attacked on the upper plain, to give certainty to the report that hostile Indians were near. The scouting-parties were sent out from the Presidio, and proclamations issued to the inhabitants to be on their guard—all for effect; and the further swoop upon the cattle was clear proof of the presence of "los barbaros" in the valley. In this foray the fiendish masquers took an opportunity of "killing two birds with one stone;" for, in addition to carrying out their general design, they gratified the mean revenge which they held against the young ranchero.

Their slaughtering his cattle in the ravine had a double object. First, the loss it would be to him gave them satisfaction; but their principal motive was that the animals might not stray back to the settlement. Had they done so, after having been captured by Indians, it would have looked suspicious. As it was, they hoped that, long before any one should discover the *battue*, the wolves and buzzard would do their work; and the bones would only supply food for conjecture. This was the more probable, as it was not likely, while the Indian alarm lasted, that any one would be bold enough to venture that way. There was no settlement or road, except Indian trails, leading in that direction.

Even when the final step was taken, and the victim carried off, she was not brought *directly* to the Presidio; for even *she* was to be hoodwinked. On the contrary, she was tied upon a mule, led by one of the ruffians, and permitted to see the way they were going, until they had reached the point where their trail turned back. She was then blinded by a leathern "tapado," and in that state carried to the Presidio, and within its walls—utterly ignorant of the distance she had travelled, and the place where she was finally permitted to rest.

Every act in the diabolical drama was conceived with astuteness, and enacted with a precision which must do credit to the head of Captain Roblado, if not to his heart. He was the principal actor in the whole affair.

Vizcarra had, at first, some scruples about the affair—not on the score of conscience, but of impracticability and fear of detection. This would indeed have done him a serious injury. The discovery of such a villainous scheme would have spread like wildfire over the whole country. It would have been ruin to him.

Roblado's eloquence, combined with his own vile desires, overruled the slight opposition of his superior; and, once entered on the affair, the latter found himself highly amused in carrying it out. The burlesque proclamations, the exaggerated stories of Indians, the terror of the citizens, their encomiums on his own energetic and valorous conduct—all these were a pleasant relief to the *ennui* of a barrack life and, during the several days' visit of "los barbaros," the Comandante and his captain were never without a theme for mirth and laughter.

So adroitly had they managed the whole matter that, upon the morning after the final *coup* of the robbers—the abduction of Rosita—there was not a soul in the settlement, themselves and their two aides excepted, that had the slightest suspicion but that real hostile Indians were the actors!

Yes, there was one other who had a suspicion—only a suspicion—Rosita's mother. Even the girl believed herself in the hands of Indians—*if belief she had.*

Chapter Thirty One

"Ha! ha! ha! A capital joke, by my honour!" continued Roblado, laughing as he puffed his cigar. "It's the only piece of fun I've enjoyed since we came to this stupid place. Even in a frontier post I find that one *may* have a little amusement if he know how to make it. Ha! ha! ha! After all, there was a devilish deal of trouble. But come, tell me, my dear Comandante—for you know by this time—in confidence, was it worth the trouble?"

"I am sorry we have taken it," was the reply, delivered in a serious tone.

Roblado looked straight in the other's face, and now for the first time noticed its gloomy expression. Busied with his cigar, he had not observed this before.

"Hola!" exclaimed he; "what's the matter, my colonel? This is not the look a man should wear who has spent the last twelve hours as pleasantly as you must have done. Something amiss?"

"Everything amiss."

"Pray what? Surely you were with her?"

"But a moment, and that was enough."

"Explain, my dear colonel."

"She is mad!"

"Mad!"

"Having mad! Her talk terrified me. I was but too glad to come away, and leave her to the care of José, who waits upon her. I could not bear to listen to her strange jabberings. I assure you, camarado, it robbed me of all desire to remain."

"Oh," said Roblado, "that's nothing—she'll get over it in a day or so. She still thinks herself in the hands of the savages who are going to murder and scalp her! It may be as well for you to undeceive her of this as soon as she comes to her senses. I don't see any harm in letting *her* know. You must do so in the end, and the sooner the better—you will have the longer time to get her reconciled to it. Now that you have her snug within earless and eyeless walls, you can manage the thing at your leisure. No one suspects— no one *can* suspect. They are full of the Indians to-day—ha! ha! ha! and 'tis said her inamorato, Don Juan, talks of getting up a party to pursue them! Ha! ha! He'll not do that—the fellow hasn't influence enough, and nobody cares either about his cattle or the witch's daughter. Had it been some one else the case might have been different. As it is, there's no fear of discovery, even were the cibolero himself to make his appearance—"

"Roblado!" cried the Comandante, interrupting him, and speaking in a deep earnest voice.

"Well?" inquired the captain, regarding Vizcarra with astonishment.

"I have had a dream—a fearful dream; and that—not the ravings of the girl—it is that is now troubling me. *Diablos!* a fearful dream!"

"You, Comandante—a valiant soldier—to let a silly dream trouble you! But come! what was it? I'm a good interpreter of dreams. I warrant I read it to your bettor satisfaction."

"Simple enough it is, then. I thought myself upon the cliff of La Niña. I thought that I was alone with Carlos the cibolero! I thought that he knew all, and that he had brought me there to punish me—to avenge *her.* I had no power to resist, but was led forward to the brink. I thought that we closed and struggled for a while; but at length I was shaken from his grasp, and pushed over the precipice! I felt myself falling—falling! I could see above me the cibolero, with his sister by his side, and on the extremest point the hideous witch their mother, who laughed a wild maniac laugh, and clapped her long bony hands! I felt myself falling—falling—yet still not reaching the ground; and this horrible feeling continued for a long, long time—in fact, until the fearful thought awoke me. Even then I could scarce believe I had been dreaming, so palpable was the impression that remained. Oh, comrade, it was a dreadful dream!"

"And *but* a dream; and what signifies—"

"Stay, Roblado! I have not told you all. Within the hour—ay, within the quarter of that time—while I was on this spot thinking over it, I chanced to look up to the cliff; and yonder, upon the extreme point, was a horseman clearly outlined against the sky—and that horseman the very image of the cibolero! I noted the horse and the seat of the rider, which I well remember. I could not trust my eyes to look at him. I averted them for a moment—only a moment; and when I looked again he was gone! So quickly had he retired, that I was inclined to think it was only a fancy—that there had been none—and that my dream had produced the illusion!"

"That is likely enough," said Roblado, desirous of comforting his companion; "likely enough—nothing more natural. In the first place, from where we stand to the top of La Niña is a good five thousand varas as the crow flies; and for you, at that distance, to distinguish Carlos the cibolero from any other horseman is a plain impossibility. In the second place, Carlos the cibolero is at this moment full five hundred miles from the tip of my cigar, risking his precious carcase for a cartload of stinking hides and a few bultos of dried buffalo-beef. Let us hope that some of his copper-coloured friends will raise his hay-coloured hair, which some of our poblanas so much admire. And now, my dear Comandante, as to your dream, that is as natural as may be. It could hardly be otherwise than that you should have such a dream. The remembrance of the cibolero's feat of horsemanship on that very cliff, and the later affair with the sister, together with the suspicion you may naturally entertain that Señor Carlos wouldn't be too kind to you if he knew all and had you in his power—all these things, being in your thoughts at one time, must come together incongruously in a dream. The old woman, too—if she wasn't in your thoughts, she has been in mine ever since I gave her that knock in the doorway. Who could forget such a picture as she then presented? Ha! ha! ha!"

The brutal villain laughed—not so much from any ludicrous recollection, as to make the whole thing appear light and trivial in the eyes of his companion.

"What does it all amount to?" he continued. "A dream! a simple, everyday dream! Come, my dear friend, don't let it remain on your mind for another instant!"

"I cannot help it, Roblado. It clings to me like my shadow. It feels like a presentiment. I wish I had left this paisana in her mud hut. By Heaven! I wish she were back there. I shall not be myself till I have got rid of her. I seem to loathe as much as I loved the jabbering idiot."

"Tut, tut, man! you'll soon change your way of thinking—you'll soon take a fresh liking—"

"No, Roblado, no! I'm disgusted—I can't tell why but I *am*. Would to God she were off my hands!"

"Oh! that's easy enough, and without hurting anybody. She can go the way she came. It will only be another scene in the masquerade, and no one will be the wiser. If you are really in earnest—"

"Roblado!" cried the Comandante, grasping his captain by the arm, "I never was more in earnest in my life. Tell me the plan to get her back without making a noise about it. Tell me quick, for I cannot bear this horrid feeling any longer."

"Why, then," began Roblado, "we must have another travestie of Indians—we must—"

He was suddenly interrupted. A short, sharp groan escaped from Vizcarra. His eyes looked as though about to start from his head. His lips grow white, and the perspiration leaped into drops on his forehead!

What could it mean? Vizcarra stood by the outer edge of the azotea that commanded a view of the road leading up to the gate of the Presidio. He was gazing over the parapet, and pointing with outstretched arm.

Roblado was farther back, near the centre of the azotea. He sprang forward, and looked in the direction indicated. A horseman, covered with sweat and dust, was galloping up the road. He was near enough for Roblado to distinguish his features. Vizcarra had already distinguished them. It was Carlos the cibolero!

Chapter Thirty Two

The announcement made by the cibolero on the bluff startled Don Juan, as if a shot had passed through him. Up to this time the simple ranchero had no thought but that they were on the trail of Indians. Even the singular fact of the trail leading back to the valley had not undeceived him. He supposed the Indians had made some other and later foray in that quarter, and that they would hear of them as soon as they should descend the cliffs.

When Carlos pointed to the Presidio, and said, "She is there!" he received the announcement at first with surprise, then with incredulity.

Another word from the cibolero, and a few moments' reflection, and his incredulity vanished. The terrible truth flashed upon his mind, for he, too, remembered the conduct of Vizcarra on the day of the fiesta. His visit to the rancho and other circumstances now rushed before him, aiding the conviction that Carlos spoke the truth.

For some moments the lover could scarce give utterance to his thoughts, so painful were they. More painful than ever! Even while under the belief that his mistress was in the hands of wild Indians he suffered less. There was still some hope that, by their strange code in relation to female captives, she might escape that dreaded fate, until he and Carlos might come up and rescue her. But now the time that had elapsed—Vizcarra's character—O God! it was a terrible thought; and the young man reeled in his saddle as it crossed his mind.

He rode back a few paces, flung himself from his horse, and staggered to the ground in the bitterness of his anguish.

Carlos remained on the bluff, still gazing down on the Presidio. He seemed to be maturing some plan. He could see the sentries on the battlements, the troopers lounging around the walls in their dark blue and crimson uniforms. He could even hear the call of the cavalry bugle, as its clear echoes came dancing along the cliffs. He could see the figure of a man—an officer—pacing to and fro on the azotea, and he could perceive that the latter had halted, and was observing him.

It was at this very moment that Vizcarra had caught sight of the horseman on the bluff—the sight that had so terrified him, and which indeed was no illusion.

The White Chief | 139

"Can it be that fiend himself?" thought Carlos, regarding the officer for a moment. "Quite likely it is he. Oh! that he were within range of my rifle! Patience—patience! I will yet have my revenge!"

And as the speaker muttered these words, he reined back from the bluff and rejoined his companion.

A consultation was now held as to what would be the best mode of proceeding. Antonio was called to their council, and to him Carlos declared his belief that his sister was a captive within the Presidio. It was telling Antonio what he had already divined. The *mestizo* had been to the fiesta as well as his master, and his keen eyes had been busy on that day. He, too, had observed the conduct of Vizcarra; and long before their halt he had arrived at an elucidation of the many mysteries that marked the late Indian incursion. He knew all—his master might have saved words in telling him.

Neither words nor time were wasted. The hearts of both brother and lover were beating too hurriedly for that. Perhaps at that moment the object of their affection was in peril,—perhaps struggling with her ruffian abductor! Their timely arrival might save her!

These considerations took precedence of all plans; in fact, there was no plan they could adopt, to remain concealed—to skulk about the place— to wait for opportunity—what opportunity? They might spend days in fruitless waiting. Days!—hours— even minutes would be too long. Not a moment was to be lost before some action must be taken.

And what action? They could think of none—none but open action. What! dare a man not claim his own sister? Demand her restoration?

But the thought of refusal—the thought of subterfuge—in fact, the certainty that such would be the result—quite terrified them both.

And yet how else could they act? They would at least give publicity to the atrocious deed; that might serve them. There would be sympathy in their favour—perhaps more. Perhaps the people, slaves as they were, might surround the Presidio, and clamour loudly;—in some way the captive might be rescued. Such were their hurried reflections.

"If not rescued," said Carlos, grinding his teeth together, "she shall be revenged. Though the *garrota* press my throat, he shall not live if she be dishonoured. I swear it!"

"I echo the oath!" cried Don Juan, grasping the hilt of his *machete.*

"Masters! dear masters!" said Antonio, "you both know I am not a coward. I shall aid you with my arm or my life; but it is a terrible business. Let us have caution, or we fail. Let us be prudent!"

"True, we must be prudent. I have already promised that to my mother; but how, comrades?—how! In what does prudence consist?—to wait and watch, while she—oh!"

All three were silent for a while. None of them could think of a feasible plan to be pursued.

The situation was, indeed, a most difficult one. There was the Presidio, and within its walls—perhaps in some dark chamber—the cibolero well knew his sister was a captive; but under such peculiar circumstances that her release would be a most difficult enterprise.

In the first place, the villain who held her would assuredly deny that she was there. To have released her would be an acknowledgment of his guilt. What proof of it could Carlos give? The soldiers of the garrison, no doubt, were ignorant of the whole transaction—with the exception of the two or three miscreants who had acted as aides. Were the cibolero to assert such a thing in the town he would be laughed at—no doubt arrested and punished. Even could he offer proofs, what authority was there to help him to justice? The military was the law of the place, and the little show of civic authority that existed would be more disposed to take sides against him than in his favour. He could expect no justice from any quarter. All the proof of his accusation would rest only on such facts as would neither be understood nor regarded by those to whom he might appeal. The return trail would be easily accounted for by Vizcarra—if he should deign to take so much trouble—and the accusation of Carlos would be scouted as the fancy of a madman. No one would give credence to it. The very atrociousness of the deed rendered it incredible!

Carlos and his companions were aware of all these things. They had no hope of help from any quarter. There was no authority that could give them aid or redress.

The cibolero, who had remained for a while silent and thoughtful, at length spoke out. His tone was altered. He seemed to have conceived some plan that held out a hope.

"Comrades!" he said, "I can think of nothing but an open demand, and that must be made within the hour. I cannot live another hour without attempting her rescue—another hour, and what we dread—No! within the hour it must be. I have formed a sort of plan—it may not be the most prudent—but there is no time for reflection. Hear it."

"Go on!"

"It will be of no use our appearing before the gate of the Presidio in full force. There are hundreds of soldiers within the walls, and our twenty

Tagnos, though brave as lions, would be of no service in such an unequal fight. I shall go alone."

"Alone?"

"Yes; I trust to chance for an interview with *him*. If I can get that, it is all I want. He is her gaoler; and when the gaoler sleeps, the captive may be freed. He shall *sleep then*."

The last words were uttered in a significant tone, while the speaker placed his hand mechanically upon the handle of a large knife that was stuck in his waist-belt.

"*He shall sleep* then!" he repeated; "and soon, if Fate favours me. For the rest I care not: I am too desperate. If she be dishonoured I care not to live, but I shall have full revenge!"

"But how will you obtain an interview?" suggested Don Juan. "He will not give *you* one. Would it not be better to disguise yourself? There would be more chance of seeing him that way?"

"No! I am not easily disguised, with my light hair and skin. Besides, it would cost too much time. Trust me, I will not be rash. I have a plan by which I hope to get near him—to see him, at all events. If it fail, I intend to make no demonstration for the present. None of the wretches shall know my real errand. Afterwards I may do as you advise, but now I cannot wait. I must on to the work. I believe it is he that is at this moment pacing yonder azotea, and that is why I cannot wait, Don Juan. If it be me—"

"But what shall we do?" asked Don Juan. "Can we not assist in any way?"

"Yes, perhaps in my escape. Come on, I shall place you. Come on quickly. Moments are days. My brain's on fire. Come on!"

So saying, the cibolero leaped into his saddle and struck rapidly down the precipitous path that led to the valley.

From the point where the road touched the valley bottom, for more than a mile in the direction of the Presidio, it ran through a thick growth of low trees and bushes forming a "chapparal," difficult to pass through, except by following the road itself.

But there were several cattle-paths through the thicket, by which it might be traversed; and these were known to Antonio the half-blood, who had formerly lived in this neighbourhood. By one of those a party of mounted men might approach within half-a-mile of the Presidio without attracting the observation of the sentries upon the walls. To this point, then, Antonio was directed to guide the party; and in due time they arrived near the edge of the jungle, where, at the command of Carlos, all dismounted keeping themselves and their horses under cover of the bushes.

"Now," said the cibolero, speaking to Don Juan, "remain here. If I escape, I shall gallop direct to this point. If I lose my horse, you shall see me afoot all the same. For such a short stretch I can run like a deer: I shall not be overtaken. When I return I shall tell you how to act.

"See! Don Juan!" he continued, grasping the ranchero by the arm, and drawing him forward to the edge of the chapparal. "It is he! by Heaven, it is he!"

Carlos pointed to the azotea of the Presidio, where the head and shoulders of a man were seen above the line of the parapet.

"It is the Comandante himself!" said Don Juan, also recognising him.

"Enough! I have no time for more talk," cried the cibolero. "Now or never! If I return, you shall know what to do. If not, I am taken or killed. But stay here. Stay till late in the night; I may still escape. Their prisons are not too strong; besides, I carry this gold. It may help me. No more. Adios! true friend, adios!"

With a grasp of the ranchero's hand, Carlos leaped back to his saddle, and rode off.

He did not go in the direction of the Presidio, as that would have discovered him too soon. But a path that led through the chapparal would bring him out on the main road that ran up to the front gate, and this path he took. Antonio guided him to the edge of the timber, and then returned to the rest.

Carlos, once on the road, spurred his horse into gallop, and dashed boldly forward to the great gate of the Presidio. The dog Cibolo followed, keeping close up to the heels of his horse.

Chapter Thirty Three

"By the Virgin, it *is* he!" exclaimed Roblado, with a look of astonishment and alarm. "The fellow himself, as I live!"

"I knew it!—I knew it!" shrieked Vizcarra. "I saw him on the cliff: it was no vision!"

"Where can he have come from? In the name of all the saints, where has the fellow—"

"Roblado, I must go below! I must go in, I will not stay to meet him! I *cannot!*"

"Nay, colonel, better let him speak with us. He has seen and recognised you already. If you appear to shun him, it will arouse suspicion. He has come to ask our help to pursue the Indians; and that's his errand, I warrant you!"

"Do you think so?" inquired Vizcarra, partially recovering his self-possession at this conjecture.

"No doubt of it! What else? He can have no suspicion of the truth. How is it possible he could, unless he were a witch, like his mother? Stay where you are, and let us hear what he has got to say. Of course, you can talk to him from the azotea, while he remains below. If he show any signs of being insolent, as he has already been to both of us, let us have him arrested, and cooled a few hours in the calabozo. I hope the fellow will give us an excuse for it, for I haven't forgotten his impudence at the fiesta."

"You are right, Roblado; I shall stay and heur him. It will be better, I think, and will allay any suspicion. But, as you say, he can have none!"

"On the contrary, by your giving him the aid he is about to ask you for, you may put him entirely off the scent—make him your friend, in fact. Ha! ha!"

The idea was plausible, and pleased Vizcarra. He at once determined to act upon it.

This conversation had been hurriedly carried on, and lasted but a few moments—from the time the approaching horseman had been first seen, until he drew up under the wall.

For the last two hundred yards he had ridden slowly, and with an air of apparent respect—as though he feared it might be deemed rude to approach the place of power by any swaggering exhibition of horsemanship. On his fine features traces of grief might be observed, but not one sign of the feeling that was at that moment uppermost in his heart.

As he drew near, he raised his sombrero in a respectful salute to the two officers, whose heads and shoulders were just visible over the parapet; and having arrived within a dozen paces of the wall, he reined up, and, taking off his hat again, waited to be addressed.

"What is your business?" demanded Roblado.

"Cavalleros! I wish to speak with the Comandante."

This was delivered in the tone of one who is soon to ask a favour. It gave confidence to Vizcarra, as well as to the bolder villain—who, notwithstanding all his assurances to the contrary, had still some secret misgivings about the cibolero's errand. Now, however, it was clear that his first conjecture was correct; Carlos had come to solicit their assistance.

"I am he!" answered Vizcarra, now quite recovered from his fright, "I am the Comandante. What have you to communicate, my man?"

"Your excellency, I have a favour to ask;" and the cibolero again saluted with an humble bow.

"I told you so," whispered Roblado to his superior. "All safe, my colonel."

"Well, my good fellow," replied Vizcarra, in his usual haughty and patronising manner, "let me hear it. If not unreasonable—"

"Your excellency, it is a very heavy favour I would ask, but I hope not unreasonable. I am sure that, if it do not interfere with your manifold duties, you will not refuse to grant it, as the interest and trouble you have already taken in the cause are but too well-known."

"Told you so," muttered Roblado a second time.

"Speak out, man!" said Vizcarra, encouragingly; "I can only give an answer when I have heard your request."

"It is this, your excellency. I am but a poor cibolero."

"You are Carlos the cibolero! I know you."

"Yes, your excellency, we have met—at the fiesta of San Juan—"

"Yes, yes! I recollect your splendid horsemanship."

"Your excellency is kind to call it so. It does not avail me now. I am in great trouble!"

"What has befallen? Speak out, man." Both Vizcarra and Roblado guessed the purport of the cibolero's request. They desired that it should be heard by the few soldiers lounging about the gate and for that reason they spoke in a loud tone themselves, anxious that their petitioner might do the same.

Not to oblige them, but for reasons of his own, Carlos replied in a loud voice. He, too, wished the soldiers, but more particularly the sentry at the gate, to hear what passed between himself and the officers. "Well, your excellency," replied he, "I live in a poor rancho, the last in the settlement, with my old mother and sister. The night before last it was attacked by a party of Indians—my mother left for dead—the rancho set on fire—and my sister carried off!"

"I have heard of all this, my friend,—nay, more, I have myself been out in pursuit of the savages."

"I know it, your excellency. I was absent on the Plains, and only returned last night. I have heard that your excellency was prompt in pursuing the savages, and I feel grateful."

"No need of that; I only performed my duty. I regret the occurrence, and sympathise with you; but the villains have got clear off, and there is no hope of bringing them to punishment just now. Perhaps some other time— when the garrison here is strengthened—I shall make an incursion into their country, and then your sister may be recovered."

So completely had Vizcarra been deceived by the cibolero's manner, that his confidence and coolness had returned, and any one knowing nothing more of the affair than could be gathered from that conversation would have certainly been deceived by him. This dissimulation both in speech and manner appeared perfect. By the keen eye of Carlos, however—with his knowledge of the true situation—the tremor of the speaker's lips, slight as it was—his uneasy glance—and an occasional hesitancy in his speech, were all observed. Though Carlos was deceiving *him*, *he* was not deceiving Carlos.

"What favour were you going to ask?" he inquired, after he had delivered his hopeful promise.

"This, your excellency; that you would allow your troops to go once more on the trail of the robbers, either under your own command—which I would much like—or one of your brave officers." Roblado felt flattered. "I would act as guide, your excellency. There is not a spot within two hundred miles I am not acquainted with, as well as I am with this valley; and though I should not say it, I assure your excellency, I can follow an Indian trail with any hunter on the Plains. If your excellency will but send the troop, I promise you I shall guide them to the robbers, or lose my reputation. I can follow their trail *wherever it may lead.*"

"Oh! you could, indeed?" said Vizcarra, exchanging a significant glance with Roblado, while both exhibited evident symptoms of uneasiness.

"Yes, your excellency, anywhere."

"It would be impossible," said Roblado. "It is now two days old; besides, *we* followed it beyond the Pecos, and we have no doubt the robbers are by this time far out of reach, of any pursuit. It would be quite useless to attempt such a thing."

"Cavalleros!"—Carlos addressed himself to both—"I assure you I could find them. They are not so far off."

Both the Comandante and his captain started, and visibly turned pale. The cibolero did not affect to notice this.

"Nonsense! my good fellow!" stammered Roblado; "they are—at least—hundreds of miles off by this—away over the Staked Plain—or to—to the mountains."

"Pardon me, captain, for differing with you; but I believe I know these Indians—I know to what tribe they belong."

"What tribe?" simultaneously inquired the officers, both with an earnestness of manner and a slight trepidation in their voices; "what tribe?—Were they not Yutas?"

"No," answered the cibolero, while he observed the continued confusion of his questioners.

"Who, then?"

"I believe," replied Carlos, "they were *not* Yutas—more likely my sworn foes, the Jicarillas."

"Quite possible!" assented both in a breath, and evidently relieved at the enunciation.

"Quite possible!" repeated Roblado. "From the description given us by the people who saw them, we had fancied they were the Yutas. It may be a mistake, however. The people were so affrighted, they could tell but little about them. Besides, the Indians were only seen in the night."

"Why think you they are the Jicarillas?" asked the Comandante, once more breathing freely.

"Partly because there were so few of them," replied Carlos. "Had they been Yutas—"

"But they were not so few. The shepherds report a large band. They have carried off immense numbers of cattle. There must have been a considerable force of them, else they would not have ventured into the valley—that is certain."

"I am convinced, your excellency, there could not have been many. A small troop of your brave soldiers would be enough to bring back both them and their booty."

Here the lounging lanzeros erected their dwarfish bodies, and endeavoured to look taller.

"*If* they were Jicarillas," continued Carlos, "I should not need to follow their trail. They are *not* in the direction of the Llano. If they have gone that way, it was to mislead you in the pursuit. I know where they are at this moment—in the mountains."

"Ha! you think they are in the mountains?"

"I am sure of it; and not fifty miles from here. If your excellency would but send a troop, I could guide it direct to the spot, and without following the trail they have taken out of the valley—which I believe was only a false one."

The Comandante and Roblado drew back from the parapet, and for some minutes talked together in a low tone.

"It would look well," muttered Roblado; "in fact, the very thing you want. The trump cards seem to drop right into your hands. You send a force at the *request* of this fellow, who is a nobody here. You do him a service, and yourself at the same time. It will tell well, I warrant you."

"But for him to act as guide?"

"Let him! So much the better—that will satisfy all parties. He won't find his Jicarillas,—ha! ha ha!—of course; but let the fool have his whim!"

"But suppose, camarado, he falls upon *our* trail?—the cattle?"

"He is not going in that direction; besides, if he did, we are not bound to follow such trails as he may choose for us; but he has said he is not going that way—he don't intend to follow a trail. He knows some nest of these Jicarillas in the mountains,—like enough; and to rout them—there's a bit of glory for some one. A few scalps would look well over the gate. It hasn't had a fresh ornament of that sort since we've been here! What say you? It's but a fifty-mile ride."

"I have no objection to the thing—it *would* look well; but I shall not go myself. I don't like being along with the fellow out there or anywhere else— you can understand that feeling, I suppose?"

Here the Comandante looked significantly at his companion.

"Oh! certainly—certainly," replied the latter.

"*You* may take the troop; or, if you are not inclined, send Garcia or the sergeant with them."

"I'll go myself," replied Roblado. "It will be safer. Should the cibolero incline to follow certain trails, I can lead him away from them, or refuse—yes it will be better for me to go myself. By my soul! I want to have a brush with these redskins. I hope to bring back some 'hair,' as they say. Ha ha! ha!"

"When would you start?"

"Instantly—the sooner the better. That will be more agreeable to all parties, and will prove our promptitude and patriotism. Ha! ha! ha!"

"You had better give the sergeant his orders to get the men ready, while I make our cibolero happy."

Roblado hastened down from the azotea, and the next moment the bugle was heard sounding "boots and saddles."

Chapter Thirty Four

During the conversation that had taken place the cibolero sat, motionless upon his horse where he had first halted. The two officers were no longer in view, as they had stepped back upon the azotea, and the high parapet concealed them. But Carlos guessed the object of their temporary retirement, and waited patiently.

The group of soldiers, lounging in the gateway, and scanning him and his horse, now amounted to thirty or forty men; but the bugle, sounding the well-known call, summoned them off to the stables, and the sentry alone remained by the gate. Both he and the soldiers, having overheard the last conversation, guessed the object of the summons. Carlos felt assured that his request was about to be granted, though as yet the Comandante had not told him.

Up to that moment the cibolero had conceived no fixed plan of action. How could he, where so much depended on chance?

Only one idea was before his mind that could be called definite—that was *to get Vizcarra alone*. If but for a single minute, it would suffice.

Entreaty, he felt, would be idle, and might waste time and end in his own defeat and death. A minute would be enough for vengeance; and with the thoughts of his sister's ruin fresh on his mind, he was burning for this. To anything after he scarce gave a thought. For escape, he trusted to chance and his own superior energy.

Up to that moment, then, he had conceived no fixed plan of action. It had just occurred to him that the Comandante himself might lead the party going out. If so he would take no immediate step. While acting as guide, his opportunity would be excellent—not only for destroying his enemy, but for his own escape. Once on the wide plains, he would have no fear of ten times the number of lancers. His true steed would carry him far beyond their reach.

The troop was going. The bugle told him so. Would Vizcarra go with it? That was the question that now engrossed his thoughts, as he sat immobile on his horse, regarding with anxious look the line of the parapet above.

Once more the hated face appeared over the wall—this time to announce what the Comandante believed would be glad news to his wretched petitioner. With all the pompous importance of one who grants a great favour he announced it.

A gleam of joy shot over the features of the cibolero—not at the announcement, though Vizcarra thought so; but at his observation of the fact that the latter seemed to be now *alone upon the azotea*. Roblado's face was not above the wall.

"It is exceedingly gracious of your excellency to grant this favour to an humble individual like myself. I know not how to thank you."

"No thanks—no thanks: an officer of his Catholic Majesty wants no thanks for doing his duty."

As the Comandante said this, he waved his hand with proud dignity, and seemed about to retire backward. Carlos interrupted his intention by putting a question: "Am I to have the honour of acting as guide to your excellency?"

"No; I do not go myself on this expedition; but my best officer, Captain Roblado, will lead it. He is now getting ready. You may wait for him."

As Vizcarra said this, he turned abruptly away from the wall, and continued his promenade along the azotea. No doubt he felt ill at ease in a *tête-à-tête* with the cibolero, and was glad to end it. Why he had condescended to give all this information need not be inquired into; but it was just what the cibolero desired to know.

The latter saw that the time was come—not a moment was to be lost, and, quick as thought, he resolved himself for action.

Up to this moment he had remained in his saddle. His rifle—its butt resting in the stirrup, its barrel extending up to his shoulder—had been seen by no one. The *"armas de aqua"* covering his legs, and the serapé his shoulders, had completely concealed it. In addition to this, his sharp hunting-knife, strapped along his left thigh, escaped observation under the hanging corner of the serapé. These were his only weapons.

During the short conversation between the Comandante and Roblado he had not been idle, though apparently so. He had made a full reconnaissance of the walls. He saw that out of the saguan, or gateway, an escalera of stone steps led up to the azotea. This communication was intended for the soldiers, when any duty required them to mount to the roof; but Carlos knew that there was another escalera, by which the officers ascended: and although he had never been inside the Presidio, he rightly conjectured that this was at the adjacent end of the building. He had observed, too, that but one sentry was posted at the gate, and that the stone banquette, inside the saguan, used as a lounging-place by the guard, was at the moment unoccupied. The guard were either inside the house, or had strayed away to their quarters. In fact, the discipline of the place was of the loosest kind. Vizcarra, though a dandy himself, was no martinet with his men. His time was too much taken up with his own pleasures to allow him to care for aught else.

All these points had passed under the keen observation of the cibolero before Vizcarra returned to announce his intention of sending the troop. He had scarce parted out of sight the second time ere the former had taken his measures.

Silently dismounting from his horse, Carlos left the animal standing where he had halted him. He did not fasten him to either rail or post, but simply hooked the bridle-rein over the "horn" of the saddle. He know that his well-trained steed would await him there.

His rifle he still carried under his serapé, though the butt was now visible below the edge, pressed closely against the calf of his leg. In this way he walked forward to the gate.

One doubt troubled him—would the sentry permit him to pass in? If not, the sentry must die!

This resolve was quickly made; and the cibolero under his serapé kept his grasp on the handle of his hunting-knife as he approached the gate.

The attempt was made to pass through. Fortunately for Carlos, and for the sentry as well, it was successful. The latter—a slouching, careless fellow—had heard the late conversation, and had no suspicion of the other's design. He made some feeble opposition, notwithstanding; but Carlos hastily replied that he had something to say to the Comandante, who had beckoned him up to the azotea. This but half satisfied the fellow, who, however, reluctantly allowed him to pass.

Once inside, Carlos sprang to the steps, and glided up with the stealthy silent tread of a cat. So little noise had his moccasins made upon the stones, that, when he arrived upon the roof, its occupant—although standing but six feet from the head of the escalera—was not aware of his presence!

There was he—Vizcarra himself—the despot—the despoiler—the violator of a sister's innocence and honour—there was he within six feet of the avenging brother—six feet from the muzzle of his ready rifle, and still ignorant of the terrible situation! His face was turned in an opposite direction—he saw not his peril.

The glance of the cibolero rested upon him but an instant, and then swept the walls to ascertain if any one was above. He knew there were two sentries on the towers. They were not visible—they were on the outer walls and could not be seen from Carlos's position. No one else was above. His enemy alone was there, and his glance again rested upon him.

Carlos could have sent the bullet into his back, and such a thought crossed his mind, but was gone in an instant. He had come to take the man's life, but not in that manner. Even prudence suggested a better plan. His knife would be more silent, and afford him a safer chance of escape when the deed was done! With this idea, he brought the butt of his rifle gently to the ground, and rested its barrel against the parapet. The iron coming in contact with the stone wall gave a tiny clink. Slight as it was, it reached the ear of the Comandante, who wheeled suddenly round, and started at the sight of the intruder.

At first he exhibited anger, but the countenance of the cibolero, that had undergone a complete metamorphosis during the short interval, soon changed his anger into alarm.

"How dare you intrude, sir?—how dare—"

"Not so loud, colonel!—not so loud—you will be heard!"

The low husky voice, and the firm tone of command, in which they were uttered, terrified the cowardly wretch to whom these words were addressed. He saw that the man who stood before him bore in his face and attitude the expression of desperate and irresistible resolve, that plainly said, "Disobey, and you are a dead man!" This expression was heightened by the gleaming blade of a long knife, whose haft was firmly grasped by the hand of the cibolero.

At sight of those demonstrations, Vizcarra turned white with terror. He now comprehended what was meant. The asking for the troop had been but a subterfuge to get near his own person! The cibolero had tracked him; his guilt was known, and the brother was now come to demand redress or have vengeance! The horrors of his night-dream returned, now mingling with the horrors of the fearful reality before him.

He scarce knew what to say—he could scarce speak. He looked wildly around in hopes of seeing some help. Not a face or form was in sight—nothing but the grey walls, and before him the frowning face of his terrible antagonist. He would have called for help; but that face—that angry attitude—told him that the shout would be his last. He gasped out at length—

"What want you?"

"*I want my sister!*"

"Your sister?"

"My sister!"

"Carlos—I know not—she is not here—I—"

"Liar! she is within these walls. See! yonder the dog howls by the door. Why is that?"

Carlos pointed to a door in the lower part of the building, where the dog Cibolo was at that moment seen, whining and making other demonstrations, as if he wanted to get inside! A soldier was endeavouring to drive him off.

Vizcarra looked mechanically as directed. He saw the dog. He saw the soldier too; but dared not make a signal to him. The keen blade was gleaming before his eyes. The question of the cibolero was repeated.

"Why is that?"

"I—I—know not—"

"Liar again! She has gone in by that door. Where is she now? Quick, tell me!"

"I declare, I know not. Believe me—"

"False villain! she is here. I have tracked you through all your paths—your tricks have not served you. Deny her once more, and this to your heart. She is here!—Where—where—I say?"

"Oh! do not murder me. I shall tell all. She—she—is—here. I swear I have not wronged her; I swear I have not—"

"Here, ruffian—stand at this point—close to the wall here.—Quick!"

The cibolero had indicated a spot from which part of the patio, or courtyard, was visible. His command was instantly obeyed, for the craven Comandante saw that certain death was the alternative.

"Now give orders that she be brought forth! You know to whom she is intrusted. Be cool and calm, do you hear? Any sign to your minions, either word or gesture, and this knife will pass through your ribs! Now!"

"O my God!—my God!—it would ruin me—all would know—ruin—ruin—I pray you—have mercy—have patience!—She shall be restored to you—I swear it—this very night!"

"This very moment, villain! Quick—proceed—all those who know—let her be brought forth!—quick—I am on fire—one moment more—"

"O Heaven! you will murder me—a moment—Stay!—Ha!"

The last exclamation was in a different tone from the rest. It was a shout of exultation—of triumph!

The face of the Comandante was turned towards the escalera by which Carlos had ascended, while that of the latter looked in the opposite direction. Carlos, therefore, did not perceive that a third person had reached the roof, until he felt his upraised right arm grasped by a strong hand, and held back! He wrenched his arm free—turning as he did so—when he found himself face to face with a man whom he recognised as the Lieutenant Garcia.

"I have no quarrel with *you*," cried the cibolero; "keep away from me."

The officer, without saying a word, had drawn a pistol, and was levelling it at his head. Carlos rushed upon him.

The report rang, and for a moment the smoke shrouded both Garcia and the cibolero. One was heard to fall heavily on the tiles, and the next moment the other sprang from the cloud evidently unhurt.

It was the cibolero who came forth; and his knife, still in his grasp, was reeking with blood!

He rushed forward towards the spot where he had parted with the Comandante, but the latter was gone! He was some distance off on the azotea, and running towards the private stairway.

Carlos saw at a glance he could not overtake him before he should reach the escalera, and make his descent; and to follow him below would now be useless, for the shot had given the alarm.

There was a moment of despair,—a short moment; for in the next a bright thought rushed into the mind of the cibolero—he remembered his rifle. There might be still time to overtake the Comandante with that.

He seized the weapon, and, springing beyond the circle of smoke, raised it to his shoulder.

Vizcarra had reached the stairway, and was already sinking into its trap-like entrance. His head and shoulders alone appeared above the line of wall, when some half-involuntary thought induced him to stop and look back. The coward had partly got over his fright now that he had arrived within reach of succour, and he glanced back from a feeling of curiosity, to see if the struggle between Garcia and the cibolero was yet over. He meant to stop only for an instant, but just as he turned his head the rifle cracked, and the bullet sent him tumbling to the bottom of the escalera!

The cibolero saw that his shot had taken effect—he saw, moreover, that the other was dead—he heard the wild shouts of vengeance from below; and he knew that unless he could escape by flight he would be surrounded and pierced by an hundred lances.

His first thought was to descend by the escalera, up which he had come. The other way only led into the patio, already filling with men. He leaped over the body of Garcia, and ran toward the stairway.

A crowd of armed men was coming up. His escape was cut off!

Again he crossed the dead body, and, running along the azotea, sprang upon the outer parapet and looked below.

It was a fearful leap to take, but there was no other hope of escaping. Several lancers had reached the roof, and were charging forward with their pointed weapons. Already carbines were ringing, and bullets whistling about his ears. It was no time to hesitate. His eye fell upon his brave horse, as he stood proudly curving his neck and champing the bit, "Thank Heaven, he is yet alive!"

Nerved by the sight, Carlos dropped down from the wall, and reached the ground without injury. A shrill whistle brought his steed to his side, and the next moment the cibolero had sprung into the saddle, and was galloping out into the open plain!

Bullets hissed after, and men mounted in hot pursuit; but before they could spur their horses out of the gateway, Carlos had reached the edge of the chapparal, and disappeared under the leafy screen of its thick foliage.

A body of lancers, with Roblado and Gomez at their head, rode after. As they approached the edge of the chapparal, to their astonishment a score of heads appeared above the bushes, and a wild yell hailed their advance!

"Indios bravos! los barbaros!" cried the lancers, halting, while some of them wheeled back in alarm.

A general halt was made, and the pursuers waited until reinforcements should come up. The whole garrison turned out, and the chapparal was surrounded, and at length entered. But no Indians could be found, though the tracks of their animals led through the thicket in every direction.

After beating about for several hours, Roblado and his troopers returned to the Presidio.

Chapter Thirty Five

Garcia was dead. Vizcarra was not, though, when taken up from where he had fallen, he looked like one who had not long to live, and behaved like one who was afraid to die. His face was covered with blood, and his cheek showed the scar of a shot. He was alive however, — moaning and mumbling. Fine talking was out of the question, for several of his teeth had been carried away by the bullet.

His wound was a mere face wound. There was not the slightest danger; but the "medico" of the place, a young practitioner, was not sufficiently master of his art to give him that assurance, and for some hours Vizcarra remained in anything but blissful ignorance of his fate.

The garrison doctor had died but a short time before, and his place was not yet supplied.

A scene of excitement for the rest of that day was the Presidio—not less so the town. The whole settlement was roused by the astounding news, which spread like a prairie fire throughout the length and breadth of the valley.

It travelled in two different shapes. One was, that the settlement was surrounded by "los barbaros," headed by Carlos the cibolero; that they must be in great numbers, since they had made an open attack upon the military stronghold itself; but that they had been beaten off by the valiant soldiers after a desperate conflict, in which many were killed on both sides; that the officers were all killed, including the Comandante; and that another attack might be looked for that night, which would most likely be directed against the town! This was the first shape of the "novedades."

Another rumour had it that the "Indios mansos" had revolted; that they were headed by Carlos the cibolero; that they had made an unsuccessful attempt upon the Presidio, in which, as before, the valiant soldiers had repulsed them with great loss on both sides, including the Comandante and his officers: that this was but the first outbreak of a great conspiracy, which extended to all the Tagnos of the settlement, and that no doubt the attack would be renewed that night!

To those who reflected, both forms of the rumour were incomprehensible. Why should "Indios bravos" attack the Presidio before proceeding against the more defenceless town as well as the several rich haciendas? And how could Carlos the cibolero be their leader? Why should he of all men,—he who had just suffered at the hands of the savages? It was well-known through the settlement that it was the cibolero's sister who had been carried off. The idea of an Indian incursion, with him at the head of it, seemed too improbable.

Then, again, as to the conspiracy and revolt. Why the tame Indians were seen labouring quietly in the fields, and those belonging to the mission were working at their usual occupations! News, too, had come down from the mines—no symptoms of conspiracy had been observed there! A revolt of the Tagnos, with the cibolero at their head, would, of the two rumours, have been the more likely to be true; for it was well-known to all that these were far from content with their lot—but at present there was no appearance of such a thing around. There were they all at their ordinary employments. Who, then, were the revolters? Both rumours, therefore, were highly improbable.

Half the town-people were soon gathered around the Presidio, and after stories of all shapes had been carried back and forward, the definite facts at length became known.

These, however, were as mysterious and puzzling as the rumours. For what reason could the cibolero have attacked the officers of the garrison? Who were the Indians that accompanied him? Were they "bravos" or "mansos"?—savages or rebels?

The most remarkable thing was, that the soldiers themselves who had taken part in the imaginary "fight" could not answer these questions. Some said this, and some that. Many had heard the conversation between Carlos and the officers; but that portion of the affair, though perfectly natural in itself when taken in connexion with after circumstances, only rendered the whole more complicated and mysterious! The soldiers could give no explanation; and the people returned home, to canvass and discuss the affair among themselves. Various versions were in vogue. Some believed that the cibolero had come with the *bona fide* desire to obtain help against the Indians—that those who accompanied him were only a few Tagnos whom he had collected to aid in the pursuit—and that the Comandante, having first promised to aid him, had afterwards refused, and that this had led to the strange conduct of the cibolero!

There was another hypothesis that gained more credit than this. It was that Captain Roblado was the man whom the cibolero had desired to make a victim; that he was guided against him by motives of jealousy; for the conduct of Carlos on the day of the fiesta was well-known, and had been much ridiculed—that, in failing to reach Roblado, he had quarrelled with the Comandante, and so forth.

Improbable as was this conjecture, it had many supporters, in the absence of the true motive for the conduct of the cibolero. There were but four men within the Presidio to whom this was known, and only three outside of it. By the general public it was not even suspected.

In one thing all agreed—in condemning Carlos the cibolero. The garotta was too good for him; and when taken, they could all promise him ample punishment. The very ingratitude of the act was magnified. It was but the day before that these same officers had gone forth with their valiant soldiers to do him a service! The man must have been mad! His mother had no doubt bewitched him.

To have killed Lieutenant Garcia!—he who was such a favourite! *Carrambo*!

This was true. Garcia was liked by the people of the settlement—perhaps not so much from the possession of any peculiar virtues, but in contrast with his superiors. He was an affable, harmless sort of person, and had won general esteem.

That night the cibolero had not one friend in San Ildefonso. Nay, we speak wrongly. He had *one*. There was one heart beating for him as fondly as ever—Catalina's—but she, too, was ignorant of the motives which had led to his mysterious conduct.

Whatever these motives were, she knew they could not be otherwise than just. What to her were the calumnies—the gibes—that were heaped upon him? What to her if he had taken the life of a fellow-creature? He had not done so without good cause—without some fearful provocation. She believed that in her soul. She knew his noble nature too well to think otherwise. He was the lord of her heart, and could do no wrong!

Sorrowful, heart-breaking news was it to her. It boded long separation—perhaps for ever! He dared no more visit the town—not even the settlement! He would be driven to the wild plains—hunted like the wolf or the savage bison—perhaps taken and slain! Bitter were her reflections. When should she see him again? Maybe, never!

Chapter Thirty Six

During all this time Vizcarra lay groaning upon his couch—not so much with pain as fear, for the fear of death still haunted him. But for that, his rage would have been boundless; but this passion was in abeyance—eclipsed by the terrors that flitted across his conscience.

Even had he been assured of recovery he would still have been in dread. His imagination was diseased by his dream and the after reality. Even surrounded by his soldiers, he feared the cibolero, who appeared able to accomplish any deed and escape its consequences. He did not even feel secure there in his chamber, with guards at the entrance, against that avenging arm!

Now, more than ever, he was desirous of getting rid of the cause—more than ever anxious that she should be got rid of; but he reflected that now more than ever was that a delicate and difficult matter. It would undoubtedly get abroad *why* the cibolero had made such a desperate attempt upon his life—it would spread until it reached high quarters—such a report could not be passed over—an investigation might be ordered; and that, unless he could destroy every trace of suspicion, might be his ruin.

These were his reflections while in the belief that he was going to recover; when a doubt of this crossed his mind, he grew still more anxious about the result.

Roblado had hinted at a way in which all might be arranged. He waited with impatience for the latter to make his appearance. The warlike captain was still engaged in beating the chapparal; but Gomez had come in and reported that he was about to give up the search, and return to the Presidio.

To Roblado the occurrences of the day had been rather pleasant than otherwise; and a close observer of his conduct could have told this. If there was anything in the whole business that really annoyed him, it was the wound of the Comandante—it was exasperating! Roblado, more experienced than the surgeon, knew this well. The friendship that existed between the two was a fellow-feeling in wickedness—a sort of felon's bond—durable enough so long as there was no benefit to either in breaking it. But this friendship did not prevent Roblado from regretting with all his heart that the bullet had not hit *his friend* a little higher up or a little lower down—either in the skull or the throat! He entertained this regret from no malice or ill-will towards the Comandante, but simply from a desire to benefit himself. It was long since Roblado had been dreaming of promotion. He was not too humble to hope he might one day command the Presidio himself. Vizcarra's death would have given him that station at once; but Vizcarra was not to die just then, and this knowledge somewhat clouded the joy he was then experiencing.

And it was joy. Garcia and he had been enemies. There had been jealousy and ill-will between them for long; therefore the lieutenant's death was no source of regret to him. But the joy of Roblado owed partly its origin to another consequence of that day's drama—one that affected him more than any—one that was nearest his heart and his hopes.

Absurd as appeared the pretensions of the cibolero in regard to Catalina, Roblado had learned enough of late to make him jealous—ay, even to give him real uneasiness. She was a strange creature, Catalina de Cruces—one who had shown proofs of a rare spirit—one not to be bought and sold like a *bulto* of goods. She had taught both her father and Roblado a lesson of late. She had taught them that. She had struck the ground with her little foot, and threatened a convent—the grave—if too rudely pressed! She had not rejected Roblado—that is, in word; but she insisted on having *her own time to make answer*; and Don Ambrosio was compelled to concede the point.

Under such circumstances her suitor felt uneasy. Not so much that he was jealous—though he did love her after his own fashion, and was piqued at the thought of such a rival—but he feared that spirit of hers, and dreaded that her splendid fortune might yet escape him. Such a woman was capable of the wildest resolve. She *might* take to a convent; or maybe *to the plains* with this base-born cibolero! Such an event in the life of such a woman would be neither impossible nor unlikely. In either case she could not take her fortune with her; but what mattered? it would not remain with him, Roblado.

The conduct of the cibolero had removed all obstacles, so far as he was concerned. There was no longer any dread of rivalry from that source. His life was now forfeited. Not only would he be cut off from all communication with her, but he would not dare to show himself in the settlement. A constant vigilance would be kept on foot to guard against that, and Roblado even promised himself the enjoyment of rare sport in hunting down his rival, and becoming at the same time his captor and executioner.

These were the ideas that crossed the mind of the savage captain, and that made him feel satisfied at the events of the day.

After scouring the chapparal, and following the track of the supposed Indians to the ceja of the table plain, he returned with his men to the Presidio, to make preparations for a more prolonged pursuit.

Chapter Thirty Seven

Roblado's arrival brought relief to Vizcarra, as he lay chafing and fretting.

Their conversation was, of course, upon the late occurrence, and Roblado gave his account of the pursuit.

"And do you really think," inquired the Comandante, "that the fellow had a party of savages with him?"

"No!" answered Roblado. "I did think so at first—that is, the men thought so, and I was deceived by their reports. I am now convinced they were not Indian bravos, but some of those Tagno friends of his: for it appears the padré was right—he had a suspicious connexion. That of itself might have been sufficient cause for us to have arrested him long ago; but now we need no cause. He is ours, when we can catch him."

"How do you propose to act?"

"Why, I have no doubt he will lead us a long chase. We must do the best we can to follow his trail. I came back to provision the men so that we can keep on for a sufficient time. The rascals have gone out of the valley by the upper pass, and perhaps have taken to the mountains. So thinks Gomez. We shall have to follow, and endeavour to overtake them. We must send express to the other settlements, so that the cibolero may be captured if he make his appearance in any of them. I don't think he will attempt that."

"Why?"

"Why! because it appears the old witch is still alive! and, moreover, he will hang around here so long as he has any hopes of recovering the sister."

"Ha! you are right; he will do so. He will never leave me till she—"

"So much the better; we shall have all the finer opportunity of laying hands on him, which, believe me, my dear colonel, will be no easy matter. The fellow will be watchful as a wolf, and on that superb horse of his can escape from our whole troop. We'll have to capture him by some stratagem."

"Can you think of none?"

"I have been thinking of one."

"What?"

"Why, it is simply this—in the first place, for the reasons I have given, the fellow will hang around the settlement. He may visit now and then the old *hechicera*, but not often. The other would be a better decoy."

"You mean her?" Vizcarra indicated the direction of the room in which Rosita was confined.

"I do. He is said to be foolishly fond of this sister. Now, were she in a place where he could visit her, I'll warrant he would come there; and then we could trap him at our pleasure."

"In a place!—where?" eagerly demanded Vizcarra.

"Why, back to her own neighbourhood. They'll find some residence. If you will consent to let her go for a while, you can easily recover her—*the more easily when we have settled with him!*"

"Consent, Roblado!—it is the very thing I desire above all things. My mind will not be easy while she is here. We are both in danger if such a report should get in circulation. If it should reach certain ears, we are ruined—are we not?"

"Why, *now* there is some truth in what you say, Garcia's death must be reported, and the cause will be inquired into. We must have *our* story as plausible as it can be made. There must be no colour of a suspicion—no rumour! It will be well to get her off our hands for the present."

"But how—that it is that troubles me—how, without increasing the chances of suspicion? If we send her home, how is it to be explained? That would not be the act of *Indians*? You said you had some plan?"

"I *think* I have. But first tell me, colonel, what did you mean by saying she was *mad*?"

"That she was so; is so still,—so says José,—within the hour, muttering strange incongruities—knows not what is said to her. I tell you, Roblado, it terrified *me*."

"You are sure she knows not what is said to her?"

"Sure of it."

"So much the better. She will then not remember where she is or *has been*. Now I *know* that I have a plan—nothing easier than to get her off. She shall go back and tell—if she can tell anything—that she has been in the hands of the Indians! That will satisfy you?"

"But how can it be arranged?"

"My dear Comandante, no difficulty in it. Listen! To-night, or before day in the morning, Gomez and José, in Indian costume as before, can carry her off to some spot which I shall indicate. In the mountains be it. No matter how far off or how near. She may be tied, and found in their company in the morning in such a way as to appear *their* captive. So much the better if she has recovered her senses enough to think so. Well; I with the troopers, in hunt after the cibolero, will come upon these Indians by accident. A few shots may be fired at sufficient distance to do them no hurt. They will make off, leaving their captive, whom we will rescue and bring back to the town, where she can be delivered out of our hands! Ha! ha! ha! What think you, Comandante, of my scheme?"

"Excellent!" replied Vizcarra, his mind seemingly relieved at the prospect of its execution.

"Why, it would blind the very devil! We shall not only be free from suspicion, but we'll get credit by it. What! a successful affair with the savages!—rescue of a female captive!—restore her to her friends!—she, too, the sister of the very man who has endeavoured to assassinate you! I tell you, Comandante, the cibolero himself, if that will be any comfort to you, will be humbugged by it! She will swear—*if her word be worth anything*—that she has been in the hands of *los barbaros* all the while! She will give the lie even to her own brother!"

"The plan is excellent. It must be done to-night!"

"To-night, of course. As soon as the men have gone to bed, Gomez can start with her. I must give over the idea of following the trail to-day and, in truth, I regard that as idle. Our only chance for taking him will be to set our trap, with her for its bait; and that we can arrange hereafter. Give yourself no farther uneasiness about it. By late breakfast to-morrow I shall make my report to you,—Desperate affair with Jicarillas, or Yutas—several warriors killed—female captive rescued—valiant conduct of troops—recommend Corporal—for promotion, etcetera. Ha! ha! ha!"

The Comandante joined in this laugh, which, perhaps, he would not have done, but that Roblado had already assured him that his wound was not of the slightest danger, and would heal in a couple of weeks.

Roblado had given him assurance of this by calling the doctor a fool, and heaping upon him other opprobrious epithets. The delivery, therefore, from the fear of apprehended death, as well as from the other thought that was torturing him, had restored Vizcarra to a composure he had not enjoyed for the twenty-four hours preceding; and he now began to imbibe, to its full extent, another passion—that of vengeance against the cibolero.

That night, after tattoo had sounded, and the soldiers had retired to their respective quarters, a small mounted party was seen to issue from the gateway of the Presidio, and take a road that led in the direction of the mountains. The party consisted of three individuals. One, closely wrapped, and mounted upon a mule, appeared to be a female. The other two, oddly attired, and fantastically adorned with paint and feathers, might have been taken for a brace of Indian warriors. But they were not Indians. They were Spanish soldiers in Indian disguise. They were Sergeant Gomez and the soldier José in charge of the cibolero's sister.

Chapter Thirty Eight

When Carlos reached the edge of the chapparal, his pursuers were still only parting from the walls of the Presidio. Of course none followed him on foot, and it had taken the men some time to get their arms and horses ready. So far as he was concerned, he no longer feared pursuit, and would have scorned to take a circuitous path. He had such confidence in the steed he bestrode, that he knew he could escape before the eyes of his pursuers, and need not have hidden himself in the chapparal.

As he rode into the ambuscade he was thinking no longer of his own safety, but of that of Don Juan and his party. Their critical situation suddenly came before his mind. How were *they* to escape?

Even before he had half crossed the open ground this thought had troubled him more than his own peril, and a plan had been before him:—to make direct for the pass of La Niña, and shun the chapparal altogether. This would have drawn the dragoons in the same direct course; and Don Juan, with his Tagnos, might have got off at their leisure.

Carlos would have put this plan in execution, could he have trusted to the prudence of Don Juan; but he feared to do so. The latter was somewhat rash, and not over-sagacious. Seeing Carlos in the act of escape, he might think it was his duty, as agreed upon, to show himself and his men on the edge of the thicket—the very thing Carlos now wished to prevent. For that reason the cibolero galloped direct to the place of ambuscade, where Don Juan and his men were waiting in their saddles.

"Thank God you are safe!" cried Don Juan; "but they are after you. Yonder they come in scores!"

"Yes!" replied Carlos, looking back; "and a good start I've gained on them!"

"What's best to be done?" inquired Don Juan. "Shall we scatter through the chapparal, or keep together? They'll be upon us soon!"

Carlos hesitated a moment before making reply. Three plans of action were possible, offering more or less chance of safety. First, to scatter through the chapparal as Don Juan had suggested; second, to make off together and at once *without showing themselves*, taking the back track, as they had come; and, third, to *show themselves* in front to the pursuers, and then retire on the back path. Of course the idea of fight was not entertained for a moment. That would have been idle, even absurd, under the circumstances.

The mind of the cibolero, used to quick action, examined these plans with the rapidity of thought itself. The first was rejected without a moment's consideration. To have scattered through the chapparal would have resulted in certain capture. The jungle was too small, not over a couple of miles in width, though extending to twice that length. There were soldiers enough to surround it, which they would do. They would beat it from side to side. They could not fail to capture half the party; and though these had made no demonstration as yet, they would be connected with the affair at the Presidio, and would be severely punished, if not shot down on the spot.

To attempt to get off through the chapparal without showing themselves at all would have been the plan that Carlos would have adopted, had he not feared that they would be overtaken before night. The Tagnos were mounted on mules, already jaded, while most of the troopers rode good and swift horses. But for that Carlos might have hoped that they would escape unseen, and thus neither Don Juan nor his people would have been suspected of having had any part in the affair. This would be an important consideration for the future; but the plan was not to be thought of. The third plan was adopted.

The hesitation of the cibolero was not half so long as the time you have occupied in reading of it. Scarce ten seconds elapsed ere he made reply, not to Don Juan alone, but to the whole band, in a voice loud enough for all to hear. The reply was in the form of a command.

"Ride through the bush, all of you! Show yourselves near the front! your heads and shoulders only, with your bows! Give your war-cry! and then back till you are out of sight! Scatter right and left!—Follow me!"

As Carlos delivered these hurried directions, he dashed forward through the underwood and soon appeared near its edge. The Tagnos, guarded by Don Juan on one side and Antonio on the other, showed almost simultaneously in an irregular line along the margin of the thicket; and flourishing their bows above their heads, they uttered a defiant war-whoop, as though they were a party of savage Indians.

It would have required a practised eye to have told from a short distance that they were not. Most of them were bare-headed, with long flowing hair; and, in fact, differing very little in appearance from their brethren of the plains. They all had bows, a weapon still carried by the Indios mansos when engaged in any hostilities; and their war-cry differed not at all from some tribes called "bravos," "wild." Many in the band had but a short time left aside the full practice of warfare. Many of them were but neophytes to the arts of peace.

The effect of the demonstration was just what the cibolero had calculated on. The soldiers, who were galloping forward in straggling knots, and some of whom had got within three hundred paces of the chapparal, reined up in surprise. Several showed symptoms of a desire to gallop back again, but these were restrained at sight of a large body of their comrades now issuing from the Presidio.

The whole of them were taken by surprise. They believed that the "Indios bravos" were in the chapparal, and no doubt in overwhelming numbers. Their belief was strengthened by the proceedings of the previous days, in which they had done nought else, as they supposed, but ride scout after "los barbaros." The latter had now come after *them*! They halted, therefore, on the plains, and waited for their fellows to come up.

That this would be the effect of his *ruse* Carlos foresaw. He now directed his companions to rein gently back, until they were once more under cover of the brush; and the whole party arrived at the spot where they had waited in ambush.

Antonio then took the trail, and guided them through the chapparal; not as they had come to La Niña, but by a path that led to the upper plain by another pass in the cliffs. From a point in this pass they obtained a distant view of the chapparal and the plain beyond. Though now full three miles from their place of ambush, they could see the valiant troopers still figuring on the open ground in front of it. They had not yet ventured to penetrate the dangerous underwood which they believed to be alive with ferocious savages!

Carlos, having reached the upper plain, struck off with his band in a direction nearly north. His object was to reach a ravine at some ten miles distance across the plain, and this was gained without a single pursuer having appeared in the rear.

This ravine led in an easterly direction as far as the Pecos bottom. It was the channel of a stream, in which water flowed in the rainy season, but was now quite dry. Its bed was covered with small pebbles, and a horse-trail upon these was scarcely to be followed, as the track only displaced the pebbles, leaving no "sign" that could be "read" to any advantage. Old and new foot-marks were all the same.

Into this ravine the party descended, and, after travelling down it for five or six miles, halted. Carlos called the halt for a special object—to detail a plan for their future proceeding, which had been occupying his attention during the last hour or two.

As yet, none of the party were compromised but himself. It would not advantage him that they should be, but the contrary. Neither Don Juan nor Antonio had shown themselves out of the thicket; and the other dusky faces, seen but for an instant through the brambles, could not have been recognised by the frightened troopers. If, therefore, Don Juan and his peons could get back to their home without observation, for them all would still be well.

This was a possible event. At starting Carlos had cautioned secrecy as to the expedition. It had left at an early hour, before any one was abroad, and no one knew of it. Indeed, no one in the valley was aware that the cibolero had returned before the news of the affair at the Presidio. His mules had been quietly unpacked, and were herded at a distance from the rancho by one of his men. If, then, the *troopers* should not visit that neighbourhood before the following day, Don Juan and his people could go back in the night and engage in their usual occupations without any suspicion. No doubt Roblado would be there in the morning, but not likely before. It was natural to suppose he would first endeavour to follow the route they had taken, and it led almost in the opposite direction from the house of Don Juan. To track them along all the windings of that route would be the work of one day at least. Then their pursuers would be no wiser as to where they had betaken themselves, for Carlos, from the point of halting, intended to adopt a plan that would be certain to throw the troopers off the trail.

It was decided, in fine, that Don Juan and his people should return home—that the peons of Carlos should also go back to the rancho; roof it on the following day—for it only wanted that; and remain by it as if nothing had occurred. They could not be made answerable for the deeds of their master.

As for the cibolero himself, his residence must remain unknown, except to one or two of his tried friends. He knew where he should find a shelter. To him the open plain or the mountain cave was alike a home. He needed no roof. The starry canopy was as welcome as the gilded ceiling of a palace.

The Tagnos were enjoined to secrecy. They were not sworn. A Tagno is not the man to talk; besides, they all knew that their own safety, perhaps their lives, depended on their silence.

All these matters were at length arranged, but the party remained where they had halted till near sunset. They then mounted, and continued on down the channel.

When they had gone a mile or so, one of them climbed out of the ravine, and, heading southward, rode off across the plain. This direction would bring him back to the valley, by a pass near the lower end of the settlement. It would be night by the time he could reach this pass, and he was not likely to encounter any one on the route—now that the "wild" Indians were abroad!

Shortly after, a second Tagno left the ravine, and rode off in a line nearly parallel to that taken by the first. Soon another imitated the example, and another, and another, until all had forsaken the ravine except Don Juan, Antonio, and the cibolero himself. The Tagnos had been instructed to reach home by different passes, and some of them, more sagacious, were sent by the most circuitous paths. There was no trooper belonging to the Presidio likely to follow that trail.

Carlos and his two companions, after riding to the farthest end of the ravine, also turned to the right, and re-entered the valley of San Ildefonso at its lower extremity. It was quite dark, but all of them knew the road well, and about midnight they arrived near the house of the young ranchero.

A reconnaissance was necessary before they dared approach. That was soon made, and the report brought back that all was right, and no troopers had yet made their appearance.

Carlos once more embraced his mother hurriedly, related what had passed, gave some instructions to Don Juan, and then, mounting his horse, rode off from the place.

He was followed by Antonio and a pack-mule loaded with provisions. They passed down the valley, and struck out in the direction of the Llano Estacado.

Chapter Thirty Nine

On the following day a new incident created a fresh surprise among the inhabitants of San Ildefonso, already excited by an unusual series of "novedades." About noon a party of lancers passed through the town on their way to the Presidio. They were returning from a scout in search of the "assassin"—so Carlos was designated. Of him they had found no traces; but they had fallen in with a large body of "Indios bravos" among the spurs of the mountains, with whom they had had a terrific conflict! This had resulted in the loss of great numbers killed on the part of the Indians, who had contrived, as usual, to carry off their dead—hence, the soldiers had returned without scalps! They had brought, however,—a far more positive trophy of victory—a young girl belonging to the settlement, whom they had re-captured from the savages, and whom Captain Roblado—the gallant leader of the expedition—*supposed* to be the same that had been carried off few days before from a rancho at the lower end of the valley!

The captain halted in the plaza, with a few men—those in charge of the recovered captive. The remainder of the troop passed on to the Presidio. Roblado's object in stopping in the town, or in coming that way—for it did not lie in his return route—was threefold. First, to deliver his charge into the hands of the civic authorities; secondly, to make sure that everybody should witness the delivery, and be satisfied by this living evidence that a great feat had been performed; and thirdly, that he might have the opportunity of a little swagger in front of a certain balcony.

These three objects the captain attained, but the last of them did not turn out quite to his satisfaction. Although the bugle had played continuously, announcing the approach of a troop—although the recovered captive was placed conspicuously in the ranks—and although his (Roblado's) horse, under the influence of sharp spurs, pitched himself into the most superb attitudes, all went for nothing—Catalina did not show in the balcony! Among the faces of "dependientes" and "criados," hers was not to be seen; and the triumphant look of the victorious leader, as soon as he had ridden past, changed to a gloomy expression of disappointment.

A few minutes after, he dismounted in front of the "Casa de Cabildo," where he delivered the girl into the hands of the alcalde and other authorities of the town. This ceremony was accompanied by a grandiloquent speech, in which an account of the recapture was given with some startling details; sympathy was expressed for the parents of the girl, *whoever they might be;* and the speaker wound up by expressing his opinion that the unfortunate captive could be no other than the young girl reported to have been carried off a few days before!

All this was very plausible and proper; and Roblado, having resigned his charge to the keeping of the alcalde, mounted and rode off amidst a storm of complimentary phrases from the authorities, and "vivas" of applause from the populace.

"*Dios lo pague, capitan!*" (God reward you, captain!) was the prayer that reached his ears as he pushed through the crowd!

A keen physiognomist could at that moment have detected in the corner of Roblado's eye a very odd expression—a mingling of irony with a strong desire to laugh. In fact, the gallant captain could hardly keep from bursting out in the faces of his admirers, and was only restrained from doing so by the desire of keeping the joke bottled up till he could enjoy it in the company of the Comandante—to whom he was now hastening.

Back to the captive.

The crowd pressed around her, all eager to gratify their curiosity. Strange to say that this feeling predominated. There was less appearance of sympathy than might have been looked for under the circumstances. The number of those that uttered the "pobrecita!"—that tender expression of Mexican pity—was few; and they were principally the poor dark-skinned native women. The well-dressed shopkeepers, both Gachupinos and Criollos, both met and women, looked on with indifference, or with no other feeling than that of morbid curiosity.

Such an indifference to suffering is by no means a characteristic of the New Mexican people—I should rather say of the females of that land—for the men are brutal enough. As regards the former, the very opposite character is theirs.

Their conduct would be unaccountable, therefore, but for the knowledge of a fact which guided it on this occasion. They knew who the captive girl was—they knew she was the sister of Carlos the cibolero—Carlos *the murderer!* This it was that checked the flow of their bettor feelings.

Against Carlos the popular indignation was strong. "Asesino," "ladron," "ingrato," were the terms used in speaking of him. A wretch! to have murdered the good lieutenant—the favourite of the place; and for what motive? Some paltry quarrel or jealousy! What motive, indeed? There seemed no motive but a thirst of blood on the part of this "demonio," this "güero heretico." Ungrateful wretch, too, to have attempted the life of the valiant Comandante—he who had been striving all he could to recover the assassin's sister from the Indian savages!

And now he had actually succeeded! Only think of it! There she was, brought safe home again by the agency of this very Comandante, who had sent his captain and soldiers for her,—this very man whom he would have killed! *Demonio! asesino! ladron!* They would all be glad to see him seated in the chair of the "garrote." No "buen Catolico" would have acted as he had done—no one but a sinful "heretico"—a blood-loving "Americano"! How he would be punished *when caught*!

Such were the feelings of all the populace, except, perhaps, the poor slaves—the *mansos*—and a very few Criollos, who, although not approving of the acts of Carlos, held revolutionary principles, and hated the Spanish *régime* with all their hearts.

With such prejudice against the cibolero, no wonder that there was but little sympathy for the forlorn creature, his sister:

That it *was* his sister no one doubted, although there were few on the spot who knew either. Up to the day of the fiesta her brother, now so notorious, was but little known to the inhabitants of the town, which he rarely visited— she less; and there were but few in the place who had ever seen her before that hour. But the identity was unmistakeable. The fair, golden hair, the white skin, the glowing red of the cheeks, though common in other parts of the world, were rare characteristics in North Mexico. The proclamation upon the walls described the "asesino" as possessing them. This could be no other than his sister. Besides, there were those who had seen her at the fiesta, where her beauty had not failed to attract both admiration and envy.

She looked beautiful as ever, though the red was not so bright on her cheek, and a singular, wild expression appeared in her eyes. To the questions put to her she either answered not or returned vague replies. She sat in silence; but several times broke forth into strange, unintelligible, exclamatory phrases, in which the words "Indios" and "barbaros" repeatedly occurred.

"*Esta loco!*" ("She is mad!") muttered one to another; "she fancies she is still with the savages!"

Perhaps it was so. Certainly she was not among friends.

The alcalde inquired if there was any one present—relative or friend— to whom he could deliver her up.

A young girl, a poblana, who had just arrived on the spot, came forward. She knew the "pobrecita." She would take charge of her, and conduct her to her home.

A half-Indian woman was in company with the poblana. It might have been her mother. Between the two the restored captive was led away; and the crowd soon dispersed and returned to their various avocations.

The girl and her conductors turned into a narrow street that led through the suburb where the poorest people lived. Passing this, they emerged into the open country; and then, following an unfrequented path through the chapparal, a few hundred yards brought them to a small mud rancho, which they entered. In a few minutes after a carreta, in which sat a peon, was driven up to the door, and stopped there.

The poblana, leading the girl by the hand, came out of the house, and both mounted into the carreta. As soon as the two were seated upon the bunches of dry "zacato" thrown into the carreta for this purpose, the driver goaded his oxen and moved off. The vehicle, after passing out of the chapparal path, took the main road leading to the lower settlements of the valley.

As they moved on the poblana regarded her companion with kind looks, and assisted her in arranging her seat, so as to defend her as much as possible against the joltings of the carreta. She added numerous expressions of a sympathising and consolatory character, but none that bespoke recognition or old acquaintance. It was evident that the girl had never seen Rosita before.

When they had got about a mile from the town, and were moving along an unfrequented part of the road, a horseman was seen coming after, and at such speed as to overtake them in a few minutes. He was mounted on a pretty mustang that bore the signs of being well cared for. Its flanks were rounded with fat, and it capered as it galloped along.

As it came close to the carreta the rider called out to the driver to stop; and it then appeared that the *horseman* was a *woman*, as the soft sweet voice at once indicated. More than that, the rider was a *señorita*, as the soft cheek, the silky hair, and the delicate features, showed. At a distance it was natural enough to have taken her for one of the opposite sex. A common serapé covered her shoulders; a broad-brimmed sombrero concealed most of her black shining hair; and she rode according to the general custom of the country—the custom of its men.

"Why, Señorita!—is it you?" asked the poblana, in a tone of surprise, and with a gesture of respect.

"Ha! ha! you did not know me, then, Josefa?"

"No, Señorita;—*ay de mi*! how could I in that disguise?"

"Disguise do you call it? Why, it is the usual costume!"

"True, Señorita; but not for a grand señora like you. *Carrambo!*"

"Well, I think I must be disguised, as I passed several acquaintances who would not bow to me! Ha! ha!"

"*Pobrecita—ita—ita!*" continued she, suddenly changing her tone, and regarding Josefa's companion with a look of kind sympathy. "How she must have suffered! Poor dear girl! I fear it is true what they have told me. *Santisima Virgen*! how like—"

The phrase was left unfinished. The speaker had forgotten the presence of Josefa and the peon, and was delivering her thoughts in too loud a soliloquy. The unfinished sentence had involuntarily escaped from her lips.

Suddenly checking herself, she looked sharply towards the two. The peon was busy with his oxen, but the poblana's face wore an expression of curiosity.

"Like whom, Señorita?" innocently inquired she.

"One whom I know. No matter, Josefa." And, as the lady said this, she raised her finger to her lips, and looked significantly towards the peon.

Josefa, who knew her secret, and who guessed the "one" meant, remained silent. After a moment the lady drew her mustang nearer the carreta, upon the side on which Josefa sat, and, bending over, whispered to the latter:—

"Remain below till the morning; you will be too late to return to-night. Remain! perhaps you may hear something. Come early—not to the house. Be in time for *oration*. You will find me in the church. Perhaps you may see Antonio. If so, give him this." A diamond set in a golden circlet sparkled a moment at the tips of the lady's fingers, and then lay hid in the shut fist of the poblana. "Tell him *for whom*—he need not know who sent it. There is money for your expenses, and some to give her; or give it to her mother, *if they will accept it*." Here a purse fell in Josefa's lap. "Bring me news! oh, bring me news, dear Josefa! *Adios! adios!*"

The last salutation was uttered hurriedly; and, as the lady pronounced it, she wheeled her glossy mustang and galloped back towards the town.

She need not have doubted that Josefa would fulfil her instructions about "remaining below until the morning!" for the poblana was nearly, if not quite, as much interested as herself in this journey. The rather pretty

Josefa chanced to be the sweetheart of the half-blood Antonio; and whether she saw Antonio or not, she was not likely to hurry back that night. If she did see him, so much the pleasanter to remain; if not, she should remain in the hope of such an event.

With a full purse of "pesos" —a sixth of which would pay all expenses— and the prospect of meeting with Antonio, the rough carreta seemed all at once transformed to an elegant coach, with springs and velvet cushions,— such as Josefa had heard of, but had never seen!

The kind-hearted girl readjusted the seats, placed the head of Rosita on her lap, spread her reboso over her to keep off the evening dew, and then told the peon to move on. The latter uttered a loud "ho-ha!" touched his oxen with the goad, and once more set them in motion along the dusty road.

Chapter Forty

Early morning prayer in the "iglesia" is a fashionable custom among the señoras of Mexico—particularly among those who dwell in cities and towns. Close upon the heels of daybreak you may see them issuing from the great doors of their houses, and hurrying through the streets towards the chapel, where the bell has already begun its deafening "ding-dong." They are muffled beyond the possibility of recognition—the richer in their silken shawls and mantas, the poorer in their slate-coloured rebosos; under the folds of which each carries a little bound volume—the "*misa.*"

Let us follow them into the sacred temple, and see what passes there.

If we arrive late, and take station near the door we shall be presented with the spectacle of several hundred backs in a kneeling position—that is, the individuals to whom the backs belong will be found kneeling.

These backs are by no means alike—no more than faces are. They are of all shapes, and sizes, and colours, and classes in the social scale. You will see the backs of ladies in shawls—some of whom have permitted that elegant garment to fall to the shoulders, while others retain it over the crowns of their heads, thus creating two very distinct styles of back. You will see the backs of pretty poblanas, with the end of their rebosos hanging gracefully over them; and the back of the poblana's mother with the reboso ill arranged, and not over clean. You will see the back of the merchant scarcely covered with a short cloth jacket, and the back of the "aguador" cased in well-worn leather; the back of the "guapo" muffled in a cloak of fine broad-cloth, and that of the "lepero" shrouded in a ragged scrape; and then you will see broad backs and slender ones, straight backs and crooked ones; and you run a good chance of beholding a hunch or two—especially if the church be in a large town. But wheresoever you enter a Mexican iglesia during prayer-time, I promise you the view of an extensive assortment of backs. Not classified, however. Quite the contrary. The back of the shawled lady may be inclusive between two greasy rebosos, and the striped or speckled back of the lepero may rise up alongside the shining broad-cloth of the dandy! I do not answer for any classification of the backs; I only guarantee their extensive number and variety. The only face that is likely to confront you at this moment will be the shaven phiz of a fat priest, in full sacerdotal robes of linen, that were once, no doubt, clean and white, but that look now as if they had been sent to the buck-basket, and by some mistake brought back before reaching the laundry. This individual, with a look as unlike heaven as the wickedest of his flock, will be seen stirring about on his little stage; now carrying a wand—now a brazen pot of smoking "incense," and anon some waxen doll—the image of a saint; while in the midst of his manipulations you may hear him "murmuring" a gibberish of ill-pronounced Latin. If you have witnessed the performance of M. Robin, or the "Great Wizard," you cannot fail to be reminded of them at this moment.

The tinkling of a little bell, which you will presently hear, has a magical effect upon the backs. For a short while you may have observed them in an odd attitude—not erect as backs ought to be, but slouching and one-sided. During this interval, too, you may catch a glance of a face—merely the profile—and if it be pretty, you will forget the back; but then the party is no longer a back in the proper sense. You won't be struck with the devotion of the profile, if you are with its prettiness. You may observe it wink or look cunningly, and, if your observation be good, you may note another profile, of coarser mould, corresponding to that wink or cunning glance. This goes on while the backs are in their "slouch" or attitude of repose. How that attitude is produced will be to you a mystery, an anatomical puzzle; but it may be explained. It is simple enough to those who know it. It is brought about by the back changing its base from the marrow-bones to the hips; and this is done so adroitly, that, under cover of shawls, mantas, rebosos, and skirts, it is no wonder you are puzzled by it.

The little bell, however, brings the backs all right again. It is to these devotees what the "Attention!" is to the rank and file of an army; and the moment the first tinkle is heard, backs up is the movement, and all become suddenly elevated several inches above their former standard. Thus they remain, stiff and erect, while the priest mumbles a fresh "Ave Maria," or "Pater noster," and goes through a fresh exhibition of pantomime. Then the backs are suddenly shortened again, the profiles appear as before—nods, and winks, and cunning glances, are exchanged—and that till the little bell sounds a second time. And then there will be a third course of this performance, and a fourth, and so on, till the worship (!) is ended.

This ridiculous genuflexion and mummery you may see repeated every morning in a Mexican "iglesia," long before the hour of breakfast. Both men and women engage in it, but by far the greater number of the devotees are of the gentler sex, and many of them the fashionable señoras of the place.

One is inclined to inquire into the motives that draw so many people out of their beds, to shiver through the streets and in the cold church at such an early hour. Is it religion? Is it superstition? Is it penance? Is it devotion? No doubt many of these silly creatures really believe that the act is pleasing to God; that these genuflexions and orisons, mechanically repeated, will give them grace in His eyes. But it is very certain that many of the most constant attendants on these morning prayers are actuated by very different feelings. In a land of jealous men you will find the women peculiarly intelligent and cunning, and the matutinal hour is to them the "golden opportunity." He is a very jealous guardian, indeed, whose vigil tempts him from his couch at so chill an hour!

Await the end of the performance by the door of the "iglesia." There stands a large vase filled with the consecrated water. Each, in passing out, takes a dip and a sprinkle. In this basin you will see the small jewelled hand immerse its finger-tips, and the next moment adroitly deliver a *carte d'amour* to some cloaked cavallero. Perhaps you may see the wealthy señora, in the safe disguise of the serapé, leave the church in a direction opposite to that by which she came. If you are curious enough to follow—which would be extremely ill-bred—you may witness under the trees of the "alameda," or some unfrequented quarter, the forbidden *"entrevista."*

The morning, in a Mexican city, has its adventures as well as the night.

The bell of the church of San Ildefonso had just commenced to ring for "oracion," when a female form was seen issuing from the gateway of one of the largest mansions of the town, and taking the direction of the church. It was yet scarce daybreak, and the person thus observed was closely muffled; but her tall upright form, the dignity and grace of her carriage, and the proud elastic step told that she was a grand señora. As she reached the portal of the church she stopped for some moments and looked around. Her face was not visible, as it was "tapada" under the folds of a closely-drawn manta; but her attitude, with her head occasionally moving around, showed that she was scanning the figures that, at the summons of the bell, approached like shadows through the grey light. She was evidently expecting some one; and from the eager scrutiny with which she regarded each new form that entered the plaza, it was some one whose presence was much desired.

The last of the devotees had arrived and entered the church. It would be idle to remain longer; and, turning on her heel with an air that betokened disappointment, the lady glided across the portal, and disappeared through the door.

In another moment she was kneeling in front of the altar, repeating her orisons and telling over the beads of her rosary.

She was not the last to enter the church; still another devotee came later. About the time that she was leaving the portal a carreta drove into the plaza, and halted in a remote corner. A young girl leaped out of the carreta, tripped nimbly across the square, in the direction of the church, and passed within the portal. The dress of this new-comer—a flaming red "nagua," broidered chemisette, and reboso—showed that she belonged to the poorer class of citizens. She was a poblana.

She entered the church, but before kneeling she threw an inquiring glance along the array of backs. Her eye became fixed upon one that was covered with a manta. It was that of the lady of whom we have spoken. This seemed to satisfy the poblana, who, gliding over the floor, knelt down in such a position that her elbow almost rested against that of the lady.

So silently had this movement been executed that the lady did not perceive her new neighbour until a slight "nudge" upon the elbow caused her to start and look round. A gleam of satisfaction lit up her features, though her lips continued to repeat the prayer, as if nothing had happened.

After a while came the cue for adopting the pose of rest, and then the two kneeling figures—señorita and poblana—dropped towards each other, so that their arms touched. A moment later and two hands became uncovered—one a little brown-skinned paw from under the reboso—the other, a delicate arrangement of white and jewelled fingers, from the manta.

They came in contact as if by a mutual understanding, and, though they were *en rapport* but a half-second, a close observer might have noticed a small roll of paper passed from one to the other—from the brown fingers to the white ones! It would have required a close observer to have noticed this manoeuvre, for so adroitly was it executed that none of those kneeling around, either in front or rear, saw anything amiss.

The two hands again disappeared under their respective covers; the little bell tinkled, and both señora and poblana once more shot into an upright position, and, with most devout looks, repeated the prayers of the misa.

When the "oracion" was over, and while sprinkling themselves at the sacred fount, a few hurried words passed between them; but they went out of the church separately, and walked off in separate directions. The poblana hastened across the square, and disappeared into a narrow street. The señora walked proudly back to the mansion whence she had come, her countenance radiant with joyful anticipation.

As soon as she had entered the house she proceeded directly to her own chamber, and, opening the little folded slip of paper, read:—

"Querida Catalina!—You have made me happy. But an hour ago I was the most wretched of men. I have lost my sister, and I feared your esteem.

Both are restored to me. My sister is by my side, and the gem that sparkles on my finger tells me that even calumny has failed to rob me of your friendship—your love. *You* do not deem me an assassin. No; nor am I one. I have been an avenger, but no assassin. You shall know all—the fearful plot of which I and mine have been the victims. It is scarce credible—so great is its atrocity! I am indeed its victim. I can no more show myself in the settlement. I am henceforth to be hunted like the wolf, and treated as one, if captured. I care not for that, so long as I know that you are not among my enemies.

"But for you I should go far hence. I cannot leave you. I would sooner risk life every hour in the day, than exile myself from the spot where you dwell—you, the only being I can ever love.

"I have kissed the gem a hundred times. In life, the sweet token can never part from me.

"My foes are after me like bloodhounds, but I fear them not. My brave steed is never out of my sight, and with him I can scorn my cowardly pursuers. But I must venture one visit to the town. I must see you once, querida. I have words for you I cannot trust to paper. Do not refuse to see me, and I shall come to the old place of meeting. To-morrow night—midnight. Do not refuse me, dearest love. I have much to explain that I cannot without seeing you face to face. You shall know that I am not an assassin—that I am still worthy of being your lover.

"Thanks!—thanks for your kindness to my poor little wounded bird! I trust to God she will soon be well again. *Mi querida. Adios!*"

When the beautiful lady had finished reading the note, she pressed it to her lips, and fervently kissed it.

"Worthy of being my lover!" she murmured; "ay, worthy to be the lover of a queen! Brave, noble Carlos!"

Again she kissed the paper, and, thrusting it into her bosom, glided softly from the apartment.

Chapter Forty One

Vizcarra's desire for revenge grew stronger every hour. The almost joyful reaction he had experienced, when relieved from the fear of death, was short-lived. So, too, was that which followed his relief from the anxiety about his captive. The thought that now tortured him was of a different character. The very breath of his existence—his personal appearance—was ruined for ever. He was disfigured for life!

When the mirror was passed before his face, it caused his heart to burn like a coal of fire. Coward though he was, he would almost as soon have been killed outright.

Several of his teeth were gone. They might have been replaced; but not so could be restored the mutilated cheek. A portion had been carried off by the "tear" of the bullet. There would be a hideous scar never to be healed!

The sight was horrible. His thoughts were horrible. He groaned outright as he contemplated the countenance which the cibolero had given him. He swore vengeance. Death and torture if he could but capture Carlos—death to him and his!

At times he even repented that he had sent away the sister. Why should he have cared for consequences? Why had he not revenged himself upon *her*? He no longer loved her. Her scornful laugh still rankled in his heart. She had been the cause of all his sufferings—of sufferings that would never end but with his life—chagrin and mortification for the rest of his days! Why had he not taken *her* life? That would have been sweet revenge upon the brother. It would almost have been satisfaction.

He tossed upon his couch, tortured with these reflections, and giving utterance at intervals to groans of anguish and horrid imprecations.

Carlos must be captured. No effort must be spared to ensure that event. And captured *alive* if possible. He should measure out the punishment. It should be death, but not sudden death. No; the savages of the plains should be his teachers. The cibolero should die like a captive Indian—by fire at the stake. Vizcarra swore this!

After him, the mother, too. She was deemed a witch. She should be punished as often witches have been. In this he would not have to act alone.

He knew that the padrés would endorse the act. They were well inclined to such fanatical cruelties.

Then the sister, alone—uncared for by any one. She would be wholly in his power—to do with her us he would, and no one to stay his will. It was not love, but revenge.

Such terrible resolves passed through the mind of the wretched caitiff.

Roblado was equally eager for the death of the cibolero. His vanity had been scathed as well, for he was now satisfied that Catalina was deeply interested in the man, if not already on terms of intimacy—on terms of love, mutually reciprocated and understood. He had visited her since the tragical occurrence at the Presidio. He had observed a marked change in her manner. He had thought to triumph by the malignant abuse heaped on the *assassin*; but she, although she said nothing in defence of the latter—of course she could not—was equally silent on the other side, and showed no symptoms of indignation at the deed. His (Roblado's) abusive epithets, joined to those which her own father liberally heaped upon the man, seemed to give her pain. It was plain she would have defended him had she dared!

All this Roblado had noticed during his morning call.

But more still had he learnt, for he had a spy upon her acts. One of her maids, Vicenza, who for some reason had taken a dislike to her mistress, was false to her, and had, for a length of time, been the confidant of the military wooer. A little gold and flattery, and a soldier-sweetheart—who chanced to be José—had rendered Vicenza accessible. Roblado was master of her thoughts, and through José he received information regarding Catalina, of which the latter never dreamt. This system of espionage had been but lately established, but it had already produced fruits. Through it Roblado had gained the knowledge that he himself was hated by the object of his regard, and that she loved some other! What other even Vicenza could not tell. That other Roblado could easily guess.

It is not strange that he desired the capture and death of Carlos the cibolero. He was as eager for that event as Vizcarra himself.

Both were making every exertion to bring it about. Already scouting-parties had been sent out in different directions. A proclamation had been posted on the walls of the town,—the joint production of the Comandante and his captain, offering a high reward for the cibolero's head, and a still higher sum for the cibolero himself if captured alive!

The citizens, to show their zeal and loyalty, had also issued a proclamation to the same effect, heading it with a large sum subscribed among them—a very fortune to the man who should be so lucky as to be the captor of Carlos. This proclamation was signed by all the principal men of the place, and the name of Don Ambrosio figured high upon the list! There was even some talk of getting up a volunteer company to assist the soldiers in the pursuit of the *heretico* assassin, or rather to earn the golden price of his capture.

With such a forfeit on his head, it was an enigma how Carlos should be long alive!

Roblado sat in his quarters busy devising plans for the capture. He had already sent his trustiest spies to the lower end of the valley, and these were to hover day and night in the neighbourhood. Any information of the haunts of the cibolero, or of those with whom he was formerly in correspondence, was to be immediately brought to him, and would be well paid for. A watch was placed on the house of the young ranchero, Don Juan; and though both Vizcarra and Roblado had determined on special action with regard to him, they agreed upon leaving him undisturbed for the present, as that might facilitate their plans. The spies who had been employed were not soldiers, but men of the town and poor rancheros. A military force appealing below would frustrate their design. That, however, was kept in readiness, but its continued presence near the rancho, thought Vizcarra and his captain, would only frighten the bird, and prevent it from returning to its nest. There was good logic in this.

Roblado, as stated, was in his quarters, completing his arrangements. A knock aroused him from the contemplation of some documents. They were communications from his spies, which had just reached the Presidio, addressed both to himself and the Comandante. They were concerning the affair.

"Who is it?" he asked, before giving the privilege to enter.

"I, captain," answered a sharp squeaky voice.

Roblado evidently knew the voice, for he called out—

"Oh! it is you? Come in, then."

The door opened, and a small dark man, of sharp weasel-like aspect, entered the room. He had a skulking shuffling gait, and, notwithstanding his soldier's dress, his sabre and his spurs, the man looked mean. He spoke with a cringing accent, and saluted his officer with a cringing gesture. He was just the sort of person to be employed upon some equivocal service, and by such men as Vizcarra and Roblado; and in that way he had more than once served them. It was the soldier José.

"Well! what have you to say? Have you seen Vicenza?"

"I have, captain. Last night I met her out."

"Any news?"

"I don't know whether it may be news to the captain; but she has told me that it was the señorita who sent her home yesterday."

"Her?"

"Yes, captain, the güera."

"Ha! go on!"

"Why, you know when you left her with the alcalde she was offered to whoever would take her. Well, a young girl came up and claimed to be an acquaintance, and a woman who was the girl's mother. She was given up to them without more ado, and they took her away to a house in the chapparal below the town."

"She did not stay there. I know she's gone down, but I have not yet heard the particulars. How did she go?"

"Well, captain; only very shortly after she arrived at the house of the woman, a carreta came up to the door, driven by a Tagno, and the girl—that is, the daughter, who is called Josefa—mounted into the carreta, taking the güera along with her; and off they went down below.

"Now, neither this girl nor her mother ever saw the güera before, and who does captain think sent them, and the carreta too?"

"Who says Vicenza?"

"The señorita, captain."

"Ha!" sharply exclaimed Roblado. "Vicenza is sure of that."

"More than that, captain. About the time the carreta drove away, or a little after, the señorita left the house on her horse, and with a common serapé over her, and a sombrero on her head, like any ranchera; and in this—which I take to be a disguise for a lady of quality like her—she rode off by the back road. Vicenza, however, thinks that she turned into the *camino abajo* after she got past the houses, and overtook the carreta. She was gone long enough to have done so."

This communication seemed to make a deep impression upon the listener. Shadows flitted over his dark brow, and gleams of some new intelligence or design appeared in his eyes. He was silent for a moment, engaged in communicating with his thoughts. At length he inquired—

"Is that all your information, José?"

"All, captain."

"There may be more from the same source. See Vicenza to-night again. Tell her to keep a close watch. If she succeed in discovering that there is a correspondence going on, she shall be well rewarded, and *you* shall not be forgotten. Find out more about this woman and her daughter. Know the Tagno who drove them. Lose no time about it. Go, José!"

The minion returned his thanks in a cringing tone, made another cringing salute, and shuffled out of the room.

As soon as he had left, Roblado sprang to his feet, and, walking about the room in an agitated manner, uttered his thoughts aloud:—

"By Heaven! I had not thought of this. A correspondence, I have no doubt. Fiends! such a woman! She must know all ere this—if the fellow himself is not deceived by us! I must watch in that quarter too. Who knows but *that* will be the trap in which we'll take him? Love is even a stronger lure than brotherly affection. Ha! señorita; if this be true, I'll yet have a purchase upon you that you little expect. I'll bring you to terms without the aid of your stupid father!"

After figuring about for some minutes, indulging in these alternate dreams of vengeance and triumph, he left his room, and proceeded towards that of the Comandante, for the purpose of communicating to the latter his new-gotten knowledge.

Chapter Forty Two

The house of Don Ambrosio de Cruces was not a town mansion. It was suburban—that is, it stood upon the outskirts of the village, some seven or eight hundred yards from the Plaza. It was detached from the other buildings, and at some distance from any of them. It was neither a "villa" nor a "cottage." There are *no* such buildings in Mexico, nor anything at all resembling them. In fact, the architecture of that country is of unique and uniform style, from north to south, through some thousand miles of latitude! The smaller kinds of houses,—the ranchos of the poorer classes,—show a variety corresponding to the three thermal divisions arising from different elevation—*caliente, templada,* and *fria.* In the hot lands of the coast, and some low valleys in the interior, the rancho is a frail structure of cane and poles with a thatch of palm-leaves. On the elevated "valles," or table-plains—and here, be it observed, dwell most of the population—it is built of "adobes," and this rule is universal. On the forest-covered sides of the more elevated mountains the rancho is a house of logs, a "log-cabin," with long hanging eaves and shingled roof, differing entirely from the log-cabin of the American backwoods, and far excelling the latter in neatness and picturesque appearance.

So much for the "ranchos." About them there is some variety of style. Not so with "casas grandes," or houses of the rich. A sameness characterises them through thirty degrees of latitude—from one extremity of Mexico to the other; and, we might almost add, throughout all Spanish America. If now and then a *"whimsical"* structure be observed, you may find, on inquiry, that the owner is some foreigner resident—an English miner, a Scotch manufacturer, or a German merchant.

These remarks are meant only for the houses of the country. In small villages the same style as the country-house is observed, with very slight modifications; but in large towns, although some of the characteristics are still retained, there is an approximation to the architecture of European cities—more particularly, of course, to those of Spain.

The house of Don Ambrosio differed very little from the general fashion of "casas grandes" of country style. It had the same aspect of gaol, fortress, convent, or workhouse—whichever you please; but this aspect was considerably lightened by the peculiar colouring of the walls, which was done in broad vertical bands of red, white, and yellow, alternating with each other! The effect produced by this arrangement of gay colours is quite Oriental, and is a decided relief to the otherwise heavy appearance of a Mexican dwelling. In some parts of the country this fashion is common.

In shape there was no peculiarity. Standing upon the road in front you see a long wall, with a large gateway near the middle, and three or four windows irregularly set. The windows are shielded with bars of wrought-iron standing vertically. That is the "reja." None of them have either sash or glass. The gateway is closed by a heavy wooden door, strongly clasped and bolted with iron. This front wall is but one storey high, but its top is continued so as to form a parapet, breast-high above the roof, and this gives it a loftier appearance. The roof being flat behind, the parapet is not visible from below. Look around the corner at either end of this front wall. You will see no gable—there is no such thing on a house of the kind we are describing. In its place you will see a dead wall of the same height as the parapet, running back for a long distance; and were you to go to the end of it, and again look around the corner, you would find a similar wall at the back closing in the parallelogram.

In reality you have not yet seen the true front of Don Ambrosio's house, if we mean by that the part most embellished. A Mexican spends but little thought on the outside appearance of his mansion.

It is only from the courtyard, or "patio," you can get a view of the front upon which the taste of the owner is displayed, and this often exhibits both grandeur and elegance.

Let us pass through the gateway, and enter the "patio." The "portero," when summoned by knock or bell, admits us by a small door, forming part of the great gate already mentioned. We traverse an arched way, the "zaguan," running through the breadth of the building, and then we are in the patio. From this we have a view of the real front of the house.

The patio itself is paved with painted bricks—a tessellated pavement. A fountain, with jet and ornamental basin, occupies its centre; and several trees, well trimmed, stand in large vessels, so that their roots may not injure the pavement. Around this court you see the doors of the different apartments, some of them glazed and tastefully curtained. The doors of the "sala," the "cuarto," and the sleeping-rooms, are on three sides, while the "cocina" (kitchen), the "dispensa" (store-room), "granero" (granary), with the "caballeriza" and coach-house, make up the remaining part of the square.

There is still an important portion of the mansion to be spoken of—the "azotea," or roof. It is reached by an "escalera," or stone staircase. It is flat and quite firm, being covered with a cement that is proof against rain. It is enclosed by a parapet running all round it—of such a height as not to hinder the view of the surrounding country, while it protects those occupying it from the intrusive gaze of persons passing below. When the sun is down, or behind a cloud, the azotea is a most agreeable promenade; and to render it still more so, that over the house of Don Ambrosio had been arranged so as to resemble a flower-garden. Richly japanned pots, containing rare flowers, were placed around, and green boughs and gay blossoms, rising above the top of the wall, produced a fine effect on viewing the building from without.

But this was not the only garden belonging to the mansion of the rich miner. Another, of oblong shape, extended from the rear of the house, enclosed by a high wall of adobes on either side. These, ending upon the bank of the stream, formed the boundary of the garden. Along the stream there was no fence, as it was here of sufficient breadth and depth to form an enclosure of itself. The garden was of large extent, including an orchard of fruit-trees at its lower part, and it was tastefully laid out in walks, flowerbeds, and arbours of different shapes and sizes. Don Ambrosio, although but a rich *parvenu*, might have been supposed to be a man of refined taste by any one viewing this garden—the more so, as such delightful retreats are by no means common in that country. But it was to another mind than his that these shadowy trees and fragrant arbours owed their existence. They were the "ideas" of his fair daughter, many of whose hours were spent beneath their shade.

To Don Ambrosio the sight of a great cavity in the earth, with huge quarries of quartz rock or scoria, and a rich "veta" at the back, was more agreeable than all the flowers in the world. A pile of "barras de plata" would be to his eyes more interesting than a whole country covered with black tulips and blue dahlias.

Not so his fair daughter Catalina. Her taste was both elevated and refined. The thought of wealth, the pride of riches, never entered her mind. She would willingly have surrendered all her much-talked-of inheritance to have shared the humble rancho of him she loved.

Chapter Forty Three

It was near sunset. The yellow orb was hastening to kiss the snowy summit of the Sierra Blanca, that barred the western horizon. The white mantle, that draped the shoulders of the mountain, reflected beautiful roseate tints deepening into red and purple in the hollows of the ravines, and seeming all the more lovely from the contrast of the dark forests that covered the Sierra farther down.

It was a sunset more brilliant than common. The western sky was filled with masses of coloured clouds, in which gold and purple and cerulean blue mingled together in gorgeous magnificence; and in which the eye of the beholder could not fail to note the outlines of strange forms, and fancy them bright and glorious beings of another world. It was a picture to gladden the eye, to give joy to the heart that was sad, and make happier the happy.

It was not unobserved. Eyes were dwelling upon it—beautiful eyes; and yet there was a sadness in their look that ill accorded with the picture on which they were gazing.

But those eyes were not drawing their inspiration from the sky-painting before them. Though apparently regarding it, the thoughts which gave them expression were drawn from a far different source. The heart within was dwelling upon another object.

The owner of those eyes was a beautiful girl, or rather a fully developed woman still unmarried. She was standing upon the azotea of a noble mansion, apparently regarding the rich sunset, while, in reality, her thoughts were busy with another theme, and one that was less pleasant to contemplate. Even the brilliant glow of the sky, reflected upon her countenance, did not dissipate the shadows that were passing over it. The clouds from within overcame the light from without. There were shadows flitting over her heart that corresponded to those that darkened her fair face.

It was a beautiful face withal, and a beautiful form—tall, majestic, of soft graces and waving outlines. The lady was Catalina de Cruces.

She was alone upon the azotea—surrounded only by the plants and flowers. Bending over the low parapet that overlooked the garden to the rear, she at the same time faced toward the sinking orb,—for the garden extended westward.

Now and then her eyes were lifted to the sky and the sun; but oftener they sought the shaded coppice of wild-china-trees at the bottom of the enclosure, through whose slender trunks gleamed the silvery surface of the stream. Upon this spot they rested from time to time, with an expression of strange interest. No wonder that to those eyes that was an interesting spot—it was that where love's first vows had been uttered in her delighted ear—it had been consecrated by a kiss, and in her thoughts it was hallowed from the "earth's profound" to the high heaven above her. No wonder she regarded it as the fairest on earth. The most famed gardens of the world— even Paradise itself—in her imagination, had no spot so sweet, no nook so shady, as the little arbour she had herself trained amid the foliage of those wild-china-trees.

Why was she regarding it with a look of sadness? In that very arbour, and on that very night, did she expect to meet him—the one who had rendered it sacred. Why then was she sad? Such a prospect should have rendered her countenance radiant with joy.

And so was it, at intervals, when this thought came into her mind; but there was another—some other thought—that brought those clouds upon her brow, and imparted that air of uneasy apprehension. What was that thought?

In her hand she held a bandolon. She flung herself upon a bench, and began to play some old Spanish air. The effort was too much for her. Her thoughts wandered from the melody, and her fingers from the strings.

She laid down the instrument, and, again rising to her feet, paced backwards and forwards upon the azotea. Her walk was irregular. At intervals she stopped, and, lowering her eyes, seemed to think intently on something that was absent. Then she would start forward, and stop again in the same manner as before. This she repeated several times, without uttering either word or exclamation.

Once she continued her walk all around the azotea, casting a scrutinising look among the plants and flower-pots on both sides, as if in search of something; but whatever it was, she was unsuccessful, as nothing appeared to arrest her attention.

She returned once more, and took up the bandolon. But her fingers had hardly touched the strings before she laid the instrument down again, and rose from the bench, as if some sudden resolution had taken possession of her.

"I never thought of that—I may have dropped it in the garden!" she muttered to herself, as she glided toward a small escalera that led down into the patio.

From this point an avenue communicated with the garden; and the next moment she had passed through this and was tripping over the sanded walks, bending from side to side, and peeping behind every plant and bush that could have concealed the object of her search.

She explored every part of the enclosure, and lingered a moment in the arbour among the china-trees—as if she enjoyed that spot more than any other—but she came back at length with the same anxious expression, that told she was not rewarded by the recovery of whatever she had lost.

The lady once more returned to the azotea—once more took up the bandolon; but after a few touches of the strings, laid it down, and again rose to her feet. Again she soliloquised.

"*Carrambo*! it is very strange!—neither in my chamber—the sala, the cuarto, the azotea, the garden!—where can it be? O Dios! if it should fall into the hands of papa! It is too intelligible—it could not fail to be understood—no—no—no! O Dios! if it should reach other hands!—those of *his* enemies! It names to-night—true, it does not tell the place, but the time is mentioned—the place would be easily discovered. Oh! that I knew where to communicate with him! But I know not, and he will come. *Ay de mi*! it cannot be prevented now. I must hope no enemy has got it. But where can it be? Madre de Dios! where can it be?"

All these phrases were uttered in a tone and emphasis that showed the concern of the speaker at the loss of some object that greatly interested her. That object was no other than the note brought by Josefa, and written by Carlos the cibolero, in which the assignation for that night had been appointed. No wonder she was uneasy at its loss! The wording not only compromised herself, but placed the life of her lover in extreme peril. This it was that was casting the dark shadows over her countenance—this it was that was causing her to traverse the azotea and the garden in such anxious search.

"I must ask Vicenza," she continued. "I like not to do it, for I have lost confidence in her of late. Something has changed this girl. She used to be frank and honest, but now she has grown false and hypocritical. Twice have I detected her in the act of deceiving me. What does it mean?"

She paused a moment as if in thought. "I must ask her notwithstanding. She may have found the paper, and, not deeming it of any use may have thrown it in the fire. Fortunately she does not read, but she has to do with others who can. Ha! I forgot her soldier sweetheart! If she should have found it, and shown it to him! *Dios de mi alma!*"

This supposition seemed a painful one, for it caused the lady's heart to beat louder, and her breathing became short and quick.

"That would be terrible!" she continued,—"that would be the very worst thing that could happen. I do not like that soldier—he appears mean and cunning and I have heard is a bad fellow, though favoured by the Comandante. God forfend he should have gotten this paper! I shall lose no more time. I shall call Vicenza, and question her."

She stepped forward to the parapet that overlooked the patio.

"Vicenza!—Vicenza!"

"*Aqui, Señorita,*" answered a voice from the interior of the house.

"*Ven aca!—Ven aca!*" (Come hither.)

"*Si, Señorita.*"

"*Anda! Anda!*" (Quickly.)

A girl, in short bright-coloured nagua, and white chemisette without sleeves, came out into the patio, and climbed up the escalera that led to the roof.

She was a *mestiza*, or half-blood, of Indian and Spanish mixture, as her brownish-white skin testified. She was not ill-looking; but there was an expression upon her countenance that precluded the idea of either virtue, honesty, or amiability. It was a mixed expression of malice and cunning. Her manner, too, was bold and offensive, like that of one who had been guilty of some known crime, and had become reckless. It was only of late she had assumed that tone, and her mistress had observed it among other changes.

"*Qué quiere V., Señorita?*" (What want you, my lady?)

"Vicenza, I have lost a small piece of paper. It was folded in an oblong shape—not like a letter, but this—"

Here a piece of paper, similarly put up, was held out for the inspection of the girl.

"Have you seen anything of it?"

"No, Señorita," was the prompt and ready answer.

"Perhaps you may have swept it out, or thrown it into the fire? It looked insignificant, and, indeed, was not of much importance, but there were some patterns upon it I wished to copy. Do you think it has been destroyed?"

"I know not that, Señorita. I know that *I* did not destroy it. I neither swept it out nor threw it into the fire. I should not do that with any paper, as I cannot read myself, and might destroy something that was valuable."

Whatever truth there was in the last part of her harangue, the mestiza knew that its earlier declarations were true enough. She had not destroyed it, either by sweeping out or burning.

Her answer was delivered with an ingenuous *naïveté*, accompanied with a slight accent of anger, as though she was not over-pleased at being suspected of negligence.

Whether her mistress noticed the latter did not appear from her answer, but she expressed herself satisfied.

"It is of no consequence, then," said she. "You may go, Vicenza."

The girl walked off, looking sulky. When her head was just disappearing below the top of the escalera, her face was towards her mistress, whose back was now turned to her. A scornful pouting of the lips, accompanied by a demoniac smile, was visible upon it. It was evident from that look that she knew something more of the lost paper than was admitted in her late declaration.

Catalina's gaze was once more turned upon the setting sun. In a few minutes he would disappear behind the snowy ridge of the mountain. Then a few hours, and then—moments of bliss!

Roblado was seated in his cuartel as before. As before, a tiny knock sounded upon the door. As before, he called out, "Quien es?" and was answered, "Yo!" and, as before, he recognised the voice and gave the order for its owner to enter. As before, it was the soldier José, who, in a cringing voice and with a cringing salute, approached his officer.

"Well, José, what news?"

"Only this," replied the soldier, holding out a slip of paper folded into an oblong shape.

"What is it?" demanded Roblado. "Who is it from?" in the same breath.

"The captain will understand it better than I can, as I can't read; but it comes from the Señorita, and looks inside like a letter. The Señorita got it from somebody at church yesterday morning: so thinks Vicenza, for she saw her read it as soon as she got back from morning prayers. Vicenza thinks that the girl Josefa brought it up the valley, but the captain most likely can tell for himself."

Roblado had not listened to half of this talk; but had instead been swallowing the contents of the paper. As soon as he had got to the end of it he sprang from his chair as if a needle had been stuck into him, and paced the room in great agitation.

"Quick! quick, José!" he exclaimed. "Send Gomez here. Say nothing to any one. Hold yourself in readiness—I shall want you too. Send Gomez instantly. *Vaya!*"

The soldier made a salute less cringing because more hurried, and precipitately retired from the apartment. Roblado continued—

"By Heaven! this is a piece of luck! Who ever failed to catch a fool when love was his lure? This very night, too, and at midnight! I shall have time to prepare. Oh! if I but knew the place! 'Tis not given here."

Again he read over the note.

"Carajo, no! that is unfortunate. What's to be done? I must not go guessing in the dark! Ha! I have it! *She* shall be watched!—watched to the very spot! Vicenza can do that while we lie somewhere in ambush. The girl can bring us to it. We shall have time to surround them. Their interview will last long enough for that. We shall take them in the very moment of their bliss. Hell and furies! to think of it—this low dog—this butcher of buffaloes—to thwart me in my purposes! But patience, Roblado! patience! to-night—to-night!—"

A knocking at the door. Sergeant Gomez was admitted.

"Gomez, get ready twenty of your men! picked fellows, do you hear? Be ready by eleven o'clock. You have ample time, but see that you be ready the moment I call you. Not a word to any one without. Let the men saddle up and be quiet about it. Load your carbines. There's work for you. You shall know what it is by and by. Go! get ready!"

Without saying a word, the sergeant went off to obey the order.

"Curses on the luck! if I but knew the place, or anything near it. Would it be about the house? or in the garden? Maybe outside—in the country somewhere? That is not unlikely. He would hardly venture so near the town, lest some one might recognise him or his horse. Death to that horse. No, no! I shall have that horse yet, or I much mistake. Oh! if I could find this place before the hour of meeting, then my game were sure. But no, nothing said of the place—yes, the *old* place. Hell and furies! they have met before—often—often—oh!"

A groan of agony broke from the speaker, and he paced to and fro like one bereft of his senses.

"Shall I tell Vizcarra now," he continued, "or wait till it is over? I shall wait. It will be a dainty bit of news along with supper. Perhaps I may garnish the table with the ears of the cibolero. Ha! ha! ha!"

And uttering a diabolical laugh, the ruffian took down his sabre and buckled the belt around his waist. He then armed himself with a pair of heavy pistols; and, after looking to the straps of his spurs, strode out of the room.

Chapter Forty Four

It wanted but an hour of midnight. There was a moon in the sky, but so near the horizon, that the bluff bounding the southern side of the valley threw out a shadow to the distance of many yards upon the plain.

Parallel to the line of the cliffs, and close in to their base, a horseman could be seen advancing up the valley from the lower end of the settlement. His cautious pace, and the anxious glances which he at intervals cast before him, showed that he was travelling with some apprehension, and was desirous of remaining unseen. It was evident, too, that this was his object in keeping within the shadow of the cliff; for on arriving at certain points where the precipice became slanting and cast no shadow, he would halt for a while, and, after carefully reconnoitring the ground, pass rapidly over it. Concealment could be his only object in thus closely hugging the bluffs, for a much better road could have been found at a little distance out from them.

After travelling for many miles in this way, the horseman at length arrived opposite the town, which still, however, was three miles distant from the cliff. From this point a road led off to the town, communicating between it and a pass up the bluffs to the left.

The horseman halted, and gazed awhile along the road, as if undecided whether to take it or not. Having resolved in the negative, he moved on, and rode nearly a mile farther under the shadow of the bluffs. Again he halted, and scanned the country to his right. A bridle-path seemed to run in the direction of the town, or towards a point somewhat above it. After a short examination the horseman seemed to recognise this path as one he was in search of, and, heading his horse into it, he parted from the shadow of the bluffs, and rode out under the full moonlight. This, shining down upon him, showed a young man of fine proportions, dressed in ranchero costume, and mounted upon a noble steed, whose sleek black coat glittered under the silvery light. It was easy to know the rider. His bright complexion, and light-coloured hair curling thickly under the brim of his sombrero, were characteristics not to be mistaken in that land of dark faces. He was Carlos the cibolero. It could be seen now that a large wolf-like dog trotted near the heels of the horse. That dog was Cibolo.

Advancing in the direction of the town, the caution of the horseman seemed to increase.

The country before him was not quite open. It was level; but fortunately for him, its surface was studded with copse-like islands of timber, and here and there straggling patches of chapparal through, which the path led. Before entering these the dog preceded him, but without noise or bark; and when emerging into the open plain again, the horseman each time halted and scanned the ground that separated him from the next copse, before attempting to pass over it.

Proceeding in this way, he arrived at length within several hundred yards of the outskirts of the town, and could see the walls, with the church cupola shining over the tops of the trees. One line of wall on which his eyes were fixed lay nearer than the rest. He recognised its outline. It was the parapet over the house of Don Ambrosio—in the rear of which he had now arrived.

He halted in a small copse of timber, the last upon the plain. Beyond, in the direction of Don Ambrose's house, the ground was open and level up to the bank of the stream already described as running along the bottom of the garden. The tract was a meadow belonging to Don Ambrosio, and used for pasturing the horses of his establishment. It was accessible to these by means of a rude bridge that crossed the stream outside the walls of the garden. Another bridge, however, joined the garden itself to the meadow. This was much slighter and of neater construction—intended only for foot-passengers. It was, in fact, a mere private bridge, by which the fair daughter of Don Ambrosio could cross to enjoy her walk in the pleasant meadow beyond. Upon this little bridge, at its middle part, was a gate with lock and key, to keep intruders from entering the precincts of the garden.

This bridge was not over three hundred yards from the copse in which Carlos had halted, and nothing intervened but the darkness to prevent him from having a view of it. However, as the moon was still up, he could distinctly see the tall posterns, and light-coloured palings of the gate, glimmering in her light. The stream he could not see—as at this point it ran between high banks—and the garden itself was hidden from view by the grove of cotton-woods and china-trees growing along its bottom.

After arriving in the copse Carlos dismounted; and having led his horse into the darkest shadow of the trees, there left him. He did not tie him to anything, but merely rested the bridle over the pommel of the saddle, so that it might not draggle upon the ground. He had long ago trained the noble animal to remain where he was placed without other fastening than this.

This arrangement completed, he walked forward to the edge of the underwood, and there stood with his eyes fixed upon the bridge and the dark grove beyond it. It was not the first time for him to go through all the manoeuvres here described—no, not by many—but, perhaps, on no other occasion were his emotions so strong and strange as on the present.

He had prepared himself for the interview he was now expecting—he had promised himself a frankness of speech his modesty had never before permitted him to indulge in—he had resolved on proposals—the rejection or acceptance of which might determine his future fate. His heart beat within his breast so as to be audible to his own ears.

Perfect stillness reigned through the town. The inhabitants had all retired to their beds, and not a light appeared from door or window. All were close shut and fast bolted. No one appeared in the streets, except the half-dozen "serenos" who formed the night-watch of the place. These could be seen muffled up in their dark cloaks, sitting half asleep on the banquetas of houses, and grasping in one hand their huge halberds, while their lanterns rested upon the pavement at their feet.

Perfect stillness reigned around the mansion of Don Ambrosio. The great gate of the zaguan was closed and barred, and the portero had retired within his "lodge," thus signifying that all the inmates of the dwelling had returned home. If silence denoted sleep, all were asleep; but a ray of light escaping through the silken curtains of a glass door, and falling dimly upon the pavement of the patio, showed that one at least still kept vigil. That light proceeded from the chamber of Catalina.

All at once the stillness of the night was broken by the loud tolling of a bell. It was the clock of the parroquia announcing the hour of midnight.

The last stroke had not ceased to reverberate when the light in the chamber appeared to be suddenly extinguished—for it no longer glowed through the curtain.

Shortly after, the glass door was silently opened from the inside; and a female form closely muffled came forth, and glided with stealthy and sinuous step around the shadowy side of the patio. The tall elegant figure could not be hidden by the disguise of the ample cloak in which it was muffled, and the graceful gait appeared even when constrained and stealthy. It was the Señorita herself.

Having passed round the patio, she entered the avenue that led to the garden. Here a heavy door barred the egress from the house, and before this she stopped. Only a moment. A key appeared from under her cloak, and the large bolt with some difficulty yielded to her woman's strength. It did not yield silently. The rusty iron sounded as it sprang back into the lock, causing her to start and tremble. She even returned back through the avenue, to make sure whether any one had heard it; and, standing in the dark entrance, glanced round the patio. Had she not heard a door closing as she came back? She fancied so; and alarmed by it, she stood for some time gazing upon the different doors that opened upon the court. They were all close shut, her own not excepted, for she had closed it on coming out. Still her fancy troubled her, and, but half satisfied, she returned to the gate.

This she opened with caution, and, passing through, traversed the rest of the avenue, and came out in the open ground. Keeping under the shadow of the trees and shrubbery, she soon reached the grove at the bottom of the garden. Here she paused for a moment, and, looking through the stems of the trees, scanned the open surface in the direction of the copse where Carlos had halted.

No object was visible but the outlines of the timber island itself, under whose shadow a human form in dark clothing could not have been recognised at such a distance.

After pausing a moment she glided among the trees of the grove, and the next moment stood, upon the centre and highest point of the bridge in front of the little gate. Here she again stopped, drew from under her cloak a white cambric handkerchief, and, raising herself to her full height, held it spread out between her hands.

The air was filled with fire-flies, whose light sparkled thickly against the dark background of the copsewood; but these did not prevent her from distinguishing a brighter flash, like the snapping of a lucifer-match, that appeared among them. Her signal was answered!

She lowered the handkerchief, and, taking out a small key, applied it to the lock of the gate. This was undone in a second, and, having thrown open the wicket, she retired within the shadow of the grove, and stood waiting.

Even in that dark shadow her eyes sparkled with the light of love, as she saw a form—the form of a man on foot, parting from the copse, and coming in the direction of the bridge. It was to her the dearest on earth; and she awaited the approach with a flushed cheek and a heart full of joyful emotion.

Chapter Forty Five

It was no fancy of Catalina's that she heard the shutting of a door as she returned up the avenue. A door in reality had been closed at that moment,—the door that led to the sleeping apartments of the maidservants. Had her steps been quicker, she might have seen some one rush across the patio and enter this door. But she arrived too late for this. The door was closed, and all was silent again. It might have been fancy, thought she.

It was no fancy. From the hour when the family had retired to rest, the door of Catalina's chamber had been watched. An eye had been bent all the time upon that ray of light escaping through the curtained glass,—the eye of the girl Vicenza.

During the early part of the evening the maid had asked leave to go out for a while. It had been granted. She had been gone for nearly an hour. Conducted by the soldier José, she had had an interview with Roblado. At that interview all had been arranged between them.

She was to watch her mistress from the house, and follow her to the place of assignation. When that should be determined she was to return with all haste to Roblado—who appointed a place of meeting her—and then guide him and his troop to the lovers. This, thought Roblado, would be the surest plan to proceed upon. He had taken his measures accordingly.

The door of the maid's sleeping-room was just opposite that of Catalina's chamber. Through the key-hole the girl had seen the light go out, and the Señorita gliding around the patio. She had watched her into the avenue, and then gently opening her own door and stolen after her.

At the moment the Señorita had succeeded in unlocking the great gate of the garden, the mestiza was peeping around the wall at the entrance of the avenue; but on hearing the other return,—for it was by the sound of her footsteps she was warned,—the wily spy had darted back into her room, and closed the door behind her.

It was some time before she dared venture out again, as the key-hole no longer did her any service. She kept her eye to it, however, and, seeing that her mistress did not return to her chamber, she concluded that the latter had continued on into the garden. Again gently opening her door, she stole forth, and, on tiptoe approaching the avenue, peeped into it. It was no longer dark. The gate was open, and the moon shining in lit up the whole passage. It was evident, therefore, that the Señorita had gone through, and was now in the garden.

Was she in the garden? The mestiza remembered the bridge, and knew that her mistress carried the key of the wicket, and often used it both by day and night. She might by this have crossed the bridge, and got far beyond into the open country. She—the spy—might not find the direction she had taken, and thus spoil the whole plan.

With these thoughts passing through her mind, the girl hurried through the avenue, and, crouching down, hastened along the walk as fast as she was able.

Seeing no one among the fruit-trees and flowerbeds, she began to despair; but the thick grove at the bottom of the garden gave her promise— that was a likely place of meeting—capital for such a purpose, as the mestiza, experienced in such matters, well knew.

To approach the grove, however, presented a difficulty. There was a space of open ground—a green parterre—between it and the flowerbeds. Any one, already in the grove, could perceive the approach of another in that direction, and especially under a bright moonlight. This the mestiza saw, and it compelled her to pause and reflect how she was to get nearer.

But one chance seemed to offer. The high adobe wall threw a shadow of some feet along one side of the open ground. In this shadow it might be possible to reach the timber unobserved. The girl resolved to attempt it.

Guided by the instinctive cunning of her race, she dropped down flat upon her breast; and, dragging herself over the grass, she reached the selvedge of the grove, just in the rear of the arbour. There she paused, raised her head, and glanced through the leafy screen that encircled the arbour. She saw what she desired.

Catalina was at this moment upon the bridge, and above the position of the mestiza—so that the latter could perceive her form outlined against the blue of the sky. She saw her hold aloft the white kerchief. She guessed that it was a signal—she saw the flash in answer to it, and then observed her mistress undo the lock and fling the wicket open.

The cunning spy was now sure that the place of meeting was to be the grove itself, and might have returned with that information; but Roblado had distinctly ordered her not to leave until she saw the meeting itself, and was certain of the spot. She therefore remained where she was, and awaited the further proceedings of the lovers.

Carlos, on perceiving the signal, had answered it by flashing some powder already prepared. He lost no time in obeying the well-known summons. A single moment by the side of his horse—a whisper which the latter well understood—and he parted from the copse, Cibolo following at his heels.

On reaching the end of the bridge he bent down, and, addressing some words in a low voice to the dog, proceeded to cross over. The animal did not follow him, but lay down on the opposite bank of the stream.

The next moment the lovers were together.

From the spot where she lay the mestiza witnessed their greeting. The moon shone upon their faces—the fair skin and curly locks of Carlos were distinctly visible under the light. The girl knew the cibolero—it was he.

She had seen all that was necessary for Roblado to know. The grove was the place of meeting. It only remained for her to get back to the officer, and give the information.

She was about to crawl away, and had already half risen, when to her dismay, the lovers appeared coming through the grove, and towards the very arbour behind which she lay!

Their faces were turned towards the spot where she was crouching. If she rose to her feet, or attempted to go off, she could not fail to be seen by one or other of them.

She had no alternative but to remain where she was—at least until some better opportunity offered of getting away—and with this intention she again squatted down close under the shadow of the arbour.

A moment after the lovers entered, and seated themselves upon the benches with which the little bower was provided.

Chapter Forty Six

The hearts of both were so agitated that for some moments neither gave utterance to their thoughts. Catalina was the first to speak.

"Your sister?" she inquired.

"She is better. I have had the rancho restored. They have returned to it, and the old scenes seem to have worked a miracle upon her. Her senses came at once, and relapse only at long intervals. I have hopes it will be all well again."

"I am glad to hear this. Poor child! she must have suffered sadly in the hands of these rude savages."

"Rude savages! Ay, Catalina, you have styled them appropriately, though you little know of whom you are speaking."

"Of whom?" echoed the lady, in surprise. Up to this moment even she had no other than the popular and universal belief that Carlos' sister had been a captive in the hands of the Indians!

"It was partly for this that I have sought an interview to-night. I could not exist without explaining to you my late conduct, which must have appeared to you a mystery. It shall be so no longer. Hear me, Catalina!"

Carlos revealed the horrid plot, detailing every circumstance, to the utter astonishment of his fair companion.

"Oh! fiends! fiends!" she exclaimed; "who could have imagined such atrocity? Who would suppose that on the earth were wretches like these? But that *you*, dear Carlos, have told me, I could not have believed in such villainy! I knew that both were bad; I have heard many a tale of the vileness of these two men; but this is wickedness beyond the power of fancy! *Santisima Madre!* what men! what monsters! It is incredible!"

"You know now with what justice I am called a murderer?"

"Oh, dear Carlos! think not of that. I never gave it a thought. I knew you had some cause just and good. Fear not! The world shall yet know all—"

"The world!" interrupted Carlos, with a sneer. "For me there is no world. I have no home. Even among those with whom I have been brought up, I have been but a stranger—a heretic outcast. Now I am worse—a hunted outlaw with a price upon my head, and a good large one too. In truth, I never thought I was worth so much before!" Here a laugh escaped from the speaker; but his merriment was of short duration. He continued—

"No world have I but you, Catalina,—and you no longer except in my heart. I must leave you and go far away. Death—worse than death—awaits me here. I must go hence. I must return to the people from whom my parents are sprung—to our long forgotten kindred. Perhaps there I may find a new home and new friends, but happiness I cannot without you—No, never!"

Catalina was silent, with tearful eyes bent upon the ground. She trembled at the thought that was passing in her mind. She feared to give it expression. But it was no time for the affectation of false modesty, for idle bashfulness; and neither were her characteristics. Upon a single word depended the happiness of her life—of her lover's. Away with womanly coyness! let the thought be spoken!

She turned toward her lover, took his hand in hers, leant forward till her lips were close to his, and, looking in his face, said in a soft, but firm voice—

"Carlos! is it your wish that *I* go with you?"

In a moment his arms were around her, and their lips had met.

"O Heavens!" he exclaimed; "is this possible? do I hear aright? Dearest Catalina! It was this I would have proposed, but I dared not do it. I feared to make the proposal, so wild does it seem. What! forsake all for me? Oh, *querida! querida!* Tell me that this is what your words mean! Say you will go with me!"

"*I will!*" was the short but firm reply.

"O God! I am too happy—a week of terrible suffering, and I am again happy. But a week ago, Catalina, and I was happy. I had met with a strange adventure, one that promised fortune. I was full of hope—hope of winning you; not you, *querida*, but your father. Of winning him by gold. See!" Here the speaker held forth his hand filled with shining ore. "It is gold. Of this I have discovered a mine, and I had hoped with it to have rivalled your father in his wealth, and then to have won his consent. Alas! alas! that is now hopeless, but your words have given me new happiness. Think not of the fortune you leave behind. I know you do not, dear Catalina. I shall give you one equal to it—perhaps far greater. I know where this precious trash is to be procured, but I shall tell you all when we have time. To-night—"

He was interrupted by Catalina. Her quick ear had caught a sound that appeared odd to her. It was but a slight rustling among the leaves near the back of the arbour, and might have been caused by the wind, had there been any. But not a breath was stirring. Something else had caused it. What could it be?

After a moment or two both stepped out, and examined the bushes whence the sound was supposed to have proceeded; but nothing was to be seen. They looked around and up towards the garden—there was no appearance of anything that could have caused the noise! It was now much darker than when they had entered the arbour. The moon had gone down, and the silvery light had turned to grey; but it was still clear enough to have distinguished any large object at several yards distance. Catalina could not be mistaken. She had heard a rustling sound to a certainty. Could it have been the dog? Carlos stepped forward on the bridge. It was not—the animal still lay where he had been placed: it could not have been he! What then? Some lizard? perhaps a dangerous serpent?

At all events they would not again enter the arbour but remained standing outside. Still Catalina was not without apprehensions, for she now remembered the loss of the note, and, later still, the shutting of the door, both of which she hastily communicated to her companion.

Hitherto Carlos had paid but little attention to what he believed to be some natural occurrence—the fluttering of a bird which had been disturbed by them, or the gliding of a snake or lizard. But the information now given made a different impression upon him. Used to Indian wiles, he was a ready reasoner, and he perceived at once that there might be something sinister in the sound which had been heard. He resolved, therefore, to examine the ground more carefully.

Once more he proceeded to the back of the arbour, and, dropping to his knees, scanned the grass and bushes. In a moment he raised his head with an exclamation of surprise.

"As I live, Catalina, you were right! Some one has been here, beyond a doubt! Some one has lain on this very spot! Where can they have gone to? By Heaven, it was a woman! Here is the trail of her dress!"

"Vicenza!" exclaimed the lady. "It can be no other—my maid, Vicenza! *Dios de mi alma!* she has heard every word!"

"No doubt it was Vicenza. She has watched and followed you from the house. What could have tempted her to such an act?"

"*Ay de mi!* Heaven only knows: her conduct has been very strange of late. It is quite annoying! Dear Carlos!" she continued, changing her tone of regret to one of anxiety, "you must stay no longer. Who knows what she may do? Perhaps summon my father! Perhaps still worse—Santisima Virgen! may it not be!"

Here Catalina hastily communicated the fact of Vicenza's intimacy with the soldier José, as well as other circumstances relating to the girl, and urged upon her lover the necessity of instant departure.

"I shall go then," said he. "Not that I much fear them; it is too dark for their carbines, and their sabres will never reach me, while my brave steed stands yonder ready to obey my call. But it is better for me to go. There may be something in it. I cannot explain curiosity that attempts so much as this girl. I shall go at once then."

And so Carlos had resolved. But much remained to be said: fresh vows of love to be pronounced; an hour to be fixed for a future meeting—perhaps the last before taking the final step—their flight across the great plains.

More than once had Carlos placed his foot upon the bridge, and more than once had he returned to have another sweet word—another parting kiss.

The final "adios" had at length been exchanged; the lovers had parted from each other; Catalina had turned towards the house; and Carlos was advancing to the bridge with the intention of crossing, when a growl from Cibolo caused him to halt and listen.

Again the dog growled, this time more fiercely, following with a series of earnest barks, that told his master some danger was nigh.

The first thought of the latter was to rush across the bridge, and make towards his steed. Had he done so, he would have had time enough to escape; but the desire to warn her, so that she might hasten to the house, impelled him to turn back through the grove. She had already reached the open parterre, and was crossing it, when the barking of the dog caused her to stop, and the moment after Carlos came up. But he had not addressed a word to her before the trampling of horses sounded outside the adobe walls of the garden—horsemen galloped down on both sides, while the confused striking of hoofs showed that some were halting outside, while others deployed around the enclosure. The rattling of the timbers of the large bridge was heard almost at the same instant; then the dog breaking into a fierce attack; and then, through the stems of the trees, the dark forms of horsemen became visible upon the opposite bank of the stream. The garden was surrounded!

Chapter Forty Seven

Long after the lovers had entered the arbour the mestiza had remained in her squatting attitude, listening to the conversation, of which not a word escaped her. It was not, however, her interest in that which bound her to the spot, but her fear of being discovered should she attempt to leave it. She had reason while it was still moonlight, for the open ground she must pass over was distinctly visible from the arbour. It was only after the moon went down that she saw the prospect of retiring unseen; and, choosing a moment when the lovers had their faces turned from her, she crawled a few yards back, rose to her feet, and ran nimbly off in the darkness.

Strange to say, the rustling heard by the señorita was not made by the girl at the moment of her leaving the arbour. It was caused by a twig which she had bent behind a branch, the better to conceal herself, and this releasing itself had sprung back to its place. That was why no object was visible to the lovers, although coming hastily out of the arbour. The spy at that instant was beyond the reach of sight as well as hearing. She had got through the avenue before the twig moved.

She did not stop for a moment. She did not return to her apartment, but crossing the patio hastily entered the zaguan. This she traversed with stealthy steps, as if afraid to awake the portero.

On reaching the gate she drew from her pocket a key. It was not the key of the main lock, but of the lesser one, belonging to the postern door which opened through the great gate.

This key she had secured at an earlier hour of the evening, for the very use she was now about to make of it.

She placed it in the lock, and then shot the bolt, using all the care she could to prevent it from making a noise. She raised the latch with like caution; and then, opening the door, stepped gently to the outside. She next closed the door after her, slowly and silently; and this done, she ran with all her speed along the road towards some woods that were outside the town, and not far from the house of Don Ambrosio.

It was in these woods that Roblado held his men in ambush. He had brought them thither at a late hour, and by a circuitous route, so that no one should see them as they entered the timber, and thus prevent the possibility of a frustration of his plans. Here he was waiting the arrival of his spy.

The girl soon reached the spot, and in a few minutes detailed to the officer the whole of what she had witnessed. What she had heard there was no time to tell, for she communicated to Roblado how she had been detained, and the latter saw there was not a moment to be lost. The interview might end before he should be ready, and his prey might still escape him.

Had Roblado felt more confidence as to time he would now have acted differently. He would have sent some men by a lower crossing, and let them approach the bottom of the garden directly from the meadow; he would, moreover, have spent more time and caution about the "surround."

But he saw he might be too late, should he adopt this surer course. A quicker one recommended itself, and he at once gave the orders to his followers. These were divided into two parties of different sizes. Each was to take a side of the garden, and deploy along the wall, but the larger party was to drop only a few of its men, while the rest were to ride hastily over the greater bridge, and gallop round to the bottom of the garden. Roblado himself was to lead this party, whose duty would likely be of most importance. As the leader well knew, the garden walls could not be scaled without a ladder, and the cibolero, if found within the garden, would attempt to escape by the bridge at the bottom. Lest he might endeavour to get through the avenue and off by the front of the house, the girl Vicenza was to conduct Gomez with several men on foot through the patio, and guide them to the avenue entrance.

The plan was well enough conceived. Roblado knew the ground well. He had often strolled through that garden, and its walls and approaches were perfectly familiar to him. Should he be enabled to surround it before the cibolero could got notice of their approach, he was sure of his victim. The latter must either be killed or captured.

In five minutes after the arrival of the spy he had communicated the whole of their duties to the men; and in five minutes more they had ridden out of the woods, crossed the small tract that separated them from the house, and were in the act of surrounding the garden! It was at this moment that the dog Cibolo first uttered his growl of alarm.

"Fly—fly!" cried Catalina as she saw her lover approach. "Oh! do not think of me! They dare not take my life. I have committed no offence. Oh, Carlos, leave me! fly! *Madre de Dios*! they come this way!"

As she spoke a number of dark forms were seen entering from the avenue, and coming down the garden. Their scabbards clanked among the bushes as they rushed through them. They were soldiers on foot! Several remained by the entrance, while the rest ran forward.

Carlos had for a moment contemplated escape in that direction. It occurred to him, if he could get up to the house and on the azotea, he might drop off on either side, and, favoured by the darkness, return to the meadow at some distant point. This idea vanished the moment he saw that the entrance was occupied. He glanced to the walls. They were too high to be scaled. He would be attacked while attempting it. No other chance offered but to cut his way through by the bridge, he now saw the error he had committed in returning. She was in no danger—at least in no peril of her life. Indeed her greater danger would arise from his remaining near her. He should have crossed the bridge at first. He was now separated from his horse. He might summon the latter by his call—he knew that—but it would only bring the noble animal within reach of his foes—perhaps to be captured. That would be as much as taking his own life. No: he could not summon his steed from where he was, and he did not utter the signal. What was he to do? To remain by the side of Catalina, to be surrounded and captured, perhaps cut down like a dog? To imperil her life as well?—No. He must make a desperate struggle to get out of the enclosure, to reach the open country if possible, and then—

His thoughts went no farther. He cried out—

"Querida, farewell! I must leave you—do not despair. If I die, I shall carry your love to heaven! Farewell, farewell!"

These words were uttered in the parting haste of the moment, and he had sprung away so suddenly that he did not hear the answering farewell.

The moment he was gone the lady dropped to her knees, and with hands clasped, and eyes raised to heaven, offered her prayer for his safety.

Half-a-dozen springs brought Carlos once more under the shadow of the grove. He saw his foes on the opposite bank, and from their voices he could tell there were many of them. They were talking loudly and shouting directions to one another. He could distinguish the voice of Roblado above the rest. He was calling upon some of the men to dismount and follow him over the bridge. He was himself on foot, for the purpose of crossing.

Carlos saw no other prospect of escape than by making a quick rush across the bridge, and cutting his way through the crowd. By that means he might reach the open plain, and fight his way until his horse could come up. Once in the saddle he would have laughed at their attempts to take him. It was a desperate resolve,—a perilous running of the gauntlet,—almost certain death; but still more certain death was the alternative if he remained where he was.

There was no time for hesitation. Already several men had dismounted, and were making towards the bridge. He must cross before they had reached it; one was already upon it. He must be beaten back.

Carlos, cocking his pistol, rushed forward to the gate. The man had reached it from the other side. They met face to face, with the gate still shut between them. Carlos saw that his antagonist was Roblado himself!

Not a word was spoken between them. Roblado also had his pistol in readiness and fired first, but missed his aim. He perceived this, and, dreading the fire from his adversary, he staggered back to the bank, shouting to his followers to discharge their carbines.

Before they could obey the order, the crack of the cibolero's pistol rang upon the air, and Roblado, with a loud oath, rolled down by the edge of the water. Carlos dashed open the gate, and was about to rush onward, when he perceived through the smoke and darkness several carbines brought to the level, and aimed at him. A sudden thought came into his mind, and he changed his design of crossing the bridge. The time was but the pulling of a trigger, but, short as it was, he effected his purpose. The carbines blazed and cracked, all nearly at the same instant, and when the smoke cleared away Carlos was no longer on the bridge! Had he gone back into the garden? No—already half-a-dozen men had cut off his retreat in that direction!

"He is killed!" cried several voices, "Carajo!—he has fallen into the river! *Mira!*"

All eyes were turned upon the stream. Certainly a body had plunged into it, as the bubbles and circling waves testified, but only these were to be seen! "He has sunk! he's gone to the bottom!" cried some.

"Be sure he hasn't swum away!" counselled a voice; and several ran along the banks, with their eyes searching the surface.

"Impossible! there are no waves."

"He could not have passed here," said one who stood a little below the bridge. "I have been watching the water."

"So have I," cried another from above. "He has not passed my position."

"Then he is dead and gone down!"

"Carajo! let us fish him out!" And they were proceeding to put this idea into execution, when Roblado, who had now got to his feet, finding that a wounded arm was all he had suffered, ordered them to desist.

"Up and down!" he thundered; "scatter both ways—quick, or he may yet escape us. Go!"

The men did as they were ordered, but the party who turned downstream halted through sheer surprise. The figure of a man was seen, in a bent attitude and crawling up the bank, at the distance of a hundred yards below. The next moment it rose into an erect position, and glided over the plain with lightning speed, in the direction of the copse of timber!

"*Hola!*" exclaimed several voices; "yonder he goes! *Por todos santos*, it is he!"

Amidst the cracking of carbines that followed, a shrill whistle was heard; and before any of the mounted men could ride forward, a horse was seen shooting out from the copse and meeting the man upon the open meadow! Quick as thought the latter vaulted into the saddle, and after uttering a wild and scornful laugh galloped off, and soon disappeared in the darkness!

Most of the dragoons sprang upon their horses and followed; but after a short gallop over the plain they gave up the chase, and one by one returned to their wounded leader.

To say that Roblado was furious would be to characterise very faintly the state he was in. But he had still one captive on which to vent his rage and chagrin.

Catalina had been captured in the garden,—taken while praying for the safe escape of her lover. José had remained in charge of her, while the rest rushed down to assist in the capture of Carlos, at which José, knowing the cibolero as he did, and not being over brave, evinced no desire to be present.

Catalina heard the shots and shouts that denoted the terrible struggle. She had heard, too, the shrill whistle and the scornful laugh that rang loudly above the din. She had heard the shouts of the pursuers dying away in the distance.

Her heart beat with joy. She knew that her lover was free!

She thought then, and then only, of herself. She thought, too, of escape. She knew the rude taunts she would have to listen to from the brutal leader of these miscreants. What could she do to avoid an encounter? She had but one to deal with—José. She knew the despicable character of the man. Would gold tempt him? She would make the trial.

It was made, and succeeded. The large sum offered was irresistible. The villain knew that there could be no great punishment for letting go a captive who could at any time be taken again. He would risk the chances of his captain's displeasure for such a sum. His captain might have reasons for not dealing too severely with him. The purse was paid, and the lady was allowed to go.

She was to close the door, locking it from the inside, as though she had escaped by flight; and this direction of José was followed to the letter.

As Roblado crossed the bridge he was met by the soldier, who, breathless and stammering, announced that the fair prisoner had got into the house. She had slipped from his side and ran off. Had it been an ordinary captive, he could have fired upon her, but he was unable to overtake her until she had passed the door, which was closed and locked before he could get near.

For a moment Roblado hesitated whether to "storm the house." His rage almost induced him to the act. He reflected, however, that the proceeding might appear somewhat ridiculous and could not much better his position; besides, the pain of his wounded arm admonished him to retire from the field.

He re-crossed the bridge, was helped upon his horse, and, summoning around him his valiant troop, he rode back to the Presidio—leaving the roused town to conjecture the cause of the alarm.

Chapter Forty Eight

Next morning the town was full of "novedades." At first it was supposed there had been an attack of Indians repelled as usual by the troops. What valiant protectors the people had!

After a while it was rumoured that Carlos the murderer had been captured, and that was the cause of the firing,—that Captain Roblado was killed in the affair. Presently Carlos was not taken, but he had been chased and came very near being taken! Roblado had engaged him singly, hand to hand, and had wounded him, but in the darkness he had got off by diving down the river. In the encounter the outlaw had shot the captain through the arm, which prevented the latter from making him a prisoner.

This rumour came direct from the Presidio. It was partly true. The wounding of Carlos by Roblado was an addition to the truth, intended to give a little *éclat* to the latter, for it became known afterwards that the cibolero had escaped without even a scratch.

People wondered why the outlaw should have ventured to approach the town, knowing as he did that there was a price upon his head. Some very powerful motive must have drawn him thither. The motive soon became known,—the whole story leaked out; and then, indeed, did scandal enjoy a feast. Catalina had been for some time the acknowledged belle of the place, and, what with envious women and jealous men, she was now treated with slight show of charity. The very blackest construction was put upon her "compromisa." It was worse even than a *mésalliance*. The "society" were horrified at her conduct in stooping to intimacy with a "lepero;" while even the lepero class, itself fanatically religious, condemned her for her association with "un asesino," but, still worse, a "heretico!"

The excitement produced by this new affair was great indeed,—a perfect panic. The cibolero's head rose in value, like the funds. The magistrates and principal men assembled in the Casa de Cabildo. A new proclamation was drawn out. A larger sum was offered for the capture of Carlos, and the document was rendered still stronger by a declaration of severe punishment to all who should give him food or protection. If captured beneath the roof of any citizen who had voluntarily sheltered him, the latter was to suffer full confiscation of his property, besides such further punishment as might be fixed upon.

The Church was not silent. The padrés promised excommunication and the wrath of Heaven against those who would stay justice from the heretic murderer!

These were terrible terms for the outlaw! Fortunately for him, he knew how to live without a roof over his head. He could maintain existence where his enemies would have starved, and where they were unable to follow him,—on the wide desert plain, or in the rocky ravines of the mountains. Had he depended for food or shelter on his fellow-citizens of the settlement he would soon have met with betrayal and denouncement. But the cibolero was as independent of such a necessity as the wild savage of the prairies. He could sleep on the grassy sward or the naked rock, he could draw sustenance even from the arid surface of the Llano Estacado, and there he could bid defiance to a whole army of pursuers.

At the council Don Ambrosio was not present. Grief and rage kept him within doors. A stormy scene had been enacted between him and his daughter. Henceforth she was to be strictly guarded—to be kept a prisoner in her father's house—to be taught repentance by the exercise of penance.

To describe the feelings of Roblado and the Comandante would be impossible. These gentlemen were well-nigh at their wits' end with mortification. Disappointment, humiliation, physical and moral pain, had worked them into a frenzy of rage; and they were engaged together during all the day in plotting schemes and plans for the capture of their outlawed enemy.

Roblado was not less earnest than the Comandante in the success of their endeavours.

Carlos had now given both of them good cause to hate him, and both hated him from the bottom of their hearts.

What vexed Roblado most was, that he was no longer able to take the field—nor was he likely to be for several weeks. His wound, though not dangerous, would oblige him to sling his arm for some time, and to manage a horse would be out of the question. The strategic designs of the Comandante and himself would have to be carried out by those who felt far less interest in the capture of the outlaw than they did. Indeed, but for the arrival of a brace of lieutenants, sent from division head-quarters at Santa Fé, the garrison would have been without a commissioned officer fit for duty. These new-comers—Lieutenants Yañez and Ortiga—were neither of them the men to catch the cibolero. They were brave enough—Ortiga in particular—but both were late arrivals from Spain, and knew nothing whatever of border warfare.

The soldiers were desirous of hunting the outlaw down, and acted with sufficient zeal. The stimulus of a large reward, which was promised to them, rendered them eager of effecting his capture; and they went forth on each fresh scout with alacrity. But they were not likely to attack the cibolero unless a goodly number of them were together. No one or two of them—including the celebrated Sergeant Gomez—would venture within range of his rifle, much less go near enough to lay hands upon him.

The actual experience of his prowess by some of them, and the exaggerated reports of it known to others, had made such an impression upon the whole troop, that the cibolero could have put a considerable body of them to flight only by showing himself! But in addition to the skill, strength, and daring which he had in reality exhibited—in addition to the exaggeration of those qualities by the fancy—the soldiers as well as people had become possessed with a strange belief—that was, that the cibolero was under the protection of his mother—under the protection of the "diablo"—in other words, that he was *bewitched,* and therefore invincible! Some asserted that he was impervious to shot, spear, or sabre. Those who had fired their carbines at him while on the bridge fully believed this. They were ready to swear—each one of them—that they had hit the cibolero, and must have killed him had he not been under supernatural protection!

Wonderful stories now circulated among the soldiers and throughout the settlement. The cibolero was seen everywhere, and always mounted on his coal-black horse, who shared his supernatural fame. He had been seen riding along the top of the cliffs at full gallop, and so close to their edge that he might have blown the stump of his cigar into the valley below! Others had met him in the night on lonely walks amid the chapparal, and according to them his face and hands had appeared red and luminous as coals of fire! He had been seen on the high plains by the hateros—on the cliff of "La Niña"—in many parts of the valley; but no one had ventured near enough to exchange words with him. Every one had fled or shunned him. It was even asserted that he had been seen crossing the little bridge that led out of Don Ambrosio's garden, and thus brought down a fresh shower of scandal on the devoted head of Catalina. The scandal-mongers, however, were sadly disappointed on hearing that this bridge no longer existed, but had been removed by Don Ambrosio on the day following the discovery of his daughter's misconduct!

In no part of the world is superstition stronger than among the ignorant populace of the settlements of New Mexico. In fact, it may be regarded as forming part of their religion. The missionary padrés, in grafting the religion of Rome upon the sun-worship of Quetzalcoatl, admitted for their own purposes a goodly string of superstitions. It would be strange if their people did not believe in others, however absurd. Witchcraft, therefore, and all like things, were among the New Mexicans as much matters of belief as the Deity himself.

It is not then to be wondered at that Carlos the cibolero became associated with the devil. His feat of horsemanship and hair-breadth escapes from his enemies were, to say the least, something wonderful and romantic, even when viewed in a natural sense. But the populace of San Ildefonso no longer regarded them in this light. With them his skill in the "coleo de toros," in "running the cock,"—his feat of horsemanship on the cliff—his singular escapes from carbine and lance, were no longer due to himself, but to the devil. The "diablo" was at the bottom of all!

If the outlaw appeared so often during the next few days to those who did not wish to see him, it was somewhat strange that those who were desirous of a sight and an interview could get neither one nor the other. The lieutenants, Yañez and Ortiga, with their following of troopers, were on the scout and look-out from morning till night, and from one day's end to the other. The spies that were thickly-set in all parts where there was a probability he might appear, could see nothing of Carlos! To-day he was reported here, to-morrow there; but on tracing these reports to their sources, it usually turned out that some ranchero with a black horse had been taken for him; and thus the troopers were led from place to place, and misled by false reports, until both horses and men were nearly worn out in the hopeless pursuit. This, however, had become the sole duty on which the soldiers were employed—as the Comandante had no idea of giving up the chase so long as there was a trooper left to take the trail.

One place was closely watched both by day and by night. It was watched by soldiers disguised, and also by spies employed for the purpose. This was the rancho of the cibolero himself. The disguised soldiers and spies were placed around it, in such positions that they could see every movement that took place outside the walls without being themselves seen. These positions they held during the day, taking others at night; and the surveillance was thus continual, by these secret sentries relieving one another. Should the cibolero appear, it was not the duty of the spies to attack him. They were only to communicate with a troop—kept in readiness not far off—that thus insured a sufficient force for the object.

The mother and sister of the cibolero had returned to live in the rancho. The peons had re-roofed and repaired it—an easy task, as the walls had not been injured by the five. It was now as comfortable a dwelling as ever.

The mother and sister were not molested—in fact, they were supposed to know nothing of the fact that eyes were continually upon them. But there was a design in this toleration. They were to be narrowly watched in their movements. They were never to leave the rancho without being closely followed, and the circumstance of their going out reported to the leader of the ambushed troop at the moment of its occurrence. These orders were of the strictest kind, and their disobedience threatened with severe punishment.

The reasons for all this were quite simple. Both Vizcarra and Roblado believed, or suspected, that Carlos might leave the settlement altogether— why should he not?—and take both mother and sister along with him. Indeed, why should he not? The place could be no more a home to him, and he would easily find another beyond the Great Plains. No time could ever release him from the ban that hung over him. He could never pay the forfeit of his life—but by that life. It was, therefore, perfectly natural in the two officers to suspect him of the intention of moving elsewhere.

But, reasoned they, so long as we hold the mother and sister as hostages, he will not leave them. He will still continue to lurk around the settlement, and, if not now, some time shall the fox be caught and destroyed.

So reasoned the Comandante and his captain, and hence the strictness of their orders about guarding the rancho. Its inmates were really prisoners, though—as Vizcarra and Roblado supposed—they were ignorant of the fact.

Notwithstanding all their ingenious plans—notwithstanding all their spies, and scouts, and soldiers—notwithstanding their promises of reward and threats of punishment—day followed day, and still the outlaw remained at large.

Chapter Forty Nine

For a long time Carlos had neither been seen nor heard of except through reports that on being examined turned out to be false. Both the Comandante and his *confrère* began to grow uneasy. They began to fear he had in reality left the settlement and gone elsewhere to live, and this they dreaded above all things. Both had a reason for wishing him thus out of the place, and until late occurrences nothing would have pleased them better. But their feelings had undergone a change, and neither the intended seducer nor the fortune-hunter desired that things should end just in that way. The passion of revenge had almost destroyed the ruffian love of the one, and the avarice of the other. The very sympathy which both received on account of their misfortunes whetted this passion to a continued keenness. There was no danger of its dying within the breast of either. The looking-glass alone would keep it alive in Vizcarra's bosom for the rest of his life.

They were together on the azotea of the Presidio, talking the matter between them, and casting over the probabilities of their late suspicion.

"He is fond of the sister," remarked the Comandante; "and mother too, for that matter, hag as she is! Still, my dear Roblado, a man likes his own life better than anything else. Near is the shirt, etcetera. He knows well that to stay here is to get into our hands some time or other, and he knows what we'll do with him if he should. Though he has made some clever escapes, I'll admit, that may not always be his fortune. The pitcher may go to the well once too often. He's a cunning rascal—no doubt knows this riddle—and therefore I begin to fear he has taken himself off,—at least for a long while. He may return again, but how the deuce are we to sustain this constant espionage? It would weary down the devil! It will become as tiresome as the siege of Granada was to the good king Fernando and his warlike spouse of the soiled chemise. *Por Dios*! I'm sick of it already!"

"Rather than let him escape us," replied Roblado, "I'd wear out my life at it."

"So I—so I, capitan. Don't fear I have the slightest intention of dropping our system of vigilance. No—no—look in this face. *Carajo*!"

And as the speaker reflected upon his spoiled features, the bitterest scowl passed over them, making them still more hideous.

"And yet," continued Vizcarra, following out the original theme, "it does not seem natural that he should leave *them* behind him, even for a short period, after what has occurred, and after the risk he ran to recover *her*; does it?"

"No," replied the other, thoughtfully, "no. What I most wonder at is his not setting off with them the night she got back,—that very night,—for by the letter he was there upon the spot! But, true, it takes some time to prepare for a journey across the prairies. He would never have gone to one of our own settlements—not likely—and to have travelled elsewhere would have required some preparation for the women at least; for himself, I believe he is as much at home in the desert as either the antelope or the prairie wolf. Still with an effort he might have gone away at that time and taken them along with him. It was bad management on our part not to send our men down that night."

"I had no fear of his going off, else I should have done so."

"How?—no fear? was it not highly probable?"

"Not in the least," replied Roblado.

"I cannot understand you, my dear capitan. Why not?"

"Because there is a magnet in this valley that held him tighter than either mother or sister could, and I knew that."

"Oh! now I understand you."

"Yes," continued Roblado, grinding his teeth against each other, and speaking in a bitter tone; "that precious 'margarita,' that is yet to be my wife,—ha! ha! He was not likely to be off without having a talk with her. They have had it. God knows whether they agreed to make it their last, but I, with the help of Don Ambrosio, have arranged that for them. *Carrai!* she'll make no more midnight sorties, I fancy. No—he's not gone. I cannot think it,—for two reasons. First, on her account. Have you ever loved, Comandante? I mean truly loved! Ha! ha! ha!"

"Ha! ha! ha! well I think I was caught once."

"Then you will know that when a man really loves—for I myself count that foolish act among my experiences,—when a man really loves, there's no rope strong enough to pull him away from the spot where the object of his love resides. No, I believe this fellow, low as he is, not only loves but worships this future wife of mine,—ha! ha!—and I believe also that no danger, not even the prospect of the garrote, will frighten him from the settlement so long as he has the hope of another clandestine *tête-à-tête* with her; and, knowing that she is ready to meet him half-way in such a matter, he will not have lost hope yet.

"But my second reason for believing he is still lurking about is that which you yourself have brought forward. He is not likely to leave them behind after what has happened. We have not blinded him; though— *Gracias à Dios*, or the devil—we have dusted the eyes of everybody besides! He knows all, as the girl Vicenza can well testify. Now, I have no belief that, knowing all this, he would leave them for any lengthened period. What I do believe is that the fellow is as cunning as a *coyote*, sees our trap, knows the bait, and won't be caught if he can help it. He is not far off, and, through these accursed peons of his, communicates with the women regularly and continually."

"What can be done?"

"I have been thinking."

"If we stop the peons from going back and forth they would be sure to know the trap that was set around them."

"Exactly so, Comandante. That would never do."

"Have you considered any other plan?"

"Partly I have."

"Let us hear it!"

"It is this. Some of those peons regularly visit the fellow in his lair. I feel certain of it. Of course they have been followed, but only in daylight, and then they are found to be on their ordinary business. But there is one of them who goes abroad at night; and all attempts at following him have proved abortive. He loses himself in the chapparal paths in spite of the spies. That is why I am certain he visits the cibolero."

"It seems highly probable."

"Now if we can find one who could either follow this fellow or track him—but there's the difficulty. We are badly off for a good tracker. There is not one in the whole troop."

"There are other ciboleros and hunters in the valley. Why not procure one of them?"

"True, we might—there are none of them over well disposed to the outlaw—so it is said. But I fear there is none of them fit, that is, none who combines both the skill and the courage necessary for this purpose—for both are necessary. They hate the fellow enough, but they fear him as well. There is *one* whom I have heard of,—in fact know something of him,—who would be the very man for us. He not only would not fear an encounter with the cibolero, but would hardly shun one with the devil; and, as for his skill in all sorts of Indian craft, his reputation among his kind is even greater than that of Carlos himself."

"Who is he?"

"I should say there are two of them, for the two always go together; one is a mulatto, who has formerly been a slave among the Americanos. He is now a runaway, and therefore hates everything that reminds him of his former masters. Among other souvenirs, as I am told, he hates our cibolero with a good stout hatred. This springs partly from the feeling already mentioned, and partly from the rivalry of hunter-fame. So much in our favour. The *alter ego* of the mulatto is a man of somewhat kindred race, a *zambo* from the coast near Matamoras or Tampico How he strayed this way no one knows, but it is a good while ago, and the mulatto and he have for long been shadows of each other; live together, hunt together, and fight for one another. Both are powerful men, and cunning as strong; but the mulatto is the zambo's master in everything, villainy not excepted. Neither is troubled with scruples. They would be the very men for our purpose."

"And why not get them at once?"

"Therein lies the difficulty—unfortunately they are not here at present. They are off upon a hunt. They are hangers-on of the mission, occasionally employed by the padrés in procuring venison and other game.

"Now it seems that the stomachs of our good abstemious fathers have lately taken a fancy to buffalo tongue cured in a certain way, which can only be done when the animal is fresh killed. In order to procure this delicacy they have sent these hunters to the buffalo range."

"How long have they been gone?—can you tell?"

"Several weeks—long before the return of our cibolero."

"It is possible they may be on the way back. Is it not?"

"I think it quite probable, but I shall ride over to the mission this very hour and inquire."

"Do so; it would be well if we could secure them. A brace of fellows, such as you describe these to be, would be worth our whole command. Lose no time."

"I shall not waste a minute," Roblado replied, and leaning over the wall he called out, "Hola! José! my horse there!"

Shortly after a messenger came up to say that his horse was saddled and ready. He was about to descend the escalera, when a large closely-cropped head—with a circular patch about the size of a blister shaven out of the crown—made its appearance over the stone-work at the top of the escalera. It was the head of the Padré Joaquin, and the next moment the owner, bland and smiling, appeared upon the azotea.

Chapter Fifty

The monk who presented himself was the same who had figured at the dinner-party. He was the senior of the two that directed the mission, and in every respect the ruler of the establishment. He was known as the Padré Joaquin, while his junior was the Padré Jorgé. The latter was a late addition to the post, whereas Padré Joaquin had been its director almost since the time of its establishment. He was, therefore, an old resident, and knew the history and character of every settler in the valley. For some reason or other he held an inveterate dislike to the family of the cibolero, to which he had given expression upon the evening of the dinner-party,—although he assigned no cause for his hostility. It could not have been because he regarded them as "hereticos," for, though the Padré Joaquin was loud in his denunciations of all who were outside the pale of the Church, yet in his own heart he cared but little about such things. His zeal for religion was sheer hypocrisy and worldly cunning. There was no vice practised in the settlement in which Padré Joaquin did not take a leading part. An adroit *monte* player he was—ready to do a little cheating upon occasions—a capital judge of game "gallos," ever ready to stake his onzas upon a "main." In addition to these accomplishments, the padré boasted of others. In his cups,—and this was nothing unusual,—he was in the habit of relating the *liaisons* and *amourettes* of his earlier life, and even some of later date. Although the neophytes of the mission were supposed to be all native Tagnos with dark skins, yet there was to be seen upon the establishment quite a crowd of young *mestizoes*, both boys and girls, who were known as the "sobrinos" and "sobrinas" of Padré Joaquin.

You cannot otherwise than deem this an exaggeration: you will imagine that no reverend father could practise such conduct, and still be held in any sort of respect by the people among whom he dwelt? So should I have thought had I not witnessed with my own eyes and ears the "priest-life" of Mexico. The immoralities here ascribed to Padré Joaquin can scarcely be called exceptional in his class. They are rather common than otherwise— some have even said *universal*.

It was no zealous feeling of religion, then, that could have "set" the monk in such hostile attitude against the family of the poor cibolero. No. It was some old grudge against the deceased father,—some cross which the padré had experienced from him in the days of the former Comandante.

As Padré Joaquin walked forward on the azotea, his busy bustling air showed that he was charged with some "novedad;" and the triumphant smile upon his countenance told that he calculated upon its being of interest to those to whom he was about to communicate it.

"Good day, father!—Good day, your reverence!" said the Comandante and Roblado speaking at the same time.

"*Buenos dias, cavalleros!*" responded the padré.

"Glad to see you, good father!" said Roblado. "You have saved me a ride. I was just in the act of starting for the mission to wait upon your reverence."

"And if you had come, capitan, I could have given you a luxury to lunch upon. We have received our buffalo-tongues."

"Oh! you have!" cried Vizcarra and Roblado in the same breath, and with an expression of interest that somewhat surprised the padré.

"Ha! you greedy *ladrones*! I see what you would be after. You would have me send you some of them. You sha'n't have a slice though—that is, unless you can give me something that will wash this dust out of my throat. I'm woeful thirsty this morning."

"Ha! ha! ha!" laughed the officers. "What shall it be, father?"

"Well—let me see.—Ah!—a cup of 'Bordeos'—that you received by last arrival."

The claret was ordered and brought up; and the padré, tossing off a glassful, smacked his lips after it with the air of one who well knew and appreciated the good quality of the wine.

"*Linda! lindisima!*" he exclaimed, rolling his eyes up to heaven, as if everything good should come and go in that direction.

"And so, padré," said the impatient Roblado, "you have got your buffalo-tongues? Your hunters, then, have returned?"

"They have; that is the business that brought me over."

"Good! that was the business that was about to take me to the mission."

"An onza we were both on the same errand!" challenged the padré.

"I won't bet, father; you always win."

"Come! you'd be glad to give an onza for my news."

"What news?—what news?" asked the officers at once, and with hurried impatience of manner.

"Another cup of Bordeos, or I choke! The dust of that road is worse than purgatory. Ah! this is a relief."

And again the padré swallowed a large glassful of claret, and smacked his lips as before.

"Now your news, dear padré?"

"*Pues*, cavalleros—our hunters have returned!"

"*Y pues?*"

"*Pues que!* they have brought news."

"Of what?"

"Of our friend the cibolero."

"Of Carlos?"

"Precisely of that individual."

"What news? Have they seen him?"

"No, not exactly *him*, but *his trail*. They have discovered his lair, and know where he is at this moment."

"Good!" exclaimed Vizcarra and Roblado.

"They can find him at any time."

"Excellent!"

"*Pues*, cavalleros; that is my news at your service. Use it to your advantage, if you can."

"Dear padré!" replied Vizcarra, "yours is a wiser head than ours. You know the situation of affairs. Our troopers *cannot catch* this villain. How would you advise us to act?"

The padré felt nattered by this confidence.

"Amigos!" said he, drawing both of them together, "I have been thinking of this; and it is my opinion you will do just as well without the help of a single soldier. Take these two hunters into your confidence—so far as may be necessary—equip them for the work—set them on the trail; and if they don't hunt down the heretic rascal, then I, Padré Joaquin, have no knowledge of men."

"Why, padré!" said Roblado; "it's the very thing we have been thinking about—the very business for which I was about to seek you."

"You had good reason, cavalleros. In my opinion, it's the best course to be followed."

"But will your hunters go willingly to work? They are free men, and may not like to engage in so dangerous an enterprise."

"Dangerous!" repeated the padré. "The danger will be no obstacle to them, I promise you. They have the courage of lions and the agility of tigers. You need not fear that danger will stand in the way."

"You think, then, they will be disposed to it?"

"They *are* disposed—I have sounded them. They have some reasons of their own for not loving the cibolero too dearly; and therefore, cavalleros, you won't require to use much persuasion on that score. I fancy you'll find them ready enough, for they have, been reading the proclamation, and, if I mistake not, have been turning over in their thoughts the fine promises it holds out. Make it sure to them that they will be well rewarded, and they'll bring you the cibolero's ears, or his scalp, or his whole carcase, if you prefer it, in less than three days from the present time! They'll track him down, I warrant."

"Should we send some troopers along with them? The cibolero may not be alone. We have reason to believe he has a half-blood with him—a sort of right-hand man of his own—and with this help he may be quite a match for your hunters."

"Not likely—they are very *demonios*. But you can consult themselves about that. They will know best whether they need assistance. That is their own affair, cavalleros. Let them decide."

"Shall we send for them? or will you send them to us?" inquired Roblado.

"Do you not think it would be better for one of you to go to *them*? The matter should be managed privately. If they make their appearance here, and hold an interview with either of you, your business with them will be suspected, and perchance get known to *him*. If it should reach his ears that these fellows are after him, their chances of taking him would be greatly diminished."

"You are right, father," said Roblado. "How can we communicate with these fellows privately?"

"Nothing easier than that, capitan. Go to their house—I should rather say to their hut—for they live in a sort of hovel by the rocks. The place is altogether out of the common track. No one will be likely to see you on your visit. You must pass through a narrow road in the chapparal; but I shall send you a guide who knows the spot, and he will conduct you. I think it like enough the fellows will be expecting you, as I hinted to them to stay at home—that possibly they might be wanted. No doubt you'll find them there at this moment."

"When can you send up the guide?"

"He is here now—my own attendant will do. He is below in the court—you need lose no time."

"No. Roblado," added the Comandante, "your horse is ready—you cannot do better than go at once."

"Then go I shall: your guide, padré?"

"Esteban! Hola! Esteban!" cried the padré, leaning over the wall.

"*Aqui, Señor,*" answered a voice.

"*Sube! sube! anda!*" (Come up quickly.)

The next moment an Indian boy appeared upon the azotea, and taking off his hat approached the padré with an air of reverence.

"You will guide the capitan through the path in the chapparal to the hunters' hut."

"Si, Señor."

"Don't tell any one you have done so."

"No, Señor."

"If you do you shall catch the 'cuarto.' *Vaya!*"

Roblado, followed by the boy, descended the escalera; and, after being helped on his horse, rode away from the gate.

The padré, at the invitation of Vizcarra, emptied another cup of Bordeos; and then, telling his host that a luncheon of the new luxury awaited him at the mission, he bade him good day, and shuffled off homeward.

Vizcarra remained alone upon the azotea. Had any one been there to watch him, they would have noticed that his countenance assumed a strange and troubled expression every time his eyes chanced to wander in the direction of La Niña.

Chapter Fifty One

Roblado entered the chapparal, the boy Esteban stepping a few paces in advance of his horse's head. For half-a-mile or so he traversed a leading road that ran between the town and one of the passes. He then struck into a narrow path, but little used except by hunters or vaqueros in search of their cattle. This path conducted him, after a ride of two or three miles, to the base of the cliffs, and there was found the object of his journey—the dwelling-place of the hunters.

It was a mere hut—a few upright posts supporting a single roof, which slanted up, with a very slight inclination, against the face of the rock. The posts were trunks of a species of arborescent yucca that grew plentifully around the spot, and the roof-thatch was the stiff loaves of the same, piled thickly over each other. There was a sort of rude door, made of boards split from the larger trunks of the yucca, and hung with strong straps of *parflèche*, or thick buffalo leather. Also a hole that served for a window, with a shutter of the same material, and similarly suspended. The walls were a wattle of vines and slender poles bent around the uprights, and daubed carelessly with a lining of mud. The smooth vertical rock served for one side of the house—so that so much labour had been spared in the building—and the chimney, which was nothing better than a hole in the roof, conducted the smoke in such a manner that a sooty streak marked its course up the face of the cliff. The door entered at one end, close in by the rock, but the window was in the side or front. Through the latter the inmates of the hut could command a view of any one approaching by the regular path. This, however, was a rare occurrence, as the brace of rude hunters had but few acquaintances, and their dwelling was far removed from any frequented route. Indeed, the general track of travel that led along the bottom line of the bluffs did not approach within several hundred yards of this point, in consequence of the indentation or bay in which the hut was placed. Moreover, the thick chapparal screened it from observation on one side, while the cliffs shut it in upon the other.

Behind the house—that is, at the hinder end of it—was a small *corral*, its walls rudely constructed with fragments of rock. In this stood three lean and sore-backed mules, and a brace of mustangs no better off. There was a field adjoining the corral, or what had once been a field, but from neglect had run into a bed of grass and weeds. A portion of it, however, showed signs of cultivation—a patch here and there—on which stood some maize-plants, irregularly set and badly hoed, and between their stems the trailing tendrils of the melon and calabash. It was a true squatter's plantation.

Around the door lay half-a-dozen wolfish-looking dogs; and under the shelter of the overhanging rock, two or three old pack-saddles rested upon the ground. Upon a horizontal pole two riding saddles were set astride— old, worn, and torn—and from the same pole hung a pair of bridles, and some strings of jerked meat and pods of chilé pepper.

Inside the house might have been seen a couple of Indian women, not over cleanly in their appearance, engaged in kneading coarse bread and stewing tasajo. A fire burnt against the rock, between two stones—earthen pots and gourd dishes lay littered over the floor.

The walls were garnished with bows, quivers, and skins of animals, and a pair of embankments of stones and mud, one at each corner of the room—there was but one room—served as bedstead and beds. A brace of long spears rested in one corner, alongside a rifle and a Spanish *escopeta*; and above hung a machete or sword-knife, with powder-horns, pouches, and other equipments necessary to a hunter of the Rocky Mountains. There were nets and other implements for fishing and taking small game, and these constituted the chief furniture of the hovel. All these things Roblado might have seen by entering the hut; but he did not enter, as the men he was in search of chanced to be outside—the mulatto lying stretched along the ground, and the zambo swinging in a hammock between two trees, according to the custom of his native country—the coast-lands of the *tierra caliente*.

The aspect of these men, that would have been displeasing to almost any one else, satisfied Roblado. They were just the men for his work. He had seen both before, but had never scrutinised them till now; and, as he glanced at their bold swarthy faces and brawny muscular frames, he thought to himself, "These are just the fellows to deal with the cibolero." A formidable pair they looked. Each one of them, so far as appearance went, might with safety assail an antagonist like the cibolero—for either of them was bigger and bulkier than he.

The mulatto was the taller of the two. He was also superior in strength, courage, and sagacity. A more unamiable countenance it would have been difficult to meet in all that land, without appealing to that of the zambo. There you found its parallel.

The skin of the former was dull yellow in colour, with a thin beard over the cheeks and around the lips. The lips were negro-like, thick, and purplish, and behind them appeared a double row of large wolfish teeth. The eyes were sunken—their whites mottled with yellowish flakes. Heavy dark brows shadowed them, standing far apart, separated by the broad flatfish nose, the nostrils of which stood so widely open as to cause a protuberance on each side. Large ears were hidden under a thick frizzled shock that partook of the character both of hair and wool. Over this was bound, turban fashion, an old check Madras kerchief that had not come in contact with soap for many a day; and from under its folds the woolly hair straggled down over the forehead so as to add to the wild and fierce expression of the face. It was a countenance that proclaimed ferocity, reckless daring, cunning, and an utter absence of all humane sentiment.

The dress of the man had little in it differing from others who lead the life of a prairie-hunter. It was a mixture of leather and blanket. The head-dress only was peculiar. That was an old souvenir of the Southern States and their negro life.

The zambo had a face as ferocious in its expression as that of his confrère. It differed in colour. It was a coppery black—combining the hues of both races from whom he derived his origin. He had the thick lips and retreating forehead of the negro, but the Indian showed itself in his hair, which scarcely waved, but hung in long snaky tresses about his neck and shoulders. He was altogether less distinguished-looking than his comrade the mulatto. His dress partook of the character of his tribe—wide trousers of coarse cotton stuff, with a sleeveless shirt of the same material,—a waist scarf, and coarse serapé. Half the upper part of his body was nude, and his thick copper-coloured arms were quite bare.

Roblado arrived just in time to witness the *finale* of an incident that would serve to illustrate the character of the zambo.

He was half sitting, half-lying in his hammock, in the enjoyment of a husk cigar, and occasionally striking at the flies with his raw-hide whip. He called out to one of the women—his wife for the time—

"Niña! I want to eat something—is the *guisado* ready?"

"Not yet," answered a voice from the hut.

"Bring me a tortilla then, with chilé Colorado."

"*Querido*—you know there is no chilé Colorado in the house," was the reply.

"Niña! come here! I want you."

The woman came out, and approached the hammock, but evidently with some mistrust.

The zambo sat perfectly silent until she was close enough for his purpose, and then, suddenly raising the raw-hide, which he had hitherto held behind him, he laid it with all his strength over her back and shoulders. A thin chemisette was all that intervened to hinder the full severity of the blows, and these fell thick end fast, until the sufferer took courage and retreated out of reach!

"Now, Niña, dear love! the next time I call for a tortilla with chilé Colorado you'll have it—won't you, dear pet?"

And then laying himself back in his hammock, the savage uttered a roar of laughter, in which he was joined by the mulatto, who would have done just the same by his better half for a like provocation!

It was just at this crisis Roblado pulled up in front of the hovel.

Both got to their feet to receive him, and both saluted him with a gesture of respect. They knew who he was. The mulatto, as the principal man, took the principal part in the conversation, while the zambo hung in the background.

The dialogue was carried on in a low tone on account of the woman and the boy Esteban. It resulted, however, in the hunters being engaged, as the padré had suggested, to track and follow the cibolero Carlos to death or capture. If the former, a large sum was to be their reward—if the latter, a sum still larger—nearly double!

With regard to assistance from the troops, neither mulatto nor zambo wished for any. Quite the contrary. They had no desire that the magnificent bounty should be diminished by subdivision. As it stood, it would be a small fortune to both of them, and the brilliant prospect whetted their appetite for the success of the job.

His errand having been thus accomplished, the officer rode back to the Presidio; while the man-hunters immediately set about making preparations for expedition.

Chapter Fifty Two

The mulatto and zambo—Manuel and Pepe were their respective names—in half-an-hour after were ready for the road. Their preparations did not cost them half that time; but a quarter of an hour was spent on the *guisado,* and each smoked a husk cigarrito, while their horses were grinding up the half-dozen heads of green maize that had been thrown them.

Having finished their cigars, the hunters leaped into their saddles, and rode off.

The mulatto was armed with a long rifle, of the kind used by American hunters, and a knife of the sort since known as a "Bowie," with a strong thick blade keenly pointed and double-edged for some inches from the point—a terrible weapon in close combat. These arms he had brought with him from the Mississippi valley, where he had learnt how to use them.

The zambo carried an escopeta strapped in a slanting direction along the flap of his saddle, a machete upon his thigh, and a bow with a quiver of arrows hung over his back. The last of these weapons—for certain purposes, such as killing game, or when a silent shot may be desirable—is preferred to any sort of fire-arms. Arrows can be delivered more rapidly than bullets, and, should the first shot fail, the intended victim is less likely to be made aware of the presence of his enemy.

In addition to these weapons, both had pistols stuck in their belts, and lazos hanging coiled from their saddle-bows.

Behind them on the croup each carried his provisions—a few strips of tasajo with some cold tortillas tied in a piece of buckskin. A double-headed calabash for water, with sundry horns, pouches, and bags, completed their equipment. A pair of huge gaunt dogs trotted behind their horses' heels, fierce and savage-looking as their masters. One was the wolf-dog of the country, the other a Spanish bloodhound.

"What road, Man'l?" inquired the zambo as they parted from the hut; "straight down to the Pecos?"

"No, Pepe boy: must climb, go round. Seen making down valley, somebody guess what we're after—send him word we're coming. He suspect—we not grow rich so easily. No—must get up by old track—cross to dry gully—down that to Pecos. Take longer—make things surer, boy Pepe."

"Carrambo!" exclaimed Pepe. "It's a murderous climb. My poor beast's so jaded with the buffalo running, that he'll scarce get up. *Carrai!*"

After a short ride through the thicket and along the bottom of the cliffs, they arrived at a point where a ravine sloped to the upper plain. Up the bottom of this ravine was a difficult pass—difficult on account of its steepness. Any other horses than mountain-reared mustangs would have refused it, but these can climb like cats. Even the dogs could scarcely crawl up this ascent. In spite of its almost vertical slope, the hunters dismounted, crawled up, and, pulling their horses after them, soon reached the table-land above.

After breathing themselves and their animals, they once more got astride, and, heading northward, rode rapidly off over the plain.

"Now, boy Pepe," muttered the mulatto, "chance meet any sheep-keepers, going after antelope; you hear?"

"Ay, Man'l; I understand."

These were the last words exchanged between them for ten miles. They rode in file—the mulatto in the lead, the zambo in his tracks, and the dogs following in the rear. These two went also in file, the bloodhound heading the wolf.

At the end of ten miles they reached a dry river channel, that ran transversely across their route. It was the same which Carlos and his party had followed on the day of their escape after the affair at the Presidio. The hunters entered it, and, turning downward, as Carlos had done, followed it to its mouth upon the banks of the Pecos. Here was a grove of timber, which they entered, and, having dismounted, tied their horses to the trees. These animals, though lately arrived from a long journey, and now having passed over more than thirty miles at a brisk rate, showed no symptoms of being done up. Lean though they were, they possessed the tough wiry strength of their race, and either of them could have gone another hundred miles without breaking down.

This their masters well knew, else they would have gone upon their man-hunt with less confidence of success.

"May gallop away on his fine black," remarked the mulatto, as he glanced at the mustangs. "Soon overhaul him again—won't we, boy Pepe?"

"*Chinga!* we will."

"Brace of hacks tire out racer,—won't they, boy Pepe?"

"*Chingara*! So they will, Man'l."

"Don't want to try that game though—do the job easier; won't we, boy Pepe?"

"I hope so, Man'l."

"Cibolero in the cave sure—stays there—no better place for him. Won't be caught sleeping,—troopers never follow him up the pass. Convenient to valley. Goes back and forward spite of spies. Tracks could lead nowhere else—sure in the cave, horse and all. When? that the trouble, boy Pepe."

"*Es verdad*! if we knew when he was in, or when he was out, either."

"Ay, knew that, no difficulty,—set our trap easy enough, boy Pepe."

"He must surely be there in daytime?"

"Just been thinking—goes to the settlements—must be by night, that's clear—goes there, boy Pepe, maybe not to rancho, somewhere near. Must go to meet Anton. Not like Anton meet him at cave—güero too sharp for that—goes out to meet Anton, sure!"

"Might we not track Anton?"

"Might track Anton—no good that—would have to deal with both together. Besides, don't want kill Anton—no ill-will to Anton—make things worse if find Anton with him. Never do, boy Pepe—have hands full with güero himself—plenty do capture him. Must not forget capture—not kill—leave that to them. No use track Anton—know where t'other keeps. If didn't know that, then might track Anton."

"Can't we get near the cave in daylight, Man'l? I don't have a good memory of the place."

"Mile—no nearer—unless he sleep—when sleep? Tell me that, boy Pepe!"

"And suppose he be awake?"

"See us enter the cañon, mile off—jump into saddle, pass up to plain above—maybe three days before find him again—maybe not find at all, boy Pepe."

"Well, brother Man'l—I have a plan. Let us get near the mouth of the cañon, and hide outside of it till night—then as soon as it is dark creep into where it narrows. He will come down that way to go out. What then? we can have a shot at him as he passes!"

"Pooh, boy Pepe! Think lose chance of half reward—risk whole by shot in dark? Dam! no—have whole or none—set us up for life—take him alive, take him alive, sure."

"Well then," rejoined the zambo, "let him pass out of the cañon, and when he's gone clear out of reach we can go up, get into the cave, and wait his return. What say you to that?"

"Talk sense now, boy Pepe—something like plan about that—what we do—but not go inside cañon till güero clear away. Only near enough see him go out, then for cave—right plan to take him. Sun near dawn, time we start—come!"

"*Vamos!*"

Both mounted, and rode forward to the bank of the river. There was no ford at the spot, but what of that? With scarce a moment's delay they plunged their horses into the stream and swam across. The dogs followed their example, and all came out dripping on the opposite bank. The evening was chill, but what was heat or cold to such men? Nothing signified their wet clothes to them; and without halting they rode straight forward to the ceja of the Llano Estacado, and having reached it turned to the right, and rode along the base of the bluffs.

After following the line of the ceja for two or three miles they approached a spur of the cliff that ran out into the plain, and gradually tapered to a point, sinking lower as it receded from the Llano. It ended in a clump, or rather several clusters, of isolated rocks and boulders that stood near each other. The place was not timbered, but the dark rocks irregularly piled upon each other gave it a shaggy appearance; and among their crevices, and the spaces between them, was ample room for even a large party both of men and horses to lie concealed.

The end of this rocky promontory was the point towards which the mulatto was steering. It formed one side of the ravine in which lay the cave, while another similar ridge bounded the ravine on its southern side. Between them a deep bay indented the cliff, from which a narrow difficult pass opened up to the high plain above. It was the same ravine in which the cattle of the young ranchero Don Juan had been slaughtered! These were no longer to be seen, but their bones were still visible, scattered over the plain, and already bleached white. The wolves, vultures, and bears, had prepared them for that.

The man-hunters at length reached their destination; and, having led their horses in among the loose boulders, fastened them securely. They then crept up through crevices in the rocks, until they had reached the crest of the ridge. From this point they commanded a view of the whole mouth of the land-bay, about three hundred yards in width, so that no object, such as a man or horse, could pass out or in without their observing it—unless the night should chance to be very dark indeed. But they expected moonlight, by the help of which not even a cat could enter the ravine without their seeing it.

Having found a spot to their liking, they lay down, with their bodies concealed from any one who might be passing on the plain below either in front of or behind them. Their horses were already hidden among the large masses of rock.

To the minds of both their purposed plan of action was clearly understood. They had their reasons for believing that the cibolero, during his period of outlawry, was dwelling in a cave that opened into this ravine, and which was well-known to the mulatto; that Carlos came out in the night, and approached the settlements—the place was but ten miles from his own rancho—and that he was met somewhere by Antonio, who gave him information of what was going on, bringing him provisions at the same time.

It was their intention to wait until Carlos should pass out, then occupy the cave themselves, and attack him on his return. True they might have waylaid him on his going forth, but that might result in a failure. Catch him they could not while mounted. They might have crept near enough to get a shot at him, but, as the mulatto had said, that would have risked their losing him altogether.

Moreover, neither wanted to take only his scalp. The mulatto in particular had resolved on earning the double price by *taking him alive*. Even though it cost them some additional risk, his capture would doubly reward them, and for money these desperadoes were ready to venture anything. Withal, they were not so daring as to have cared for an open encounter. They knew something of the mettle of "el güero," but they trusted to the advantage they should obtain over him by stratagem. On starting out they had resolved to follow him up, and steal upon him when asleep—and the plan which they had now formed had been the result of cogitations by the way. In Manuel's mind it had been developed long before the suggestion of the zambo.

They rested their hopes upon the belief that their victim would not know that they were after him—he could not have heard of their return from the buffalo-hunt, and therefore would be less on the alert. They knew if Carlos became aware that they were upon his trail he would pursue a *very* different course from that observed towards his soldier-pursuers. From these he could easily hide at any time upon the Llano Estacado, but it was different with men like the hunters, who, though they might not overtake him at the first burst, could follow on and find him again wherever he should ride to.

But both mulatto and zambo believed that their presence would be unsuspected by the güero, until they had laid hands upon him. Hence their confidence of success.

They certainly had taken measures that promised it, supposing their hypothesis to be correct—that is, supposing the cibolero to be in the cave at that moment, and that during the night he should come out of the ravine.

They were soon to know—the sun had already gone down. They would not have long to watch.

Chapter Fifty Three

Carlos *was* in the cave, and at that very moment. Ever since the affair at the Presidio he had made it his dwelling, his "lair," and for reasons very similar to those which the mulatto had imparted to his companion. It afforded him a safe retreat, and at a convenient distance from his friends in the valley. Out of the ravine he could pass with safety by night, returning before day. During the day he slept. He had little fear of being tracked thither by the troopers; but even had they done so, his cave entrance commanded a full view of the ravine to its mouth at nearly a mile's distance, and any one approaching from that direction could be perceived long before they were near. If a force of troopers should enter by the mouth of the ravine, though both sides were inaccessible cliffs, the cibolero had his way of escape. As already stated, a narrow pass, steep and difficult, led from the upper end of the gully to the plain above. Steep and difficult as it was, it could be scaled by the black horse; and, once on the wide plain of the Llano Estacado, Carlos could laugh at his soldier-pursuers.

The only time his enemies could have reached him would be during his hours of sleep, or after darkness had fallen. But Carlos was not afraid even then. He went to sleep with as much unconcern as if he had been surrounded by a body-guard! This is explained by a knowledge of the fact that he *had* his guard—a faithful guard—the dog Cibolo; for although Cibolo had received some lance-thrusts in his last terrible encounter, he had escaped without any fatal wound. He was still by the side of his master. While the latter slept the sagacious animal sat upon the ledge, and watched the ravine below. The sight of a soldier's uniform would have raised the hair along Cibolo's back and drawn from him the warning growl. Even in the darkness no one could have got within several hundred yards of the cave without attracting the notice of the dog, who would have given his master time to get off from the most rapid pursuers.

The cave was a large one, large enough to hold both men and horses. Water, pure crystal water, dripped from the rocks near its inner end, and lay collected in a tank, that from its round bowl-like shape seemed to have been fashioned by the hand of man. But it was not so. Nature had formed this bowl and filled it with choicest water. Such a formation is by no means uncommon in that region. Caves containing similar tanks exist in the Waco and Guadalupe Mountains lying still farther to the south.

It was just the spot for a hiding-place—a refuge for either robber, outlaw, or other fugitive; and circumstanced as Carlos was it was the very dwelling for him. He had long known of its existence, and shared that knowledge only with hunters like himself and the wild Indians. No settlers of the valley ever ventured up that dark and dismal ravine.

In his lair Carlos had ample time for reflection, and bitter often were his reflections. He had information of all that passed. Antonio managed that. Nightly did he meet Antonio at a point on the Pecos, and receive from him the "novedades" of the settlement. The cunning mulatto had guessed correctly. Had Antonio brought his news direct to the cave, he might have been followed, and the hiding-place of Carlos have been thus discovered. To prevent that the cibolero nightly went forth to meet him.

Antonio, in collecting the news of the settlement, found in the young girl Josefa an able adjutant. Through her he learnt that Catalina de Cruces was kept under lock and key—that Roblado had only been wounded, and would recover—that new officers went out with the scouting-parties—and that his master's head had risen in price. The shallow artifice of the spies around the rancho had long been known to Carlos. Shallow as it was, it greatly annoyed him, as by these he was prevented from visiting his mother and sister. Through Antonio, however, he kept up almost daily communication with them. He might have been apprehensive in regard to his sister after what had occurred, but the villain Vizcarra was an invalid, and Carlos rightly judged why Rosita was permitted to go unmolested. He had little fear for her—at least for a time—and ere that time expired he should bear her away, far out of the reach of such danger.

It was for that opportunity he was now waiting. With, all the vigilance of his foes, he had no fear but that he could *steal* his own mother and sister almost at any time. But another was to be the companion of their flight—another dear as they, and far more closely guarded!

For her only did he risk life daily—for her only did he sit hour after hour in that lone cave brooding over plans, and forming schemes of desperate peril.

Kept under lock and key—closely watched from morn to night, and night till morning—how was she to be rescued from such a situation? This was the problem upon which his mind now dwelt.

She had given him the assurance of her willingness to go. Oh! why had he not proposed instant flight? Why did he neglect that golden moment?

Why should either have thought of delay? That delay had been fatal—might retard their purpose for months, for years—perhaps for ever!

But little cared Carlos for the anger of his enemies—little for the contempt in which he was held throughout the settlement—she alone was his care—his constant solicitude. His waking hours were all given to that one thought—how he would rescue, not himself, but his mistress.

No wonder he looked anxiously for the night—no wonder he rode with impatient eagerness towards that lone rendezvous on the Pecos.

Night had come again; and, leading his horse down the slope in front of the cave, he mounted and rode off toward the mouth of the cañon. The dog Cibolo trotted in advance of him.

Chapter Fifty Four

The man-hunters had not long to wait. They had anticipated this. There was a moon which they had also expected. It was a bright moon at intervals, and then obscured—for minutes at a time—by the passage of dark clouds over the canopy.

There was no wind, however, and the air was perfectly still. The slightest noise could have been heard for a long distance in the atmosphere of that elevated region—so pure and light that it vibrated afar with the slightest concussion.

Sounds were heard, but they were not made by either the dogs or horses of the hunters—well-trained to silence—nor by the hunters themselves. Both lay stretched in silence; or if they spoke, it was only in whispers and low mutterings.

The sounds were those of nature—such as it exists in that wild region. The "snort" of the grizzly bear from the rocky ledge—the howling bark of the coyote—the "hoo-hoop" of the burrowing owl, and the shrill periodical cries of the bull-bat and goatsucker. For a while these were the only sounds that fell upon the ears of the ambushed hunters.

Half-an-hour elapsed, and during all that time never permitted their eyes or ears to rest for a moment. They gazed up the ravine, and at intervals glanced outwards upon the plain. There was a probability that their victim might be abroad—even in the day—and with such men no probability was allowed to pass without examination. Should it prove to be so, and he were to return at that time, it would frustrate the plan they had arranged. But for such a contingency the mulatto had conceived another—that was, to steal during the night as near the cave as possible—within rifle-shot if he could—wait until the güero should make his appearance in the morning, and *wing* him with a bullet from his rifle—in the use of which weapon the yellow hunter was well skilled. To shoot the horse was another design. The horse once killed or crippled, the cibolero would be captured to a certainty; and both had made up their minds, in case a good opportunity offered, to despatch the noble animal.

These men knew a certain plan by which their victim could be killed or captured—that is, supposing they had been certain he was in the cave—a plan which could scarce have failed. But yet, for reasons of their own, they would not adopt it.

It would have been simple enough to have conducted a party of dragoons to the head of the pass, and there have stationed them, while another party entered the cañon from below. As the sides of the ravine were impassable precipices, the retreat of the cibolero would have been thus cut off at both ends. True, to have reached the upper plain, without going through the ravine itself—and that, as we have seen would have defeated such a plan—would have cost a journey to the troop to be stationed above. But neither Vizcarra nor Roblado would have grudged either the time or the men to have rendered success thus sure. The mulatto and his dusky camarado knew all this perfectly, but to have caused such a plan to be put in execution was the last thought in their minds. Such a course would have been attended with but little peril to them, but it would have brought as little pay, for every trooper in the whole band would have claimed equal share in the promised reward. That would not be satisfactory to the hunters, whose heads and knowledge had furnished the means and the ways.

Neither entertained any idea of following such a course. Both were confident in their ability to effect their object without aid from any quarter.

From the time they had taken their station on the rock, half-an-hour was all they had to wait. At the end of that period the quick ears of both caught the sound of some one coming from the direction of the ravine. They heard a horse's hoof striking upon loose shingle, and the rattling of the displaced pebbles. A débris of broken fragments filled the bottom of the ravine, brought there during rain-torrents. Over this ran the path. A horseman was coming down it.

"The güero!" muttered the mulatto; "be sure, boy Pepe."

"Trust you for a guess, brother Man'l: you were right about the tracks we first fell in with. The cave's his hiding-place to a certainty. We'll have him sure when he comes back. *Carrai!* yonder he comes!"

As the zambo spake, a tall dark form was perceived approaching down the ravine. By the moon gleaming upon it, they could make out the figure of a horse and rider. They had no longer any doubt it was their intended victim.

"Brother Man'l," whispered the zambo, "suppose he passes near! why not bring down the horse? you can't miss in this fine light—both of us can aim at the horse; if we stop him we'll easily overtake the güero."

"Won't do, boy Pepe—not easily overtake güero afoot. Get off among rocks—hide for days—can't track *him* afoot—be on his guard after—give us trouble—old plan best—let pass—have him safe when he come back—have him sure."

"But Man'l—"

"Dam! no need for buts—always in a hurry, boy Pepe—have patience—no buts, no fear. See, now!"

This last exclamation was intended to point out to Pepe that his suggestion, even though a wise one, could not have been carried out, as the horseman was not going to pass within range of either rifle or escopeta.

It was plain he was heading down the middle of the cañon, keeping equally distant from the sides, and this course would carry him out into the open plain two hundred yards from the ambush of the hunters.

So did it, for in a few moments he was opposite the spot where they lay, and at full that distance from them. A shot from a hunter's rifle would not have reached him, and the bullet of an escopeta would have been an uncertain messenger. Neither thought of firing, but lay in perfect silence, firmly holding their dogs down in the crevice of the rocks, and by gestures enjoining them to be still.

The horseman advanced, guiding his horse at a slow pace, and evidently observing caution as he went. While passing, the moon shone full upon him, and the bright points of his harness and arms were seen sparkling under her light. His fair complexion, too, could be distinguished easily, as also his fine erect figure, and the noble outlines of his horse.

"The güero!" muttered Manuel; "all right, boy Pepe!"

"What's yon ahead?" inquired the zambo.

"Ha! didn't notice that. Dam! a dog! dog, sure."

"It is a dog. *Malraya!*"

"Devil roast that dog!—heard of him before—splendid dog, boy Pepe. Dam! that dog give us trouble. Lucky, wind t'other way. Safe enough now. Dam! see!"

At this moment the horseman suddenly stopped, looking suspiciously in the direction of the rocky spur where they lay. The dog had given some sign.

"Dam!" again muttered the mulatto; "that dog give us trouble yet—thank our luck, wind t'other way."

There was not much wind either way, but what there was was in the faces of the hunters, and blowing from the horseman. Fortunately for them it was so, also Cibolo would have scented them to a certainty.

Even as things stood, their ambush was near enough discovery. Some slight noise from that quarter—perhaps the hoof of one of their horses against the turf—had awakened the dog's suspicions—though nothing had been heard by his master. Neither was the dog sure—for the next moment he threw down his head and trotted on. The horseman followed and in a few minutes both were out of sight.

"Now, boy Pepe, for the cave!"

"*Vamos!*"

Both descended from the ridge, and, mounting their horses, rode through among the scattered rocks. They entered the ravine, and kept up its edge until the gradual narrowing brought them into the same path by which the horseman had lately descended. Up this they rode, keeping their eyes bent on the cliff to the right—for on that side was the cave.

They had no fear of their tracks being discernible, even should the güero return by daylight, for the path lay over hard rock already marked by the hoofs of his own horse. For all that the mulatto was uneasy; and at intervals repeated half to himself, and half in the hearing of his companion—

"Dam! dog give trouble, sure give trouble—dam!"

At length the mouth of the cave, like a dark spot upon the rock, appeared on one side. After silently dismounting, and leaving his horse with Pepe, the mulatto crawled up the ledge and reconnoitred the entrance. Even the probability that some one might have been left there was not overlooked by this keen hunter, and every precaution was taken.

After listening a moment at the entrance he sent in the dogs, and, as neither bark nor howl came out again, he was satisfied that all was safe. He then crawled in himself, keeping on the shadowy side of the rock. When he had got fairly within the cavern, he struck a light, at the same time shading it so that the gleam might not fall on the outside. With this he made a hurried examination of the interior; and, now satisfied that the place was untenanted, he came out again, and beckoned his comrade to bring up the horses.

These were led into the cave. Another reconnaissance was made, in which the few articles used by Carlos for eating and sleeping were discovered upon a dry ledge. A serapé, a small hatchet for cutting firewood, an olla for cooking, two or three cups, some pieces of jerked meat and fragments of bread, were the contents of the cavern.

The best of these were appropriated by the intruders; and then, after fastening their horses in a secure corner, and making themselves thoroughly acquainted with the shape and position of the rocky interior, the light was extinguished, and, like beasts of prey, they placed themselves in readiness to receive their unsuspecting victim.

Chapter Fifty Five

Carlos, on leaving his cave, proceeded with the caution natural to one circumstanced as he was. But this night he was more than usually careful. He scanned every bush and rock that stood near his path, and that might have sheltered an enemy. Why to-night more cautious than before? Because a suspicion had crossed his mind—and that, too, having reference to the very men who were at the moment in ambush so near him!

At various times of late had his thoughts reverted to these men. He knew them well, and knew the hostile feelings with which both, but particularly the mulatto, regarded him. He thought of the probability of their being set upon his trail, and he knew their capability to follow it. This had made him *more* uneasy than all the scouting of the dragoons with their unpractised leaders. He was aware that, if the cunning mulatto and his scarce less sagacious comrade were sent after him, his cave would not shelter him long, and there would be an end to his easy communication with the settlement.

These thoughts were sources of uneasiness; and would have been still more so, had he not believed that the hunters were absent upon the plains. Under this belief he had hopes of being able to settle his affairs and get off before their return. That morning, however, his hopes had met with discouragement.

It was a little after daylight when he returned to his hiding-place. Antonio, watched closely by the spies, had not been able to reach the rendezvous until a late hour,—hence the detention of Carlos. On going back to his cave he had crossed a fresh trail coming in from the northern end of the Llano Estacado. It was a trail of horses, mules, and dogs; and Carlos, on scrutinising it, soon acquainted himself with the number of each that had passed. He knew it was the exact number of these animals possessed by the yellow hunter and his comrade; and this startled him with the suspicion that it was the return trail of these men from their hunt upon the prairies!

A further examination quite assured him of the truth of this. The footprints of one of the dogs differed from the rest; and although a large one, it was not the track of the common wolf-dog of the country. He had heard that the yellow hunter had lately become possessed of a large bloodhound. These must be *his* tracks!

Carlos rode along the trail to a point where it had crossed an old path of his own leading to the ravine. To his astonishment he perceived that, from this point, one of the horsemen, with several of the dogs, had turned off and followed his own tracks in that direction! No doubt the man had been trailing him. After going some distance, however, the latter had turned again and ridden back upon his former course.

Carlos would have traced this party farther, as he knew they must have passed on the evening before. But as it was now quite day, and their trail evidently led to the settlements, he dared not ride in that direction, and therefore returned to his hiding-place.

The incident had rendered him thoughtful and apprehensive throughout the whole of that day; and as he rode forth his reflections were upon this very subject—hence the caution of his movements.

As he emerged from the ravine, the dog, as stated, made a demonstration, by suddenly turning toward the rocks, and uttering a low growl. This caused Carlos to halt, and look carefully in that direction. But he could see nothing that appeared suspicious; and the dog, after a moment's pause, appeared satisfied and trotted on again.

"Some wild animal, perhaps," thought Carlos, as he set his horse in motion, and continued on over the plain.

When fairly out into the open ground, he quickened his pace; and after a ride of about six or seven miles arrived on the banks of the Pecos. Here he turned down-stream, and, once more riding with caution, approached a grove of low timber that grew upon the bank. This grove was the point of rendezvous.

When within a hundred yards of it, the cibolero halted upon the plain. The dog ran on before him, quartered the grove, and then returned to his master. The horseman then rode boldly in under the shadow of the trees, and, dismounting, took station upon one side of the timber, to watch for the coming of his expected messenger.

His vigil was not of long duration. In a few minutes a man on foot, bent into a crouching attitude, was seen rapidly advancing over the plain. When he had arrived within three hundred yards of the grove, he stopped in his tracks, and uttered a low whistle. To this signal the cibolero replied, and the man, again advancing as before, was soon within the shadow of the grove. It was Antonio.

"Were you followed, amigo?" asked Carlos.

"As usual, master; but I had no difficulty in throwing them off."

"Hereafter it may not be so easy."

"How, master?"

"I know your news—the yellow hunter has got back?"

"Carrambo! it is even so! How did you hear it, master?"

"This morning, after you had left me, I crossed a trail—I knew it must be theirs."

"It was theirs, master. They came in last evening but I have worse news than that."

"Worse!—what?"

"They're after *you!*"

"Ha! already? I guessed that they would be, but not so soon. How know you, Anton!"

"Josefa—she has a brother who is a kind of errand-boy to Padré Joaquin. This morning the Padré took him over to the Presidio, and from there sent him to guide Captain Roblado to the yellow hunter's hut. The Padré threatened the boy if he should tell any one; but on his return to the mission he called on his mother; and Josefa, suspecting he had been on some strange errand—for he showed a piece of silver—got it all out of him. He couldn't tell what Roblado and the hunters talked about, but he fancied the latter were preparing to go somewhere as he left them. Now, putting one thing with another, I'm of the mind, master, they're on your trail."

"No doubt of it, amigo—I haven't the slightest doubt of it. So—I'll be chased out of my cave—that's certain. I believe they have a suspicion of where I am already. Well, I must try to find another resting-place. 'Tis well I have got the wind of these rascals—they'll not catch me asleep, which no doubt they flatter themselves they're going to do. What other news?"

"Nothing particular. Josefa saw the girl Vicenza last night in company with José, but she has had no opportunity of getting a word with the señorita, who is watched closely. She has some business with the portero's wife to-morrow. She hopes to hear something from her."

"Good Antonio," said Carlos, dropping a piece of money into the other's hand, "give this to Josefa—tell her to be active. Our hopes rest entirely with her."

"Don't fear, master!" replied the half-blood. "Josefa will do her best, for the reason that," smiling, "*her* hopes, I believe, rest entirely upon *me.*"

Carlos laughed at the *naïve* remark of his faithful companion, and then proceeded to inquire about other matters,—about his mother and sister, about the troopers, the spies, and Don Juan.

About the last Antonio could give him no information that was new. Don Juan had been arrested the day after the affair at the Presidio, and ever since had been kept a close prisoner. The charge against him was his having been an accomplice of Carlos, and his trial would take place whenever the latter should be captured.

Half-an-hour was spent in conversation, and then Carlos, having received from the half-blood the packages containing provisions, prepared to return to his hiding-place in the Llano Estacado.

"You will meet me here to-morrow night again, Anton," said he at parting. "If anything should happen to prevent me coming, then look for me the night after, and the night after that. So *buenas noches, amigo!*"

"*Buenos noches, mi amo!*" ("Good night, master!")

And with this salutation the friends—for they were go—turned their backs on each other and parted.

Antonio went crouching back in the direction of the valley; while the cibolero, springing to his saddle, rode off toward the frowning bluffs of the Llano.

Chapter Fifty Six

The "report" delivered by Antonio was of a character to have caused serious apprehension to the cibolero—fear, in fact, had he been the man to have such a feeling. It had the effect of still further increasing his caution, and his mind was now bent with all its energies upon the craft of taking care of himself.

Had he contemplated an open fight, even with the two strong men who were seeking him, he would have been less uneasy about the result; but he knew that, strong as they were, these ruffians would not attack him without some advantage. They would make every effort to surprise him asleep, or otherwise take him unawares. Against their wiles he had now to guard himself.

He rode slowly back to the ravine, his thoughts all the while busied about the yellow hunter and his companion.

"They must know of the cave," so ran his reflections. "Their following my trail yesterday is an evidence that they suspected something in the direction of the ravine. They had no doubt heard of late affairs before getting so far. Some *hatero* on the outer plains has told them all, very like; well, what then? They have hastened on to the mission. Ha! the Padré Joaquin took the boy over to the Presidio. I see—I see—the Padré is the 'patron' of these two ruffians. They have told him something, else why should he be off to the Presidio so early? News from them—and then Roblado starting directly after to seek them! Clear—clear—they have discovered my hiding-place!"

After a pause:—

"What if they have reached the ravine in my absence? Let me see. Yes, they've had time enough to get round; that is, if they started soon after Roblado's interview. The boy thinks they did. By Heaven! it's not too soon for me to be on the alert."

As this thought passed through the cibolero's mind, he reined up his horse; and, lowering his head, glanced along the neck of the animal into the darkness before him. He had now arrived at the mouth of the cañon, and nearly on the same track by which he had ridden out of it; but the moon was under thick clouds, and the gloom of the ravine was no longer relieved by her light.

"It would be their trick," reflected he, "to get inside the cañon, at its narrow part, and wait for me to come out of the cave. They would waylay me pretty handy there. Now suppose they *are* up the cañon at this moment!"

For a moment he paused and dwelt upon this hypothesis. He proceeded again.

"Well, let them; I'll ride on. Cibolo can beat the rocks a shot's range ahead of me. If they're ambushed there without him finding them, they'll be sharper fellows than I take them to be; and I don't consider them flats, either, the scoundrels! If he start them, I can soon gallop back out of their reach. Here! Cibolo!"

The dog, that had stopped a few paces in front, now came running back, and looked up in his master's face. The latter gave him a sign, uttering the simple word "Anda!"

At the word the animal sprang off, and commenced quartering the ground for a couple of hundred yards in advance.

Following him, the horseman moved forward.

In this way he approached the point where the two walls converging narrowed the cañon to a space of little more than a hundred yards. Along the bases of the cliffs, on both sides, lay large loose rocks, that would have given cover to men in ambush, and even horses might have been concealed behind them.

"This," thought Carlos, "would be the place chosen for their cowardly attack. They might hit me from either side with half an aim. But Cibolo makes no sign.—Ha!"

The last exclamation was uttered in a short sharp tone. It had been called forth by a low yelp from the dog. The animal had struck the trail where the yellow hunter and his companion had crossed to the middle of the ravine. The moon had again emerged from the clouds, and Carlos could see the dog dashing swiftly along the pebbles and up the ravine towards the mouth of the cavern!

His master would have called him back, for he was leaving the loose rocks unsearched, and, without that being done, Carlos felt that it would be perilous to proceed farther; but the swiftness with which the dog had gone forward showed that he was on a fresh trail; and it now occurred to the cibolero that his enemies might be within the cave itself!

The thought had hardly crossed his mind when the dog uttered several successive yelps! Although he had got out of sight, his master knew that he was at that moment approaching the mouth of the cave, and running upon a fresh scent.

Carlos drew up his horse and listened. He dare proceed no farther. He dared not recall the dog. His voice would have been heard if any one were near. He reflected that he could do no better than wait till the dog should return, or by his attack give some sign of what he was after. It might, after all, be the grizzly bear, or some other animal, he was pursuing.

The cibolero sat upon his horse in perfect silence—not unprepared though for any sudden attack. His true rifle lay across his thighs, and he had already looked to its flint and priming. He listened to every sound, while his eyes pierced the dark recesses of the ravine before and around him.

For only a few moments this uncertainty lasted, and then back down the chasm came a noise that caused the listener to start in his saddle. It resembled the worrying of dogs, and for a moment Carlos fancied that Cibolo had made his attack upon a bear! Only a moment did this illusion last, for his quick ear soon detected the voices of more dogs than one; and in the fierce confusion he distinguished the deep-toned bark of a *bloodhound*!

The whole situation became clear to him at once. His enemies had been awaiting him in the cave—for from it he was certain that the sounds proceeded.

His first instinct was to wheel his horse and gallop out of the cañon. He waited a moment, however, and listened.

The worrying noise continued, but, amid the roar find barking of the dogs, Carlos could distinguish the voices of men, uttered in low hurried tones, as if addressing the dogs and also one another.

All at once the conflict appeared to cease, for the animals became silent, except the hound, who at intervals gave out his deep loud bray. In a moment more he, too, was silent.

Carlos knew by this silence that Cibolo had either been killed upon the spot, or, having been attacked by men, had sheered off. In either case it would be of no use waiting his return. If alive, he knew that the dog would follow and overtake him. Without further delay, therefore, he turned his horse's head, and galloped back down the ravine.

Chapter Fifty Seven

On arriving at the month of the ravine he halted—not in the middle of the plain, but under the shadow of the rocks—the same rocks where the hunters had placed themselves in ambush. He did not dismount, but sat in his saddle, gazing up the cañon, and listening for some token of the expected pursuit.

He had not been long in this spot when he perceived a dark object approaching him. It gave him joy, for he recognised Cibolo coming along his trail. The next moment the dog was by his stirrup. The cibolero bent down in his saddle, and perceived that the poor brute was badly cut and bleeding profusely. Several gashes appeared along his side, and one near his shoulder exhibited a flap of hanging skin, over which the red stream was pouring. The animal was evidently weak from loss of blood, and tottered in his tracks.

"Amigo!" said Carlos, "you have saved my life to a certainty. It's my turn to save yours—if I can."

As he said this he dismounted, and, taking the dog in his arms, climbed back into the saddle.

For a while he sat reflecting what to do, with his eyes turned in the direction from which he expected the pursuit.

He had now no doubt as to who were the occupants of the cave. The bay of the hound was satisfactory evidence of the presence of the yellow hunter, and of course the zambo was along with him. Carlos knew of no other bloodhound in the settlement—the one heard must be that of the mulatto.

For some minutes he remained by the rocks, considering what course he had best take.

"I'll ride on to the grove," reflected he, "and hide in it till Antonio comes. They can't track me this night—it will be too dark. The whole sky is becoming clouded—there will be no more moon to-night I can lie hid all day to-morrow, if they don't follow. If they do, why, I can see them far enough off to ride away. My poor Cibolo, how you bleed! Heavens, what a gash! Patience, brave friend! When we halt, your wounds shall be looked to. Yes! to the grove I'll go. They won't suspect me of taking that direction, as it is towards the settlements. Besides they can't trail me in the darkness. Ha!

what am I thinking of?—not trail me in the darkness! What! I had forgotten the bloodhound! O God, preserve me! These fiends can follow me were it as dark as pitch! God preserve me!"

An anxious expression came over his countenance, and partly from the burden he held in his arms, and partly from the weight of his thoughts, he dropped into an attitude that betokened deep depression. For the first time the hunted outlaw showed symptoms of despair.

For a long while he remained with his head leaning forward, and his body bent over the neck of his horse.

But he had not yet yielded to despair.

All at once he started up, as if some thought, suddenly conceived, had given him hopes. A new resolution seemed to have been taken.

"Yes!" he soliloquised, "I shall go to the grove—direct to the grove. Ha! you bloodthirsty yellow-skin, I'll try your boasted skill. We shall see—we shall see. Maybe you'll get your reward, but not that you are counting upon. You have yet something to do before you take the scalp of Carlos the cibolero!"

Muttering these words he turned his horse's head, renewed his hold of the dog and the bridle, and set off across the plain.

He rode at a rapid pace, and without casting a look behind him. He appeared to be in a hurry, though it could not be from fear of being overtaken. No one was likely to come up with him, so long as he kept on at such a pace.

He was silent, except now and then when he addressed some kind word to the dog Cibolo, whose blood ran over his thighs, and down the flanks of the horse. The poor brute was weak, and could no longer have kept his feet.

"Patience, old friend!—patience!—you shall soon have rest from this jolting."

In less than an hour he had reached the lone grove on the Pecos—the same where he had lately parted with Antonio. Here he halted. It was the goal of his journey. Within that grove he had resolved on passing the remainder of the night, and, if not disturbed, the whole of the following day.

The Pecos at this point, and for many miles above and below, ran between low banks that rose vertically from the water. On both sides its "bottom" was a smooth plain, extending for miles back, where it stepped up to a higher level. It was nearly treeless. Scattered clumps grew at distant intervals, and along its margin a slight fringing of willows. This fringe was not continuous, but broken here and there by gaps, through which the water might be seen. The timber clumps were composed of cotton-wood trees and live-oak, with acacias forming an underwood, and occasionally plants of cactus growing near.

These groves were so small, and so distant from each other, that they did not intercept the general view of the surface, and a person occupying one of them could see a horseman, or other large object, at a great distance. A man concealed in them could not have been approached by his enemy in daylight, if awake and watching. At night, of course, it was different, and the security then afforded depended upon the degree of darkness.

The "motte" at which the cibolero had arrived was far apart from any of the others, and commanded a view of the river bottom on both sides for more than a mile's distance. The grove itself was but a few acres in size, but the fringe of willows running along the stream at both ends gave it, when viewed from a distance, the appearance of a wood of larger dimensions. It stood upon the very bank of the stream, and the selvedge of willows looked like its prolongation. These, however, reached but a few feet from the water's edge, while the grove timber ran out several hundred yards into the plain.

About this grove there was a peculiarity. Its central part was not timbered, but open, and covered only with a smooth sward of gramma-grass. It was, in fact, a glade, nearly circular in shape, and about a hundred yards in diameter. On one side of this glade the river impinged, its bank being almost a tangent line to it. Here there was a gap in the timber, so that out of the glade could be obtained a view of the bottom on the other side of the stream. Diametrically opposite to this gap another opening, of an avenue-like form, led out into the adjacent plain, so that the grove was in reality bisected by an open line, which separated it into two groves, nearly equal in extent. This separation could only be observed from certain positions in the plain—one on each side of the river.

The glade, the avenue of a dozen yards loading from it to the outside plain, and the plain itself, were all perfectly level, and covered with a smooth turf. Any object upon their surface would be easily perceptible at a distance. The grove was thickly stocked with underwood—principally the smaller species of "mezquite." There was also a network of vines and llianas that, stretching upward, twined around the limbs of the live-oaks—the latter forming the highest and largest timber of all. The underwood was impenetrable to the eye, though a hunter could have crept through it in pursuit of game. At night, however, even under moonlight, it appeared a dark and impassable thicket.

On one side of the glade, where the ground was dry and sandy, there stood a small clump of *pitahaya* cactus. There were not over a dozen plants in all, but two or three of them were large specimens, sending up their soft succulent limbs nearly as high as the live-oaks. Standing by themselves in massive columns, and so unlike the trees that surrounded them, they gave a peculiar character to the scene; and the eye, unaccustomed to these gigantic candelabra, would scarce have known to what kingdom of nature they belonged—so unlike were they to the ordinary forms of vegetation.

Such were the features of the spot where the hunted outlaw sought shelter for the night.

Chapter Fifty Eight

Carlos spoke the truth, when he gave his dog the credit of having saved his life, or, at all events, his liberty, which in the end amounted to the same thing. But for the sagacious brute having preceded him, he would certainly have entered the cave, and as certainly would he have been captured.

His cunning adversaries had taken every step necessary for securing him. They had hidden their horses far back in the cavern. They had placed themselves behind the jutting rocks—one on each side of the entrance—so that the moment he should have shown himself they were prepared to spring upon him like a brace of tigers.

Their dogs, too, were there to aid them—crouched by the side of their masters, and along with them, ready to seize upon the unsuspecting victim.

It was a well-planned ambuscade, and so far well-executed. The secrecy with which the hunters had left the settlement, and made their roundabout journey—their adroit approach to the ravine—their patient behaviour in watching till Carlos had ridden out of the way, and their then taking possession of the cave, were all admirably executed manoeuvres.

How was it possible the cibolero could be aware of, or even suspect, their presence? They did not for a moment fancy that he knew of their return from their hunting expedition. It was quite dark the night before, when they had passed up the valley to the mission; and after unpacking the produce of their hunt, which had been done without observation, the Padré Joaquin had enjoined on them not to show themselves in the town before he should send them word. But few of the mission servants, then, knew of their return; and for the rest, no one knew anything who would or could have communicated it to Carlos. Therefore, reasoned they, he could have no suspicion of their being in the cave. As to their trail up the ravine, he would not notice it on his return. He would only strike it where it led over the shingle, and, of course, there it would not be visible even in daylight.

Never was a trap better set. He would walk into the cave unsuspectingly, and perhaps leading his horse. They would spring upon him—dogs and all—and pinion him before he could draw either pistol or knife! There seemed no chance for him.

For all that there *was* a chance, as the yellow hunter well knew; and it was that which caused him at intervals to mutter—

"Dam! fear dog give us trouble, boy Pepe."

To this the zambo's only response was the bitter shibboleth—"*Carajo!*" showing that both were uneasy about the dog. Long before this time both had heard of the fame of Cibolo, though neither had a full knowledge of the perfect training to which that sagacious animal had attained.

They reflected that, should the dog enter the cave first, they would be discovered by him, and warning given to his master. Should he enter it before the latter had got near, the chances were that their ambuscade would prove a failure. On the other hand, should the dog remain in the rear, all would go right. Even should he approach at the same time with his master, so that the latter might get near without being alarmed, there would still be a chance of their rushing out upon and shooting either horse or rider.

Thus reasoned these two treacherous ruffians in the interim of the cibolero's absence.

They had not yet seated themselves in the positions they designed to take by the entrance of the cave. They could occupy these at a moment's warning. They stood under the shadow of the rocks, keeping watch down the ravine. They knew they might be a long time on their vigil, and they made themselves as comfortable as possible by consuming the meagre stock of provisions which the cibolero had left in the cave. The mulatto, to keep out the cold, had thrown the newly appropriated blanket upon his shoulders. A gourd of chingarito, which they had taken care to bring with them, enabled them to pass the time cheerfully enough. The only drawback upon their mirth was the thought of the dog Cibolo, which every now and again intruded itself upon the mind of the yellow hunter, as well as upon that of his darker confrère.

Their vigil was shorter than either had anticipated. They fancied that their intended victim might make a long ride of it—perhaps to the borders of the settlement—that he might have business that would detain him, and that it might be near morning before he would get back.

In the midst of those conjectures, and while it still wanted some hours of midnight, the mulatto, whose eyes were bent down the ravine, was seen suddenly to start, and grasp his companion by the sleeve.

"Look!—yonder, boy Pepe! Yonder come güero!"

The speaker pointed to a form approaching from the plain, and nearing the narrow part of the ravine. It was scarce visible by the uncertain light, and just possible to distinguish it as the form of a man on horseback.

"Carr-rr-a-ai! it is—carr-r-ai!" replied the zambo, after peering for some time through the darkness.

"Keep close in, boy Pepe! hwish! Pull back dog! take place—lie close—I watch outside—hwish!"

The zambo took his station according to the plan they had agreed upon; while the yellow hunter, bloodhound in hand, remained by the entrance of the cave. In a few moments the latter was seen to start up with a gesture of alarm.

"Dam!" he exclaimed. "Dam! told you so—till lost—ready, boy Pepe— dog on our trail!"

"Carajo, Man'l! what's to be done?" eagerly inquired the zambo.

"In—in—let come in—kill 'im in cave—in!"

Both rushed inside and stood waiting. They had hastily formed the design of seizing the cibolero's dog the moment he should enter the cave, and strangling him if possible.

In this design they were disappointed; for the animal, on reaching the mouth of the cave, refused to enter, but stopped upon the ledge outside and commenced barking loudly.

The mule uttered a cry of disappointment, and, dropping the bloodhound, rushed forward, knife in hand, to attack Cibolo. At the same moment the hound sprang forward, and the two dogs became engaged in a desperate conflict. This would have terminated to the disadvantage of the hound, but, in another moment, all four—mulatto, zambo, hound, and wolf—were assailing Cibolo both with knives and teeth. The latter, seeing himself thus overmatched, and having already received several bad cuts, prudently retreated among the rocks.

He was not followed, as the ruffians had still some hopes that the cibolero, not suspecting what it could mean, might yet advance towards the cave. But these hopes were of short duration. Next moment through the dim light they perceived the horseman wheel round, and gallop off towards the mouth of the ravine!

Exclamations of disappointment, profane ejaculations, and wild oaths, echoed for some minutes through the vaulted cavern.

The excited ruffians at length became more cool, and, groping about in the darkness, got hold of their horses, and led them out upon the ledge. Here they stopped to give farther vent to their chagrin, and to deliberate on their future course.

To attempt immediate pursuit would not avail them, as they well know the cibolero would be many a mile out of their reach before they could descend to the plain.

For a long time they continued to give utterance to expressions of chagrin, mingled with anathemas upon the head of the dog, Cibolo. At length becoming tired of this, they once more set their heads to business.

The zambo was of opinion it would be useless to go farther that night—they had no chance of coming up with the cibolero before morning—in daylight they would more easily make out his trail.

"Boy Pepe, fool!" was the mulatto's reply to these observations. "Track by daylight—be seen—spoil all, fool Pepe!"

"Then what way, brother Man'l?"

"Dam! forgot bloodhound? Trail by night fast as ride—soon overtake güero."

"But, brother Man'l, he's not going to stop short of ten leagues from here! We can't come up with him to-night, can we?"

"Fool again, boy Pepe! Stop within ten miles—stop because won't think of bloodhound—won't think can trail 'im—stop, sure. Dam! that dog played devil—thought he would—dam!"

"Malraya! *he* won't trouble us any more."

"Why think that, boy Pepe?"

"Why, brother Man'l! because I had my blade into him. He'll not limp much farther, I warrant."

"Dam! wish could think so—if could think so, give double onza. But for dog have güero now. But for dog, get güero before sun up. Stop soon—don't suspect us yet—don't suspect hound—stop, I say. By mighty God—sure!"

"How, brother Man'l? you think he'll not go far off?"

"Sure of it. Güero not ride far—nowhere to go—soon trail 'im—find 'im asleep—crawl on 'im but for dog—crawl on 'im sure."

"If you think so, then I don't believe you need trouble yourself about the dog. If he lives twenty minutes after the stab I gave him, he's a tough brute, that's all. You find the güero, I promise you'll find no dog with him."

"Hope so, boy Pepe—try anyhow. Come!" Saying this, the yellow hunter straddled his horse, and followed by the zambo and the dogs commenced moving down the rocky channel of the ravine.

Chapter Fifty Nine

Having arrived at the point where the horseman had been last seen, the mulatto dismounted, and called up the bloodhound. He addressed some words to the dog, and by a sign set him on the trail. The animal understood what was wanted, and, laying his nose to the ground, ran forward silently. The hunter again climbed back to his saddle, and both he and his companion spurred their horses so as to keep pace with the bloodhound.

This was easy enough, though the moon was no longer seen. The colour of the dog—a very light red—rendered him conspicuous against the dark greensward, and there were neither bushes nor long grass to hide him. Moreover, by the instruction of his master, he moved slowly along the trail—although the scent was still fresh, and he could have gone at a much faster rate. He had been trained to track slowly in the night, and also to be silent about it, so that the "bay" peculiar to his race was not heard.

It was two hours, full time, before they came in sight of the grove where the cibolero had halted. The moment the mulatto saw the timber, he pointed to it, muttering to his companion:—

"See, boy Pepe! dog make for island—see! Bet onza güero there. Dam! there sure!"

When they had arrived within five or six hundred yards of the grove—it was still but dimly visible under the darkening sky—the yellow hunter called the dog off the trail, and ordered him to keep behind. He knew that the horseman must have passed either into the grove or close beside it. In either case his trail could be easily taken up again. If—as the mulatto from his excited manner evidently believed—their victim was still in the grove, then the dog's sagacity was no longer needed. The time was come for them to take other measures.

Diverging from his forward course, the yellow hunter rode in a circle, keeping at about the same distance from the edge of the timber. He was followed by his companion and the dogs.

When opposite the gap made by the avenue, a bright blaze struck suddenly upon their eyes, causing both to rein up with an exclamation of surprise. They had arrived at a point commanding a view of the glade, in the centre of which they perceived a large fire!

"Told so, boy Pepe! fool's asleep yonder—never dream could trail him by night—don't like cold—good fire—believe safe enough. Know that glade—cunning place—only see fire from two points. Ha! yonder horse!"

The figure of a horse standing near the fire was plainly discernible under the light.

"Dam!" continued the hunter; "güero bigger fool than thought 'im. Mighty God, see! believe 'im sleep yonder! him, sure!"

As the mulatto uttered these words, he pointed to a dark form by the fire. It appeared to be the body of a man, prostrate and asleep.

"*Santisima*, it is!" replied the zambo. "Snug by the fire too. He *is* a fool! but, sure enough, he could have no thought of our following him in a night so dark as this."

"Hwish, dam! dog not there, güero ours! No more talk, boy Pepe! follow me!"

The mulatto headed his horse, not direct for the grove, but for a point on the bank of the river some distance below. They rode silently, but now with more rapidity.

Their victim was just where they would have wished him, and they were in a hurry to take advantage of his situation. The nature of the ground was well-known to both, for they had shot deer from the cover of that very copse.

On arriving at the river bank, both dismounted; and having tied both their horses and dogs to the willows, they commenced moving forward in the direction of the grove.

They observed less caution than they might otherwise have done. They felt certain their victim was asleep by the fire. Fool, they thought him! but then how was he to have suspected their presence? The most cunning might have deemed himself secure under such circumstances. It was natural enough that he had gone to sleep, wearied as no doubt he was. Natural, too, that he had kindled a fire. The night had become unpleasantly cold, and it would have been impossible to sleep without a fire. All that seemed natural enough.

They reached the edge of the grove, and without hesitation crawled into the underwood.

The night was still, the breeze scarce turned a leaf, and the slightest rustling among the bushes could have been heard in any part of the glade. A low murmur of water from a distant rapid, a light ripple in the nearer stream, the occasional howl of the prairie wolf, and the dismal wailing of nightbirds, were the only sounds that fell upon the ear.

But although the man-stalkers were making their way through thick underwood, not a sound betokened their advance. There was no rustling of leaves, no snapping of twigs, no crackling of dead sticks under the pressure of hand or knee, no signs of human presence within that dark shrubbery. These men well knew how to thread the thicket. Silent, as the snake glides through the grass, was their advance.

In the glade reigned perfect silence. In its very centre blazed a large fire that lit up the whole surface with its brilliant flames. It was easy to distinguish the form of a fine steed—the steed of the cibolero—standing near the fire; and, nearer still, the prostrate form of his master, who seemed asleep! Yes, there were the manga, the sombrero, the botas and spurs. There was the lazo reaching from the neck of the horse, and, no doubt, wound around the arm of the sleeper! All these points could be determined at a glance.

The horse started, struck the ground with his hoof and then stood still again!

What had he heard? Some wild beast moving near?

No, not a wild beast—worse than that.

Upon the southern edge of the glade a face looked out from the underwood—a human face! It remained but a moment, and was then drawn back behind the leaves. That face could easily have been recognised, his yellow complexion, conspicuous under the glare of the blazing wood, told to whom it belonged. It was the face of Manuel the mulatto.

For some moments it remained behind the leafy screen. Then it was protruded as before, and close beside it another face of darker hue. Both were turned in the same direction. Both regarded the prostrate form by the fire, that still appeared to be sound asleep! The eyes of both were gleaming with malignant triumph. Success seemed certain—their victim was at length within their power!

The faces were again withdrawn, and for a minute neither sound nor sight gave any indication of their presence. At the end of that minute, however, the head of the mulatto was again protruded, but this time at a different point, close to the surface of the ground, and where there was an opening in the underwood.

In a moment more his whole body was drawn through, and appeared in a recumbent position within the glade.

The head and body of the zambo followed; and both now glided silently over the grass in the direction of the sleeper. Flat upon their bellies, like a pair of huge lizards, they moved, one following in the other's trail!

The mulatto was in the advance. His right hand grasped a long-blade, knife, while his gun was carried in the left.

They moved slowly and with great caution—though ready at any moment to spring forward should their victim awake and become aware of their presence.

The unconscious sleeper lay between them and the fire. His form cast a shadow over the sward. Into this they crept, with the view of better concealment, and proceeded on.

At length the mulatto arrived within three feet of the prostrate body; and gathering himself, he rose upon his knees with the intention of making a spring forward. The sudden erection of his body brought his face full into the light, and rendered it a conspicuous object. His time was come.

The whip-like crack of a rifle was heard, and at the same instant a stream of fire shot out from the leafy top of a live-oak that stood near the entrance of the avenue. The mulatto suddenly sprang to his feet, threw out his arms with a wild cry, staggered a pace or two, and, dropping both knife and gun, fell forward into the fire!

The zambo also leaped to his feet; and, believing the shot had come from the pretended sleeper, precipitated himself upon the latter, knife in hand, and drove his blade with desperate earnestness into the side of the prostrate form.

Almost on the instant he leaped back with a yell of terror; and, without stopping to assist his fallen comrade, rushed off over the glade, and disappeared into the underwood. The figure by the fire remained prostrate and motionless.

But at this moment a dark form was seen to descend through the branches of the live-oak whence the shot had come; a shrill whistle rang through the glade; and the steed, dragging his lazo, galloped up under the tree.

A man, half-naked, and carrying a long rifle, dropped upon the horse's back; and the next instant both horse and man disappeared through the avenue, having gone off at full speed in the direction of the plain!

Chapter Sixty

Who was he then who lay by the fire? Not Carlos the cibolero! It was his manga—his botas—his hat and spurs—his complete habiliments!

True, but Carlos was not in them. He it was who, half-naked, had dropped from the tree, and galloped off upon the horse! A mystery!

Less than two hours before we left him where he had arrived—upon the edge of the grove. How had he been employed since then? A knowledge of that will explain the mystery.

On reaching the grove he had ridden direct through the avenue and into the glade, where he reined up his horse and dismounted. Cibolo was gently laid upon the soft grass, with a kind expression; but his wounds remained undressed for the present. His master had no time for that. He had other work to do, which would occupy him for the next hour.

With a slack bridle his horse was left to refresh himself on the sward, while Carlos proceeded to the execution of a design that had been matured in his mind during his long gallop.

His first act was to make a fire. The night had grown chill enough to give excuse for one. It was kindled near the centre of the glade. Dry logs and branches were found among the underwood, and these were brought forward and heaped upon the pile, until the flames blazed up, illuming the glade to its very circumference. The huge pitahayas, gleaming in the red light, looked like columns of stone; and upon these the eyes of the cibolero were now turned.

Proceeding towards them, knife in hand, he commenced cutting through the stem of the largest, and its tall form was soon laid prostrate upon the grass. When down, he hewed both stem and branches into pieces of various length, and then dragged them up to the side of the fire. Surely he did not mean to add them to the pile! These green succulent masses would be more likely to subdue the flame than contribute to its brilliancy.

Carlos had no such intention. On the contrary, he placed the pieces several feet from the fire, arranging them in such a manner as to imitate, as nearly as possible, the form and dimensions of a human body. Two cylindrical pieces served for the thighs, and two more for the arms, and these were laid in the attitude that would naturally be adopted by a person in repose or asleep. The superior shoulder was represented by the "elbow" of the plant; and when the whole structure was covered over with the ample "manga" of the cibolero, it assumed a striking resemblance to the body of a man lying upon his side!

The head, lower limbs, and feet, were yet wanting to complete the design—for it *was* a design. These were soon supplied. A round clew of grass was formed; and this, placed at a small distance from the shoulders by means of a scarf and the cibolero's hat, was made to look like the thing for which it was intended—a human head. The hat was slouched over the ball of grass so as nearly to conceal it, and seemed as if so placed to keep the dew or the musquitos from the face of the sleeper!

The lower limbs and feet only remained to be counterfeited. With these considerable pains had to be taken, since, being nearest to the fire— according to the way in which hunters habitually sleep—they would be more exposed to observation than any other part.

All these points had been already considered by the cibolero; and, therefore, without stopping for a moment he proceeded to finish his work. His leathern "botas" were pulled off, and adjusted at a slight angle to the thighs of pitahaya, and in such a way that the rim of the ample cloak came down over their tops. The huge spurs were allowed to remain on the boots, and could be seen from a distance gleaming in the blaze of the fire.

A few more touches and the counterfeit was complete.

He that had made it now stepped back to the edge of the glade, and, passing around, examined it from different points. He appeared satisfied. Indeed, no one would have taken the figure for anything but that of a sleeping traveller who had lain down without taking off his spurs.

Carlos now returned to the fire, and uttering a low signal brought the horse up to his hand. He led the animal some paces out, and tightened the bridle-rein by knotting it over the horn of the saddle. This the well-trained steed knew to be a command for him to give over browsing, and stand still in that same place until released by the hand of his master, or by a well-known signal he had been taught to obey. The lazo fastened to the bit-ring was next uncoiled. One end of the rope was carried to the prostrate figure, and placed under the edge of the manga, as though the sleeper held it in his hand!

Once more the cibolero passed round the circumference of the glade, and surveyed the grouping in the centre. Again he appeared satisfied; and, re-entering the thicket, he brought out a fresh armful of dry wood and flung it on the fire.

He now raised his eyes, and appeared to scrutinise the trees that grew around the glade. His gaze rested upon a large live-oak standing at the inner entrance of the avenue, and whose long horizontal limbs stretched over the open ground. The top branches of this tree were covered thickly with its evergreen frondage, and laced with vines and *tillandsia* formed a shady canopy. Besides being the tallest tree, it was the most ample and umbrageous—in fact, the patriarch of the grove.

"'Twill do," muttered Carlos, as he viewed it. "Thirty paces—about that—just the range. They'll not enter by the avenue. No—no danger of that; and if they did—but no—they'll come along the bank by the willows—yes, sure to do so:—now for Cibolo."

He glanced for a moment at the dog, that was still lying where he had been placed.

"Poor fellow! he has had it in earnest. He'll carry the marks of their cowardly knives for the rest of his days. Well—he may live long enough to know that he has been avenged—yes! that may he. But what shall I do with him?"

After considering a minute, he continued:—

"Carrambo! I lose time. There's a half-hour gone, and if they've followed at all they'll be near by this time. Follow they can with their long-eared brute, and I hope he'll guide them true. What can I do with Cibolo? If I tie him at the root of the tree, he'll lie quiet enough, poor brute! But then, suppose they should come this way! I don't imagine they will. I shouldn't if I were in their place; but suppose they should, the dog would be seen, and might lead them to suspect something wrong. They might take a fancy to glance up the tree, and then—No, no, it won't do—something else must be done with Cibolo."

Here he approached the root of the live-oak, and looked inquiringly up among its branches.

After a moment he seemed to be satisfied with his scrutiny. He had formed a new resolution.

"It will do," he muttered. "The dog can lie upon those vines. I'll plait them a little for him, and cover them with moss."

Saying this, he caught hold of the lower limbs, and sprang up into the tree.

After dragging down some of the creeping vines, he twined them between the forks of a branch, so as to form a little platform. He next tore off several bundles of the *tillandsia*, and placed it over the spot thus wattled.

When the platform was completed to his satisfaction, he leaped down again; and, taking the animal in his arms, carried him up to the tree, and placed him gently upon the moss, where the dog lay quietly down.

To dispose of himself was the next consideration. That was a matter of easy accomplishment, and consisted in laying hold of his rifle, swinging his body back into the tree, and seating himself firmly among the branches.

He now arranged himself with care upon his seat. One branch, a stout one, supported his body, his feet rested upon another, while a third formed a stay for his arms. In a fork lay the barrel of his long rifle, the stock firmly grasped in his hands.

He looked with care to this weapon. Of course it was already loaded, but, lest the night-dew might have damped the priming, he threw up the pan-cover, with his thumb-nail scraped out the powder, and then poured in a fresh supply from his horn. This he adjusted with his picker, taking care that a portion of it should pass into the touch-hole, and communicate with the charge inside. The steel was then returned to its place, and the flint duly looked to. Its state of firmness was felt, its edge examined. Both appeared to be satisfactory, so the piece was once more brought to its rest in the fork of the branch.

The cibolero was not the man to trust to blind chance. Like all of his calling, he believed in the wisdom of precautions. No wonder he adopted them so minutely in the present instance. The neglect of any one of them might be fatal to him. The flashing of that rifle might cost him his life! No wonder he was particular about the set of his flint, and the dryness of his powder.

The position he occupied was well chosen. It gave him a view of the whole glade, and no object as large as a cat could enter the opening without being seen by him.

Silently he sat gazing around the circle of green shrubbery—silently and anxiously—for the space of nearly an hour.

His patient vigil was at length rewarded. He saw the yellow face as it peered from the underwood, and for a moment hesitated about firing at it then. He had even taken sight upon it, when it was drawn back!

A little longer he waited—till the mulatto, rising to his knees, offered his face full in the blazing light. At that moment his finger pressed the trigger, and his unerring bullet passed through the brain of his treacherous foeman!

Chapter Sixty One

The zambo had disappeared in the underwood almost at the same instant that Carlos had mounted and galloped out through the avenue. Not a living creature remained in the glade.

The huge body lay with arms outstretched, one of them actually across the blazing pile! Its weight, pressing down the faggots, half-obscured their light. Enough there was to exhibit the ghastly face mottled with washes of crimson. There was no motion in either body or limbs—no more than in that of the counterfeit form that was near. Dead was the yellow hunter—dead! The hot flame that licked his arm, preparing to devour it, gave him no pain. Fire stirs not the dead!

Where were the others? They had gone off in directions nearly opposite! Were they flying from each other?

The zambo had gone back in the same direction whence he had come. He had gone in a very different manner though. After disappearing behind the leafy screen, he had not halted, but rushed on like one terrified beyond the power of controlling himself. The cracking of dead sticks, and the loud rustling among the bushes, told that he was pressing through the grove in headlong flight. These noises had ceased—so, too, the echo of hoofs which for a while came back from the galloping horse of the cibolero.

Where were they now—zambo and cibolero? Had they fled from each other? It would have seemed so from the relative directions in which they had gone.

It was not so in reality. Whatever desire the zambo might have felt to get away from that spot, his antagonist had no such design. The latter had galloped out of the glade, but not in flight.

He knew the zambo well enough to tell that his courage was now gone. The sudden loss of his comrade, and under such mysterious circumstances, had terrified the black, and would paralyse him almost beyond the power of resistance. He would think of nothing else but making his escape. Carlos knew that.

The quick intellect of the latter had taught him whence his enemies had come—from the lower or southern side of the grove. He had, indeed, been loosing for them in that direction, and, while scrutinising the underwood, had given most attention to that edge of the glade lying to the south. He conjectured that they would deem this the safest way to approach him, and his conjectures proved true.

Their horses would be left at some distance off, lest the stroke of their hoofs might alarm him. This, too, was his conjecture, and a just one. Still another, also just, was that the zambo was now making for the horses! This last occurred to Carlos as he saw the other rushing off into the underwood.

Just what the zambo was doing. Seeing his leader fall so mysteriously, he thought no longer of an encounter. Flight was his only impulse—to get back to the horses, mount and ride off, his one purpose. He had hopes that Carlos would not hastily follow—that he might escape under cover of the darkness.

He was mistaken. It was just to defeat this purpose that Carlos had galloped forth. He, too, was resolved to make for the horses!

Once in the open plain, he wheeled to the right, and rode round the grove. On reaching a point where he could command a view of the river he reined up. His object in doing so was to reload his rifle.

He threw the piece into a vertical position, at the same time groping for his powder-horn. To his surprise he could not get his hands upon it, and on looking down he saw that it was gone! The strap by which it had been suspended was no longer over his shoulders. It had been caught upon a branch, and lifted off as he had leaped from the tree!

Annoyed with this misfortune, he was about turning his horse to hurry back to the live-oak, when his eye fell upon a dark figure gliding over the plain, and close in to the fringe of willows by the river. Of course it was the fleeing zambo—there could be no doubt of that.

Carlos hesitated. Should he return for the powder-horn, and then waste time in reloading, the zambo might escape. He would soon reach the horses, and mount. Had it been day Carlos could easily have overtaken him, but not so under the night darkness. Five hundred yards' start would have carried him safe out of sight.

The cibolero was full of anxiety. He had ample reasons to wish that this man should die. Prudence as well as a natural feeling of revenge prompted this wish. The cowardly manner in which these hired ruffians had dogged him had awakened his vengeance. Besides, while either lived, the outlaw knew he would have a dangerous enemy. The zambo must not escape!

It was but for a moment that Carlos hesitated. Should he wait to reload his rifle the other would get off. This reflection decided him. He dropped the piece to the ground, turned his horse's head, and shot rapidly across the plain in the direction of the river. In a dozen seconds he reined up in front of his skulking foe.

The latter, seeing himself cut off from the horses, halted and stood at bay, as if determined to fight. But before Carlos could dismount to close with him, his heart once more gave way; and, breaking through the willows, he plunged into the river.

Carlos had not calculated upon this. He stood for some moments in a state of surprise and dismay. Would the fiend escape him? He had come to the ground. Whether should he mount again or follow on foot?

He was not long irresolute. He chose the latter course, and, rushing through the willows where the other had passed, he paused a moment on the edge of the stream. Just then his enemy emerged upon the opposite bank, and, without a moment's halt, started off in full run across the plain. Again Carlos thought of following on horseback, but the banks were high,—a horse might find it difficult to ford at such a place,—perhaps impossible. There was no time to be lost in experiments.

"Surely," thought Carlos, "I am swift as he. For a trial then!"

And as he uttered the words he flung himself broad upon the water.

A few strokes carried him across the stream; and, climbing out on the opposite bank, he sprang after his retreating foe.

The zambo had by this time got full two hundred yards in the advance, but before he had run two hundred more, there was not half that distance between them. There was no comparison in their speed. Carlos fairly doubled upon his terrified antagonist, although the latter was doing his utmost. He knew that he was running for his life.

Not ten minutes did the chase continue.

Carlos drew near. The zambo heard his footsteps close behind. He felt it was idle to run any longer. He halted, and once more stood at bay.

In another instant the two were face to face, within ten feet of each other!

Both were armed with large knives—their only weapons—and, dim as the light was, the blades of these could be seen glittering in the air.

The foes scarce waited to breathe themselves. A few angry exclamations passed between them; and then, rushing upon each other, they clutched in earnest conflict!

It was a short conflict. A dozen seconds would have covered its whole duration. For a while, the bodies of the combatants seemed turned around each other, and one of them fell heavily upon the plain. A groan was uttered. It was in the voice of the zambo. It was he who had fallen!

The prostrate form wriggled for a moment over the ground—it half rose and fell again—then writhed for a few seconds longer, and then lay still in death!

The cibolero bent over it to be assured of this. Death was written upon the hideous face. The marks were unmistakeable. The victor no longer doubted; and, turning away from the corpse, he walked back towards the river.

Having regained his rifle and powder-horn, and reloaded his gun, Carlos now proceeded to search for the horses.

These were soon found. A bullet was sent through the head of the bloodhound, and another through that of his more wolf-like companion, and the horses were then untied and set free.

This done, Carlos once more returned to the glade, and, after lifting Cibolo down from his perch, he approached the fire, and gazed for a moment at the corpse of the yellow hunter. The fires were blazing more brightly than ever. These were fed by human flesh!

Turning in disgust from the sight, the cibolero collected his garments, and, once more mounting into the saddle, rode off in the direction of the ravine.

Chapter Sixty Two

Three days had elapsed from the time that the yellow hunter and his companion had started on their expedition. Those who sent them were beginning to grow impatient for some news of them. They did not allow themselves to doubt of the zeal of their employes,—the reward would secure that,—and scarce did they doubt of their success. The latter seemed to all three—Roblado, Vizcarra, and the Padré—but a consequence of the former. Still they were impatient for some report from the hunters—if not of the actual capture, at least that the outlaw had been seen, or that they were upon his trail.

On reflection, however, both Padré and officers saw that it would not be likely they should have any report before the hunters themselves came back, either with or without their captive.

"No doubt," suggested the monk, "they are after him every hour, and we shall hear nothing of them until they have laid hands upon the heretic rascal."

What a startling piece of news it was to this charming trio, when a *hatero* brought the information to the settlement that he had seen two dead bodies upon the plain, which he recognised as those of the Mission hunters—Manuel and Pepe.

His report was that he had seen them near a grove upon the Pecos,—that they were torn by the wolves and vultures—but that what still remained of their dress and equipments enabled him to make out who they were—for the hatero had chanced to know these men personally. He was sure they were the mulatto and Zambo, the hunters of the mission.

At first this "mysterious murder," as it was termed, could not be explained—except upon the supposition that the "Indios bravos" had done it. The people knew nothing of the duty upon which the hunters had been lately employed. Both were well enough known, though but little notice was taken of their movements, which lay generally beyond the observation of the citizen community. It was supposed they had been out upon one of their usual hunts, and had fallen in with a roving band of savages.

A party of dragoons, guided by the hatero, proceeded to the grove; and these returned with a very different version of the story.

They had ascertained beyond a doubt that both the hunters had been killed, not by Indian arrows, but by the weapons of a white man. Furthermore, their horses had been left, while their dogs had been killed— the skeletons of the latter were found lying upon the bank of the river.

It could not have been Indians, then. They would have carried off the animals, both dogs and horses, and, moreover, would have stripped the dead of their equipments, which were of some value. Indians? No.

There was not much difficulty in deciding who had committed this murder. Where the skeletons of the dogs were found the ground was soft, and there were hoof-tracks that did not belong to the horses of the hunters. These were recognised by several. They were the tracks of the well-known horse of Carlos the cibolero.

Beyond a doubt Carlos had done the deed. It was known that he and the yellow hunter had not been on friendly terms, but the contrary. They had met and quarrelled, then; or, what was more likely, Carlos had found the hunters asleep by their camp-fire, had stolen upon them, and thus effected his purpose. The mulatto had been shot dead at once, and had fallen into the fire, for part of the body was consumed to a cinder! His companion, attempting to make his escape, had been pursued and overtaken by the bloodthirsty outlaw!

New execrations were heaped upon the head of the devoted Carlos. Men crossed themselves and uttered either a prayer or a curse at the mention of his name; and mothers made use of it to fright their children into good behaviour. The name of Carlos the cibolero spread more terror than the rumour of an Indian invasion!

The belief in the supernatural became strengthened. Scarce any one now doubted that the cibolero's mother was a witch, or that all these deeds performed by her son were the result of her aid and inspiration.

There was not the slightest hope that he would either be captured or killed. How could he? Who could bind the devil and bring him to punishment? No one any longer believed that he could be caught.

Some gravely proposed that his mother—the witch should be taken up and burnt. Until that was done, argued they, he would set all pursuit at defiance; but if she were put out of the world, the murderer might then be brought to justice!

It is probable enough that the counsels of these and they were the majority of the inhabitants—would have prevailed; especially as they were openly approved of by the padrés of the mission; but before the public mind became quite ripe for such a violent sacrifice, an event occurred which completely changed the currant of affairs.

It was on the morning of a Sunday, and the people were just coming out of the church, when a horseman, covered with sweat and dust, galloped into the Plaza. His habiliments were those of a sergeant of dragoons; and all easily recognised the well-known lineaments of the sergeant Gomez.

In a few minutes he was surrounded by a crowd of idlers, who, although it was Sunday, were heard a few moments after breaking out into loud acclamations of joy. Hats were uptossed and *vivas* rent the air!

What news had Gomez announced? A rare bit of news—*the capture of the outlaw*! It was true. Carlos had been taken, and was now a prisoner in the hands of the soldiers. He had been captured neither by strength nor stratagem. Treachery had done the work. He had been betrayed by one of his own people.

It was thus his capture had been effected. Despairing for the present of being able to communicate with Catalina, he had formed the resolution to remove his mother and sister from the valley. He had prepared a temporary home for them far off in the wilderness, where they would be secure from his enemies, while he himself could return at a better opportunity.

To effect their removal, watched as they were, he knew would be no easy matter. But he had taken his measures, and would have succeeded had it not been for treason. One of his own people—a peon who had accompanied him in his last expedition—betrayed him to his vigilant foes.

Carlos was within the rancho making a few hasty preparations for the journey. He had left his horse hidden some distance off in the chapparal. Unfortunately for him Cibolo was not there. The faithful dog had been laid up since his late encounter at the cave. To a peon had been assigned the duty that would otherwise have been intrusted to him—that of keeping watch without.

This wretch had been previously bought by Roblado and Vizcarra. The result was, that, instead of acting as sentinel for his master, he hastened to warn his enemies. The rancho was surrounded by a troop; and, although several of his assailants were killed by the hand of Carlos, he himself was finally overpowered and taken.

Gomez had not been five minutes in the Plaza when a bugle was heard sounding the advance of a troop, which the next moment defiled into the open square. Near its middle was the prisoner, securely tied upon the back of a saddle-mule, and guarded by a double file of troopers.

An arrival of such interest was soon known, and the Plaza became filled with a crowd eager to gratify its curiosity by a sight of the notorious cibolero.

But he was not the only one upon whom the people gazed with curiosity. There were two other prisoners—one of whom was regarded with an interest equal to that felt at the sight of the outlaw himself. This prisoner was his mother. Upon her the eyes of the multitude turned with an expression of awe mingled with indignation; while jeering and angry cries hailed her as she passed on her way to the *Calabozo*.

"*Muera la hechicera! muera!*" (Death to the witch—let her die!) broke from ruffian lips as she was carried along.

Even the dishevelled hair and weeping eyes of her young companion—her daughter—failed to touch the hearts of that fanatical mob, and there were some who cried, "*Mueran las dos! madre y hija!*" (Let both die—mother and daughter!)

The guards had even to protect them from rude assault, as they were thrust hastily within the door of the prison!

Fortunately Carlos saw nought of this. *He was not even aware that they were prisoners!* He thought, perhaps, they had been left unmolested in the rancho, and that the vengeance of his enemies extended no farther than to himself. He knew not the fiendish designs of his persecutors.

Chapter Sixty Three

The female prisoners remained in the Calabozo. Carlos, for better security, was carried on to the Presidio, and placed in the prison of the guard-house.

That night he received a visit. The Comandante and Roblado could not restrain their dastard spirits from indulging in the luxury of revenge. Having emptied their wine-cups, they, with a party of boon companions, entered the guard prison, and amused themselves by taunting the chained captive. Every insult was put upon him by his half-drunken visitors—every rudeness their ingenuity could devise.

For long all this was submitted to in silence. A coarse jest from Vizcarra at length provoked reply. The reply alluded to the changed features of the latter, which so exasperated the brute, that he dashed, dagger in hand, upon the bound victim, and would have taken his life, but that Roblado and others held him back! He was only prevented from killing Carlos by his companions declaring that such a proceeding would rob them of their anticipated sport! This consideration alone restrained him; but he was not contented until with his fists he had inflicted several blows upon the face of the defenceless captive!

"Let the wretch live!" said Roblado. "To-morrow we shall have a fine spectacle for him!"

With this the inebriated gang staggered out, leaving the prisoner to reflect upon this promised "spectacle."

He did reflect upon it. That he was to be made a spectacle he understood well enough. He had no hopes of mercy, either from civil or military judges. His death was to be the spectacle. All night long his soul was tortured with painful thoughts, not of himself, but about those far dearer to him than his own life.

Morning glanced through the narrow loophole of his gloomy cell. Nothing else—nought to eat, to drink—no word of consolation—no kind look from his ruffian gaolers. No friend to make inquiry about him—no sign that a single heart on earth cared for him.

Midday arrived. He was taken, or rather dragged, from his prison. Troops formed around, and carried him off. Where was he going? To execution?

His eyes were free. He saw himself taken to the town, and through the Plaza. There was an unusual concourse of people. The square was nearly filled, and the azoteas that commanded a view of it. All the inhabitants of the settlement seemed to be present in the town. There were haciendados, rancheros, miners, and all. Why? Some grand event must have brought them together. They had the air of people who expected to witness an unusual scene. Perhaps the "spectacle" promised by Roblado! But what could that be? Did they intend to torture him in presence of the multitude? Such was not improbable.

The crowd jeered him as he passed. He was carried through their midst, and thrust into the Calabozo.

A rude *banqueta* along one side of his cell offered a resting-place. On this the wretched man sank down into a lying posture. The fastenings on his arms and legs would not allow him to sit upright.

He was left alone. The soldiers who had conducted him went out, turning the key behind them. Their voices and the clink of their scabbards told him that some of them still remained by the door. Two of them had been left there as sentinels. The others sauntered off, and mingled with the crowd of civilians that filled the Plaza.

Carlos lay for some minutes without motion—almost without thought. His soul was overwhelmed with misery. For the first time in his life he felt himself yielding to despair.

The feeling was evanescent; and once more he began to reflect—not to hope—no! Hope, they say dies but with life: but that is a paradox. He still lived, but hope had died. Hope of escape there was none. He was too well guarded. His exasperated enemies, having experienced the difficulty of his capture, were not likely to leave him the slightest chance of escape. Hope of pardon—of mercy—it never entered his thoughts to entertain either.

But reflection returned.

It is natural for a captive to glance around the walls of his prison—to assure himself that he is really a prisoner. It is his first act when the bolt shoots from the lock, and he feels himself alone. Obedient to this impulse, the eye of Carlos was raised to the walls, his cell was not a dungeon—a small window, or embrasure, admitted light. It was high up, but Carlos saw that, by standing upon the banqueta, he could have looked out by it. He had no curiosity to do so, and he lay still. He saw that the walls of his prison were not of stone. They were *adobe* bricks, and the embrasure enabled him to tell their thickness. There was no great strength in them either. A determined man, with an edge-tool and time to spare, could make his way through them easily enough. So Carlos reflected: but he reflected, as well, that he had neither the edge-tool nor the time. He was certain that in a few hours—perhaps minutes—he would be led from that prison to the scaffold.

Oh! he feared not death—not even torture, which he anticipated would be his lot. His torture was the thought of eternal separation from mother, sister, from the proud noble girl he loved—the thought that he would never again behold them—one or other of them—this was the torture that maddened his soul.

Could he not communicate with them? Had he no friend to carry to them a last word?—to convey a dying thought? None.

The sunbeam that slanted across the cell was cut off at intervals, and the room darkened. Something half covered the embrasure without. It was the face of some idle lepero, who, curious to catch a glimpse of the captive, had caused himself to be hoisted upon the shoulders of his fellows. The embrasure was above the heads of the crowd. Carlos could hear their brutal jests, directed not only against himself, but against those dear to him—his mother and sister. While this pained him, he began to wonder that they should be so much the subject of the conversation. He could not tell what was said of them, but in the hum of voices their names repeatedly reached his ear. He had lain about an hour on the banqueta, when the door opened, and the two officers, Vizcarra and Roblado, stepped within the cell. They were accompanied by Gomez.

The prisoner believed that his hour was come. They were going to lead him forth to execution. He was wrong. That was not their design. Far different. They had come to gloat over his misery. Their visit was to be a short one. "Now, my brave!" began Roblado. "We promised you a spectacle to-day. We are men of our word. We come to admonish you that it is prepared, and about to come off. Mount upon that banqueta, and look out into the Plaza; you will have an excellent view of it; and as it is near you will need no glass! Up then! and don't lose time. You will see what you will see. Ha! ha! ha!"

And the speaker broke into a hoarse laugh, in which the Comandante as well as the sergeant joined; and then all three, without waiting for a reply, turned and went out, ordering the door to be locked behind them.

The visit, as well as Roblado's speech, astonished and puzzled Carlos. For some minutes he sat reflecting upon it. What could it mean? A *spectacle*, and he to be a *spectator*? What spectacle but that of his own execution? What could it mean?

For a time he sat endeavouring to make out the sense of Roblado's words. For a good while he pondered over the speech, until at length he had found, or thought he had found, the key to its meaning.

"Ha!" muttered he; "Don Juan—it is he! My poor friend! They have condemned him, too; and he is to die before me. That is what I am called upon to witness. Fiends! I shall not gratify them by looking at it. No! I shall remain where I am."

He threw himself once more prostrate along the banqueta, determined to remain in that position. He muttered at intervals:—

"Poor Don Juan!—a true friend—to death—ay, even to death, for it is for me he dies—for me, and—oh! love—love—"

His reflections were brought to a sudden termination. The window was darkened by a face, and a rough voice called in:—

"Hola! Carlos, you butcher of buffaloes! look forth! *Carajo*! here's a sight for you! Look at your old witch of a mother! What a figure she cuts! Ha! ha!"

The sting of a poisonous reptile—a blow from an enemy—could not have roused Carlos more rapidly from his prostrate attitude. As he sprang to an upright position, the fastenings upon his ankles were forgotten; and, after staggering half across the floor, he came down upon his knees.

A second effort was made with more caution, and this time he succeeded in keeping his feet. A few moments sufficed for him to work himself up to the banqueta; and, having mounted this, he applied his face to the embrasure and looked forth.

His eyes rested upon a scene that caused the blood to curdle in his veins, and started the sweat in bead-drops over his forehead. A scene that filled his heart with horror, that caused him to feel as if some hand was clutching and compressing it between fingers of iron!

Chapter Sixty Four

The Plaza was partially cleared—the open space guarded by lines of soldiers. The crowds, closely packed, stood along the sides of the houses, or filled the balconies and azoteas. The officers, alcalde, magistrates, and principal men of the town, were grouped near the centre of the Plaza. Most of these wore official costumes, and, under other circumstances, the eyes of the crowd would have been upon *them*. Not so now. There was a group more attractive than they—a group upon which every eye was gazing with intense interest.

This group occupied a corner of the Plaza in front of the Calabozo, directly in front of the window from which Carlos looked out. It was the first thing upon which his eyes rested. He saw no more—he saw not the crowd, nor the line of soldiers that penned it back—he saw not the gaudy gentry in the square; he saw only that group of beings before him. That was enough to keep his eyes from wandering.

The group was thus composed. There were two asses—small shaggy brown animals,—caparisoned in a covering of coarse black serge, that hung nearly to their feet. Each had a coarse hair halter held in the hand of a lepero driver, also fantastically dressed in the same black stuff. Behind each stood a lepero similarly attired, and carrying "cuartos" of buffalo-skin. By the side of each ass was one of the padrés of the mission, and each of these held in his hand the implements of his trade—book, rosary, and crucifix. The priests wore an official look. They were in the act of officiating. At what? Listen!

The asses were mounted. On the back of each was a form—a human form. These sat not freely, but in constrained attitudes. The feet were drawn underneath by cords passed around the ankles; and to a sort of wooden yoke around the necks of the animals the hands of the riders were tied—so as to bring their backs into a slanting position. In this way their heads hung down, and their faces, turned to the wall, could not yet be seen by the crowd.

Both were nude to the waist, and below it. The eye needed but one glance at those forms to tell they were women! The long loose hair—in the one grey, in the other golden—shrouding their cheeks, and hanging over the necks of the animals, was further proof of this. For one it was not needed. The outlines were those of a Venus. A sculptor's eye could not have detected a fault. In the form of the other, age had traced its marks. It was furrowed, angled, lean, and harsh to the eye of the observer.

Oh, God! what a sight for the eye of Carlos the cibolero! Those involuntary riders *were his mother and sister*!

And just at that moment his eye rested upon them—ay, and recognised them at a glance. An arrow passing through his heart could not have inflicted keener pain. A sharp, half-stifled scream escaped his lips—the only sign of suffering the ear might detect. He was silent from that moment. His hard quick breathing alone told that he lived. He did not faint or fall. He did not retreat from the window. He stood like a statue in the position he had first taken, hugging the wall with his breast, to steady himself. His eyes remained fixed on the group, and fixed too in their sockets, as if glued there!

Roblado and Vizcarra, in the centre of the square, enjoyed their triumph. They saw him at the embrasure. He saw not them. He had for the moment forgotten that they existed.

At a signal the bell rang in the tower of the parroquia, and then ceased. This was the cue for commencing the horrid ceremony.

The black drivers led their animals from the wall, and, heading them in a direction parallel to one side of the Plaza, stood still. The faces of the women were now turned partially to the crowd, but their dishevelled hair sufficiently concealed them. The padrés approached. Each selected one. They mumbled a few unintelligible phrases in the ears of their victims, flourished the crucifix before their faces, and then, retiring a step, muttered some directions to the two ruffians in the rear.

These with ready alacrity took up their cue, gathered the thick ends of their cuartos around their wrists, and plied the lash upon the naked hacks of the women. The strokes were deliberate and measured—they were counted! Each seemed to leave its separate weal upon the skin. Upon the younger female they were more conspicuous—not that they had been delivered with greater severity, but upon the softer, whiter, and more tender skin, the purple lines appeared plainer by contrast.

Strange that neither cried out. The girl writhed, and uttered a low whimpering, but no scream escaped her lips. As for the old woman, she remained quite motionless—no sign told that she suffered!

When ten lashes each had been administered, a voice from the centre of the Plaza cried out—

"*Basta por la niña!*" (Enough for the girl.)

The crowd echoed this; and he, whose office it was to flog the younger female, rolled up his cuarto and desisted. The other went on until twenty-five lashes were told off.

A band of music now struck up. The asses were d along the side of the square, and halted at the next corner.

The music stopped. The padrés again went through their mumbling ceremony. The executioners performed their part—only one of them this time—as by the voice of the crowd the younger female was spared the lash, though she was still kept in her degraded and shameful position.

The full measure of twenty-five stripes was administered to the other, and then again the music, and the procession moved on to the third angle of the Plaza. Here the horrid torture was repeated, and again at the fourth and last corner of the square, where the hundred lashes—the full number decreed as the punishment—were completed.

The ceremony was over. The crowd gathered around the victims—who, now released from official keeping, were left to themselves.

The feeling of the crowd was curiosity, not sympathy. Notwithstanding all that had passed before their eyes, there was but little sympathy in the hearts of that rabble.

Fanaticism is stronger than pity; and who cared for the witch and the heretic?

Yes—there were some who cared yet. There were hands that unbound the cords, and chafed the brows of the sufferers, and flung rebosos over their shoulders and poured water into the lips of those silent victims—silent, for both had fainted!

A rude carreta was there. How it came there no one knew or cared. It was getting dusk, and people, having satisfied their curiosity, and hungry from long fasting, were falling off to their homes. The brawny driver of the carreta, directed by a young girl, and aided by two or three dusky Indians, lifted the sufferers into his vehicle, and then, mounting himself, drove off; while the young girl, and two or three who had assisted him, followed the vehicle.

It cleared the suburbs, and, striking into a byroad that traversed the chapparal, arrived at a lone rancho, the same where Rosita had been taken before—for it was Josefa who again carried her away.

The sufferers were taken inside the house. It was soon perceived that one no longer suffered. The daughter was restored to consciousness, only to see that that of her mother had for ever fled!

Her temples were chafed—her lips moistened—her hand pressed in vain. The wild utterance of a daughter's grief fell unheard upon her ears. Death had carried her spirit to another world.

Chapter Sixty Five

From the embrasure of his prison Carlos looked upon the terrible spectacle. We have said that he regarded it in silence. Not exactly so. Now and then, as the blood-stained lash fell heavier than usual, a low groan escaped him—the involuntary utterance of agony extreme.

His looks more than his voice betrayed the fearful fire that was burning within. Those who by chance or curiosity glanced into the embrasure were appalled by the expression of that face. Its muscles were rigid and swollen, the eyes were fixed and ringed with purple, the teeth firmly set, the lips drawn tight over them, and large sweat-drops glistened upon the forehead. No red showed upon the cheeks, nor any part of the face—not a trace to tell that blood circulated there. Pale as death was that face, and motionless as marble.

From his position Carlos could see but two angles of the Plaza—that where the cruel scene had its commencement, and that where the second portion was administered. The procession then passed out of sight; but though his eyes were no longer tortured by the horrid spectacle, there was but little relief in that. He knew it continued all the same.

He remained no longer by the window. A resolve carried him from it,—the resolve of self-destruction!

His agony was complete. He could endure it no longer. Death would relieve him, and upon death he was determined.

But how to die?

He had no weapon; and even if he had, pinioned as he was, he could not have used it.

But one mode seemed possible—to dash his head against the wall!

A glance at the soft mason-work of *adobes* convinced him that this would not effect his purpose. By such an effort he might stun, but not kill himself. He would wake again to horrid life.

His eyes swept the cell in search of some mode of self-destruction.

A beam traversed the apartment. It was high enough to hang the tallest man. With his hands free, and a cord in them, it would do. There was cord enough on them for the purpose, for they were bound by several varas of a raw-hide thong.

To the fastenings his attention was now directed; when, to his surprise and delight, he perceived that the thong had become slack and loose! The hot sweat, pouring from his hands and wrists, had saturated the raw-hide, causing it to melt and yield; and his desperate exertions, made mechanically under the influence of agony and half-madness, had stretched it for inches! A slight examination of the fastenings convinced him of the possibility of his undoing them; and to this he applied himself with all the strength find energy of a desperate man. Had his hands been tied in front, he might have used his teeth in the endeavour to set them free; but they were bound fast together across his back. He pulled and wrenched them with all his strength.

If there is a people in the world who understand better than any other the use of ropes or thongs, that people is the Spanish-American. The Indian must yield to them in this knowledge, and even the habile sailor makes but a clumsy knot in comparison. No people so well understand how to bind a captive *without iron*, and the captive outlaw had been tied to perfection.

But neither ropes of hemp nor hide will secure a man of superior strength and resolution. Give such an one but time to operate, and he will be certain to free himself. Carlos knew that he needed but time.

The effect produced by the moistening of the raw-hide was such, that short time sufficed. In less than ten minutes it slipped from his wrists, and his hands were free!

He drew the thong through his fingers to clear it of loops and snarls. He fashioned one end into a noose; and, mounting upon the banqueta, knotted the other over the beam. He then placed the noose around his naked threat—calculating the height at which it should hang when drawn taut by the weight of his body! and, placing himself on the elevated edge of the banqueta, he was prepared to spring out—

"Let me look on them once more before I die—poor victims!—once more!"

The position he occupied was nearly in front of the embrasure, and he had only to lean a little to one side to get a view of the Plaza. He did so.

He could not see them; but he saw that the attention of the crowd was directed towards that angle of the square adjacent to the Calabozo. The horrid ceremony would soon be over. Perhaps they would then be carried within sight. He would wait for the moment, it would be his last—

"Ha! what is that? Oh God: it is—"

He heard the "weep" of the keen cuarto as it cut the air. He thought, or fancied, he heard a low moan. The silence of the crowd enabled him to distinguish the slightest sounds.

"God of mercy, is there no mercy? God of vengeance, hear me! Ha! vengeance! what am I dreaming of, suicidal fool? What! my hands free— can I not break the door? the lock? I can but die upon their weapons! and maybe—"

He had flung the noose from his neck, and was about to turn away from the window, when a heavy object struck him on the forehead, almost stunning him with the blow!

At first he thought it was a stone from the hand of some ruffian without; but the object, in falling upon the banqueta, gave out a dull metallic clink. He looked down, and in the dim light could make out that the thing which had struck him was of an oblong shape. He bent hastily forward, and clutched it.

It was a parcel, wrapped in a piece of silken scarf and tied securely. The string was soon unfastened, and the contents of the parcel held up to the light. These were a roleau of gold onzas, a long-bladed knife, and a folded sheet of paper!

The last occupied his attention first. The sun was down, and the light declining, but in front of the window there was still enough to enable him to read he opened the paper and read:—

"*Your time is fixed for to-morrow. I cannot learn whether you will be kept where you are all night, or be taken back to the Presidio. If you remain in the Calabozo, well. I send you two weapons. Use which you please, or both. The walls can be pierced. There will be one outside who will conduct you safe. Should you be taken to the Presidio, you must endeavour to escape on the way, or there is no hope. I need not recommend courage and resolution to you—the personification of both. Make for the rancho of Josefa. There you will find one who is now ready to share your perils and your liberty. Adieu! my soul's hero, adieu!*"

No name appeared. But Carlos needed none—he well knew who was the writer of that note.

"Brave, noble girl!" he muttered as he concealed the paper under the breast of his hunting-shirt; "the thought of living for you fills me with fresh hope—gives me new nerve for the struggle. If I die, it will not be by the hands of the *garrotero*. No, my hands are free. They shall not be bound again while life remains. I shall yield only to death itself."

As the captive muttered these thoughts he sat down upon the banqueta, and hurriedly untied the thongs that up to this time had remained upon his ankles. This done, he rose to his feet again; and, with the long knife firmly clutched, strode up and down the cell, glancing fiercely towards the door at each turning. He had resolved to run the gauntlet of his guards, and by his manner it was evident he had made up his mind to attack the first of them that entered.

For several minutes he paced his cell, like a tiger within its cage.

At length a thought seemed to suggest itself that caused a change in his manner, sudden and decided. He gathered up the thongs just cast off; and seating himself upon the banqueta, once more wound them around his ankles—but this time in such a fashion, that a single jerk upon a cunningly-contrived knot would set all free. The knife was hidden under his hunting-shirt, where the purse had been already deposited. Last of all, he unloosed the raw-hide rope from the beam, and, meeting his hands behind him, whipped it around both wrists, until they had the appearance of being securely spliced. He then assumed a reclining attitude along the banqueta, with his face turned towards the door, and remained motionless as though he were asleep!

Chapter Sixty Six

In our land of cold impulses—of love calculating and interested—we cannot understand, and scarcely credit, the deeds of reckless daring that in other climes have their origin in that strong passion.

Among Spanish women love often attains a strength and sublimity utterly unfelt and unknown to nations who mix it up with their merchandise. With those highly-developed dames it often becomes a true passion—unselfish, headlong, intense—usurping the place of every other, and filling the measure of the soul. Filial affection—domestic ties—moral and social duty—must yield. Love triumphs over all.

Of such a nature—of such intensity—was the love that burned in the heart of Catalina de Cruces.

Filial affection had been weighed against it; rank, fortune, and many other considerations, had been thrown into the scale. Love out-balanced them all; and, obedient to its impulse, she had resolved to fling all the rest behind her.

It was nearing the hour of midnight, and the mansion of Don Ambrosio was dark and silent. Its master was not at home. A grand banquet had been provided at the Presidio by Vizcarra and Roblado, to which all the grandees of the settlement had been invited. Don Ambrosio was among the number. At this hour he was at the Presidio, feasting and making merry.

It was not a ladies' festival, therefore Catalina was not there. It was, indeed, rather an extemporised affair—a sort of jubilee to wind up the performances of the day. The officers and priests were in high spirits, and had put their heads together in getting up the improvised banquet.

The town had become silent, and the mansion of Don Ambrosio showed not a sign of life. The portero still lingered by the great gate, waiting his master's return; but he sat inside upon the banqueta of the zaguan, and seemed to be asleep.

He was watched by those who wished him to sleep on.

The large door of the *caballeriza* was open. Within the framework of the posts and lintels the form of a man could be distinguished. It was the groom Andres.

There was no light in the stable. Had there been so, four horses might have been seen standing in their stalls, saddled and bridled. A still stranger circumstance might have been observed—around the hoofs of each horse were wrapped pieces of coarse woollen cloth, that were drawn up and fastened around the ankles! There was some design in this.

The door of the caballeriza was not visible from the zaguan; but at intervals the figure within the stable came forth, and, skulking along, peeped around the angle of the wall. The portero was evidently the object of his scrutiny. Having listened a while, the figure again returned to its place in the dark doorway, and stood as before.

Up to a certain time a tiny ray of light could be detected stealing through the curtains of a chamber-door—the chamber of the señorita. All at once the light silently disappeared; but a few moments after, the door opened noiselessly. A female figure glided softly forth, and turned along under the shadow of the wall, in the direction of the caballeriza. On reaching the open doorway she stopped, and called in a low voice—

"Andres!"

"*Aqui, Señorita!*" answered the groom, stepping a little more into the light.

"All saddled?"

"Si, Señorita."

"You have muffled their hoofs?"

"Every one, Señorita."

"Oh! what shall we do with him," continued the lady in a tone of distress, and pointing toward the zaguan. "We shall not be able to pass out before papa returns, and then it may be too late. *Santisima!*"

"Señorita, why not serve the portero as I have done the girl? I'm strong enough for that."

"Oh, Vicenza! how have you secured her?"

"In the garden-house,—tied, gagged, and locked up. I warrant she'll not turn up till somebody finds her. No fear of her, Señorita. I'll do the same for the portero, if you but say the word."

"No—no—no! who would open the gate for papa? No—no—no! it would not do." She reflected. "And yet, if he gets out before the horses are ready, they will soon miss—pursue—overtake him. He *will* get out, I am sure of it. How long would it occupy him? not long. He will easily undo his cord fastenings. I know that—he once said he could. Oh, holy Virgin! he may now be free, and waiting for me! I must haste—the portero—Ha!"

As she uttered this exclamation she turned suddenly to Andres. A new plan seemed to have suggested itself.

"Andres! good Andres! listen! We shall manage it yet!"

"Si, Señorita."

"Thus, then. Lead the horses out the back way, through the garden—can you swim them across the stream?"

"Nothing easier, my lady."

"Good! Through the garden take them then. Stay!"

At this she cast her eyes toward the entrance of the long alley leading to the garden, which was directly opposite to, and visible from, the zaguan. Unless the portero were asleep, he could not fail to see four horses passing out in that way—dark as was the night. Here, then, a new difficulty presented itself.

Suddenly starting, she seemed to have thought of a way to overcome it.

"Andres, it will do. You go to the zaguan. See whether he be asleep. Go up boldly. If asleep, well; if not enter into conversation with him. Get him to open the little door and let you out. Wile him upon the street, and by some means keep him there. I shall lead out the horses."

This was plausible, and the groom prepared himself for a strategic encounter with the portero.

"When sufficient time has elapsed, steal after me to the garden. See that you manage well, Andres. I shall double your reward. You go with me—you have nothing to fear."

"Señorita, I am ready to lay down my life for you."

Gold is powerful. Gold had won the stout Andres to a fealty stronger than friendship. For gold he was ready to strangle the portero on the spot.

The latter was not asleep—only dozing, as a Spanish portero knows how. Andres put the stratagem in practice, he offered a cigar; and in a few minutes' time his unsuspicious fellow-servant stepped with him through the gate, and both stood smoking outside.

Catalina judged their situation by the hum of their voices. She entered the dark stable; and gliding to the head of one of the horses, caught the bridle, and led the animal forth. A few moments sufficed to conduct it to the garden, where she knotted the rein to a tree.

She then returned for the second, and the third, and the fourth and last—all of which she secured as she had done the first.

Once more she went back to the patio. This time only to shut the stable-door, and lock that of her own chamber; and, having secured both, she cast a look towards the zaguan, and then glided back into the garden. Here she mounted her own horse, took the bridle of another in her hand, and sat waiting.

She had not long to wait. Andres had well calculated his time, for in a few minutes he appeared in the entrance; and, having closed the gate behind him, joined his mistress.

The *ruse* had succeeded admirably. The portero suspected nothing. Andres had bidden him "buenas noches," at the same time expressing his intention of going to bed.

Don Ambrosio might now return when he pleased. He would retire to his sleeping-room as was his wont. He would not know before morning the loss he had sustained.

The mufflings were now removed from the feet of the horses, and, plunging as silently as possible into the water, the four were guided across the stream. Having ascended the opposite bank, they were first headed towards the cliffs, but before they had proceeded far in that direction they turned into a path of the chapparal leading downward. This path would conduct them to the rancho of Josefa.

Chapter Sixty Seven

From the position he occupied, Carlos did not fail to observe the outlines of his prison, and search for that point that might be pierced with least trouble. He saw that the walls were of adobe bricks—strong, enough to shut in an ordinary malefactor, but easily cut through by a man armed with the proper tool, and the determination to set himself free. Two hours' work would suffice, but how to work that two hours without being interrupted and detected? That, was the question that occupied the mind of the captive.

One thing was very evident; it would be unwise to commence operations before a late hour—until the relief of the guard.

Carlos had well calculated his measures. He had determined to remain as he was, and keep up the counterfeit of his being fast bound until such time as the guard should be changed. He knew that it was the duty of the old guard to deliver him to the relief; and these would assure themselves of his being in the cell by ocular inspection. He guessed that the hour of guard-mounting must be near. He would, therefore, not have long to wait before the new sentries should present themselves in his cell.

One thought troubled him. Would they keep him in the Calabozo that night, or take him back to the Presidio for better security? If the latter, his only chance would be—as she had suggested—to make a desperate effort, and escape on the route. Once lodged in the guard-house prison, he would be surrounded by walls of stone. There would be no hope of cutting his way through them.

It was probable enough he should be taken there; and yet why should they fear his escape from the Calabozo—fast bound as they believed him—unarmed, guarded by vigilant sentinels? No. They would not dream of his getting off. Besides, it would be more convenient to keep him all night in the latter prison. It was close to the place of his intended execution, which no doubt was to take place on the morrow. The garrote had been already erected in front of his gaol!

Partly influenced by such considerations, and partly that they were occupied with pleasanter matters, the authorities had resolved on leaving him where he was for the night, though Carlos was ignorant of this.

He had, however, prepared himself for either contingency. Should they convey him back to the Presidio, he would seek the best opportunity that offered, and risk his life in a bold effort to escape. Should he be permitted to remain in the Calabozo, he would wait till the guard had visited him—then set to work upon the wall after they had gone out. In the event of being detected while at work, but one course remained,—run the gauntlet of the guard, and cut his way through their midst.

His escape was not an affair of such improbability. A determined man with a long knife in his grasp—one who will yield only to death—is a difficult thing to secure under any circumstances. Such an one will often effect his freedom, even when hemmed in by a host of enemies. With Carlos, however, the probabilities of escape were much greater. He was individually strong and brave, while most of his enemies were physically but pigmies in comparison. As to their courage, he knew that once they saw him with his hands free and armed, they would make way for him on all sides. What he had most to fear was the bullets of their carbines; but he had much to hope from their want of skill, and the darkness would favour him.

For more than an hour he lay along the banqueta, turning over in his mind the chances of regaining his liberty. His reflections were interrupted by an unusual stir outside his prison. A fresh batch of soldiers had arrived at the door.

Carlos' heart beat anxiously. Was it a party come to conduct him to the Presidio? It might be so. He waited with painful impatience listening to every word.

To his great joy it proved to be the arrival of the relief-guard; and he had the satisfaction of hearing, by their conversation, that they had been detailed to guard him all night in the Calabozo. This was just the very thing he desired to know.

Presently the door was unlocked and opened, and several of the men entered. One bore a lantern. With this they examined him—uttering coarse and insulting remarks as they stood around. They saw that he was securely bound! After a while all went out and left him to himself. The door was of course re-locked, and the cell was again in perfect darkness.

Carlos lay still for a few minutes, to assure himself they were not going to return. He heard them place the sentries by the door, and then the voices of the greater number seemed borne off to some distance.

Now was the time to begin his work. He hastily cast the cords from his hands and feet, drew the long knife from his breast, and attacked the adobe wall.

The spot he has chosen was at the corner farthest from the door, and at the back side of the cell. He knew not what was the nature of the ground on the other side, but it seemed most likely that which would lie towards the open country. The Calabozo was no fortress-prison—a mere temporary affair, used by the municipal authorities for malefactors of the smaller kind. So much the better for his chances of breaking it. The wall yielded easily to his knife. The adobe is but dry mud, toughened by an admixture of grass, and although the bricks were laid to the thickness of twenty inches or more, in the space of an hour Carlos succeeded in cutting a hole large enough to pass through. He could have accomplished this feat, in still shorter time, but he was compelled to work with caution, and as silently as possible. Twice he fancied that his guards were about to enter the cell, and both times he had sprung to his feet, and stood, knife in hand, ready to assail them. Fortunately his fancies were without foundation. No one entered until the hole was made, and the captive had the satisfaction to feel the cold air rushing through the aperture!

He stopped his work and listened. There was no sound on that side of the prison. All was silence and darkness. He pressed his head forward, and peered through. The night was dark, but he could see weeds and wild cactus-plants growing close to the wall. Good! There were no signs of life there.

He widened the aperture to the size of his body, and crawled through, knife in hand. He raised himself gradually and silently. Nothing but tall rank weeds, cactus-plants, and aloes. He was behind the range of the dwellings. He was in the common. He was free!

He started towards the open country, skulking under the shadow of the brushwood. A form rose before him, as if out of the earth, and a voice softly pronounced his name. He recognised the girl Josefa. A word or two was exchanged, when the girl beckoned him to follow, and silently led the way.

They entered the chapparal, and, following a narrow path, succeeded in getting round the village. On the other side lay the ranche, and in half-an-hour's time they arrived at and entered the humble dwelling.

In the next moment Carlos was bending over the corpse of his mother!

There was no shock in this encounter. He had been half prepared for such an event. Besides, his nerves had been already strained to their utmost by the spectacle of the morning. Sorrow may sometimes eclipse sorrow, and drive it from the heart; but that agony which he had already endured could not be supplanted by a greater. The nerve of grief had been touched with such severity that it could vibrate no longer!

Beside him was one who offered consolation—she, his noble preserver.

But it was no hour for idle grief. Carlos kissed the cold lips—hastily embraced his weeping sister—his love.

"The horses?" he inquired.

"They are close at hand—among the trees."

"Come, then! we must not lose a moment—we must go hence.—Come!"

As he uttered these words, he wrapped the serapé around the corpse, lifted it in his arms, and passed out of the rancho.

The others had already preceded him to the spot where the horses were concealed.

Carlos saw that there were five of these animals. A gleam of joy shot from his eyes as he recognised his noble steed. Antonio had recovered him. Antonio was there, on the spot.

All were soon in the saddles. Two of the horses carried Rosita and Catalina; the other two were ridden by Antonio and the groom Andres. The cibolero himself, carrying his strange burden, once more sprang upon the back of his faithful steed.

"Down the valley, master?" inquired Antonio.

Carlos hesitated a moment as if deliberating.

"No," replied he at length. "They would follow us that way. By the pass of La Niña. They will not suspect us of taking the cliff road. Lead on, Antonio:—the chapparal path—you know it best. On!"

The cavalcade started, and in a few minutes had passed the borders of the town, and was winding its way through the devious path that led to the pass of La Niña. No words were exchanged, or only a whisper, as the horses in single file followed one another through the chapparal.

An hour's silent travel brought them to the pass, up which they filed without halting till they had reached the top of the ravine. Here Carlos rode to the front, and, directing Antonio to guide the others straight across the table-land, remained himself behind.

As soon as the rest were gone past, he wheeled his horse, and rode direct for the cliff of La Niña. Having reached the extremity of the bluff, he halted at a point that commanded a full view of San Ildefonso. In the sombre darkness of night the valley seemed but the vast crater of an extinct volcano; and the lights, glittering in the town and the Presidio, resembled the last sparks of flaming lava that had not yet died out!

The horse stood still. The rider raised the corpse upon his arm; and, baring the pale face, turned it in the direction of the lights.

"Mother! mother!" he broke forth, in a voice hoarse with grief. "Oh! that those eyes could see—that those ears could hear!—if but for a moment—one short moment—that you might bear witness to my vow! Here do I swear that you shall be revenged! From this hour I yield up my strength, my time, my soul and body, to the accomplishment of vengeance. Vengeance! why do I use the word? It is not vengeance, but justice—justice upon the perpetrators of the foulest murder the world has ever recorded. But it shall not go unpunished. Spirit of my mother, hear me! *It shall not.* Your death shall be avenged—your torture shall have full retribution. Rejoice, you ruffian crew! feast, and be merry, for your time of sorrow will soon come—sooner than you think for! I go, but to return. Have patience—you shall see me again. Yes! once more you shall stand face to face with Carlos the cibolero!"

He raised his right arm, and held it outstretched in a menacing attitude, while a gleam of vengeful triumph passed over his countenance. His horse, as if actuated by a similar impulse, neighed wildly; and then wheeling round at a signal from his rider, galloped away from the cliff!

Chapter Sixty Eight

After having witnessed the disgusting ceremony in the Plaza, the officers returned to their quarters at the Presidio.

As already stated, they did not return alone. The principal men of the place had been invited to dine with them—cura, padrés, alcalde, and all. The capture of the outlaw was a theme of public gratulation and rejoicing; and the Comandante and his captain—to whom was due the credit—were determined to rejoice. To that end the banquet was spread in the Presidio.

It was not thought worth while to remove Carlos to the soldiers' prison. He could remain all night in the Calabozo. Fast bound and well guarded as he was, there was not the slightest danger of him making his escape.

To-morrow would be the last day of his life. To-morrow his foes should have the pleasure of seeing him die—to-morrow the Comandante and Roblado would enjoy their full measure of vengeance.

Even that day Vizcarra had enjoyed part of his. For the scorn with which he had been treated he had revenged himself—though it was he who from the centre of the Plaza had cried "*Basta!*" It was not mercy that had caused him to interfere. His words were not prompted by motives of humanity—far otherwise.

His designs were vile and brutal. To-morrow the brother would be put out of the way, and then—

The wine—the music—the jest—the loud laugh—all could not drown some bitter reflections. Ever and anon the mirror upon the wall threw back his dark face spoiled and distorted. His success had been dearly purchased—his was a sorry triumph.

It prospered better with Roblado. Don Ambrosio was one of the guests, and sat beside him.

The wine had loosened the heart-strings of the miner. He was communicative and liberal of his promises. His daughter, he said, had repented of her folly, and now looked with indifference upon the fate of Carlos. Roblado might hope.

It is probable that Don Ambrosio had reasons for believing what he said. It is probable that Catalina had thrown out such hints, the better to conceal her desperate design.

The wine flowed freely, and the guests of the Comandante revelled under its influence. There were toasts, and songs, and patriotic speeches; and the hour of midnight arrived before the company was half satiated with enjoyment.

In the midst of their carousal, a proposal was volunteered by some one, that the outlaw Carlos should be brought in! Odd as was this proposition, it exactly suited the half-drunken revellers. Many were curious to have a good sight of the cibolero—now so celebrated a personage.

The proposal was backed by many voices, and the Comandante pressed to yield to it.

Vizcarra had no objection to gratify his guests. Both he and Roblado rather liked the idea. It would be a further humiliation of their hated enemy.

Enough. Sergeant Gomez was summoned, the cibolero sent for, and the revelry went on.

But that revelry was soon after brought to a sudden termination, when Sergeant Gomez burst into the saloon, and announced in a loud voice that—

The prisoner had escaped!

A shell dropping into the midst of that company could not have scattered it more completely. All sprang to their feet—chairs and tables went tumbling over—glasses and bottles were dashed to the floor, and the utmost confusion ensued.

The guests soon cleared themselves of the room. Some ran direct to their houses to see if their families were safe; while others made their way to the Calabozo to assure themselves of the truth of the sergeant's report.

Vizcarra and Roblado were in a state bordering upon madness. Both stormed and swore, at the same time ordering the whole garrison under arms.

In a few minutes nearly every soldier of the Presidio had vaulted to his saddle, and was galloping in the direction of the town.

The Calabozo was surrounded.

There was the hole through which the captive had got off. How had he unbound his fastenings—who had furnished him with the knife?

The sentries were questioned and flogged—and flogged and questioned—but could tell nothing. They knew not that their prisoner was gone, until Gomez and his party came to demand him!

Scouring parties were sent out in every direction—but in the night what could they do? The houses were all searched, but what was the use of that? The cibolero was not likely to have remained within the town. No doubt he was off once more to the Plains!

The night search proved ineffectual; and in the morning the party that had gone down the valley returned, having found no traces either of Carlos, his sister, or his mother. It was known that the *hechicera* had died on the previous night, but where had the body been taken to? Had she come to life again, and aided the outlaw in his escape? Such was the conjecture!

At a later hour in the morning some light was thrown on the mysterious affair. Don Ambrosio, who had gone to rest without disturbing his daughter, was awaiting her presence in the breakfast-room. What detained her beyond the usual hour? The father grew impatient—then anxious. A messenger was at length sent to summon her—no reply to the knocking at her chamber-door!

The door was burst open. The room was entered—it was found untenanted—the bed unpressed—the señorita had fled!

She must be pursued! Where is the groom?—the horses? She must be overtaken and brought back!

The stable is reached, and its door laid open. No groom! no horse!—they, too, were gone!

Heavens! what a fearful scandal! The daughter of Don Ambrosio had not only assisted the outlaw to escape, but she had shared his flight, and was now with him. "*Huyeron!*" was the universal cry.

The trail of the horses was at length taken up, and followed by a large party, both of dragoons and mounted civilians. It led into the high plain, and then towards the Pecos, where they had crossed. Upon the other side the trail was lost. The horses had separated, and gone in different directions, and their tracks, passing over dry shingle, could no longer be followed.

After several days' fruitless wandering, the pursuing party returned, and a fresh one started out; but this, after a while, came back to announce a similar want of success. Every haunt had been searched; the old rancho—

the groves on the Pecos—even the ravine and its cave had been visited, and examined carefully. No traces of the fugitives could be discovered; and it was conjectured that they had gone clear off from the confines of the settlement.

This conjecture proved correct, and guessing was at length set at rest. A party of friendly Comanches, who visited the settlement, brought in the report that they had met the cibolero on their way across the Llano Estacado—that he was accompanied by two women and several men with pack-mules carrying provisions—that he had told them (the Indians) he was on his way for a long journey—in fact, to the other side of the Great Plains.

This information was definite, and no doubt correct. Carlos had been often heard to express his intention of crossing over to the country of the Americanos. He was now gone thither—most likely to settle upon the banks of the Mississippi. He was already far beyond the reach of pursuit. They would see him no more—as it was not likely he would ever again show his face in the settlements of New Mexico.

Months rolled past. Beyond the report of the Comanches, nothing was heard of Carlos or his people. Although neither he nor his were forgotten, yet they had ceased to be generally talked of. Other affairs occupied the minds of the people of San Ildefonso; and there had lately arisen one or two matters of high interest—almost sufficient to eclipse the memory of the noted outlaw.

The settlement had been threatened by an invasion from the Yutas—which would have taken place, had not the Yutas, just at the time, been themselves attacked and beaten by another tribe of savages! This defeat had prevented their invasion of the valley—at least for that season, but they had excited fears for the future.

Another terror had stirred San Ildefonso of late—a threatened revolt of the Tagnos, the *Indios mansos*, or *tame* Indians, who formed the majority of the population. Their brethren in several other settlements had risen, and succeeded in casting off the Spanish yoke.

It was natural that those of San Ildefonso should dream of similar action, and conspire.

But their conspiracy was nipped in the bud by the vigilance of the authorities. The leaders were arrested, tried, condemned, and shot. Their scalps were hung over the gateway of the Presidio, as a warning to their dusky compatriots, who were thus reduced to complete submission!

These tragic occurrences had done much to obliterate from the memory of all the cibolero and his deeds. True, there were some of San Ildefonso who, with good cause, still remembered both; but the crowd had ceased to think of either him or his. All had heard and believed that the outlaw had long ago crossed the Great Plains, and was now safe under the protection of those of his own race, upon the banks of the Mississippi.

Chapter Sixty Nine

And what had become of Carlos? Was it true that he had crossed the great plains? Did he never return? What became of San Ildefonso?

These questions were asked, because he who narrated the legend had remained for some time silent. His eyes wandered over the valley, now raised to the cliff of La Niña, and now resting upon the weed-covered ruin. Strong emotion was the cause of his silence.

His auditory, already half guessing the fate of San Ildefonso, impatiently desired to know the end. After a while he continued.

Carlos *did* return. What became of San Ildefonso? In yonder ruin you have your answer. San Ildefonso fell. But, you would know how? Oh! it is a terrible tale—a tale of blood and vengeance, and Carlos was the avenger.

Yes—the cibolero returned to the valley of San Ildefonso, but he came not alone. Five hundred warriors were at his back—red warriors who acknowledged him as their leader—their "White Chief." They were the braves of the Waco band. They knew the story of his wrongs, and had sworn to avenge him!

It was autumn—late autumn—that loveliest season of the American year, when the wild woods appeal painted, and Nature seems to repose after her annual toil—when all her creatures, having feasted at the full banquet she has so lavishly laid out for them, appear content and happy.

It was night, with an autumnal moon—that moon whose round orb and silvery beams have been celebrated in the songs of many a harvest land.

Not less brilliant fell those beams where no harvest was ever known—upon the wild plain of the Llano Estacado. The lone *hatero*, couched beside his silent flock, was awakened by a growl from his watchful sheep-dog. Raising himself, he looked cautiously around. Was it the wolf, the grizzly bear, or the red puma? None of these. A far different object was before his eyes, as he glanced over the level plain—an object whose presence caused him to tremble.

A long line of dark forms was moving across the plain. They were the forms of horses with their riders. They were in single file—the muzzle of each horse close to the croup of the one that preceded him. From east to west they moved. The head of the line was already near, but its rear extended beyond the reach of the hatero's vision.

Presently the troop filed before him, and passed within two hundred paces of where he lay. Smoothly and silently it glided on. There was no chinking of bits, no jingling of spurs, no clanking of sabres. Alone could be heard the dull stroke of the shoeless hoof, or at intervals the neigh of an impatient steed, suddenly checked by a reproof from his rider. Silently they passed on—silent as spectres. The full moon gleaming upon them added to their unearthly appearance!

The watcher trembled where he lay—though he knew they were not spectres. He knew well what they were, and understood the meaning of that extended deployment. They were Indian warriors upon the march. The bright moonlight enabled him to distinguish farther. He saw that they were all full-grown men—that they were nude to the waist, and below the thighs—that their breasts and arms were painted—that they carried nought but their bows, quivers, and spears—in short, that they were braves *on the war-trail!*

Strangest sight of all to the eyes of the hatero was the leader who rode at the head of that silent band. He differed from all the rest in dress, in equipments, in the colour of his skin. *The hatero saw that he was white!*

Surprised was he at first on observing this, but not for long. This shepherd was one of the sharpest of his tribe. It was he who had discovered the remains of the yellow hunter and his companion. He remembered the events of that time. He reflected; and in a few moments arrived at the conclusion that the *White Chief* he now saw could be no other than Carlos the cibolero! In that conjecture he was right.

The first thought of the hatero had been to save his own life by remaining quiet. Before the line of warriors had quite passed him, other thoughts came into his mind. The Indians were on the *war-trail!*—they were marching direct for the settlement,—they were headed by Carlos the cibolero!

The history of Carlos the outlaw now came before his mind—he remembered the whole story; beyond a doubt the cibolero was returning to the settlement to take vengeance upon his enemies!

Influenced partly by patriotism, and partly by the hope of reward, the hatero at once resolved to defeat this purpose. He would hasten to the valley and warn the garrison!

As soon as the line had filed past he rose to his feet, and was about to start off upon his errand; but he had miscalculated the intelligence of the white leader. Long before, the flanking scouts had enclosed both him and his charge, and the next moment he was a captive! Part of his flock served for the supper of that band he would have betrayed.

Up to the point where the hatero had been encountered, the White Chief and his followers had travelled along a well-known path—the trail of the traders. Beyond this, the leader swerved from the track; and without a word headed obliquely over the plain. The extended line followed silently after—as the body of a snake moves after its head.

Another hour, and they had arrived at the *ceja* of the Great Plain—at a point well-known to their chief. It was at the head of that ravine where he had so oft found shelter from his foes. The moon, though shining with splendid brilliance, was low in the sky, and her light did not penetrate the vast chasm. It lay buried in dark shade. The descent was a difficult one, though not to such men, and with such a guide.

Muttering some words to his immediate follower, the White Chief headed his horse into the cleft, and the next moment disappeared under the shadow of the rocks.

The warrior that followed, passing the word behind him, rode after, and likewise disappeared in the darkness; then another, and another, until five hundred mounted men were engulfed in that fearful-looking abysm. Not one remained upon the upper plain.

For a while there struck upon the ear a continued pattering sound—the sound of a thousand hoofs as they fell upon rocks and loose shingle. But this noise gradually died away, and all was silence. Neither horses nor men gave any token of their presence in the ravine. The only sounds that fell upon the ears were the voices of nature's wild creatures whose haunts had been invaded. They were the wail of the goatsucker, the bay of the barking wolf, and the maniac scream of the eagle.

Another day passes—another moon has arisen—and the gigantic serpent, that had all day lain coiled in the ravine, is seen gliding silently out at its bottom, and stretching its long vertebrate form across the plain of the Pecos.

The stream is reached and crossed; amidst plashing spray, horse follows horse over the shallow ford, and then the glittering line glides on.

Having passed the river lowlands, it ascends the high plains that overlook the valley of San Ildefonso.

Here a halt is made—scouts are sent forward—and once more the line moves on.

Its head reaches the cliff of La Niña just as the moon has sunk behind the snowy summit of the Sierra Blanca. For the last hour the leader has been marching slowly, as though he waited her going down. Her light is no longer desired. Darkness better befits the deed that is to be done.

A halt is made until the pass has been reconnoitred. That done, the White Chief guides his followers down the defile; and in another half-hour the five hundred horsemen have silently disappeared within the mazes of the chapparal!

Under the guidance of the half-blood Antonio, an open glade is found near the centre of the thicket. Here the horsemen dismount and tie their horses to the trees. The attack is to be made on foot.

It is now the hour after midnight. The moon has been down for some time; and the cirrus clouds, that for a while had reflected her light, have been gradually growing darker. Objects can no longer be distinguished at the distance of twenty feet. The huge pile of the Presidio, looming against the leaden sky, looks black and gloomy. The sentinel cannot be seen upon the turrets, but at intervals his shrill voice uttering the *"Centinela alerte!"* tells that he is at his post. His call is answered by the sentinel at the gate below, and then all is silent. The garrison sleeps secure—even the night-guard in the zaguan with their bodies extended along the stone banqueta, are sleeping soundly.

The Presidio dreads no sudden attack—there has been no rumour of Indian incursion—the neighbouring tribes are all *en paz*; and the Tagno conspirators have been destroyed. Greater vigilance would be superfluous. A sentry upon the azotea, and another by the gate, are deemed sufficient for the ordinary guardianship of the garrison. Ha! the inmates of the Presidio little dream of the enemy that is nigh:

"Centinela alerte!" once more screams the watcher upon the wall. *"Centinela alerte!"* answers the other by the gate.

But neither is sufficiently on the alert to perceive the dark forms that, prostrate upon the ground, like huge lizards, are crawling forward to the very walls. Slowly and silently these forms are moving, amidst weeds and grass, gradually drawing nearer to the gateway of the Presidio.

A lantern burns by the sentinel. Its light, radiating to some distance, does not avail him—he sees them not!

A rustling noise at length reaches his ear. The *"quien viva?"* is upon his lips; but he lives not to utter the words. Half-a-dozen bowstrings twang simultaneously, and as many arrows bury themselves in his flesh. His heart is pierced, and he falls, almost without uttering a groan!

A stream of dark forms pours into the open gateway. The guard, but half awake, perish before they can lay hand upon their weapons!

And now the war-cry of the Wacoes peals out in earnest, and the hundreds of dark warriors rush like a torrent through the zaguan.

They enter the patio. The doors of the *cuartos* are besieged—soldiers, terrified to confusion, come forth in their shirts, and fall under the spears of their dusky assailants. Carbines and pistols crack on all sides, but those who fire do not live to reload them.

It was a short but terrible struggle—terrible while it lasted. There were shouts, and shots, and groans, mingling together—the deep voice of the vengeful leader, and the wild war-cry of his followers—the crashing of timber, as doors were broken through or forced from their hinges—the clashing of swords and spears, and the quick detonation of fire-arms. Oh! it was a terrible conflict!

It ends at length. An almost total silence follows. The warriors no longer utter their dread cry. Their soldier-enemies are destroyed. Every cuarto has been cleared of its inmates, who lie in bleeding heaps over the patio and by the doors. No quarter has been given. All have been killed on the spot.

No—not all. There are two who survive—two whose lives have been spared. Vizcarra and Roblado yet live!

Piles of wood are now heaped against the timber posterns of the building, and set on fire. Volumes of smoke roll to the sky, mingling with sheets of red flame. The huge pine-beams of the azotea catch the blaze, burn, crackle, and fall inwards, and in a short while the Presidio becomes a mass of smoking ruins!

But the red warriors have not waited for this. The revenge of their leader is not yet complete. It is not to the soldiers alone that he owes vengeance. He has sworn it to the citizens as well. The whole settlement is to be destroyed!

And well this oath was kept, for before the sun rose San Ildefonso was in flames. The arrow, and the spear, and the tomahawk, did their work; and men, women, and children, perished in hundreds under the blazing roofs of their houses!

With the exception of the Tagno Indians, few survived to tell of that horrid massacre. A few whites only—the unhappy father of Catalina among the rest—were permitted to escape, and carry their broken fortunes to another settlement.

That of San Ildefonso—town, Presidio, mission, haciendas, and ranchos—in the short space of twelve hours had ceased to exist. The dwellers of that lovely valley were no more!

It is yet but noon. The ruins of San Ildefonso are still smoking. Its former denizens are dead, but it is not yet unpeopled. In the Plaza stand hundreds of dusky warriors drawn up in hollow square, with their faces turned inward. They are witnessing a singular scene—another act in the drama of their leader's vengeance.

Two men are mounted upon asses, and tied upon the backs of the animals. These men are stripped—so that their own backs are perfectly bare, and exposed to the gaze of the silent spectators! Though these men no longer wear their flowing robes, it is easy to distinguish them. Their close-cut hair and shaven crowns show who they are—the padrés of the mission!

Deep cuts the cuarto into their naked skin, loudly do they groan, and fearfully writhe. Earnestly do they beg and pray their persecutors to stay the terrible lash. Their entreaties are unheeded.

Two white men, standing near, overlook the execution. These are Carlos the cibolero and Don Juan the ranchero.

The priests would move them to pity, but in vain. The hearts of those two men have been turned to stone.

"Remember my mother—my sister!" mutters Carlos.

"Yes, false priests—remember!" adds Don Juan.

And again is plied the cutting lash, until each corner of the Plaza has witnessed a repetition of the punishment!

Then the asses are led up in front of the parroquia—now roofless and black; their heads are fastened together, so that the backs of their riders are turned toward the spectators.

A line of warriors forms at a distance off—their bows are bent, and at a signal a flight of arrows goes whistling through the air.

The suffering of the padrés is at an end. Both have ceased to exist.

I have arrived at the last act of this terrible drama; but words cannot describe it. In horror it eclipses all the rest. The scene is La Niña—the top of the cliff—the same spot where Carlos had performed his splendid feat on the day of San Juan.

Another feat of horsemanship is now to be exhibited. How different the actors—how different the spectators!

Upon the tongue that juts out two men are seated upon horseback. They are not free riders, for it may be noticed that they are tied upon their seats. Their hands do not grasp a bridle, but are bound behind their backs; and their feet, drawn together under the bellies of their horses, are there spliced with raw-hide ropes. To prevent turning in the saddle, other thongs, extending from strong leathern waist-belts, stay them to croup and pommel, and hold their bodies firm. Under such a ligature no horse could dismount either without also flinging the saddle, and that is guarded against by the strongest girthing. It is not intended that these horsemen shall lose their seats until they have performed an extraordinary feat.

It is no voluntary act. Their countenances plainly tell that. Upon the features of both are written the most terrible emotions—craven cowardice in all its misery—despair in its darkest shadows!

Both are men of nearly middle age—both are officers in full uniform. But it needs not that to recognise them as the deadly enemies of Carlos—Vizcarra and Roblado. No longer now his enemies. They are his captives!

But for what purpose are they thus mounted? What scene of mockery is to be enacted? Scene of mockery! Ha! ha! ha!

Observe! *the horses upon which they sit are wild mustangs!* Observe! *they are blinded with tapojos!*

For what purpose? You shall see.

A Tagno stands at the head of each horse, and holds him with difficulty. The animals are kept fronting the cliff, with their heads directed to the jutting point of La Niña.

The Indians are drawn up in line also facing to the cliff. There is no noise in their ranks. An ominous silence characterises the scene. In front is their chief mounted upon his coal-black steed; and upon him the eyes of all are fixed, as though they expected some signal, his face is pale, but its expression is stern and immobile. He has not yet reached the completion of his vengeance.

There are no words between him and his victims. All that has passed. They know their doom.

Their backs are towards him, and they see him not; but the Tagnos who stand by the horses' heads have their eyes fixed upon him with a singular expression. What do these expect? A signal.

In awful silence was that signal given. To the right and left sprang the Tagnos, leaving free the heads of the mustangs. Another signal to the line of mounted warriors, who, on receiving it, spurred their horses forward with a wild yell.

Their spears soon pricked the hips of the mustangs, and the blinded animals sprang towards the cliff!

The groans of agonised terror that escaped from their riders were drowned by the yells of the pursuing horsemen.

In a moment all was over. The terrified mustangs had sprung out from the cliff—had carried their riders into eternity!

The dusky warriors pulled up near the brink, and sat gazing upon each other in silent awe.

A horseman dashed to the front; and, poising his horse upon the very edge, looked down into the abysm. It was the White Chief.

For some moments he regarded the shapeless masses that lay below. He saw that they moved not. Men and horses were all dead crushed, bruised, and shattered—a hideous sight to behold!

A deep sigh escaped him, as though some weight had been lifted from his heart, and, turning around he muttered to his friend—

"Don Juan! I have kept my oath—*she is avenged!*"

The setting sun saw that long line of Indian warriors filing from the valley, and heading for the plain of the Llano Estacado. But they went not as they had come. They returned to their country laden with the plunder of San Ildefonso—to them the legitimate spoils of war.

The cibolero still rode at their head, and Don Juan the ranchero was by his side. The fearful scenes through which they had just passed shadowed the brows of both; but these shadows became lighter as they dwelt on the prospect before them. Each looked forward to a happy greeting at the end of his journey.

Carlos did not remain long among his Indian friends. Loaded with the treasure they had promised, he proceeded farther east, and established a plantation upon the Red River of Louisiana. Here, in the company of his beautiful wife, his sister, Don Juan, and some of his old servants, he led in after years a life of peace and prosperity.

Now and then no made hunting excursions into the country of his old friends the Wacoes—who were over glad to see him again, and still hailed him as their chief.

Of San Ildefonso there is no more heard since that time. No settlement was ever after made in that beautiful valley. The Tagnos—released from the bondage which the padrés had woven around them—were but too glad to give up the half-civilisation they had been taught. Some of them sought other settlements, but most returned to their old habits, and once more became hunters of the plains.

Perhaps the fate of San Ildefonso might have attracted more attention in other times; but it occurred at a peculiar period in Spanish-American history. Just then the Spanish power, all over the American continent, was hastening to its decline; and the fall of San Ildefonso was but one episode among many of a character equally dramatic. Near the same time fell Gran Quivira, Abo, Chilili, and hundreds of other settlements of note. Each has its story—each its red romance—perhaps far more interesting than that we have here recorded.

Chance alone guided our steps to the fair valley of San Ildefonso,—chance threw in our way one who remembered its legend—the legend of the *White Chief*.

Appendix

Notes

"*Sierra Blanca.* The Sierra Blanca is so called because the tops of this range are usually covered with snow. The snow of the Sierra Blanca is not "eternal." It only remains for about three parts of the year. Its highest peaks are below the snow-line of that latitude. Mountains that carry the eternal snow are by the Spanish Americans denominated "Nevada."

"*The Grand Prairie*". This name is somewhat indefinite, being applied by some to particular portions of prairie land. Among the hunters it is the general name given to the vast treeless region lying to the west of the timbered country on the Mississippi. The whole longitudinal belt from the Lower Rio Grande to the Great Slave Lake is, properly speaking, the Grand Prairie; but the phrase has been used in a more restricted sense, to designate the larger tracts of open country, in contra-distinction to the smaller prairies, such as those of Illinois and Louisiana, which last are separated from the true prairie country by wide tracts of timbered surface.

"*Settlements of Nuevo Mexico*". The settlements of New Mexico covered at one time a much wider extent of country than they do now. The Indians have been constantly narrowing the boundaries for the last fifty years. At present these settlements are almost wholly restricted to the banks of the Del Norte and a few tributary streams.

"*Gramma grass.*" The *Chondrosium,* a beautiful and most nutritions herbage that covers many of the plains of Texas and North Mexico. There are several species of grass known among Mexicans as "gramma"; one in particular, the *Chondrosium foeneum,* as a food for horses, is but little inferior to oats.

"*Cackle of his fighting-cock*". There is no exaggeration in all this. Every traveller in Mexico has witnessed such scenes, and many have borne testimony to these and similar facts. I have often seen the fighting chanticleer carried inside the church under the arm of its owner, while the latter entered to pray!

"*Fiestas principales*". The more noted Saints' days, or religious festivals, as Saint John's, Good-Friday, Guadalupe, etcetera, are so styled to distinguish them from the many others of lesser celebrity.

"Tailing the bull". "Bull-tailing" (*coleo de toro*) and "running the cock" (*correr el gallo*) are favourite sports in most parts of Mexico, but particularly in the Northern provinces. They were also Californian games while that country was Spano-Mexican.

"The Apache". One of the largest tribes of the "Indios bravos" or wild Indians, *i.e.* Indians who have never submitted to the Spanish yoke. Their country lies around the heads of the Gila, extending from that stream to the Del Norte, and down the latter to the range of another large and powerful tribe—the Comanches—also classed as "Indios bravos."

"Familias principales." The "first families," a United States phrase, is the synonym of "familias principales" of Mexico.

"Comerciante." Merchant or extensive trader. Merchandise is not degrading in Mexico. The rich merchant may be one of the "familias principales." Although there is still an old *noblesse* in the Mexican republic, the titles are merely given by courtesy, and those who hold them are often outranked and eclipsed in style by the prosperous parvenu.

"Alcalde." Pronounced Alkalde. The duties of the Alcalde are very similar to those of a magistrate or justice of the peace. Every village has its Alcalde, who is known by his large gold or silver-headed cane and tassel. In villages where the population is purely Indian, the Alcalde is usually either of Indian or mixed descent—often pure Indian.

"Mode de Paris!" The upper classes in Mexico, particularly those who reside in the large cities, have discarded the very picturesque national costume, and follow the fashions of Paris. In all the large towns, French tailors, modistes, jewellers, etcetera, may be met with. The ladies wear French dresses, but without the bonnet. The shawl is drawn over the head when it becomes necessary to cover it. The hideous bonnet is only seen upon foreign ladies residing in Mexico. The city gentleman of first-class wears a frock-coat, but the cloth jacket is the costume of the greater number. A long-tailed dress-coat is regarded as an *outré* affair, and never appears upon the streets of a Mexican town.

"Gachupino." A Spaniard of Old Spain. The term is used contemptuously by the natives, or Creoles (Criollos), of Mexico, who hate their Spanish cousins as the Americans hate Englishmen, and for a very similar reason.

"Hijo de algo." Literally, "son of somebody." Hence the word *hidalgo*. The "blue blood" (*sangre azul*) is the term for pure blood or high birth.

"Poblanas." A *poblana* is, literally, a village girl or woman, but in a more specific sense it signifies a village belle, or beauty. It is nearly a synonyme of the Spanish "maja."

"Don Juan Tenorio." Don Juan Tenorio—a celebrated character of Spanish romance and drama. He is the original from which Byron drew his conception of Don Juan. He is the hero of a thousand love-scrapes and *"desafios,"* or duels. The drama of "Don Juan Tenorio" still keeps the Spanish stage, and Spaniards can hardly find words to express their admiration of its poetry. It requires two nights to play this piece, which is about twice the length of a regular five-act play.

"Teniente." "Lugar-teniente" is lieutenant in Spanish, but the "lugar" is left out, and "teniente" stands for the title of the subaltern.

"Quien sabe!." A noted phrase which figures largely in Spanish dialogue. Literally, "Who knows?"

"Gambucinos and rancheros!" Gambucino, a petty miner, who digs or washes gold on his own account. *Ranchero*, the dweller in a *rancho*, or country hut. The ranchero class corresponds pretty nearly to that known as "small farmers," though in Mexico they are more often graziers than agriculturists.

"Enaguas." Sometimes written "nagua,"—the petticoat, usually of coarse blue or red cotton stuff, with a list of white or some other colour forming the top part.

"Reboso." The scarf of greyish or slaty blue, worn by all women in Mexico, except the ladies of the Upper Ten Thousand, who use it only on occasions.

"Allegria." A singular custom prevails among the women of New Mexico, of daubing their faces all over with the juice of a berry called by them the "allegria," which gives them anything but a charming look. The juice is of a purplish red colour, somewhat like that of blackberries. Some travellers allege that it is done for ornament, as the Indians use vermilion and other pigments. This is not a correct explanation. The "allegria" is used by the New Mexican belles to preserve the complexion, and get it up towards some special occasion, such as a grand *fiesta* or "fandango," when it is washed off, and the skin comes out clear and free from "tan." The "allegria" is the well known "poke-weed" of the United States (*Phytolacca decandra.*)

"Sombrero." The black *glaze* hat with low crown and broad leaf is a universal favourite throughout Mexico. It is often worn several pounds in weight, and that, too, under a hot tropic sun. Some sort of gold or silver lace-band is common, but frequently this is of heavy bullion, and costly.

"Pueblos." There are many towns in New Mexico inhabited exclusively by "Pueblos," a name given to a large tribe of civilised Indians,—*Indios*

mansos (tame Indians) such tribes are called, to distinguish them from the *Indios bravos*, or savages, who never acknowledged the sway of the Spanish conquerors.

"*Peons.*" The labouring serfs of the country are *peons*. They are not slaves by the wording of the political law, but most of them are in reality slaves by the law of debtor and creditor.

"*Petates,*" etcetera A "petate" is a small mat about the size of a blanket, woven out of palm-strips, or bulrushes, according to the district; it is the universal bed of the Mexican peasant.

Tunas and *pitahayas* are fruits of different species of cactus.

Sandias are water-melons.

Dulces are preserves.

Agua-miel and *limonada*, refreshing drinks peculiar to Mexico.

Piloncillos, loaves of coarse brown sugar, met with in all parts of Mexico, and very much like the maple-sugar of the States.

Tortillas, the often-described daily bread of the Mexican people.

Chili Colorado, red pepper.

Ollas, earthen pots of all sizes—almost the only sort used in the Mexican kitchen.

Atole, a thin gruel resembling flour and water, but in reality made out of the finer dust of the maize, boiled and sweetened.

Pinole, parched maize mixed with water and sweetened.

Clacos, copper cents, or half-pence,—the copper coin of Mexico.

Punche, a species of native-grown tobacco.

Aguardiente, whisky distilled from maize, or sometimes from the aloe—literally, *agua ardiente*, hot or fiery water. It is the common whisky of the country, and a vile stuff in most cases.